# THE
# SCAPEGRACERS

## HANNAH ABIGAIL CLARKE

EREWHON

THE SCAPEGRACERS
Copyright © 2020 by Hannah Abigail Clarke

Edited by Liz Gorinsky

Erewhon Books
2 W. 29th Street, Suite 3S
New York, NY 10001
www.erewhonbooks.com

Erewhon books are available at special discounts when purchased in bulk for premiums and sales promotions as well as for fund-raising or educational use. Special editions or book excerpts can also be created to specification. For details, send an email to specialmarkets@workman.com.

Library of Congress Control Number: 2019956225

ISBN 978-1-64566-000-2 (hardcover)
ISBN 978-1-64566-005-7 (ebook)

Cover art by Anka Lavriv
Cover and interior design by Dana Li

Printed in the United States of America

First US Edition: September 2020
10 9 8 7 6 5 4 3 2 1

Y'all know who you are.

*"Magic kills industry."* —*Francis Bacon*

*"Hell is a teenage girl."* —Jennifer's Body

# THE SCAPEGRACERS

# BY THE PRICKING OF MY THUMBS

The punch was the color of my first and second knuckles and it tasted like lye. It singed off the surface of my tongue. Between sips, if I angled my wrist just right, I could make my reflection glint off the surface, and warped little me could stare up from the depths of my Solo cup like an overgrown jackdaw. Which, like. Yikes. I made myself look literally anywhere else and ground on a last bit of chalk.

My sigil was enormous, six feet wide, maybe more. I'd drawn the lines on bold and thick, but it was anything but elegant. It looked like an astrolabe that'd been hit by a truck. White lines spiraled, switchbacked, zigzagged back and forth in a cacophonous mess, and all the jaggedy lines only just managed to squeeze themselves inside my gigantic hand-drawn circle. The chalk looked rough against the concrete floor, weathered like a three-day-old game of hopscotch. I could've done better, but this was my second cup of jungle juice. So.

Parties are too fucking loud. Like, I understand the bass is heavy and we're drunk and whatever, but that doesn't make shrieked lyrics of nasty bubblegum bop any easier on my ears. I pulled my knees to my chest and toyed with the frets in the denim. Soon enough, the unholy trinity would meander over here, and we could start things. My throat itched from the lack of starting things. I soothed the itch with more booze and fought back the urge to retch.

This was the first weekend in October, and the township of Sycamore Gorge doesn't fuck around where Halloween is concerned. This was the dawn of scare-party season. First weekend was pre-costumes but well within the realm of the macabre, and house parties had to thematically follow suit to garner any interest whatsoever. Three years back, a little ridiculousness with a Ouija board and some rounds of Bloody Mary might've sufficed, but that sort of thing reeked of amateur hour now. Jing and Yates and Daisy were the longest-standing monarchs our school had ever seen, and I couldn't fathom them tarnishing their reputations with a mind-numbing three hours of sitting around in silence, shoving a flimsy plastic planchette back and forth in hopes that Elvis might shimmy in from beyond the veil and tell them what was up. They needed something real to stay relevant, something genuine. Something that couldn't be purchased at Party City for under twenty bucks.

Jing and Yates and Daisy are a whole lot of things, but they aren't stupid.

They'd paid me forty.

Fog machines frosted the crowd in a milky, dreamy haze, and bodies twisted together under the strobe lights like a great meaty knot. Torsos flickered and drifted, denim-clad pelvises clattered together, and countless long, glow-stick-spangled arms waved red cups like beacons through the fog. Worn sneakers scuffed the ground. The partygoers all looked a little smudged, a little sickly, like they were either going to keel over or float away any second, and when I let my eyes fall out of focus, the whole bopping crowd blurred together into one churning mass, like a monster's four-chambered heart. To my right, a straight couple I didn't recognize dipped their tongues down each other's throats. To my left, a leggy girl tossed her head back, neck impossibly long like a goose, falsies fluttering up over the whites of her eyes like she had a Hollywood devil inside her. A dudebro slopped punch on her Vans.

Daisy Brink came out of the darkness. She was dressed something like a pleated Creamsicle, and her lip gloss looked so sticky under the seizing LEDs that I nearly forgot for a second why I shouldn't tangle with girls like her, no matter how tempting the prospect might be. Daisy dropped, sat crisscross, and gnawed on her poison-colored Ring Pop. It stained her incisors blue. She lowered the Ring Pop, waggled her brows, and toyed with the glow-stick choker around her throat. I made myself stare intently at the chalk. Right. No. There'd be no straight girls for me.

Yates and Jing emerged from the same gap of darkness as Daisy and took spots beside her, marking the third and fourth points on the circle. Yates had black-eyed Susans tucked in the curls of her afro and Jing wore an oversized hoodie and not much else. They both had a glossy sheen of boredom around them, heavy eyed and languid. Jing rolled her shoulders and slid her hands out of her pockets, eased her glow-bracelet-bangled wrists to the ground, and traced her bitten-down nails over the chalk lines. "So. Sideways. When do we start this thing?"

I skimmed my tongue over my teeth. I'd drawn out a five-pointed sigil. Hard to tell, because it wasn't exactly Ye Olde Average Pentagram, but it was still five pointed in an abstract sense. You know, for tradition's sake, or whatever.

There were four of us.

I cleared my throat. "Yeah, so. We need a fifth person for the fifth point. Doesn't matter who."

"Couldn't you have made a four-person spell?" Jing pulled a face and jerked one of her slash-straight eyebrows up into her hairline. "Whatever." She smacked her lips. Her gaze whipped over my head and her pupils fixed on some lucky sucker behind me. She stabbed one of her fingers at whoever stood behind me, and her mouth curled up at the edges. "Hey. You. You like magic?"

I jerked myself around, craned my neck. My heart hurled itself against my rib cage and stuck there.

She must be new or something. I didn't know her.

She was lanky, probably taller than me. Long and narrow. There were Band-Aids on her shins. She wore high-waisted shorts and a satiny basketball jacket. The fitted cap she wore cast shadows under her brows, and on top of that cap was a woven glow-stick halo. It shimmered down on her shoulders with a ghostly violet glow. Her hair was velvety black, so black it glinted blueish under the LEDs, and it hung in two raggedy fishtails that swayed around her waist when she moved. They swung back a little when she rocked on her heels, which she did presently, jabbing an inquisitive finger at her chest. *Me?* She snapped her bubblegum between her teeth and gave us a slow nod. "I sure do."

"What's your name?" Jing leaned back, shook her hair out with one hand, and loosened up the other into a lazy come-hither motion. "You should hang with us. This here is Sideways Pike. She's a real bona fide witch, and she's gonna show us something special."

"Dope," said the stranger. "I'm Madeline."

"Well then, Madeline." Jing waved her hand over the blank space on the floor beside her. "Take a seat."

I was on the other side of that blank space. Jing, me, blank space. Madeline would be sitting next to me. Fuck.

Madeline sat down and sprawled back, pulled one of her thighs toward her chest. She hugged her arms around it and rested her chin on her knee. "So. We're playing witchcraft?" Her voice was slow, a little raw, and she looked at my seedy sigil like it was a stained-glass window. Something glinted deep in her sockets, but it was gone before I could place it. She sniffed, knotted her eyebrows. "I could fuck with that."

I opened my jaws and felt myself almost say something awful and significantly gayer than I intended, but I drowned the words before they could slither out. The last of my punch scorched my esophagus and burned off the lining of my stomach. Very gross, very fruit-punch-y. Reality fell a little out of focus. My limbs felt vaguely numb. I licked the grime off my teeth and crunched the Solo cup in my fist, thrust it aside, shook out my wrists and my fingers. Gooseflesh bloomed down the length of my spine.

I felt it now. The world was starting to prickle. Slowly, steadily, the air started to fizzle, and the radio-static air vibrated louder and louder until every follicle on my head stood on end. The feeling seeped from my pores inward, thrummed into my capillaries, my spider veins, the very meat of me, and the feeling went pitter-pat, itched for a strike or a spark. My eyes swiveled up in my skull and my vision swam. I couldn't see anything but the milky fog and strobe lights crashing above us. The air was pale, bruise-lavender blue. It pulsed like it was alive, and I couldn't see the ceiling above it. I clawed at either side of me, felt around for hands and found them with a lurch. On my left, that was Madeline. Her fingers were dead cold and calloused, and she took me by my wrist and held me tight. Jing grabbed my right hand. She gave me a little squeeze.

This was it. It was the crackle before a storm. My lungs pinwheeled and my body quaked, and my fake leather jacket was suddenly three sizes too small for me. The sleeves were bindingly tight, tight enough to jeopardize my circulation, and strips of fabric clung to my back like wet papier-mâché. It was suffocatingly hot and there was no chance I could shuck off my jacket now. Once a spell starts, I'm not so good at stopping it. I'd warned the three of them before I got paid.

The space between the five of us felt thicker, and particles science hasn't named yet went ricocheting infinitely fast in the vacuum between our kneecaps. I couldn't peel my eyes off the ceiling, but I knew what was in front of me without having to look. There was a presence in this basement. The shapeless, electric something shimmered over the chalk.

"Do you feel that?" The words whistled through the gap between my front teeth before I could stop them. The incantation had been brewing in my throat since this started. Now it fluttered up in my jaws, and I was just keyed up enough to open wide, to let it pour out. "All that power, do you feel that? All that bristling? The Pop Rocks in your skin? That's it. That's the magic crawling in. It's that slow and raw and buzzing thing. If your bones are aching, let them ache. Let all of this sizzle and fester." The misty air was blooming red spots above our heads—or maybe that was the blood in my temples. Adrenaline rammed through my ribs. My pulse quickened, thickened, turned into something else.

There was an inscription imbedded in my sigil. The incantation. I'd only practiced it a few times, but I knew it like a reflex, like a Hexennacht Hail Mary. It dripped off my tongue without effort or intention, and I didn't self-edit, didn't think about how anything looked, anything sounded, anything seemed. The words bled out and I didn't stop to breathe.

"We're inviting the liquid night, the molten magic. We're inviting the star-spiked darkness inside and calling it to this circle. Our hands entwined are a chalice. Flow through us and spill. All this dancing is in triumph and our booze is all libations. We've brought you beats and lights and glamour, we brought fresh meat, new blood, and booze, and in return, we want some chaos. We want havoc. Bring us hell."

A sound tore the crowd down the middle. The sound was thin and itchy, like dead skin tearing, and something wet splashed the back of my hands. I jerked my head down, hissed a breath through my teeth. The glow sticks: all of them had snapped clean in half. Plastic tubes sprang off limbs and clattered to the floor, and dancers' wrists splattered rat-poison blue and scalding pink liquid from wrists to elbows. Madeline's glow halo split and fell. Lavender chemicals trickled down her temples like from a candied head wound. Acid green pooled above Daisy's collarbone. Jing's forearms splashed phosphorescence on the chalk.

Yates balked. She tore her hands away from Jing and Daisy, yanked them to her chest with a force that propelled her backward, away from the circle. Her eyes stretched wide with terror.

I felt it like a smack.

The magic snapped back like a rubber band. It struck hard and all at once. I pitched forward, caught my hands on the concrete just in time to keep my head from cracking. My lungs slammed against my sternum and went ragged, and my nerves all twinged at once. My vision speckled like I'd stared at the sun. A jagged, painful pulse reverberated from my limbs to my core, and I heaved in a breath through my teeth, wheezed a cough. There was a whistling in my ears loud enough to rupture my skull. The crowd howled. People yelped and laughed, and someone was screaming, and it all blended into a single thorny cacophony. Voices had no definition. It was loud enough to cleave my brain into bits. I'd have covered my ears with my fists if I could, but I couldn't seem to pull them off the concrete.

The world looked inverted and garish. I blinked a few times, tried to snap myself out of it, but all I could see were Jing's teeth and how long and sharp they looked as she laughed. She jumped to her feet and out of sight, and she let out a triumphant cry just loud enough to cut through the ringing. "Fuck *all* of y'all. That was some *magic.*"

The room roared in response. Everybody eased up. Grimaces flipped into smiles . . . or most of them did, anyway. An out-of-sight DJ changed tracks, and the crowd sprang to life again. The glow on their splatted throats and arms made their already shadowy torsos look like voidspace. I couldn't name the song that was playing, but I knew all the words, and so did everybody else, apparently. They all shouted along as they thrashed together, bobbing in the darkness, in the heat. The room sweltered and smelled like brine.

Magic doesn't do well with being cut off early.

I wanted to throw up.

In the periphery of my vision, Jing shot finger guns my way and seized Daisy by the waist. She hauled her into the dancing throng. Yates scrambled close behind them, ducking between swaying couples in an attempt to match their pace. She didn't bother making eye contact with me. Amid the waves of bodies, I thought I saw Austin Grass, whom I hated more than any other person who I knew in real life, put his arms around all three of them at once. *Didn't know you girls were into lezzie shit. Nice to have some hot ones around here with that East High piece, huh?*

Usually, I'd be pissed, but fuck. It had worked. It actually worked. It worked with fucking *witnesses.*

I wiggled my fingertips against the floor, mostly to prove to myself that I still had fingers. My body felt pinched and cotton stuffed. Pins and needles shot down my shins and my body screamed *stay down, stay down,* but I didn't. I put my feet underneath me, made myself crouch. My tongue felt thick between my teeth, and my cheeks felt raw. I forced my right hand off the ground and pressed it to my mouth, snagged the corner of my sleeve between my teeth.

Something dead cold and calloused locked around my wrist.

Madeline crouched in front of me. The strobe lights flashed on her eyes and her hair, and her whole body flickered like a phantom's. If her hand wasn't so icy, I'd think she was a dream. She wasn't real enough to be real. Madeline ducked her head, forced herself into my line of sight, and her mouth twisted up into a grin. It was a weary half-grin, but a grin regardless. Teeth and everything. Her lips moved, but I couldn't hear her. She didn't let go of my wrist. The way my skin pinched, she must've gripped it tighter.

Dull pain bloomed around her fingers, and I cleared my throat, tried to fish my voice out of my stomach. "I can't hear you," I said. It sounded like a mouthful of gravel. I tried to smile, but my face hurt too much to do it properly. I landed somewhere around a grimace. The strobe lights felt like rapid-fire ice picks to my temples and looking at her dead-on was tricky. She shimmered too much. I felt like my soul was leaking out of my shoes.

Her mouth moved slower. The syllables were syrupy and distinct. *Follow me.* She rose to her feet and dragged me up with her, cast a glance over her shoulder as she moved. She pressed her back against the kissing couple, who didn't notice, and then she turned in slow motion, took a bracing step through the crowd. She led me toward the stairs, and I let myself be leashed along, my feet moving faster than my head. My heart twisted itself to bits in my chest, and I had the notion that it'd be a useless fist of cells by the end of the night, too worn to go on beating, because I was going to have a panic attack if this girl—or, really, any girl—liked me. I wasn't built for this kind of emotional wear, I swear to God. I was built for skulking under bridges. This was too much.

Madeline walked with a tired sort of swagger. She squared her shoulders, slid through the mess with a cool stride in her step, and the crowd just oozed apart for her. No shoulder checking, no getting clotheslined by random flailing limbs. The people she passed didn't even look up, didn't react; they just gravitated away. Their backs made a tunnel and she eased through the space with me tailing behind her like a leather kite. She didn't look behind her when she reached the stairs, simply pulled me up with her, and I let myself stagger behind her two steps at a time. The music dulled as we got higher. She opened the door and I flinched.

Upstairs and downstairs were different dimensions, because in a past life, Jing's house just might have been a yacht. It was a chrome-and-cream magazine photoshoot, all brocade drapes and matching pillows. Black-and-white balloons polka-dotted the Persian rug. A strung-out redhead was spinning in the corner, singing a song that was popular when we were little. It wasn't the song playing downstairs. A couple across from her smoked weed and hacked like consumption victims, and, as we passed, they stopped their story swapping to look up at her and clap. Normally I'd stick around for a little while to eavesdrop. Stoner hearsay is usually true.

Madeline didn't seem keen on stopping for hearsay.

Her sneakers stopped in front of a set of French doors that served as the living room's back wall. These doors were the only barrier of separation between the inside's warmth and the outside's frigidness. She coiled her fingers around the gilded knob and twisted. The night air blew inward, ruffled her braids, and the two of us stepped into the dark.

The night was clean and dark and scalpel sharp. It cut deep, slid through my jacket and my scissor-cropped t-shirt to my stomach. As soon as both of my feet landed on the deck, the doors closed tight behind me and clicked. I zipped up my jacket and mouthed a cussy prayer that my vegan leather might suddenly be warmer than it was, but it wasn't, because of course it fucking wasn't. I crossed my arms over my chest and tried not to shiver like a fucking baby.

The seafoam corpse of Jing's pool was eerie in the moonlight. It was long, vaguely elliptical, about twenty feet back from the deck. The pool lights were on, but without thousands of gallons of water to coat them, they looked as harsh and bleak as surgical lamps. Dead leaves heaped like plague bodies along the pool's edge. A family of pale deer grazed between a set of lemony lawn chairs and odd jutting pink plastic flamingos. I rocked back and sucked on my teeth.

"So. How did you do it? Explain it to me." Madeline didn't look cold. On the contrary, the way she leaned her forearms against the deck railing looked as breezy as a June afternoon. Not a single shiver in sight. Her basketball jacket remained unzipped and drifted like a flag around her waist. The moonlight washed her out, made her corpsey. She looked at me unblinking and drummed her fingers on the rail.

Christ.

"You saw how I did it. You were there." My tongue was clumsy in my mouth. Lips moved oddly. I didn't mean to sound snide, but I did, because I guess I can't even scrape the bitter off my tone for a cute girl. My insides felt gooey and raw. The chill was weirdly abrasive after party heat. I wrapped my arms around my rib cage and tried to hold my body together with my fists, because I had caved and was now shivering so hard I thought bits of me might shake off and fly over the deck. "I don't know how to explain it in shorthand. It's complicated." I jammed my stupid tongue in my stupid cheek. I mean, that wasn't a lie, by any stretch. It was genuinely hard to explain. It was like explaining how to fall in love with something: There wasn't a way to do it that didn't sound like flowery bullshit, and even if you half managed it, the explanation wouldn't make it any easier to *do*. It wasn't a checklist sort of affair. My spell book was good, but brief, it was not.

"Can you show me?" Madeline slipped her fingers through the frets of her braid and poked them out the other side. The knuckles caught inside the braid vanished for a moment, like she'd dipped her hand through dark water. Her fingertips were hypnotic. I scratched at my jacket seams and chewed on my tongue. Madeline watching me was a physical thing. I felt it like an X-ray, like she was mapping my skull for craters.

"Huh." I looked out over the yard and tried to seem significantly cooler than I am. It's cool when people give the yard a casual, devil-may-care surveying gaze because eye contact freaks them out, yeah? The dizziness from the spell getting yanked earlier still tasted sour in the back of my throat. Or maybe that was the jungle juice. Probably equal parts spell and juice. Madeline was curious. She was genuinely curious and had pulled us somewhere we could be alone, and opportunities like this don't just happen. If I'm attention-starved enough to show off my magic at a fucking Jing/Daisy/Yates party, surely I'm thirsty enough to show a gorgeous stranger something killer. She wanted some magic. I had magic. I fought the urge to retch. "I could potentially show you a trick or two, yeah."

"No tricks. I want the real magic, flesh-and-blood magic, like you did down there. They said you're legit, and you are. What you did down there, there's no way you could have faked that," she said. She pulled her hand out of her hair, shoved herself off the deck rail and tossed that hand in my direction. "I'm Madeline Kline. Let's start with that. East High. I'm a senior. Your name is *Sideways?*"

"They call me that, yeah. Sideways Pike. West High. Also a senior." I reached for her hand and clapped it. It shocked me, like jumping the wrong kind of fence. Pain zapped down my fingers toward my palm and I jumped, jerked back, shook my hand at the wrist.

"What happened? You alright?" Madeline scrunched her brows into a V. She looked between my hand and my face and back again.

"Fine. You just shocked me. I'll live." A thin, nervous cackle creaked out of me. I pressed my hand up against my stomach under my shirt. My fingertips throbbed, but the throbbing simmered down to a tingling. My palm itched.

My heartbeat crashed faster. The tingling washed up my arm and into my chest, and the dead energy zapped back to life in my gut. Every single synapse twinged at once. Lightning marrow deep. I hitched a breath and swayed against the railing, braced myself with my free hand. My vision bruised. Madeline gripped my shoulder, sank her nails into my jacket to keep me from falling off the rail. Her touch was fire. It shocked through the fake leather, through vinyl and cotton and sinew, and I felt it soak into my bloodstream like a drug. My ribs contracted, and every breath was bigger than the last. The world was seizing up on me. The night was speckled red.

I was so happy I could sing.

"Sideways? What's up?" One of Madeline's braids swung

forward and dangled by my cheek. Her voice was low, measured. Moderately concerned. The hand on my shoulder moved to my back, just below my neck. I wasn't cold anymore. I was starting to sweat. Something was blooming in my throat, and if I didn't open my mouth, it might strangle me from the inside out.

"You want to see some magic?" I panted. I eyeballed her with a little twitch at the corners of my mouth. It felt like telling the most spectacular secret. My mind blazed. I wanted to scream.

She dimpled when she smiled.

I took her by the wrists and yanked her downward until we were both kneeling, shins on the cold, crispy deck. Wind picked up and tossed our hair, and it felt like celestial validation, like the entire night was primed for whatever I was going to do. *Wreak havoc,* said Nature. *Raise hell.* Our hands vibrated where they touched. This didn't feel like a liquor-dusted parlor trick; this was ancient, opulent, invincible. It was the realest thing in the world. I clawed around my memory for the circle in the basement, but I didn't need to dig for long. The image floated to mind. Long chalk lines, glow splattered but still unbreakably looped. I pictured it so vividly that the circle superimposed itself in our laps, not tangibly, but in a way that was undeniably real, and the words summoned themselves up to finish it off. "I call the chill in the air. I call down the lightning, the star fire, the dead summer sun. I call down the screaming cosmos and I cry for chaos. We want something impossible. We want something the papers can't explain, something so wild and gorgeous that nothing could doubt it, not ever. Douse our revelry with magic. Change the way we are."

The wind swept circles around us. Leaves whipped around our waists. A strange, desperate smile flooded Madeline's face. She opened her mouth to laugh, but there were only straight teeth and blackness stretching all the way down. No sound. Her hair pulled free of its braids and tumbled loose around her jaw. Something glistened in my ribs. My pulse hurtled forward. I squeezed her wrists so hard my knuckles popped.

"Give us decadence!" I threw back my head and addressed the stars directly, heartbeat heavy in my ears. A laugh broke out of me, gutted me from throat to belt, and I couldn't stop to swallow, couldn't stop to breathe. I was practically screaming. The words flew out of their own accord. "Give us something obscene! Give us something to sink our teeth into! We demand magic! Fuck you, reality! Tonight is a dream!"

My skull hit the deck with a smack.

✳

Something had me by the wrists.

I don't know who was dragging me, not specifically. But whoever they were, they clamped hard and their palms were warm, and they dragged me over something that scraped against my spine, something blunt and metallic. Something like a door track. It hurt like a mother. I squirmed myself awake.

A ceiling rolled above me. There was a wooden fan that spun in slow, psychedelic circles, and everything was scaldingly bright. I winced, scrunched up my face. Daylight slapped me like I was goddamned Dracula.

Morning. Daylight meant it was morning. How the hell? Discordant birdsong hammered at my temples. I heaved in a breath and wheezed.

"God, she's awake!" It was a feminine voice, a familiar one.

My arms hit the floor with a thud.

I spat, swore, and lugged myself into a sitting position. Every isolated muscle twitch weighed one billion pounds. I shrunk in on myself, winced away from lights and sounds and everything within ten feet. Covered my head with my arms. My entire body felt like a gigantic bruise. My skin was probably purple. All of it. I wasn't a girl anymore. I was a human welt. I curled my knees to my chest.

"Sideways. Sideways Pike, I swear to God." A different voice. Also a girl's. Also familiar. Why wasn't I connecting names to voices? I splayed my fingers across my face and peeked between them. There, looking supremely pissed, was Jing. Or her knees, anyway. I was eye level with her knees, and something told me that looking up was going to be a bad idea, because I didn't need to look up to understand the level of pissed she was. It radiated off her in waves. She was the Chernobyl of being pissed.

I furrowed my brows. "What the *fuck?*" Speaking felt slimy. I licked the inside of my shirt to scrape the sleep-film off my tongue.

"Good question." Jing tapped her foot. "Care to explain what the hell you did?"

"I don't know what you're talking about," I groaned, scowling into my sleeve. I was way too tired for tact. Besides. Fuck 'em for dragging me. Bastards.

"Cute. Sorry, no. You're explaining now, and I mean *now*," hissed Jing as she knelt in front of my face. She lowered her cheek until it rested on the cherrywood floors, angling herself so that I couldn't avoid eye contact. Her gaze locked on mine. I could just make out my scraggly reflection across her blackboard irises.

"By the way, Sideways, I don't know how you pulled all that off, but color me impressed." It was the first voice. Daisy. I had zero doubts. Only Daisy would be so smug in overriding Jing's authority like that. Also, her voice was way more nasal than Yates', who was the only other member of the Jing triumvirate I could think of in my state of groggy semiconsciousness. Wait, "triumvirate" meant three. That was all three of them. So yeah, definitely Daisy. What the fuck.

I pressed the heels of my hands against my temples and swore.

"*Listen.* I swear to God. I don't know what you're talking about. I don't know what you put in that punch, Daisy, but whatever it was really beat the ever-loving shit out of me. I must have been *blitzed*. I don't remember anything post hanging with that East High girl." Madeline. Where was Madeline? What had happened there? I silently prayed that drunk Sideways didn't screw everything up for me. It wouldn't be the first time.

"Damn it," said Jing. She looked me over, scowled, and stood up. "Goddamn it. You really don't remember."

"Where's Yates?" I rubbed my temples and looked over at Daisy, who had tossed herself across a studded leather armchair and was currently scrolling some blog on her phone. Her pleated Creamsicle was creased in odd places and her hair, which currently resembled a tumbleweed, was twisted into a ratty bun. One sock on, the other sock in the void, probably.

Daisy wrinkled her nose and huffed. "God, I'm not Yates' babysitter. She left. I don't know where. She's a big girl now." There was a waver in her voice that suggested she wasn't entirely sober yet.

That was how she normally sounded.

"You freaked her out. She went home," Jing corrected. She clicked her tongue. "Okay. Up. If you don't remember, I'll give you a little tour of the disaster zone. See if that clears some of those cobwebs." Jing didn't wait for me to stand on my own. Her hands found my shoulders, gripped fistfuls of faux cow hide, and jerked me to my feet.

"Jesus, ease up on me, alright?" I rubbed my left shoulder with a scowl.

She gave me a once-over and spun on her heel, and for some godforsaken reason, I followed her. There was a snicker from my left, so Daisy must have tagged along. Man. Something about this was making my flesh crawl, and it was too early for anything as uncomfortable as that.

The house, all things considered, wasn't in terrible shape. A few crushed cups, some popped balloons, a disembodied bra, and trampled confetti, but nothing impossible to clean up before the folks came home. The yachty living room still looked yachty. There was no vomit on the floor, which was a step above most party venues come morning. Jing picked up her pace and so did I. She stopped at the threshold between the hallway and the staircase to hell, aka the basement door.

Something flickered in Jing's expression, something that made Daisy stiffen behind me. I couldn't parse it. Jing flared her nostrils, pushed the door wide, and descended the staircase two steps at a time, and Daisy and I followed suit.

The walls were dripping with chalk.

Matrixes of spindly lines crisscrossed the floor, the ceiling, every inch of concrete in sight. Sigils, spirals, all varieties of rune and glyph. Sketchy symbols tattooed overtop of posters and streamers. None of them matched. Every mark had a different size, different shape, different level of intricacy. In the upper right corner of the room, there was something vaguely like an esoteric alchemical array, only it didn't match any array I'd ever read about. Across from it was a distinctly Crowley-ish set of stars, which bordered a random smattering of Enochian letters and something that looked like stupid failed cuneiform. And then there were the scribbles. Jagged, careless scribbles, the sort of absent doodling a loser goth might give their homework margins. Layered Xs, eyeballs, flowers. A heart punctured by twenty-something arrows.

The only commonality to the sigils was their orientation,

the slight slanting they all had toward the center of the room. They were pointing toward the circle. The circle was pristine.

"It was about midnight, maybe after. I was damn sure you'd gone upstairs. It was after the glow-stick thing," said Jing. She put her hands on her hips. "We were screwing around, having fun. I'll give you this, the glow-stick thing was rad. Everyone was majorly impressed. But then the chalk started. No one drew the shapes. They appeared on their own. I'm not screwing with you. All the drawings just showed up under our feet. Then the music got louder. Painfully loud. I had Alexis DJ for us, and it busted her speakers, it was so loud. It wasn't her music, either. It switched mid-song. It was this freaky retro doo-wop. It was damned weird, Sideways."

"I think it was the Chordettes," said Daisy.

"It was not the Chordettes," said Jing. "So, we're all wincing and cussing, and the lights cut out. All of them. But it wasn't the power, because the music kept playing and there was light under the door upstairs."

"You could only see people's hands. The broken glow bracelets, you know? It was wicked cool. Hands down, best scare party ever. I can't wait until next weekend. Costumes won't be tacky by then." Daisy, impervious to Jing's acid glare, looked monstrously pleased with herself. "The chalk drawings glowed, too. It was spooky as hell. I'm sure that Austin Grass pissed himself, he was so scared. Serves the bastard right for dumping Alexis like that."

"I filmed it." Jing flared her nostrils. Last night's mascara had flaked under her eyes, and the smudges reminded me of kiddy skeleton face paint. She pursed her lips. "People are still posting about it. It's a pretty big deal. Speculation abounds. You'd be surprised how many people are trying to write it off as some trick you learned in Drama, Sideways. As if the ragtag Drama Club could pull off a stunt like this."

"Watch it. That's my ragtag Drama Club you're talking about," I grumbled into the back of my wrist. The Sycamore Gorge West High Drama Club was the most the school had to offer, thanks. I loved it even if it was shitty and poorly directed and none of the folks involved were talking to me anymore. I scratched the back of my neck and took a step closer to the wall. A chalk drawing comprised of Vs and Cs loomed inches from my nose. Lines drawn on thick. Angles sharp. Curves heavy. "Holy hell. This is my handwriting."

"Yeah. I figured." Jing crossed her arms. "Explain how the hell you did it."

"I don't know." A smile broke over my face. My heartbeat rammed faster. I reached out and brushed the marks with my fingertips, brushed them as softly as I might stroke a cat. The swirling line work felt cool against my fingertips. Lovely, delicate lines, tangled and stretched tight atop the bricks. "God, this is so cool. I did this. I am *so cool*."

"Right," said Daisy.

"Look. Sideways." Jing struck a pose like she was praying: fingertips pressed together, palms parallel, expression hard as the walls or the floor. Her voice was sweet and buttery. "When I invited you to do your witch thing, I was expecting something small. I was going to let you wiggle your fingers and say something rhymey and weird. Hell. I thought it wouldn't work, but you're creepy and I figured just having you here would put people in the Halloween mood. This. I was not expecting all of this."

"Is that your way of saying that I'm banned from your house parties?" I leaned against the wall, shoulder to my accidental masterpiece. The stupid, giddy grin was here to stay. My face kind of hurt from smiling this hard. Good.

Jing looked me in the face, her gaze lasering through my skull. She grinned with teeth. "Are you kidding? I nearly got my scare party trending, and it's only the third. Everyone is talking about it. Conversation Monday morning will be strictly about the baddest haunted house ever."

I cocked a brow. "You're giving me whiplash, Jing."

"Look. I'm pissed because there's chalk all over my goddamn basement. You're staying the night and helping me clean up. My parents come home on Tuesday, and it needs to be spotless by then. I'm not pissed because of the magic. I just want to know how you did it. I want in."

My mind flashed to Madeline again. My smile slipped a little. If the casting worked, then what had happened with Madeline? I shoved my hands into my pockets and stared at my shoes. There was a crumpled leaf stuck in the laces. The gap from midnight 'til now was starting to leave a strange taste in my mouth. "Did you see Madeline, by any chance?"

"Madeline? Like, the extra chick on the circle? No." Jing snaked her hand through her hair. "Why?"

"She wanted to see how it worked, too. She dragged me

upstairs and we sat on the deck, and she was insistent about it. Not that I minded. I like showing off. Something struck me when we were out there, and I felt this sort of zinging queasiness, the sort that always comes with magic. So, I maybe recklessly jumped into it. It was a huge rush, but I blamed the alcohol for that. I didn't think about it. I mean, it shouldn't have worked. I drew a five-pointed circle, and Yates broke the circle, so the spell should have died. I don't know how the two of us could have done all this. I really don't remember." I jammed my tongue in my cheek. I tried to rewind the tapes in my head, but it was like there wasn't a gap at all. Inhale at midnight, exhale at noon.

"We found you on the deck. Just you, though. Madeline must have left," Jing said.

"Do you have her number?"

Daisy yowled and clapped her hands.

"Not like that." I rolled my eyes so hard that they nearly fell out of my head. "I'm just saying that she might know what happened. I'm plenty curious myself, believe it or not."

Admittedly, the Daisy line of thought was also appealing. A significant part of me wanted to buy Madeline coffee. All the coffee in the damned world. Even if she *had* left me on a freezing deck. Wait. Maybe not, then. Goddamn it. I clawed the hair off my forehead and cringed at how stringy it felt.

"I don't. I barely know her. She came with someone else." Jing stood beside me and rocked back against the wall. Her hair, tousled and bleached, fell in a jagged fringe across her forehead, and the way it frayed around her collarbone was the stuff of daydreams. If she told me that she'd spent the morning at the beach, I'd have believed her.

"Random," I said mostly to myself, "but your hair looks mega-kickass. Thought you should know." I scuffed the sole of my boot across the cement. "When I do the messy hair thing, I look like a junkie."

"Thanks," said Jing. She blinked, and something like a smile twitched on her cheeks. "And you always look like a junkie. It just kind of works on you."

Right. I took a cursory scan of the room and cleared my throat. "I have no idea what any of these lines mean. Like, any of them. It makes zero sense."

"I can't believe I'm asking this, but what did the actual spell do? Like, what were you trying to do when we were all holding hands?" Daisy was sizing up the St. Sebastian heart doodle. "Because I've seen *The Craft* like six times, and they never drew hearts on stuff."

"I don't really know what I was trying to do. I just kind of did it. I don't normally draw hearts and shit, but it doesn't matter so much what you draw, so long as you believe it. I mean, there's got to be a circle, but you can scribble like a five-year-old with lipstick on a wall, and it'll still work as long as your incantation doesn't suck."

Actually, no. It barely ever works, and when it does, it can usually be debunked by killjoy skeptics on the internet, and that's when I'm following spell book advice to the letter. *This* was absurd. I didn't draw any of these on purpose, so there wasn't any intention to drive them. And it wasn't like I had a hell of a lot of intention in the first place. I was trying to make the lights flicker. Something simple, flashy, manageable. These sigils shouldn't have been capable of this.

I cracked my knuckles, click-click-click, but my left ring finger was stuck un-cracked, and it took a substantial amount of willpower not to snap it trying. My mood rings smudged green. Thinking hurt. "Hey. Jing. Can I see that video you took? There's gotta be something in there."

"Yeah." Jing pulled the latest iPhone out of nowhere and fluttered her fingertips across the screen. She gave me a tight little smirk and thrust it in my direction.

The quality, for a shitty phone recording, was remarkable. The bass was distorted, but the laughter and off-key singing sounded genuine. Glow-splotchy bodies writhed in on themselves. Then the chalk drawings rippled into existence, floating like bodies to the brick wall's surface. The music cut out, then skidded back with an old vinyl crackle. A scream tore through the crowd, and dark shadows, only people-shaped where the neon splatters lit them up, threw themselves on top of each other as they scrambled toward the stairs. Jing's voice, jagged as glass, carved through the crowd: *Bet you losers thought we couldn't scare you!* The angle fell crooked and blacked out.

I watched it three times.

"I have no idea what I did," I said. "But, holy hell, I did a damn good job of it."

"I'd say." Daisy yawned, stretched on relevé. She folded her arms behind her head. "You should come to our parties more often. Jing, I'm inviting Sideways to all our parties. Na-na *na* na-na. Nothing you can do about it. Sideways Pike at all our parties. Can you imagine?"

Yikes. Alright. My crooked, stupid smile fell right off, but I crossed my arms, made like I hadn't heard her. I'd just materialized magic chicken scratch on Jing Gao's walls without trying to. Daisy would have to rack up a lot more nasty to faze me at this point.

"Give my phone back."

I uncrossed my arms long enough to hand it over and promptly resumed my stance.

"Right," said Jing as she pocketed her phone and rocked back on her heels. "Whatever."

"Look." I wasn't sure what point I was trying to make, but a nagging voice in my head said it was the wrong one. I cleared my throat. "I can try to revamp that spell, reverse engineer it or something. I can show you how I did it in the first place. Us plus Yates and Madeline pack quite the supernatural punch. No way we couldn't re-create this. Hell, we could make it bigger. I wager we could do a lot more than party tricks. We could do something really cool."

Something cool. A horrible, tantalizing fantasy swam up in my mind's eye: the four of us in a clique, strutting meanly in lockstep in matching jackets, our nails sharp, our lips dark, our heels clacking in tandem with our heartbeats. The unholy trinity alchemizing into a quartet. I imagined us shocking people speechless. They'd look at us like we were teenage Erinyes. Like we were untouchable. I felt ill and giddy imagining it, imagining Yates and Jing and Daisy wanting to be near me, wanting to talk to me and be close to me. Best friends like the movies.

Jing's phone exploded. Her phone was at its peak volume, and the ringing was so jarring that I jumped. She sighed, rolled her eyes, and declined the call. "It was just Yates," she said to Daisy. She flickered her focus back to me. "So. If you think we can do that again, I'm in. Nothing is cool in this town, and that was cool. Bring it. We can—god*damn* it," she spat. Her phone lit up again. The ringer blasted. Jing scowled, swiped, and cradled it to her ear.

Daisy and I exchanged silent question marks.

"What the fuck. Slow down. Start over."

Someone was sobbing on the other side.

"I can't understand you, babe. What's wrong?"

The sobbing grew louder.

"What do you mean, in the pool? You're talking nonsense. Okay. Okay, I get it. I'll come see the pool. Hush, I know."

"The pool?" Daisy looked ravenous. "Like, as in *your* pool?"

Jing shot a seething glance in Daisy's direction, but she nodded nonetheless.

Daisy looked lupine. She grabbed me by the wrist and bounced from foot to foot. "Come on, Sideways. If it's gremlins, you can witch them to death." She dragged me back toward the stairs.

Daisy held my hand differently than Madeline had. Tighter grip, almond nails poised to prick. Her hands were softer. Even so, the similarity made me roil. Cold sweat on the back of my neck. I let her pull me across the threshold. I heard Jing, still whispering into her phone, at our heels.

We trekked through the party ruins, through the black balloons, through the deck door, past the place where my skull had smacked, down the rickety stairs. We crossed the lawn and weaved between flamingos.

We stopped precariously close to the edge of the pool, toes on the rim, and peered over the edge at the cavernous turquoise hole below. It went down and down and down.

My stomach flipped.

There were bodies at the bottom.

Four slender bodies, two does and a fawn, lay dead in the deep end of the pool. Necks stretched. Eyes dull. Their legs stuck out at stiff angles. There were no bullet holes or cherry splatters. Their insides were not out. It was just the stillness, the inexplicable sickening stillness. Their bodies were arranged in neat rows. The bottom doe, the bigger of the two, had her head to the left and her tail to the right, and the middle doe was arranged in the opposite fashion. The fawn, still milky-speckled, was stretched like the first doe, left to right.

The fourth body, curled up right next to the fawn, was Yates, her phone cradled to her cheek.

# TWO

# WHO PUT BELLA IN THE WYCH ELM?

Yates whispered to herself. She shuddered, ghosted her
fingertips across her sides and her arms. Her mascara was
horror-flick thick under her eyes and her curls were still
peppered with flowers from last night, but the petals were
limper now, shrunken. Her feet were a shade bluer than the
pool's belly beneath her feet. Her left knee was bruised like a
Jawbreaker.

"Yates. Baby girl. Talk to us."

"What happened?"

"Are you hurt?"

"Are you okay?"

"Jesus fucking Christ, does she look like she's okay?"

"If someone laid a single finger on you, I'll chainsaw
massacre them. I'll carve their guts out. I'll feed them to your
dog."

Daisy squeezed my hand so tight I could hardly stand it.
My bones were threatening to crack. She'd cut off circulation
at this rate, but I couldn't bring myself to jerk my hand away,
couldn't pry my eyes off Yates for that long.

A sob tore out of her, a seam-splitting sob. It set my jaw on edge.

Jing's expression flickered and her mouth opened, but the sound caught somewhere in her throat. She dropped, hoisted herself over the ledge of the pool, and jumped down into the cavern. Her feet hit the ground with a smack. Her mouth was pulled taut. Jing maneuvered around the deer in an arc, and she fell to a crouch when she reached Yates. She wrapped her arms around Yates' shoulders and whispered something in her ear. I couldn't make out the words, only the harsh, low raggedness of Jing's voice. Yates hid her face in her knees.

"Hey, Sideways," said Daisy. She sank her nails into my skin. "How'd the deer die?"

"No idea. I didn't do it." My tongue felt brittle. I shook my head, curled my lip, tried to make my heart beat slower, beat at a human pace, but it just got harder. I pulled my arm back, but Daisy's grip was inescapable. "I don't know how they died. I really don't."

"If you did this to Yates," Daisy said, "they won't find your fucking body, Sideways."

Jing's gaze cut away from Yates. She looked at me out of the corner of her eye. I blistered where her eyes met mine, and I shook my head, opened my mouth. My voice box wasn't working.

Three little deer, all laid in a row. Acid lurched up the back of my throat. There weren't any wounds on them. There should be gory bullet holes or arrows jutting from their stomachs, or knife wounds, gashes, lesions. But the bodies were pristine. If their eyes were shut, they could have been sleeping, but they weren't. The whole thing smacked of magic.

Jing moved her mouth against Yates' temple. Her lips moved. She kept looking at me, her gaze fixed on my face. Yates shook her head. She moved her head to murmur something into Jing's hair, then tossed her arms around Jing's shoulders and collapsed against her. Jing pulled her tight, furrowed her brow, tore her gaze away from me. She kissed her forehead. "It wasn't Sideways," she said.

It felt like a sip of cold water. Daisy loosened her grip and I pulled myself free, shook off the sting with a hiss. Angry red welts bloomed up where her fist had been.

Jing hauled Yates upright. She went boneless, crumpled against Jing's sternum, and Jing braced herself against the wall with a sharp inhale. Yates wrapped one arm around Jing's waist and the other around her shoulders and patted her arm, looking up at us beseechingly.

My throat tied itself up in knots.

I stepped off the ledge. It was a six-foot drop, maybe seven, and the impact threw me. My boots skidded on the cement. The impact wrenched the breath out of me, and I sucked in a hard breath, tossed an arm around my stomach. I took a step forward and froze, recoiled. A wave of nausea struck me. The toe of my right boot was an inch from the first doe's nose. My ankle was reflected in its glossy black eye.

My palms dewed up.

I shifted my weight to the balls of my feet. My steps were lighter, quicker than felt natural, but stomping felt inappropriate. What if I woke them up? I shivered. Gritted my teeth. Yates was under the diving board, at the deep end's deepest point, and the ground sloped under my feet, drew me down to where she sat. I stopped beside the two of them and shoved my hands in my pockets. Words didn't come. I wasn't good at helping people. I wasn't good at any of that. I swallowed, gave Jing a tight little nod.

Yates threw herself at my chest. The impact rocked me. Her arms looped around my neck and she shuddered, heaved a ragged breath into my hair. Her cheek felt wet on my collarbone. My mouth popped open. I looked at Jing, eyes wide, but she didn't look up to tell me how to deal with this. Her eyes were on Yates' back. I swallowed, awkwardly placed my hand between her shoulder blades, and patted her spine.

"The way you were laying there, I thought you were dead."

I looked down. Yates' eyes were enormous. They consumed my entire line of sight. Deer eyes, living deer eyes. Her lids were magenta and raw.

"Lila. Hey." Jing rocked toward us, jammed her tongue in her cheek. "Hey. Let's go. Sideways and I are going to walk you over to the stairs over there, okay?" She shot me a glance. I nodded, shifting so that Jing could slide her arm around Yates' shoulders. We braced her between us. I gnawed my bottom lip.

Lila. I wasn't sure I'd ever heard Yates called by her first name before. Lila Yates.

One of the flowers slipped from her temple and fell to the concrete floor.

Daisy edged around the pool, displacing mounds of

blackened leaves as she went. She stopped by the shallow end's staircase and sat on the topmost step. She reached out a hand, wiggled her fingertips. The snarl from earlier melted off her face and she softened, gave Yates a strange, crooked smile. "Come on, Baby Yates. Come inside."

We led Yates forward. She wasn't walking, but she let herself be whisked. Between Jing and me, she felt like air. Her breathing was easier, still raw, but measured. I tried not to look at the deer as we went around them, but the fawn's eyes followed us as we went.

When we drew close enough, Yates reached out and took Daisy's hand. Daisy pulled her away from us, guided her up the stairs. She kept her fingers twined with Yates'.

Jing closed the French doors behind us.

We brought Yates to the bathtub.

Jing had drawn the water steaming hot. She dropped a little asteroid into the water, which bubbled violet and pink, and we all sat on the countertop and watched the water rise. The bath bomb smelled like blackberries and something ambiguously sugary. The mirror clouded. Water droplets beaded on the lilac wall tiles.

"Did someone attack you?" Jing stuffed her hands in her pockets. Her face looked vaguely green.

"Not like that," said Yates. She raked the fabric of her dress off her back, lifted it over her shoulders. It crumpled on the floor in a yellow heap. "It wasn't like that."

Jing crossed her arms, gave her a curt nod. "In you go, then."

Yates blew out slow, shivered once, and stepped into the tub. Her calves disappeared into red-violet bubbles and she lowered herself into the steaming water, drew her knees to her chest. "I love you guys."

A bizarre prickling sensation bubbled up in my chest, and I rubbed my thumb across my collarbone, the salty spot where she'd cried on me. *Guys,* plural. She didn't know me, so she didn't mean me, but the phrase stabbed between my fourth and fifth ribs and burrowed deep, took root. My face felt hot. I forced my gaze down, stared at the dress on the floor.

"You're not into this, are you?" Daisy dropped her voice and poked me in the ribs. A smile flickered on her lips.

"Fuck you," I snapped.

"She's not being creepy, Daze." Yates sank a little lower into the tub. She rested the back of her neck on the rim of the tub and stared up at the ceiling. "Sideways didn't climb into that pool to try and get with me." She rolled her head to the side, gave me a little smile. It was weak, and fleeting, but I felt it like sunlight. "Right?"

"Yeah." I rubbed the tiles with my boot.

Jing leaned forward. The drawstrings on her hoodie swung back and forth like the spindle on a metronome, and she cleared her throat, bit her lip. "I need to know what happened, Lila. I need you to tell me everything." She didn't sound unkind, but she was Jing. Everything she said sounded like her left hook, but there was a note of raw softness that I hadn't heard come out of her before.

"Right." Yates splashed her face with pink water, and some

of last night's eyeliner blurred off. She looked at the faucet like she was trying to make something out, but the faucet was still a faucet. Her expression fell. She rubbed her hands over her knees and cleared her throat. "It feels like a fever dream now. Christ. It was after the glow-stick bit. Look, I've seen all your stupid horror movies, and I wasn't about last night. We're hot girls. I'm a hot *black* girl. Hot girls at parties who play with ghosts end up dead in horror movies, particularly girls like me. Chopped into ribbons dead. Inviting the local devil worshiper over to your place felt like a particularly stupid idea, Jing, but I thought it was bullshit, so I didn't say anything. I guess it was harmless enough when it wasn't going to work. But then it *worked*. I was like, no thanks. I just wanted to have a good time and not be axe murdered by the devil, so I slipped off to get tipsy and avoid this nonsense like the plague.

"So, I was on the dance floor and there was this East High boy that I hadn't seen before. He was angel-faced, but he wasn't my type. Too preppy, I guess. But preppy felt safe, and I was just trying to distance myself from the weirdness. He was kind of handsy, but I like that. Mind was in dirty places, you know? So, I drag him into that back closet in the basement, the one behind the punch table, and we'd not quite closed the door when the drawings showed up on the wall.

"Then he . . . switched. It was like Jekyll and Hyde, just like that. His face curled up, and he started screaming about someone named Addie. 'Where's Addie, how do you know Addie, Addie, Addie.' He just kept screaming about it. I'm not sure I've ever met someone named Addie in my life. I told him again and again, but he just kept snarling at me. I couldn't hear him over the music. And the music was wrong. It was this vintage stuff, all staticky and brassy, and it wasn't on the playlist for the party—I helped Alexis make that playlist. I thought I was losing it.

"I thought he was going to kill me. There was something wrong with his eyes. They were too big for his face. He said something else, but I still couldn't hear him. He took me by the shoulders and pulled me out of the closet, and he took me through the crowd and up the stairs, but everyone was too busy freaking out about the chalk drawings to notice anything, or it was too dark, or everyone was stoned past heaven or straight up unconscious. Sideways was out cold on the patio. Her eyes were open. I thought you were dead, Sideways. We stepped over you."

I shifted a little. Daisy shot me a look.

"So, he takes me into the pool. He shoves me against the wall under the diving board, and then he starts acting weird. And I mean *weird*. He starts talking nonsense, and I can't understand a word out of his mouth. Something about whoever the hell Addie is, I don't know. And then he takes a permanent marker out of his pocket and writes something above my knee, and then, nothing. Seriously, nothing. Until I woke up and there were fucking deer in the pool with me, and I was freezing and alone." Yates paused and splashed more pink water on her face. "Thank God my phone wasn't dead. I just don't get it. It was just so freaky. And the deer? What the fuck is that about?"

46

"You sure it was a preppy kid? Sounds like some hick jock who thought he was clever," said Daisy with a snarl. She slid off the counter and bounced on her toes, shifted her weight back and forth like a boxer. "It's fucking sick. Who the hell puts a girl in an empty pool and arranges deer around her? What even is that? I swear to God, when I find out which miserable douchebag did this, I'm going to slit his throat with a goddamned bobby pin."

"*Daisy,*" Jing said.

Daisy scowled and crossed her arms over her chest.

I shoved my fists in my pockets. "He drew something on your leg, right?"

"Yeah." Yates frowned, and she stuck her sudsy leg out of the bath. She pressed her pointer finger against a smudge above her kneecap. "It was here."

I coughed. "Can I see it?"

She let go of a breath and gave me a nod. I crouched by the side of the tub.

The mark was faded now. It was quick, sketchy, blurred past the point of distinction, but I thought I saw switchbacks and spirals in the lines. "It's a sigil." No question about that much. "Not sure what it means, though."

"Oh." Yates' face fell, but I shook my head, cut off the apology before it came out of her mouth.

"There isn't an inscription. I wouldn't know even if you hadn't washed it off. I guess he knew a thing or two, whoever he was." I didn't like that. It conjured a sour taste.

I'd never met someone else who could draw sigils. I'd been

under the impression that I was the only one around these parts. It was undeniably a sigil, though, and whoever had drawn it on her was good enough to skip the chants. That wasn't supposed to be a thing.

Yates reached out of the bath and caught one of my hands, gave it a squeeze. My heart cartwheeled. I jerked my gaze away. Her thumb rubbed circles around my knuckles, and it ached, but I didn't tell her not to. She didn't ask about the bruising. I felt the question hang in the air, but I wasn't in the mood to answer.

"Sideways." It was Jing's voice behind me. Raked a shiver down my spine.

"Yeah?"

"Can you curse people?"

Something constricted in my chest.

"I mean. Theoretically, yeah. Never tried before," I sounded out. It was true. I hadn't. When I had a problem with someone, I usually explained it to them with the backs of my hands.

"Let's curse him, then. Magic works. You can do it. I want him to suffer for this." Jing's voice was cool, but I felt her seethe without even looking. It pulsated in the air. "Tonight, that's what we're going to do. Chalk be damned—I'll deal with that in the morning. I want to curse this prick so severely he never even ponders touching a girl again." Then, softer: "Would you like that, Lila?"

Yates frowned. She gave my hand a squeeze. "I think so."

"Badass," said Daisy. "I'll order pizza."

\*

Daisy did not order pizza. Pizza is singular. She ordered *pizzas*. Three pizzas with every combination of sauce and topping the pizzeria could supply, with the addition of salad and buffalo wings and two two-liter bottles of orange soda. She put it all on a heavy-looking credit card without asking what it cost.

We sat on Jing's bedroom floor, the four of us in a circle. Daisy had eaten most of a pizza by herself. The sauce on her cheek looked like a war wound. Yates had her curls wrapped up in a sky-colored scarf, and she sat with her knees to her chest, absently toying with the furry carpet. Jing sat across from me. She hadn't touched the food, hadn't looked away from my face. She stared at me so intensely I felt like she was fiddling with my synapses.

My guts felt hollow. I took a second slice.

"So," I said. "Yates. Do you know his name? It helps if you do."

I didn't have my spell book at hand, but there wasn't much of it I didn't know by heart. The curse section of my *Vade Mecvm Magici* was brief and vague, but that was how it was about everything. It wouldn't help me here. The name would, though. Might aim this thing properly.

"I don't think I asked." She shrugged, squeezed fistfuls of fluffy carpet. "I don't think I cared. He was an East High loser. He wasn't exactly interesting."

"His name was probably Chett. Every other guy at East High is named Chett. Douchebag name." Daisy opened the second box of pizza, which had a few toppings I didn't recognize. I didn't ask. I'd eat it regardless.

"Yeah. He looked like he could've been a Chett." Yates picked at the pizza without much interest. "That works, I guess."

"That might work. I don't know. Do you remember what his face looked like?" I dropped the crust on one of Jing's porcelain plates and crossed my legs.

Yates nodded. "Don't think I could forget."

"Can you focus on that while we do this? We're going to need a poppet. A poppet . . . like, a symbol for Chett. An idol. It could be a spoon, a hairbrush, doesn't matter. Something that we can pass around while we work."

Jing clucked her tongue. "Hold on." There was a horrible, anticipatory beat while she looked at me dead on, said something vicious with her eyes, and then fell backward and rolled onto her stomach. She shimmied under her bed, movements low and lizard-like, and clawed around for something out of my line of sight. A breath later, she emerged with a battered Rubbermaid container in her hands. She sat up, popped the lid, flipped the container over. A hail of naked Barbies clattered to the floor.

These were not virile Barbies. They were half headless, limbless, tattooed with Magic Marker and floral stickers. Hair hacked to bits. A few faces had been scrubbed off and redrawn. They looked like Jack the Ripper victims. The Ken dolls were in equally rough shape, if not worse. Those were the dolls Jing was sorting through now. She pulled all the buff-colored plastic boyfriends out and laid them in a row, shoulder to shoulder, and tapped her nails over each of their abdomens with a frown. "These oughta work, yeah?"

"Christ, Jing, I didn't know you still had these." Daisy clapped one of her hands over her heart and snatched up a Ken doll with the other. She pinched its ankle between her fingers and held it at arm's length, eyeballed it from head to toe. This was a blond Ken. Its left eye was worn away, but its perpetual smile was untouched. If *Toy Story* was right, and toys were sentient beings capable of suffering, this Ken was one unlucky bastard, indeed. Daisy pressed it to her sternum and fanned her fingers over its back. "I haven't seen these since second grade. Do you remember their names? I feel like this one was Eric. My first boyfriend. It's so sweet I could die."

"Pick a Chett," Jing said with a leer. She looked at me for a long minute, like I might say something to contradict her, but there was nothing to say. She was right. Barbies would work damn well. Curse dolls were a trope for a reason.

Yates ran her fingertips over every battered doll boy. She pressed her prints into the notches between neck and chin, danced over their nipple-less plastic pecs, prodded hollow faces until they squished. Yates bit her bottom lip, scrunched up her brows, pondered every plastic body with equal consideration. Her eyes moved from left to right and left again, textbook-reading style, until they froze mid-motion.

Her gaze drifted up an inch at a time.

It settled on the doll in Daisy's fists.

Daisy scoffed. "Really? Yates, this is my boyfriend, Eric. He'd never put anyone in a pool. You've got the wrong guy."

Yates turned that gaze on me and fluttered her lashes.

Damn.

I ripped my hand through my hair. "Yates called it. Eric is moonlighting as Chett tonight. Sorry, Daisy."

"Ugh. Screw you guys." Daisy, pouting, tossed Eric/Chett onto the faux fur carpet and crossed her arms over her chest.

Yates delicately picked it up, placed it on her lap. She squeezed its head between her thumb and forefinger. "How did you even manage to smudge its eye? I thought the paint on these things was immortal. I've never seen a smeared one before."

"Bug spray," said Jing. She wagged her eyebrows. "Melts the paint right off."

"Alright." I cleared my throat. "Do we know what we're doing to him? Have you decided for sure, Yates?"

"I don't know. I don't want to put him in the hospital or anything."

"I want to put him in the hospital," said Jing and Daisy in unison.

"It'd look really bad to colleges if we killed the guy, so I'm drawing a hard line with anything that could fuck up and result in murder. Besides, that's a tad complicated. Let's go with something easier to pull off. Mental anguish, something like that," I said. I ran my thumbnail over a chicken bone on my plate. There was a cold, queasy feeling in my gut. I tried to ignore it. My palms clammed up anyway.

Jing considered for a moment and gave us a nod. "I could work with mental anguish."

"I mean. I want to implode his gonads," Daisy said, "but I could settle for psychological torture, if y'all are going to be boring about it. You game, Yatesy?"

Yates sucked in her cheeks, and after a long pause, she set the doll on the floor. "I'm game."

"Alright." I wiped my mouth with my sleeve. "Here's what we're going to do. We need a piece of paper to draw our sigils on, and a cup or some such to trace a circle with. Don't overthink it. We're all going to lay down a few curse lines, Thou Shalt Nots—actions you want to stop and their consequences. It doesn't matter what they are, so long as they feel right in your gut, alright? Just, again: zero murder. We're going with mind games. Then we draw shapes over the lines to lash them in place. The shapes can be literally anything. You guys saw the basement. Seriously. Anything genuine goes. Questions?"

"Yeah," said Jing. "What if we just wrote it all on the doll? I want them sticking to him forever. We can make it like we're tattooing our grievances on him. Make it count."

Shit. That was clever, and would totally work. I nodded, shoved my hands under my armpits. A nasty, cloying thought writhed around in my stomach like a long, icy centipede, squirming, twisting, and I felt it threaten to clamber up my esophagus and batter itself through my teeth. It was the urge to fuck up this whole thing and say something like the truth:

If Jing was as good at magic as I was, would that be the end of whatever this was? If they didn't need me, why keep me around? This, the four of us, was hardly anything, but I felt attached to it now. I set my teeth in a hard line and forced it back down. "Yeah." I swiped my tongue over my teeth. "I guess that'll work, too."

Daisy fetched a Sharpie from Jing's bedside table.

Jing picked up the Chett poppet and flipped it over a few times in her hands. "He's fucking small. Where do we draw the circle?"

"Around his neck," I breathed. I reached for another slice of pizza. The cheese was approaching room temperature, but the litany of mismatched toppings smelled bizarrely delicious. I sank my teeth in and tried to steel my nerves. Chew. Swallow. Take comfort in the fact that it tastes fantastic. "If you draw it around the doll's neck, then everything we draw on the body is technically inside of the circle. There isn't enough room on his chest to draw a decent circle, even if we crammed our writing as small as we could."

"Cool," said Jing. She passed the Sharpie from Daisy to Yates.

Yates, looking pensive, uncapped the pen. Pop goes the toxic Sharpie smell. Nausea lurched in my gut. Yates drew a skinny black ring around his neck. It resembled a nineties choker. She shook her head and put him down, pulled her knees to her chest. "Someone else write first."

"I'll do the honors," Daisy said. She gingerly plucked up the doll and the marker and laid them both innocently across her lap. She lofted the Sharpie, poised as Marie Antoinette with a teacup, and tattooed where the doll's clavicle should be. "Thou Shalt Not Look at Girls with Nasty Intentions." She took the Thou Shalt Not thing literally, I suppose. Works. She used hearts to dot her *i*s. "If you do, you'll go blind looking at them."

Jing took the doll out of Daisy's hands and flipped him over, poised the Sharpie between his plastic shoulder blades. "Thou Shalt Not Lay Hands on Unconsenting Girls. So much as an accidental brush in the hallway, and it'll trigger more panic than a cavity kid at a dentist."

Yates nodded at me.

The doll and the marker were placed in my hands.

I hovered the Sharpie over its abdomen. "Thou Shalt Not Be Prideful for Harming Girls. Any happiness gleaned from harming girls will rebound threefold as shame."

Yates flashed me a nervous smile.

I handed Chett over.

"Thou Shalt Not Stalk. That Addie chick included. If you even think about stalking a girl again, you'll feel double the paranoia you inflict," said Yates, who wrote across the doll's plastic thighs.

"Alright, then." I drew my knees to my chest, reached for another wing, and gnawed on it. "Yates, you can draw the sigils. First thing that comes to mind, draw that."

She drew daisies and butterflies across his Four Commandments.

Yates, when she'd finished girlying up the lyrics to our

curse, set Chett on the floor between the four of us. His shiny body caught the light and glared. Daisy smoothed his hair and repositioned him, spread his arms and his legs so that he looked like a store-brand Vitruvian Man.

I hacked into my sleeve and cast down my chicken bone like a gauntlet, seized the hands on either side of me. "Time for the invocation."

I squeezed them tight. Forty fingers tangled together, heartline to heartline, and magic knocked me up the backside of my head. My eyes swelled in their sockets. Sinews stiffened. Blood welled up in my ribs. The circle on Chett's neck thrummed with a livid, liquid power, and it charred its way through my bones, lacerated tissue, and seeped into marrow. The words bubbled up in my stomach, and I felt the incantation vibrate in my teeth.

Chett, ever smiling, stared vaguely toward the door.

"The four of us bind ourselves together to curse a toxic fuck. Where our hands are clasped, where skin touches skin, power flows through. As long as our fingers are tangled, the entire universe is trapped here between us. We're naming this doll our poppet. We've got some scores to settle."

Jing leaned forward with her teeth set on edge. "No one fucks with us. The bastard who did so needs to suffer, and we're determined to see to it." Her voice snapped—harsh fricatives, clipped vowels, throaty slides to the tonic. I didn't have time to be jarred. She was doing this right. She was spitting *magic*. Those words had charge in them, had darkness. They prickled the hair on my neck. "One of ours was screwed with by a certain fuckboy. We're going to call this asshole *Chett*. Chett needs to be made an example, and our clique is henceforth putting a permanent end to this kind of disgustingness. This doll is Chett. He's going to help modify all that hell Yates had to suffer through." Jing spoke with brittle straightforwardness. Her voice had edges. This incantation felt different than last night. It felt like a *curse* now, like ancient, honest vengeance.

My chest thrummed like a beehive. The tension in me was redistributing. Normally, all the elastic power fizzled in me and me alone, but I felt it radiate out of my fingertips, felt it ooze into the three girls beside me. Every word out of Jing's mouth took some weight off my shoulders. I didn't feel like I was tap-dancing on a scythe blade. There was balance, calibration. Breathing was easier.

"I don't want anyone else to go through that, not ever. I don't want him to be capable of it anymore. He needs to simmer in what he did," Yates said. Her eyes, under inky lashes, drifted back and forth across Chett's stiff stomach. I held her hand tighter, and she held mine tighter still.

Daisy let out a high, crooked laugh, like she'd been punched in the stomach. Her eyes stretched to take up half her face. She balled her hand up in a fist around my fingers, and she leaned forward, locked her gaze on the Chett doll's body. "He's gonna do more than *simmer*."

"The four of us invite the chaos into our arms and charge it thus: where wrong has been inflicted, the scales have to tip. The four of us have four prongs for Chett. May he feel where we jab him forever," I breathed, white-knuckled, as I clutched at either girl beside me, "and may he think about exactly what the fuck he's done."

"First prong. Dear Chett," said Daisy, licking her teeth like a cat with a canary, "Thou Shalt Not Look at Girls with Nasty Intentions. One sick glance in a girl's direction, and it'll sting your eyes like a splash of battery acid. Don't even glance their way with one of your filthy thoughts. Or, better yet, do it. I *really* hope you do. I want you to find out what happens." There was a weird cast of puckish delight on Daisy's features. Every word out of her mouth struck her face like an eerie spotlight: the mocking curve of her smile, the upturn of her nose, the triangle of peach blush that peaked her cheeks. Was she getting off on this? Magic fucks with my perception, so I'm not sure if it was real, but out of the corner of my eye her skirt looked like it was fluttering. Her fringe drifted off her face. Whether she was serious about the spell casting, I didn't know, but Daisy's smirking gave the room a strange static. I felt it prickle the follicles on my arms, tease the hair to stand on end.

"Second." Jing slammed her brows into a V. She bristled with the sort of determination that I imagined Bonnie and Clyde had, righteously illegal and dripping with love. She rubbed her thumb over Yates' knuckles. "Thou Shalt Not Touch Unconsenting Girls. I don't care if it's innocent. I don't care if it was the single least harmful thing in the entire world. I don't care if you bump into a girl at the supermarket. Unless they expressly say so, I want it to shock you like an exposed wire. I want you to feel it in your stomach for hours afterward. Not only that, but I want you to be so sick over what you did, so nauseous with it, that you couldn't even fathom touching them twice. Not a single fucking finger."

"Third." My words, my voice, my heart spasming at twice its normal rate. Everything was racing faster. My tongue moved too fast behind my teeth. "Thou Shalt Not Be Prideful for Harming Girls. You won't be cocky or smug, not even for a second. The second something snide or misogynistic comes out of your mouth, it'll scald your tongue and taste like rot. You'll choke on it, every single ugly syllable."

"Fourth and final." Yates let out a breath, closed her eyes. "Thou Shalt Not Stalk. Leave Addie the hell alone, and leave everyone else alone, too. Don't look for me, or you'll only get lost. And if you look for me or Addie or anyone else, you'll feel awful for it, worse than I do right now. Three times the paranoia. It'll be like the walls have eyes just for you."

"This is our hex," I said. "You earned every inch."

A pungent, acidic smell split the air. Something like burning plastic. I looked down and my throat closed. The doll had moved, and not in a way it could've. The arms had snapped in half. The place where its elbows should be were cleanly broken, and thin, Sharpied filaments held the forearms to the upper arms. Its fuse-fingered hands rested over its face, covered its melty eyes. The sigil, the inscription, and the doodles had seeped into the plastic itself. They looked like a molded feature, like he'd come this way.

The tension melted away. Now there was just the

afterlights, the magic embers. I let go of Yates and Daisy.

We all exhaled in unison.

There was a bottomless moment where we couldn't speak. We stared at each other, at the doll, at our hands. There was something impossible between us. It was thin and invisible and honeyed raw, and it had an unspeakable gravity. There were hooks in it and it had put hooks in me. We'd torched the world for a second there. Reality was still flickering in its wake.

This wasn't what magic was ever like. Magic before had been like lying on my back and clawing at the sky, trying for a fistful of stars and ending up with the occasional lightning bug. Even following my spell book by the letter, the most I could do was burn paper, unbreak dishes, make scrapes and cuts scab faster. What the four of us could do was something else. I felt seasick and disgustingly in love with it, with them.

Jing put her hands over her mouth. She stared at the doll, which didn't feel like a doll anymore, and put on a meticulously neutral expression. "So." She slipped her hand inside her sleeve and picked the doll up slowly, delicately, like it might spring to life and bite her. It might. I wasn't sure. "What do we do with it?"

"I want to burn it." Daisy looked at the poppet like it was a reliquary. Her face broke into a grin, and she tossed her arms around her stomach, dug her nails into her sides. "Can we burn it, Sideways?"

"Absolutely not." I skittered my fingertips up and down my thighs. "I wouldn't want to breathe the smoke. Besides, whatever we put in there, I don't want it getting out. We need to keep an eye on it. Put it someplace safe."

"Define safe," said Jing. She held it closer to her face, eyes sharp on its makeshift elbows. A vein twitched in her cheek. "God. It made little tendons. They're bunched and notched and everything."

I cracked my neck. "Safe like a jar filled with nails."

"Nails. We can do that." Jing sucked her teeth. "Daze. The bat. It's in my closet."

Daisy lit up and sprung to her feet. She sidestepped Jing and half skipped to the sliding closet door, yanked it open, and dove her hands into some unseen back corner. She stuck her tongue out of the corner of her mouth, screwed up her face in concentration, and then eased into a smile. She pulled the bat out slowly. Jing's clothes slid to either side like curtains.

It was a Louisiana Slugger. It was a Louisiana Slugger peppered with twenty-something railroad spikes. Daisy leaned on it, crossed her toe behind her ankle. She waggled her brows.

My mouth popped open like a codfish. "What the *fuck?*"

"I get bored." Jing shrugged. She set down the poppet, shoved the spare Barbies back in the Rubbermaid container, and slithered back under the bed with it, reemerged with a ribbon-handled hammer. "Does it matter if the jar's been used for anything before?"

"Nah," I said. My tongue felt dry.

Was it appropriate here to ask her if she was straight?

"Dope," she said. She tucked the hammer under her arm

and strode over to her desk, where she picked up a mason jar that'd been holding pens, dumped the pens out, and then sat back on the floor. She put down the jar, took up her hammer, and reached for the Slugger with her free hand. "This spell thing is more convenient than I thought it'd be."

Yates had been silent. She didn't look at the doll. She looked at the rug instead, knotting her hands in tufts of purple fur like it'd anchor her in place. "Hey, Sideways," she breathed. "Can you come here for a second?"

I sucked my teeth, shoved my hands in my pockets, and gave her a stiff nod. I mean, I was already beside her. I'd listen, though, if that's what she meant.

Yates scooted closer and positioned herself in front of me. She leaned back. Her spine aligned with my sternum, and she let herself melt, went soft against my chest. She pressed her cheek against my neck. I forgot how to swallow. "Thank you." There was a tickling, mothy sensation at my jawline, and I nearly jerked away until I realized it was her lashes, blinking slow. "I needed that," she said. "I seriously needed that."

Thank me. Thank me for what? I didn't ask her, just nodded and said, "No problem." My voice sounded weird and raw, like it wasn't mine. My entire body felt grimy—it had all morning, but now it was hitting me how disgusting I was. There was a twig in my hair. Probably dead crickets, too. Yates felt too clean, too soft to be on me. My arms fit funny in my sleeves. I didn't pull my hands out of my pockets and I didn't wrap them around her, because I wasn't sure I'd do it right. I'd fuck it up somehow. I awkwardly leaned my cheek against her forehead, just barely, just enough that she'd feel it.

Yates made a sound in the back of her throat. She shifted a little, made herself comfortable, and wiggled her toes in the faux purple fur. "Can I ask you a question?"

"Shoot."

"Is Sideways mean? I mean, I know why they call you that. I don't want to be like that. I could call you Eloise instead."

"Well, damn." I felt my face contort. "No. I like Sideways. I picked it myself and it just kind of stuck. No one calls me Eloise. My dads don't call me Eloise." Then, with a hesitant little cough, "Thanks for asking, though."

Jing jerked her head up. She was halfway through the process of yanking the spikes out of her Slugger, and the hammer slipped out of her hand and banged against the side of her bed. The noise made Daisy jump. "Jesus fucking Christ, Sideways, your name is *Eloise?*"

# THREE

# LIKE BLOOD AND WATER

Seeing Jing's room, now that I properly had time to see Jing's room, screwed with my expectations of who she was. Jing at school was slick and nonchalant, dismissive, authoritative, slacking in classrooms but commanding social office, slim as a whippet and twice as quick. There was little room for adoration in her public image. That wasn't the case up close. Under her electric chandelier was a poster of Eartha Kitt, and a stack of battered paperbacks—*Ariel, The Woman Warrior, Alias Grace*—sat dog-eared and unsuspecting atop her bedside table. A pair of sneakers dangled by the laces from a blade of her ceiling fan, unworn, stuffed with lavender springs, and swung in lazy circles as the fan blade made its rounds. There was a whiteboard adhered to the closet door labeled PEOPLE I'M IN LOVE WITH, and all the entries had been scratched out save three names: Daisy, Yates, and Rico Nasty. There were tally marks etched in her footboard and a crack in her TV screen.

The four of us sat on the rug again. Daisy and I had taken showers, but unlike Daisy, I'd crept back into yesterday's crusty clothes. Not like I'd brought a spare set. We were watching a movie, but I hadn't been paying enough attention to know which movie it was. A teenage girl was about to be hacked to pieces on-screen, and Jing was bad-mouthing her for locking herself in a cabinet instead of running out the front door. Yates was texting someone and elbowing Jing from time to time, but Jing didn't seem to notice. Either that, or she was too invested in coaching the slasher victim through How Not to Be Slashed to acknowledge whatever was going on with Yates' phone.

My mind was elsewhere. Nowhere in particular, but somewhere else, somewhere in a vague, hazy plane of existence at the periphery of our own.

Daisy Brink was braiding my hair.

"Hey, Sideways," said Yates, who looked up from her phone and over her shoulder at me. "Can I ask you something?"

"Can you?" I snorted, but I couldn't muster anything cleverer than that. Daisy's nails against my scalp were mesmerizing. The easy, repetitive motion wrung out my nerves. I felt on the verge of hysteria, and I couldn't place why. Maybe it was just the attention. I'm not used to attention. This was the first time in a while I didn't feel angry, not even a little. "Yeah, sure."

"The legendary West High Fight Club. I heard it was coordinated by the Drama kids before it was broken up. You're a Drama kid. Is all that true? Please say it's true." She said this politely, though her tone was overshadowed by Daisy's snickering above my head.

"Those rumors were wildly exaggerated." I grimaced, and Daisy gave my hair a little tug, which I ignored. "You shouldn't believe everything you hear."

"Exactly. See, I'd heard you were a militant vegan/cannibal who favored human farming over cattle husbandry," said Jing, pausing long enough in her horror rapture to shoot me a glance. "And that was clearly bull."

"I'll say. If I'm a militant vegan, then I really screwed myself with those chicken wings, man." My eyes rolled back in my head. Daisy had her own kind of sorcery, and this was it.

"Those rumors are always so vicious. God, I hate this town sometimes. We're all so bored that we just pick at each other for entertainment, and that doesn't do anything for me. It's like eating bubblegum for dinner." Yates set her phone on her lap. "And the teachers all wonder why this is such a party town. What else is there to do?"

"Suffer." Jing slammed her hands on the floor, eyes stretched wide. "Run the other way, asshole, the *other* way! Jesus fucking *Christ*, it's like you're asking him to knife you. The door is on the left, the *left!*"

"Yates, ask my boyfriend if he misses me at college." Daisy punctuated her sentence by tapping the crown of my head. She sounded smug. I missed the joke.

Yates put her face in her hands. "Akeem isn't going to date you, Daze. He still thinks you're, like, twelve."

"He's my true love," said Daisy. I heard the smirk in her voice. "Only man I could ever love at all, I think."

"He's literally engaged, Daze." Yates sighed, glanced at me through her fingers. "Akeem is my older brother. He's graduating from Yale this spring."

"Yale?" Damn. I was hoping to get into the artsy private school Julian had attended. It was nice and all, but it sure as hell wasn't Yale.

"Yeah. It's kind of a thing. Both my parents are alumni. If everything goes according to plan, I'll be going, too. Akeem is a total dork and wants me to recreate all the stupid pictures he took as a freshmen." Yates said this matter-of-factly, but a wave of palpable stress rolled off her and dissipated into the air like smoke. She waved a hand at the phone in her lap. "He and his roommate have just illegally snuck a rabbit into their strictly anti-pet apartment. He's been asking me for 'cool' name suggestions. That's the level of dork he is."

"I voted for Abunninable," said Jing. She leaned closer to the screen just as the slasher plunged his cleaver into a frat boy's shoulder. "But apparently, Akeem doesn't have a sense of humor."

"It's hard to say and isn't cute." Yates screwed her face up. "I feel like a rabbit needs a name that you can baby talk. You can't baby talk *Abunninable*."

"It's punny." Jing scowled. "Puns are cute."

"You're cute," Daisy said.

"Fuck you," Jing replied.

"Cute is in the eye of the beholder. I like Abunninable." I scratched at my shins, and Daisy kneed me in the back, presumably because I kept squirming. I stilled up. "Makes it sound mysterious. Like a jackalope."

"She gets me." Jing jerked a thumb in my direction. "Sideways gets me."

"I vote Bunnicula," said Daisy.

Yates shrugged, pulled her phone up and danced her fingers over the screen. A moment later, she gave Daisy a nod. "He says that Bunnicula works."

"See? Soulmates."

Yates stuck out her tongue. She set her phone aside, produced a vial of nail polish from seemingly nowhere, and swished the brush over her forefinger.

I wrapped my arms around my chest. My ribs felt weirdly honeyed, and my stomach fluttered, purred with something next to happiness. This wasn't what I thought these three were like. I didn't think they were much like anything. In school, they were dangerous angels, sugar-coated rattlesnakes, the kind of girls who everybody adored, who sucked up said adoration without giving any in turn. The triumvirate's power was unparalleled. Rules had exclusion clauses for them. If they wore something too short, or cut too deep, no one batted a lash. If there was an election for student council, for prom, for extracurricular leadership, they won as soon as they wrote their name on the ballot. Outside of that, though, they vanished. They had these parties, sure, but I'd never been to one before last night. In the iron-clad West High social pyramid, they were on the thrones up top and I was skulking near the bottom, lurking behind bleachers, doing magic tricks for bottles of Coke. I wasn't supposed to fit in their paradigm.

I wasn't fit for friendship.

"So. Sideways. Where did the witch thing come from? Tell me," Daisy commanded as she weaved the hair at the nape of my neck. I think she was going for twin braids, the style she'd been wearing the night before. That meant I had another fifteen minutes or so of paradise. I made myself comfortable. "Made a deal with the devil?"

"That sounds sick. But no." Witchcraft questions are always locked and loaded, and I could blow myself away if I worded the answer wrong. I opted for a half-truth. Half-truths are easier to swallow. "My dads own an antique shop. Lots of weird vintage shit in there. I found a lot of occult texts and esoteric lexicons in the back room. That, and the internet."

"Whoa, your folks own an antique shop? Which one?" Yates perked up and peered at me over her shoulder.

"Rothschild & Pike. It's the *Addams Family*–looking place on Main."

"For real? I love Rothschild & Pike! I buy all my jewelry from there. Is your dad Julian? I was just about to ask him for a job, because my mom thinks I need more work experience on my résumé. It's a drag, but that's fair, I guess. If I must work, I'd like it to be for him. He's human sunshine." Yates punctuated her sentence with a little shrug and a wink in my direction before she seized Jing's foot by the ankle and swished a generous portion of nail polish across her big toe. Not the nail. The knuckle.

"Twat," Jing said with a jolt.

"Yeah. Julian is my dad. One of them, anyway." I snickered

a little, rocked my head forward to make Daisy's reach easier. The second braid was nearing the back of my neck, and I tried not to shiver when her nails brushed my spine. "Boris is the other half of it. The Rothschild half, that is. Also dad."

Daisy's hands were on the tips of my shoulders, and my scalp still sang under phantom fingertips. I was going to be hooked on this like nicotine, whatever this was. Affection, maybe. Wasn't sure. "So, were you adopted?" Daisy's voice was distant, twinged with something chilly. It sounded like a challenge, but I couldn't fathom what that challenge could possibly be.

"Fucking obviously." I made a sound in the back of my throat.

The silence behind me was so coarse I could feel it. It felt like steel wool shoved up against my chest. Jing and Yates looked at each other for a second, then at me, and then pointedly at the slasher flick. My throat tensed up. Dread slipped down my sternum like a dry-swallowed ice cube, and the heaven Daisy was weaving into the back of my head dissolved into nothing. She finished my braids without a word. When she tied them off, she lowered them between my shoulder blades and leaned forward, rested her elbows on either side of my neck.

"Tell me more," she said.

The back of my throat felt like tar.

"Daisy, don't," Jing said under her breath. Something shifted in her shoulders. "Just don't."

"No. It's fine." I jammed my tongue against my gums. "My

mom's dead. Julian is Mom's brother. He and his husband took me in."

A couple in a convertible was hacked to pieces, and their awful, campy shrieking echoed through the room. There wasn't any other sound. The bedroom was a vacuum. I felt Daisy's breath rustle the wispies on the back of my neck, but I couldn't hear her breathing. Her nose was needle-close to my skull. Daisy's body ran a few degrees warmer than mine, and it radiated like a faint young sun, faint but unmistakable down my back and around my sides.

She was waiting for something. I wasn't sure what.

"Must be something in the weather," Daisy said. "My mom croaked, too. She's under that smug angel in the boneyard on Hickory Street. The one with all the garlands and Annabel Lee." Her voice was hushed, just loud enough that I'd hear her. There was a crookedness in her tone, something sharp and red and raw. I recognized that tone of voice. It sounded a lot like mine.

My mouth twisted upward. It wasn't out of mirth. "We should start a club."

She extended her arms, crossed them over my sternum and twined them around my ribs. Her body burned. It let off a strange, violent energy, something that jolted through my bones like a fever. Daisy's arms were a bit like witchcraft. It was almost too warm to breathe.

"You're nervous," she whispered. "Don't be. I just decided not to bite." Then she released me. Cold air flooded my pores, and Daisy gave the room a drawn-out yawn. "I don't like these braids." Lazy, cocky. "I'm redoing them. Does anyone have any gum?"

No one had any gum.

Daisy clicked her tongue. Cracked her knuckles. She started unraveling the undoubtedly perfect braids she had just finished. I didn't say anything to contradict her.

Yates chanced a glance in my direction. "Which lunch period do you have?"

I chewed on the inside of my cheeks. "C." The suckiest one, naturally. "Why?"

"Who do you usually sit with?"

Fucking, I sat with *nobody*, that's who. Just me and myself by the stage. Who the hell was there to sit with, anyway? There were the Drama kids, but we weren't friends-friends even when we did hang out. I hadn't been forgiven by most of the actors for being given an understudy part despite being an oh-so-lowly crew kid. One of only *two* crew kids, to be specific, and the only one who can even lift the planks of wood when we're building sets. Also, there was still beef over the time when I might've gotten into a physical altercation with the stage manager. The person I was the closest to was Mickey-Dick (technically Michael Richardson), who I was friends with in a class-partner way but not a hanging-out-after-school way. He was still weird about the fact that I might've fooled around with his ex-girlfriend at the world's most terrible improv camp last summer. Not that there are . . . like, great improv camps. And they weren't even together at the time! Anyway, the point is that none of them had any interest in sitting with me, and I didn't particularly covet them, either. "I move around," I said. "Why d'you ask?"

"We have C lunch, too." Yates gave me a little nod. "So, you should sit with us, if you want."

"Yeah, I'll think about it." I tangled my fists in the carpet. The fur was about the same consistency as a Valentine's Day bear, cheap and sugary. Something told me that if I gave it a good tug, it'd come out by the bushel. I fought the urge.

"Think about it? Excuse me, Sideways, but did I just hear you say you'll think about it?" You would've thought I'd called Daisy every slur in the book, the way she bristled. Her voice was nasal, accusatory. I didn't have to see the snarl to feel it.

The air knocked out of my lungs.

Daisy weighed substantially more than she looked. She slammed me down face-first, and she rolled me over before she pinned me. Her fringe swung with momentum. Daisy broke into a grin, and she braced her knee against my diaphragm, leered down over my face. "You have to sit with us. You can't curse a fuckboy with us and share a sob story without being one of us, Sideways Pike. You ain't got a choice."

My stomach split its seams. I bucked, grabbed her around the middle and tossed her on the rug beside me. She hit the floor with an *oof.* She flashed a grin.

"Y'all should've warned me that friendship with you three was mandatory. Is there a contract? Are there terms and conditions for me to reckon with?"

"Yeah. Rule one: I always win play fights." Daisy

clambered back on top of me, moved like she was going to shoulder check my neck. I broke into a laugh, but my laugh flatlined before the sound could leave my mouth. Daisy's body crushed against mine. Her ribs poked my ribs. She made a sound like a squeak toy underfoot.

A slender, bracelet-bound wrist flopped by the side of my face.

Yates. The extra weight was Yates.

The air squished out of my lungs.

"Jesus," I wheezed. I jerked one of my arms out from under Daisy's stomach and reached out to absently claw at the carpet, but it was damn clear where the leverage was here. The leverage was not with me. I couldn't toss them off. A sloppy smile slapped across my face. "Mercy. Fucking have mercy. Yates. Daisy. I'm dying."

"Yeah, guys. You heard the woman. *She's dying.*" Jing, out of the corner of my eye, cast her arms behind her head and kicked her feet up on the pile, suave as a pinup at a tropical resort. Give her a Bloody Mary and beach towel and she'd be perfect. She pursed her lips into a faux smile.

Laughing hurt. Goddamn, did I hurt.

Brightly, from the corner of a table, warbled Morrissey.

That'd be my ringtone.

"Off," I moaned, wriggling under the triple girl weight. "That's my phone! Off. Daisy, damn it . . ."

Jing reached one of her long arms over to my phone and plucked it up. She nonchalantly tapped at the screen, and the ringing stopped. She pressed it to her ear.

She'd guessed my password.

I was as horrified as I was impressed.

"Hi. Eloise can't come to the phone right now. Can I take a message?" Jing twirled a lock of hair around her finger. She spoke with the high, over-polite timbre of a girly receptionist, and her expression twisted into something grotesque. Smug bastard. I contemplated punching her squarely in the neck. Lucky for her, I couldn't presently move my arms.

Muffled surprise from the other end. I couldn't make out the words.

"Oh! One second." Jing cradled my phone against her heart and gave me her best patronizing whisper: "Sideways, it's your father."

Fuck. That could be either really good or really bad. "Which father?" I hissed between my teeth.

She returned the phone to her cheek. "Right. Which father?" She paused, nodded, then cleared her throat and resumed her previous pose, iPhone to sternum, lashes fluttering like a bird mid-flight. "It's Julian."

Shit.

Jing looked me in the face and wordlessly understood. Her eyes stretched wide. She pressed my phone to my cheek and I coughed once, scrambled to hook my hand around the quickly slipping phone.

"Hey. Right. What's up?" I pressed my cheek against the rug in an act of submission to whatever righteous onslaught heaven was about to deal me for being a bad kid. I probably deserved it, whatever it was. Julian Pike was the single most kind-hearted human being on the face of the earth, and anyone who made him nervous deserved to rot. Fucking Julian. Why couldn't it have been Boris?

"Eloise?" I cringed, shaped a string of compound cuss words that didn't leave my mouth. *Eloise.* He was definitely nervous. "Sweetie, could you kindly tell me where you are and that you're not dead? Your father has been up all night worrying about you," he said slowly, sugarly, sounding earnest. He was not *being* earnest. The father he was referring to was Boris, and Boris was a huge advocate for me "experiencing my youth uninhibited." He always went on about measured indulgence in "whatever my spirit told me to pursue," which included all the nonsense I'd tangled myself in, the fight club that didn't happen, and my habit of disappearing for a night whenever I was too tense to be home. Boris sure as hell wasn't worried. He wouldn't be worried until two days from now. Julian, on the other hand? The fact that he was framing it this way stung like a boot to the face. He was being polite, which meant he didn't want me to feel yelled at, which means he really ought to be yelling at me. Which of course yanked the bubblegum off the hole on my Hoover Dam of guilt. It sloshed out cold and soaked my insides, and I was drenched in it.

I gritted my teeth. "Oh, man. Look, I'm sorry, I'm sleeping over at a friend's house. I thought I'd texted you. Must not have. Sorry about that. Wouldn't want Boris to worry or anything, I really wouldn't," I said, but I felt myself trail off.

Silence buzzed on the other end.

Me running away to live in Cuba with a washed-up rock star would've sounded more plausible than me sleeping over at a friend's house.

Julian didn't ask who those friends might be, thank God. He went quiet for a moment, and after an agonizing breath, he cleared his throat, sounding as dad-like as can be. "Well, then. Are you having fun?"

"Oodles," I said.

Daisy cackled.

"When will you be home? Will you need a ride?"

Yates, from the top of the stack, hiked her voice up an octave higher than it usually was. "I'll give her a ride! She'll be home tomorrow! Thanks, Julian!"

A weary half chuckle from Dad's end. "Right. Okay, well. Text me if you need anything at all, Lamby."

Lamby. Yikes.

"Capisce. Gotta scram. Love you," I said, and I hung up directly after. I released the phone. It clattered to the floor beside my cheek.

"If he isn't the nicest guy! He's so chill about things. Envious," Yates yawned. She repositioned herself on top of Daisy and made herself comfortable, which triggered a line of impressively prickly cuss words out of Daisy. For some reason, I hadn't thought that pretty girls could curse like the rest of us. Misconception noted.

"Language," Yates said breezily.

"Life is hell," Daisy snapped.

I coughed into my shoulder. "Says the chick in the middle of the stack."

Jing swung her feet off our girl pyre. She popped upright, slinked across the room, and slid open her closet door, and there was a rustling, a shuffling of fabric against fabric. A thunk as something hit the bed. Her voice, when she spoke, had royal gravity to it. Genuine confidence. "Sideways. What's your dress size?"

"Why?"

"We're going out. You're still in crusty booze-smelling clothes from yesterday. I wagered you might want to borrow a dress," she mused. There was a swish sound as she pulled more fabric from her closet and flung it on her bed.

"What, that new slasher flick you keep going on about? The showing was at eight thirty," Daisy said. "Why get dressed so early?"

"Because it's already seven o'clock, Daze. Did you losers not notice it get dark outside?"

"Kind of hard from down here," said Daisy with a groan. She writhed under Yates, which drove her elbow into my guts. I jolted, but didn't shove her back. Even with her cheer abs, Daisy was smaller than me, and accidentally snapping her in half wouldn't bode well for this newfound friendship. Assuming this was a friendship.

"Right," I said. "Yeah. I'm not your dress size."

"We'll see." Jing leaned down beside us. A lock of her bleach-blond hair dangled by my cheek. Then, with a sneer, she seized Daisy by her shoulder and her waistband and hurled her off me, sending Yates toppling in her wake. Yates and Daisy hit the ground beside me with matching sounds of pain. Jing took me by the hand and hauled me upright.

"You've got a helluva arm," I said.

"I know," she replied. She cocked her brow and gestured behind her. "Now, try this on, would you?"

*

The dress was mighty tight. Mighty tight and very short. Dangerously short.

I'd seen Jing in this dress before. When she wore it, it barely touched her. The bloody violet velvet always drifted a half centimeter over her skin and fell around her knees in a loose, easygoing line. It made her look elegant. On me, it was tight. It fit snugly over my ribs and my stomach and my hip bones, and the knee-length hem was suddenly thigh length, and only just. Spaghetti straps threatened to snap.

Daisy and Yates had their hands clasped over their hearts.

"Jesus, Sideways." There was an element of genuine awe in Daisy's voice. Her eyes fixed on my torso, and I shifted, crossed my arms over my chest. The braids on either side of my head swung off my shoulders and dangled down my back. Daisy leaned closer. "You're kind of a babe in that, you know. You could get so much dick in that dress," she said. She smacked her lips. "Making me question myself, girl."

Ha, no. "Getting dick has never been a big concern of mine," I snapped. Well, getting girl dick, maybe, but whatever.

Wasn't what she'd meant. I crossed my arms over my chest and rocked back on my heels, made a point of not looking in the mirror. Looking in the mirror felt like a potentially catastrophic move.

"Daze, get it right. Sideways is dressed to be a *lady*-killer. She's a lezzie magnet," Jing drawled, and she rotated her pointer finger in little circles. *Spin for me.*

Stupid. This was stupid. My body was obedient, nonetheless. I pivoted, half expecting all the seams to pop, and Jing let a smirk flash across her face.

"Erm. Jing. Should you *say* that word? Isn't it a tad inappropriate for a straight girl to say that sort of thing?" Yates cocked her head to the side and knotted her brows. She slipped her pinky between her lips and gnawed on the nail. "I feel like it is."

Jing shrugged. She leaned back against the vanity table and watched me for a long moment, evidently satisfied with herself. She narrowed her eyes a touch. Bit the corner of her lip. "Probably," she said.

"Jing," Yates started, but she trailed off.

"I don't know, man. It's, whatever," said Jing. She leaned back, stretched her arms above her head, and gave me a look that sank somewhere deep in my core. Wordless, with feline fluidity, she turned her back on us and plucked up a vial of lipstick. She uncapped it and leaned toward her reflection, pressed the rouge to her bottom lip.

"Cool," I said.

Yates and Daisy looked at each other, and then at me, as if I would tell them what they hadn't telepathically understood. I shrugged.

"Yeah." Jing put down the lipstick and leaned back, gave herself a once-over in the mirror. Her reflection met my gaze. "I'm bisexual. I'm pretty goddamn sure about that." Her tone was casual, nonchalant, but I heard the edge in it and understood. "Discreetly, that is. For now."

"Roger." I nodded, and Yates and Daisy gave their scattered agreements.

Jing snapped three pale clips in her hair, tossed her head back, and looked down her nose at herself. "Good," she sneered. She bounced on the balls of her feet and whirled around, snatched a jacket off her chair. "Let's go seize the world."

# AT THE LATE-NIGHT DOUBLE FEATURE PICTURE SHOW

There were three theaters within a reasonable drive from Sycamore Gorge. Two of them were part of huge chain corporations, their tickets were expensive, and the snacks were subpar. No one went to either. Instead, the dive of choice was the Gorge's own dilapidated Queen's Cinema. It ought to be condemned. It was a crumbling ramshackle slot at the end of Main Street, splattered with spray paint and dripping hairy vines, and the second light-up E in QUEEN'S had been broken for the past three years. A group of cardinals had nested inside it. Through the industrial doors, the inside smelled like pickle brine and caramel. Outdated movie posters sat crooked and warped behind cracked glass cases, and seedy pop music mixed with the techno jingle of arcade games. The staff wasn't paid enough to give a damn about mopping up the slushy splatters or the crushed popcorn, so every step on the bowling-alley carpet crunched underfoot.

I am *such* a *sucker* for Queen's Cinema.

The four of us stood between the stained red stanchions

and passed a bottle of Coke back and forth. I was still in the velvet dress, but it felt a little less like wearing nothing now that I was back in my leather jacket. The jacket put a barrier between my velvety self and the sharp, cold world. The Coke tasted flat. I drank it anyway. We meandered a little farther down the line, and I let myself tune back into the conversation.

Daisy was explaining the reportedly God-shattering hookup she'd had in the single stall bathroom around the back. "I had to lather myself with rubbing alcohol afterward," she said smoothly, "but it was completely worth it."

"You're a public menace," Jing said. It sounded bizarrely like praise.

"Four tickets to the cheesy horror movie." Yates bounced on her toes, smoothed her hands against the ticket counter and smiled up at the employee with the radiance of twenty thousand cherubim. The employee behind the ticket counter yawned. Said employee was a poster child for mono symptoms, or maybe for cocaine addiction. It was hard to tell in this town.

"Together or separate?" said Dark Under-eye Circles Girl. Her voice was completely devoid of inflection. I thought she might croak as soon as we looked away. Her name tag might have said Kaylee or Baylee or Shaylee, something like that, but I didn't pay too much attention.

"Together," said Daisy as she slapped down her credit card.

I opened my mouth to protest.

Jing shot me a look.

"IDs?" said D.U.C. Girl. "We're supposed to ID folks for R-rated movies."

I reached for my wallet, but Jing waved a hand at me. She looked up at D.U.C. Girl and cocked a brow. "Do you care?"

"That's a good point," said D.U.C. Girl. Her eyes rolled up in her head. "Last theater to the left. Enjoy your film."

The four of us ambled onward toward the snack line, which was where most people seemed to be haphazardly slapped together. They held processed snack food in their claws. Someone in line was vaping, and their breath bleached the air above them like smokestack exhaust. Jing breathed some comment about *losers* that I didn't quite catch. I saw a barrage of letter jackets. Vineyard Vines. Tattered jeans. A trio of older women, primed with matching Coach bags and feathered bobs, were interrogating a second D.U.C. girl about whether popcorn was gluten free. A kid bawled at their feet.

Yates tossed her arm around my shoulders.

Daisy knelt beside the candy racks and ogled at the baggies like senior boys ogle freshman girls. Her tongue dipped out of the corner of her mouth. She reached her hands into the racks and dragged her fingertips across the surface of every single package, touching everything, coffin nails warping the plastic wrap as she dragged them along. It was a motion I associated with selecting tarot cards, but on Daisy, the typical tarot introspection was replaced with something ravenous and canine. She plucked three boxes from the back of each stack, sprang upright and tucked them against her ribs. It was more candy than we could possibly eat. Her eyes burned bright. "Don't worry, guys," she said. "I picked the best ones."

"I can believe it," said Jing.

I could believe it, too.

It was the rest of this whole *going to a place I like with people who like me* bit that I was having trouble with.

Jing shoulder-checked her way through a group of jock types to the front of the line. "XL popcorn and XL slushy, please. White cherry. No butter on the popcorn." She paused, rolled her eyes toward me. "You don't like butter on your popcorn, do you?"

"All popcorn is good popcorn. Do what you will," I said. I shoved my hands in my pockets.

She pursed her lips. I took that as affirmation.

The bag of popcorn was roughly the size of Jing's torso. Yates reached inside it, hooked a golden fistful between her fingers, and tossed it between her teeth with an audible crunch. Daisy did the same, which was impressive, considering how constricted her arms were by the candy she was carrying.

I let my hands stay put.

Daisy shifted forward, pulling out not her credit card again, but instead a fistful of twenty-dollar bills, looking as cool as if she was tucking said twenties into a stripper's G-string. I offhandedly assumed that those twenties covered Jing's slushy and her popcorn. If they didn't, then Jing's snacks were technically stolen. Not that D.U.C. girl seemed to give even a single fuck about that.

We took our snacks and hauled them down the hallway to

the left. We passed an animated reimagining/slaughtering of some eighties cartoon and the fourth sequel to an action series that I didn't care about. After that there was a shitty-looking spy movie, a rom-com that was miasmic to even walk by, an Oscar-baiting bore fest. Our movie, naturally, was in the backmost projector room.

*Ghastly.* The dripping letters on the poster taped above the door were bubblegum pink and featured an ambiguous white boy with a gag between his teeth. The trailers were already rolling inside.

Daisy cut to the front of our pack and brought us deeper and deeper into the belly of the theater. We sat in one of the first rows, dead center in the buttery darkness. Moviegoing for me had historically been my dads and me toward the back at the latest sci-fi matinee. Sitting in the front felt different on my skin. It was vaguely like spell casting. Too loud, too hot, as hyper as an intravenous caffeine drip.

The lights dropped, and the screen lit up.

And they say there's no such thing as love at first sight.

Cue the muffled screaming. The camera swept over electric-blue eyes and panned outward to reveal the boy from the poster, an overly handsome blond boy with a ribbon in his teeth. He thrashed in his letter jacket, eyes whirling around and around in their sockets, but the zip-ties didn't snap. He tried to heave himself upright, but the minty turf was slick. He slipped, fell on his hip. One of the football floodlights flicked on, and long shadows fell across him. His rabbit eyes popped wide. A group of countless girls in hooded pastel robes stood around him in a circle, and the leader, marked by her distinctive Barbie-pink cloak, took a step toward him. She withdrew a mean pair of scissors from her sleeve and the hooded figures clapped, jeered, pulled out their iPhones, and hit record. "The sisterhood has identified you as a cheating asshole," said the leader girl. She brandished the scissors like an athame. "So, like, die." The scissors flew across the jock's throat and red splashed across the screen.

G-H-A-S-T-L-Y.

Yates smothered a laugh with her hand, and Jing punched her in the shoulder.

The camera panned over Main Character, a horrifically generic new girl who was Not Like Those Other Slutty Girls. She naturally didn't have friends, because that's what happens to people who act like condescending pricks to everyone who approaches them, so she logically set her heart on befriending conventionally attractive Jock Boy for some reason. Unfortunately for her, Jock Boy was revealed to be the newest boyfriend of Bitchy Cheerleader, the school's uncontested tyrant who ran the student body like some sort of forties Mafioso. Bitchy Cheerleader was, from my perspective, ridiculously hot and deeply cool.

Despite his relationship with Bitchy Cheerleader, Jock Boy flirted with Main Character, and the two of them acquired some sort of instant magic love connection despite having zero chemistry. I wasn't sure if that was a legit thing with heterosexual kids, but it wasn't any more convincing in this movie than it had been in any other movie Hollywood ever made prior to this one. Main Character and Jock Boy nearly screw in the passenger's seat of his Italian car. Of course, they don't commit the deed, because Main Character feels the need to remind him and the audience that she's Not Like Those Other Sluts. It broke Jock Boy's heart. He called Bitchy Cheerleader to voice his doubts about their relationship, outright admitting to cheating in the process, an admission which spelled out his obvious and much deserved demise.

Bitchy Cheerleader took it upon herself to correct the whole situation. She invited Main Character to a party of hers, which Main Character attended in the hopes of flirting with Jock Boy some more, but when Main Character arrived at the ritzy Victorian mansion she'd been directed to, she didn't arrive at a party. Instead, Bitchy Cheerleader and all her friends stood waiting. They'd donned their pastel robes. They all smiled at her. They offered her a pink robe of her very own.

"Join the sisterhood," said Bitchy Cheerleader. She handed over the scissors. "We used to make Valentines with these. Stupid gifts for stupid boys who use us, screw us, leave us. Now we use them for better things. I know you cheated with him, but I will forgive you if you kill him for us. For yourself. For the sisterhood. We don't need boys like him. They're better off dead."

Main Character hesitantly accepted the scissors. She used them to slash at Bitchy Cheerleader's face.

The finale of the movie was a tempest of jump scares and

bloodbaths, but it was ultimately uninspiring, as Main Character found obviously hidden Jock Boy, who had been tied up and left on Bitchy Cheerleader's bed. The camera shook as Main Character cut off his zip-ties and led him downstairs, where a pissed-off group of hooded girls laid in wait. They ran, hid, screamed too loudly. They both miraculously made it out alive. A few of the sisters didn't. Bitchy Cheerleader stared down the camera and vowed revenge.

Credits rolled.

Lights went up.

The four of us unceremoniously climbed to our feet.

"Lame," I said. Every single vertebra in my spine popped when I stood up. My back sounded like Rice Krispies. I rolled my shoulders, snatched up my bag. "She shoulda joined the cult. The sisterhood had their collective shit together. Fuckboy wasn't worth it."

"Agreed," said Jing. "Also, that was gross as all hell, Sideways. Tell your skeleton to chill."

Yates had a huge, weary smile on her face. She glued herself to my side and pressed her face to my shoulder. "I'm not going to sleep tonight," she said. "I'm never going to sleep again. Or turn off the lights. Or touch scissors."

Daisy snickered. Somehow, over the course of the movie, she'd managed to eat the vast majority of that mega-jumbo popcorn without snagging any in her hair or teeth. She was still tossing candy in her mouth faster than moms around here pop Xanax. "*Aw*, was Yatesy scared by the *big bad movie?*"

"Bite me!"

Daisy made grabby hands at Yates' shoulder and smacked her lips, wagged her brows, cackled like a cartoon robber. "Better run, pretty kitty. I *vant* to *suck* your *blood*!"

Yates squeaked, and without warning me beforehand, scrambled halfway up my back. She tossed her arms around my neck, looped her legs around my waist, and said, "Sideways, save me!" into the hair above my ear.

I toppled forward. *Fuck.* I grappled at the back of the seat in front of me and sucked in a breath. Yates adjusted herself on my back, and I coughed once, twice, thrice, until it occurred to her that her headlock was choking me to death.

When I could breathe again, she felt like next to nothing. She was annoyingly light, and, let's call me stocky.

I piggybacked her out into the aisle.

Jing had started down it ahead of us. She slammed to a stop mid-step.

I hovered a step behind her. My brows screwed into a V.

Blocking our way was a boy built like an ice chest. His friends were identical, all Ralph Lauren generics with snapbacks and matching haircuts. They stood behind him in a loose formation, and their laughter curdled something in my stomach.

It was the Austin fucking Grass posse.

I fucking hate the Austin Grass posse.

Wasn't sure if Austin recalled kneeling on my hair and markering slurs all over my face after PE when we were fourteen. Wasn't sure if he recalled any of the subsequent little torture bouts, either. I knew this, though: I sure as fuck remembered.

He gave Jing a sloppy little chuckle, the kind of chuckle that all high school boys of this delineation seemed to possess: two isolated *huh-huhs* that triggered a round of answering *huh-huhs* from the rest of his pack. "*Jing.* So, what was that party about, baby? You into some sorta Satanist shit now? That shit was *legit* freaky. Man, my boy Tony nearly pussied out and went home, he got so freaked. How'd you do it? Does scissoring give you magic fucking powers, now?"

"As if I'd spill how I did it to the likes of you." Jing's expression hardened into an icy, imposing smile. That exact look had terrified me when I was twelve, rendered me slack-jawed and reverent at fifteen. I was quickly growing to admire that look as the world's most unparalleled statement of *Fuck you, I'm the true Plantagenet here.* "Didn't *you* scream like a little kid when the lights cut out? I think you and your boys have something in common."

"Nah. No way. You got it wrong," Austin snickered, and his buddies snickered with him, but the snickers shriveled when Jing pulled out her phone and conjured up the video she had shown me. She didn't start it, but the sight of it alone was enough for his face to fall off-kilter.

She twisted her lips into a smile.

Austin's mouth twitched. His gaze lasered over her shoulder and rested on me, and then the hyena laughter was back. He looked behind him at his friends. The group of them shared some wordless affirmation—I swear, West High boys have a hive mind—and looked back at Jing like we'd just dealt him a Royal Flush. He cleared his throat and smiled. "Playing for Team Lesbo now? It's a damn shame. You're hot as hell, you know that, Jing. You could bone *any* guy you wanted. You're too pretty to play on that team."

"Better watch out," chimed Yates, the parrot on my shoulder. "Sideways might curse you for being such an asshole."

"She made all that chalk crawl on Jing's walls," Daisy added from behind me. "Who's to say she couldn't make your pecker shrivel up like a raisin?"

An image of my new friends at the party, laughing with his arms around their shoulders, wandered back to my mind.

Jing put her hands on her hips. "Ladies, please. That'd be such a waste of Sideways' time. Alexis told me *all* about Austin, here. He's got nothing for Sideways to shrivel." She rolled her eyes and shouldered past him, and the three of us, Yates and Daisy and I, moved to follow behind her. I could feel my pulse in the soles of my shoes.

"Whatever. Too many fags around here, man."

There it was. That one little syllable was a teakettle screaming in my ears. My vision speckled and a big black hole ripped open under the velvet and sucked up all my insides, erased any thought I'd had of leaving, of being quiet, of stuffing all this down in the back of my head and mostly forgetting it. Everything was pulsating. The floor throbbed under my feet. The ceiling warped above me. The whole world tasted vile. I shouldered off Yates, felt her skitter to the floor behind me. I spun on my heel, spat on the carpet.

Austin's eyes went round as Easter eggs.

My knuckles met his nose with a crunch.

✳

Jing killed the radio.

Daisy cussed her out for killing the radio, because it was her turn with the AUX chord, goddamn it.

Jing respectfully ignored everything that came out of Daisy's mouth.

"Eloise," said Jing. Her eyes met mine in the rearview mirror. Her face was sharp, but it was always sharp. Her tone was impossible to parse. With a look like that, it might have been my death rattle.

"It's Eloise Marie, if you're gonna full-name me," I said, fumbling around my jacket pockets like there might be an anxiety antidote just lying around in there. My knuckles skimmed my zipper. My lungs tied themselves up in knots. The thing about fracturing a bone is that it heals stronger than before. Damn hard to break the same bone twice. By this point, my knuckles had diamond cores, but that didn't mean I couldn't jack up the skin on top. Austin's face had really jacked up the skin on top, old maroon bruises turning scarlet. The back of my hand smelled like salt. "What?"

"You know that if he'd called the cops, you'd have been fatally fucked. *Orange Is the New Black* isn't cute in real life. That could've been you."

I leaned my temple on the window, let my eyes roll back in my head. "Yeah, well, he didn't, and Queen's doesn't have any cameras in the theaters, just in the lobby. So, it doesn't matter."

"I didn't know you had the guts," said Jing. "I thought Daisy was our only berserker. Look. He fucking deserved it. You let him off easy. I know that you already know he's worthless. So I'm gonna say this instead. Daisy's the most vicious bitch you know, yes?"

"Yeah," I said.

Daisy tossed her hair over her shoulder.

"Well, she told me that I should just give that dress to you, because it looks so damn good on you that people would accuse *me* of wearing *your* dress instead of the other way around," said Jing.

I sat for a moment in silence.

"She really did say that," Yates quietly added from the seat to my left.

"You don't have to make shit up to make me feel better," I snapped. "I'm fine. I can take it. He's nothing new, and it's, whatever." There was a horrible buzzing heat in my cheeks, and I tried to hide it against the window glass. My cheeks rubied up.

Screw. That. I'm supposed to be teen Rasputin or some suburban Circe, not a sniveling loser who chokes up at casual assholery. The compliment just didn't change anything. My throat felt tight and I focused on the flat darkness outside.

"Eloise," Jing started, but she didn't finish.

"What's with calling me Eloise all of a sudden?" I felt myself overenunciating the fricatives, which was stupid, and I knew it, because I'd been so damn excited about being friends with these three all of twenty minutes ago. Now, I deeply wanted nothing more but for them to shut up and keep their fingers out of my papercut. I fought the impulse to slam my bad hand against the car door. Same impulse that'd ruined my quasi-friendships with the Drama kids, actually.

Why couldn't I just be good at this?

Jing slammed the brakes at the red light, and my seat belt lashed my stomach. She turned her head to look at me and scowled. Or smiled. Her face was a riddle, and I didn't have the bandwidth to parse it. "Do you want me to drop you off at home?"

"She's sleeping over," said Yates.

"I didn't ask you, Lila," Jing hissed, but Yates cut her off with a wave of her hand.

"She's sleeping over. She's gotta. She's protecting me from Daisy, because Daisy's being a biting weirdo and I wanna make sure I'm safe at night. I am *so* not in the mood to be cannibalized." To illustrate her point, she swung her feet up on my lap, as if the presence of her shoes on my thighs staked a claim on me. In the low light, the white Vans almost glowed. Ghost shoes.

Something twisted under my ribs, knotted tight. Something warm and radiant. I placed a hand across Yates' ankle and gave it a squeeze. She didn't recoil, didn't grimace when my skin touched hers.

I kept my temple to the glass.

"My house it is," said Jing. The light flashed green, and we rolled on.

# FEVERLESS FEVER DREAMS

The katydids were dead by now, so the four of us sat in total silence out by the pool. We perched on the edge with our legs dangling into the depths, and the stillness was thick in the air. The flamingoes balanced on their skinny plastic legs. My skinless knuckles stiffened in the cold. The only light fell from the deck behind us, and our shadows stretched like fingers over the pale deer down below. We didn't speak, as though breaking the silence might wake the darkness and solidify it into something that could grab our ankles and yank us off the ledge.

Daisy rocked her head back and stared at the night. "There's trash bags in the kitchen. We could stash them inside, carry them up the stairs, and toss them in the back of your car, Jing. Leave them in the woods somewhere."

"I don't want them in my car," said Jing. "I don't want them anywhere near anything that belongs to me."

"They'd be heavy," I said. "I could lift them, but it wouldn't be clean." I imagined their stomachs bent around my neck, heaved fireman style over my shoulders with their hooves dangling near my hip bones. I wasn't sure what deadweight felt like. My insides felt hoarfrosted.

"I want to bury them," said Yates. She looked greenish out of the corner of my eye, the blood gone from her face. "We can't just put them in trash bags and dump them somewhere. That feels wrong."

"Burying them is harder than leaving them somewhere. They're just deer. It shouldn't matter," said Daisy.

But it did matter. If Yates said so, it did. So, it did.

"Sideways," said Jing. Her voice was hushed. "Can I ask you something?"

"Shoot." I ran my nails up and down my knees. Tripped the rough edges over ingrown hairs. It stung a little.

"Do you know how they died?"

The fawn's eyes reflected the porchlight. For a second, it looked almost aware, like it was glancing back at me. There wasn't a single mark on any of them, and the flawlessness spoke of supernatural influence. They were so carefully spaced, so tenderly arrayed, so meticulously aligned with each other and the wall. This was ritualistic. These were magic killings.

Yates and the real Chett had stepped over me. She'd said my eyes were open.

I looked at the fawn and forgot how to swallow.

"No," I said.

But that wasn't what she was asking me.

"Let's just go inside," said Yates. "We'll scrub the walls tonight and finish this tomorrow. I'd feel better about things that way. I don't know if I can sleep if we touch them tonight."

Jing slumped her shoulders and her hair fell in her face. "Fine," she said. "Let's go inside, then."

We went inside. Yates and I carried washrags and bleach water down the stairs to the basement, but we needn't have. Jing and Daisy were ghost-faced on the landing. All the chalk glyphs on the walls were gone.

✳

I was achingly awake. I was bleeding, too. I didn't know how long I'd been awake, only that the darkness was as thin and milky as a Sleeping Beauty hex; an invisible fishnet of unconsciousness that swathed everyone except myself, the woozy witch in the corner, who was too busy seeping blood and scowling to succumb.

It was the bleeding that woke me up: the taste in my mouth, the slickness down my throat, the molten crust of drying blood that collected on my pillow. I drifted out of sleep to find the stickiness down my jaw. My heart wrenched and my adrenaline pricked, and I slammed myself upright, patting my face, spitting.

I'd been dreaming of that incantation I'd cast on the porch. About Madeline. About something she had said. Whatever it was, it evaporated as soon as I opened my eyes, and all at once I was jarringly alone in the darkness in Jing's basement.

I clamped my hand across my nose.

It was a dry October. Nosebleeds just randomly assault

people, no questions asked, when the weather withers, and this was that. This was that. I groped in the darkness for the tissue box Jing had brought downstairs until my fingertips found cool cardboard. I audibly hissed a sigh of relief. I ripped a tissue free, and then two more, and shoved them against my gory nose.

My mouth filled up with blood.

I was not quite sure how to find the bathroom from here, so I stayed on my sleeping bag and dragged my legs to my chest. Yates and Jing and Daisy were eerily motionless. My eyes adjusted and their stillness tugged at me, and I made myself look away. They were sleeping across where the chalk circle had been.

Daisy was snoring.

Thank God for Daisy snoring.

If she didn't snore—if the three of them were stiff and still and completely silent under their blankets—my mind would've fed me the worst sort of paranoia. They were breathing. All three of them were breathing. They were breathing, and they definitely hadn't been laid out in neat little rows like the deer had been. They were just sleeping that way by chance. Correlation, not causation.

My stomach turned sour, and I blamed it on the blood.

I wasn't sure if it was morning yet.

The copper taste was nauseating. I spat more red and grimaced.

The was a rustling, a whisper of fabric on fabric. It came from beside me and sent a lurching into my gut.

Hands on my back.

"Sideways, you okay?"

I sucked a breath between the gap in my teeth. It was Yates. Yates was not whatever I'd been tensing for. I twisted back toward her and found her tucked neatly at my flank, eyes half mooned and dreamy, her blankets whorled around her waist like some sort of downy nest. She had a sleeping bag, but she hadn't been sleeping on it. Rather, she had rolled it out on top of her blow-up mattress and used it for extra padding. It crinkled as she shifted.

"I just have a nosebleed, s'all," I said, a solid octave lower than I normally would. My throat was all gravel and grossness. I sounded like a grumpy dragon.

"Come," she said, and with a silent, catlike motion, she rolled onto her feet. One of her fleece blankets rose with her about her shoulders, which gave her an unintentional likeness to a carnival mystic: silky bonnet, billowing shawl, and a misty disposition. She weaved her way between pillows and extra comforters, and I crawled to my feet and trudged behind her with the tissue box in hand.

It occurred to my still half-sleeping self that maybe the staircase to Jing's basement jinxed reality, so that every time you crossed, you were a little less on earth. It must be some kind of thin space: walking through it meant something wicked materialized at the other end. I walked down these stairs and drew that circle. I walked up these stairs and cast that spell. Down again and sigils dripped down walls, up again and deer were dead in the swimming pool. I tiptoed over the top three steps and shut the door behind me.

"*Jesus,*" Yates breathed, jumping at the abruptness of the door closing.

"Sorry." I crossed my arms over my chest.

She shook her head and slipped down the hallway. Her feet, unlike mine, were deathly quiet as they padded over the planked floor. She looked back at me for a moment, tossed me a sleepy smile, and slipped through a door to her left.

I glanced over my shoulder at the bottomless, human-less hallway, and the dark stretched all the way back. It was a witchy, electric darkness. It was the darkness that had lived on the porch with Madeline, and now it was inside with me. Breathing, willful, impish darkness. Darkness that might slip under the crack in the door and smother Jing and Daisy while they slept, or else trickle in through their mouths and ears and take root in the pink of their brains. Darkness that I might be carrying around in my lungs. It was darkness as vivid and thick as outer space, and now it was here, and all I could do was scramble forward into the half bath and shut the door behind me.

The bathroom light was scalding. I winced like it was rapture.

"It's spooky up here, isn't it? Ugh, be glad you weren't friends with us when Jing and Daisy started their slasher phase. They were obsessed. We were thirteen, I think. Some of those films were so atrociously bad that they didn't bother me, but every once in a while, there'd be some movie—usually one that Jing found out about on some forum—that was just petrifying to me. It was always the ones where they don't show the creep, you know? If we saw the creep, then I knew it was just an ugly weirdo, and I could cover my ears and not worry too much. But when you couldn't see the threat, it could be anything. I wouldn't see it coming. I would wait until Jing and Daisy fell asleep and I'd hide up here with the lights on until I calmed down." Yates closed the toilet and perched on the lid, knees to chest, and scratched the side of her cheek with one of her polished nails.

"I used to do that sort of thing." I leaned against a wall and skimmed my gums with my tongue. My reflection was cringeworthy. I was a damn horrorshow. When I lifted the tissues, there were red ochre splotches smudged down my lips, down my chin, down my throat. They painted my teeth pink and clumped in my hair. Globs speckled my cleavage. "My dad—Boris, that is—is a pulp-horror junkie. He collects these old paperback novels, has all these first editions and signed prints. Splatterpunk, psycho thrillers, classic horror, he has it all. Whenever he finished a new one, my other dad would try to read it, and half the time he'd put it down because it was just too much for him. Those were the ones I'd read. I think it helped that I read them under the bed. Made the whole thing more atmospheric," I said as I vise-gripped a new tissue over my nose. I tossed the old ones in the little waste bin, which, like the rest of the room, was almost surgically white. Polar-white walls, polar-white tiles, polar-white lights that cast anemic shadows under my cheek- and brow bones.

"God, why'd you read them under the bed? That's horrific all by itself," Yates said, folding a hand over her mouth. "You probably could've read them like a normal person, you know."

"Ha. I thought I'd get caught. I wasn't supposed to read them at all. Julian would panic that I'd have nightmares or some such rot, so I had to sneak them from Boris' bookshelf and smuggle them into my room under my shirt. In retrospect, I think you're probably right—my dads weren't exactly going to psychically sense that I'd been reading forbidden horror novels, and they probably wouldn't have stopped me even if they did catch me. So I totally could have read them like a normal person. I just didn't. Besides, it was harder to scare myself under the covers, and I wanted to be scared. Everything is safer under the blankets, you know? And what kind of fourteen-year-old wants to feel safe?"

"I did." Yates rubbed her eyes with her forefingers and yawned, which made me yawn in turn. She traced her hand down the back of her neck with a sigh. "So, you're in that Drama Club, right? You an actress?"

I doubted she really cared—this was the sort of getting-to-know-you stuff that I usually tried to dodge at Boris' folks' house and things like that—but it was better than silence, so I obliged. Besides. Talking about myself isn't all bad. "Ah, no," I said. "I'm head of crew. I build the sets and do all the heavy lifting. I got to be Lady Mac for one night last semester, but that was only because Ashleigh Smith caught mono and flaked out on us two days before open, and her understudy broke her foot in a parkour accident. I wasn't about it. I'm not a good actress, and playing straight isn't easy for me. But I got to do the Unsex Me speech, so. There's that."

"Excuse me, the what?" Yates stifled a laugh. Her eyes popped wide and she splayed her fingers across her heart. The sparkles on her nails gleamed green.

I gave her a half shrug. "*Come, you spirits that tend on mortal thoughts, unsex me here.* It's a prayer, really. Or a spell. She's invoking magic to fill her and make her something other than what she is. Girls are supposed to be nice. Nice and soft and nurturing. She couldn't stay that way if she was going to get what she wanted. She needed to be genderless and limitless."

"Can girls not be soft and still be powerful?"

"Girls can. Girls are. Just not her, I think." The blood felt like it was slowing down. I pulled the tissue away from my nose and a clot stretched between my skin and the paper. "Not me, either."

"Oh," said Yates. "I see."

"It's, whatever."

Yates folded her hands neatly in her lap, instantly as dainty as a primrose. I licked the blood off my teeth. What kind of divine creature was she, looking lovely at three in the fucking morning? I looked like a gargoyle, and that wasn't even self-deprecating. She was a heavenly being. It felt like a privilege just to breathe her air.

"I think I've talked myself around about magic." Yates' hands shifted a little, refolded. "I wasn't comfortable with it, but I've been mulling a few things over."

"Yeah?" A bit of blood slipped down my throat. "Things like what?"

"The ambiguity of it almost makes sense." Her gaze softened. She looked toward me, but not at me. "I don't know. We're at an ambiguous age and we're ambiguously nice and there's a lot about us that's sort of gray or weird, I think. Our bodies in Sycamore Gorge. The kinds of relationships we have."

I looked at her for a moment. There was a ringing I didn't care to name in my stomach. "Relationships?"

"I mean." Earnest uncertainty. She looked at her wrists. "The friendships we have. Other things, maybe. I think I'm maybe queer. I've talked to Akeem about it, but I don't think my friends need to know, not right now. Or at least, I don't think I want to have a conversation about it. There's a lot of things in my life that are tricky, and being queer isn't the most pressing of those things. It just sort of *is*. But I'm not sure. Anyway, my point is that there's always been things about me that rub edges with everything else, and I know that Jing and Daisy are the same way.

"I guess my point is that teenage girls aren't supposed to be powerful, you know? Everybody hates teenage girls. They hate our bodies and hate us if we want to change them. They hate the things we're supposed to like but hate it when we like other things even more, because that means we're ruining their things. We're somehow this great corrupting influence, even though we've barely got legal agency of our own. But the three of us—the four of us, counting you— we're powerful. Maybe not in the ways that people are supposed to be, maybe in ways that people think are scary or hard to understand, but we are. Magic is ambiguous. It's scary and flashy and everybody wants it and it really freaks people out. I guess it fits with the rest."

I opened my mouth and shut it. My whole body thrummed like it'd been plucked. I couldn't find words to string together a definition for the haziness in my head. It was a warm, whirling feeling. It was like swing rides in carnivals. Slow flight, rocking and easy and far off the ground. *I'm ambiguous,* I wanted to say. *I'm like you. Am I allowed to be like you?*

"They like you, you know." Her change in topic snapped my focus back. "Jing and Daisy? They can be hard to read, I know that. But they do. Jing has told me as much, and it's implied with Daisy."

"Implied."

"I mean, she hasn't done anything too Daisy-ish to you, which means she probably likes you. If she didn't, you'd know." She waved her hands to insinuate exactly what she meant by Daisy-ish. I caught her meaning quick. I'd heard the stories. Everyone knew about Daisy tossing drunk boys into the pool, Daisy smearing toothpaste on the inside of Oreos and doling them out to rude teachers, Daisy pouring ice water down the back of someone's shirt for flirting with someone who wasn't their girlfriend, Daisy taking a wrench to someone's bike for tripping Jing, Daisy intentionally calling boys by their best friend's name while she was making out with them—the stories were endless, and by mass alone, at least half of them had to be true.

Huh.

Yates pursed her lips and quirked an eyebrow, and then she *hmphed* and rose to her feet. "Sit," she said, dimples blooming on her cheeks. She gestured at the toilet seat with Vanna White levels of enthusiasm. "Seriously. Sit."

I sat.

Yates knelt before the sink and opened the cabinet beneath, eyes swiveling, and reached inside and plucked a washrag from some unseen bin. She closed the cabinet, stood up, doused the rag with water, and wrung it out. She turned to me with her tongue in her cheek. "May I?"

I tugged a lock of my hair. "You planning on de-Dracula-ing my face?"

"Bet your life," she said. "You need it. The Carrie look needs to go."

Despite myself, I leaned my head back, waited for the washcloth onslaught. My eyes fell half-shut as Yates descended on my cheek. The rag was deliciously warm, warmer than I expected, and she swept it over every stitch of my expression. The rough texture was good. Vaguely hypnotic. She scrubbed the blood out of my smile lines. She dabbed the blood off my chin. She washed away spots that I hadn't even noticed, and my skin felt smoother in her wake.

"You have a pretty nose. Did you know that?" said Yates as she rubbed circles down my jawline. She turned up the corners of her mouth. "You have such a strong profile. You should model for me sometime; I'd love to draw you if you'd let me.

Jing never lets me. It's the only time I've seen her clam up."

I snickered. That was rich. I had a nose like the sharp side of a kitchen knife. It had a thick horizontal scar on the bridge from dumbassery at the age of seven, and a bump from breaking it in some tussle or the next.

"I'm serious." She tapped the rag between my eyes. "Let me draw you. I love portrait sketching. I'd die for a model who doesn't fidget around when I'm trying to draw. You're holding still. You'd totally be good at it. All you have to do is sit and be your pretty self."

"If you want someone pretty, make Daisy do it," I said with a sneer, but Yates thwacked me across the cheek with the rag.

"Don't do that. Never do that. Don't ever say you're not beautiful, not ever, okay? Girls are just beautiful. That's the way they are."

"Right," I breathed, yanking my hand through my hair. I felt all the blood in my body amass in my cheeks. What do you even say to that? I crossed and uncrossed my ankles. "I mean. I agree that girls are pretty great. I'm a fan."

Yates rolled her eyes.

"I'm going back to sleep, Sideways." Yates brushed her fingertips over my shoulder and moved to hang up the rag. The rag she'd been using was three shades darker than the rest of the towelettes on the rack, an odd pink where white should be.

"Thanks. I'll be down in a second. Don't wait up. I'm gonna rinse the blood taste out of my mouth."

"Alright," she said. "Watch your step on the way down."

✳

The faucet, a faceless snake head to my 3:30 imagination, must siphon water directly from the *Titanic's* belly. It was cold to the bone where it splashed my wrists, cold and sharp as needles. It would probably give me hypothermia. I stood blankly in the dark at the kitchen sink, pelvis shoved up against the countertop and shoulders hunched forward like a question mark, and filled a wineglass I'd managed to find with glacial water. The longer the faucet stream tumbled down, the less I remembered why I was there. The silvery churning at the bottom of the cup was mesmerizing. I watched the bubbles sparkle, split, burst into more bubbles. The froth looked like magic in old, scratchy cartoons. It belonged in an oozing beaker or a churning cauldron. Maybe it wasn't water at all. Fingers of moonlight stretched in between the blinds and stroked the surface of the water, which filled the glass to the brim and spilled over.

"*Fuck*," I spat aloud. I yanked the glass away. Winter water sloshed over onto my wrists and stung my skin where it touched. I put the glass down and twisted the knobs until the stream stopped. The silence sans faucet hissing triggered shivers between my shoulder blades. My wrist dripped. I rubbed it on the front of my shirt, which was Jing's shirt. She'd let me borrow it to sleep in, and it smelled like her, like matches and metal and raspberry cream. I shivered, sucked in my cheeks.

The shadows took on odd shapes in the kitchen, casting themselves from nothing. Stretches of black lined the floor, but they didn't quite match the blinds, and I couldn't think of anything rational to explain it away. I'm not the sort to be afraid of the dark. When I was little, I used to sit in my bathroom sink with the door shut and the light switched off, and I'd chant Bloody Mary until the thrill was gone and all that remained was how boring it was to sit in a sink. I genuinely like lurking around in the dark. It was just that the dark felt different here than it did at my usual haunts. It had eyes. It was prickly. Around the corner from Jing's kitchen was her yacht-like living room, and the basement door was in sight. I'd drink the water up here then go back downstairs, sleep all this off.

I made my way to the yacht-parlor and sat in one of the creamy leather armchairs, the one closest to the patio door. It felt very Gatsby and much less eerie than the kitchen. The view of the patio deck wasn't exactly sexy, but it beat spooky shadows. I kicked my feet up on the coffee table and took a sip of my water like wine.

Something shifted just outside. It barely registered, but there was something different just past the deck railing, something that darted in and out of sight.

I stopped with the cup against my mouth.

There it was again. Nothing, nothing, but it was real enough to make my heart wind a little tighter.

I swung my feet off the coffee table and stood up, leaned closer to the glass.

There was absolutely nothing outside. Which should have been obvious. I saw the balcony, planked railing washed blue by moonlight, the far edges of the fence and half-naked trees. From this angle, the swimming pool was out of sight, but so was everything else. If there really had been movement, it was probably a goddamned deer. Maybe it was a deer come to mourn her dead deer pals. Nothing for me to stress over.

The pain struck down my spine.

It was instant, electric. It surged down my sides and I pitched forward against the door, lungs constricting, heart carving itself up into bits. The cup flew out of my hands and smashed between my feet. I barely noticed. My vision twisted. I slammed my hand against the door to steady myself, but my knees buckled and my back gave way. Every nerve wire in my body twinged and cool sweat pricked the back of my neck. My body rocked with shivers, pounded like I'd been struck all over with hammers. My skin crawled—I imagined tangled centipedes squirming between my sinews, worming between my muscle ropes—and my stomach convulsed, flipped inside out. I toppled forward.

My knees slammed the hardwood and pain scissored up my shins. A gasp knifed out of my throat, barely audible, and then my voice gave out. I hacked a cough and dry-retched, my shoulders heaving over and over until my ribs were sore. Everything was sticky. A pool of water trickled away from me in glass-studded tendrils. Something dark had tinted the water, flowing in gradients from black to rust. I must have landed in the glass. The pain from that hadn't quite registered yet. I dragged myself to my feet and sucked in a ragged breath, because all at once that pain was registering. My shins screamed. Black slits scored my knees, and blood dripped like rain on a windshield.

I knew what this felt like.

This felt like magic rebound.

But that wasn't fucking possible. There was no magic to be broken.

All the throbbing in my body dragged itself toward my chest and solidified into something the size of a fist, something dark and slick and magnetic. I felt its pull like a meat hook in my sternum. It ached like nothing else. It was carnal, visceral, unstoppable. It lugged me toward the French doors, threatened to bust me through the panes. I felt my fingers loop around the doorknob. My wrist twisted. The door clicked.

Wind blasted inside and tore through me. I felt the chill marrow deep. My teeth chattered and I wound my arms around my stomach, but magic compelled my feet to move one after the other. I walked through the glass and water and onto the deck. I couldn't bring myself to shut the door behind me.

The deck was agony to walk on. The water on my soles threatened to frost. The weight in my stomach slammed; it said *lower, go lower*, and it took my nails in the railing and all my might not to pitch over the side. I forced myself down the stairs. Every step was progressively colder, bitterer. The tips of my toes numbed. Blood shook loose and made stains the size of pennies along the wooden planks. The blood was black as ink.

I knew where I was headed, because I knew my goddamned luck.

My body was being lured to the poolside.

Proximity to whatever was drawing me here was skull-splittingly tense. The nearness made me nauseous. The wind whorled my hair across my face. I could barely see through the tangles, so I dragged it off my cheeks with both fists and slammed my palms against my temples. My toes hooked over the edge of the pool and I slammed myself to a halt just before I stepped into the deep end, resisted the urge to continue with every fiber of my being. My voice snagged in my throat.

There were no longer three bodies in the swimming pool. There were seven.

# SIX

# HAVE YOU HEARD THE GOOD NEWS?

There were four of them, and they lounged around in slacks and blazers, looking as shellacked and jolly as a Pencey Prep debate team. They snickered, whispered to each other, prodded the deer with the toes of their Vans. They looked like misprints of the same boy, with just the slightest alterations to distinguish them as separate entities—a mole here, a scar there, a smattering of extra freckles—but the same sugar-blond hair, strong jaw, skinny lips, and colorless complexion. Something about the way they leered at each other with button-blue eyes set me on edge. Every stitch of my body thrummed. I watched, openmouthed, palms twitching, chest ablaze.

"Levi, you showy son of a bitch. Who were you measuring your cock against, huh? Who were you trying to best? This is so sloppy—even *I* know that. We're supposed to use stupid little rats or birds or something. Why in Christ's name would it even occur to you to use goddamn deer? I don't care if it worked, there's no flipping way someone from that party didn't see it all. And what about the girl you used to activate it?

Don't you think she's gonna snitch about it? Dad's gonna gut you. He's gonna gut you like a mackerel. He's gonna gut you, and I'm gonna watch. Think about how many witnesses there could've been! Think about how much you could have fucked everything up. It was a damn bad move, Levi. We're gonna fry you for supper." It was the shortest boy who spoke, a boy whose ears peeked out from under his hair like freshly sliced strawberries. His voice cracked every other syllable. There were at least two octaves in his monologue, and with every spike in pitch, his strawberry ears grew increasingly pink.

"*Language*," scolded the boy to his right. He was tall, but that had more to do with how broadly he held his shoulders and how high his chin raised toward the sky than his actual height. He wore his hair slicked back, and there was something like a laugh in his voice. "We don't take the Lord's name in vain, David. We don't snitch, neither. Levi was right to come to me. He knew he had done wrong by us, and he knew he needed help. There's no need to involve Dad. We can handle this smoothly. It'll be over and done with."

"Sounds like your girlfriend," added the third boy, kneeling on the ground beneath the others so I could not see his face. He spoke flatly. Devoid of inflection.

"Sure." The tall one sighed, gingerly crossed his arms over his chest. "Or it would, assuming David here had a girlfriend, which he does not. Now. Levi. How are our results coming?"

That third speaker, the one I could only half see, shifted, and his hair blinded me for a second—he was searingly blond, far blonder than the rest of them. He knelt with the fawn's head propped in his lap. His fingers fished between its jaws. "Hush," he said. "I'm close."

My stomach soured.

A smile cracked over the kneeling boy's—Levi's—mouth. He jerked his wrist, breathed something that sounded like pillow talk under his breath, and withdrew what he'd been looking for like a magician producing a dove from his sleeve. The object glittered in his grip. It was spherical, glistening red—red like a slap to the face, crushed cherries, rubies on snow—and it sparkled in the darkness like a chunk of fallen star. His smile flickered, then abruptly dropped.

"It should be violet," he said. The smug, vulpine sharpness slid off his face and left him looking wounded. He shoved the fawn's head off his lap in disgust. Its skull made a dull thud as it dropped against the concrete. If he noticed, he didn't care. He stood up, paced the length of the pool, and returned to deliver a solid kick to the base of the fawn's neck. Something inside it snapped. The *snap* echoed in my skull. The marble radiated red between his knuckles. "It wasn't her. She was violet. I'd been so damn *sure*. Fuck it all."

"It couldn't have been her. Levi, listen to me. We knew she wasn't the caster when we came here. You thoroughly eradicated any possibility of that, remember? It doesn't mean she wasn't involved. They congregate. They travel in packs. She might have found herself a new circle. Most respectable flocks wouldn't admit someone like her, I'd wager, so she must have found some loser stragglers willing to accept the handicap of keeping her around. She's deadweight. Deadweight is easy to spot. We'll find her. Don't lose faith." The oldest boy adjusted his cuff links, and Levi responded with a scoff. David looked thrilled just to be there.

"I frankly don't give a fuck." It was the last boy, the one who'd been silent the entire time. Whatever genetic anomalies had distinguished the rest of them, this boy seemed to lack. If anything, he looked so like Levi that it would've been hard to distinguish them, were it not for the long, blunt scar on the bridge of his nose. He rolled his shoulders and slipped his thumbs through his belt loops. "I don't care about her, or how you're stuck on her, or your everlasting angst parade. The *mimic* is glowing and that's what matters. Eyes on the prize." He traced his teeth with his tongue, swiveled on his heel, and looked at me head-on. He gave me the smallest of nods. "Good evening, ma'am."

The other three boys turned in tandem.

"God, that was quick! Is she the witch?" asked David.

"Don't be rude," said the tallest. He clapped his hands together, raised his brows, and beamed at me. Dimples bloomed in his cheeks. It was the sort of look that I imagine would murder a straight girl. It made my skin feel grimy. "Hello there! My name is Abel, and these are my brothers. Terribly sorry if we startled you, miss. Wasn't our intention. You were at that party last night, weren't you?"

Words tangled themselves in my throat. Intricate, vinegar-soaked paragraphs detailing every sort of *fuck you* imaginable bubbled up my esophagus, but I couldn't make myself open my jaws, much less spit insults. There was something skincrawlingly wrong about that. Whatever was happening to me felt like magic. Magic *forces* the words out of you. It drags up poetry with every exhalation. It takes a jackhammer to any floodgates blocking thought. Trying to bite back an incantation is a solid way to knock a few teeth out, and I wasn't even sure if I could slide my tongue across my hard palate. It was bizarrely numb, and lay in my mouth like a dead thing. It should be impossible *not* to scream at them. What the fuck was happening to me?

The fourth boy, the one who'd first noticed me, strolled to Levi's side. He unfolded Levi's arms, yanked his wrist away from his chest with one hand, and worked at prying the marble from Levi's fist with the other. His face remained a dead neutral—hollow eyes, flat mouth, the unnerving stillness of dissatisfaction—and he was seemingly deaf to the little hisses and winces Levi made when he squeezed too hard. He pulled Levi's fingers farther back than he needed to, past the threshold of release and into potential dislocation territory. He finally plucked the glowing marble from Levi, but took his time letting go. Levi, whey-faced, yanked his battered hand to his chest. The other boy rolled his gaze over to me.

Three long strides and he was below me.

My instinct was to kick his teeth in, but I couldn't make my leg obey. The closer I was to the marble, the harder it was to breathe.

He extended his hand, translucent marble tucked between his fore and middle fingers, and held it to my ankle.

It swirled opaque as a maraschino cherry.

He gave a barely perceivable nod. "Found our witch-girl."

"Caleb." Abel spoke slowly, gently, as if he was addressing a half-tame pit bull instead of his brother. "Put the mimic away. We have what we need."

Caleb's eyes rolled up in his head, and he pocketed the marble—the mimic—with a sigh of resignation.

Abel rubbed his hands together and cleared his throat like he was about to drop a sermon. I decided right then that I hated him, and that I'd hate him even if he wasn't being a freaky lurker. When people preach at me, they tend to get hit. He deserved a fucking hit. He flashed me a smile. "This all must be terribly confusing for you, miss. I'm sorry about that. Fortunately, it's our custom to explain these things to you to minimize whatever discomfort you might be feeling. We—the four of us—are the brothers Chantry. Our family and those who follow us are devoted to purifying the world of anathemas and witchcraft. We want to help you. That little stone Caleb was holding? It's called a mimic. Handy little things, mimics. They copy the magic signature of the nearest active caster, and then they play that signature back at a frequency that compels its caster to approach it. My little brother Levi was attempting to find a wayward friend of his, a girl who's lost her way. She goes by the name of Addie. The poor thing is a danger to herself and everyone around her, and it's very important for us to locate her before someone is seriously injured. Rumors circulated that a magical reckoning was to transpire at this residence yesterday evening. Levi believed that Addie might wish to attend such a gathering, so he went as well, and planted a mimic in hopes that it might draw her back to this spot for retrieval, in the event that she had acquired the means to cast on her own. Now, I admit that he might have gone about that in a tactless way—we would never aim to make such a scene on a stranger's property—but trust that his intentions were just.

"It did not reveal her. Instead, it brought you to us. That's really excellent, miss.

"We know that you likely did not intend to be malevolent. You weren't trying to hurt anyone, and we'd never accuse you of anything of the sort. You were just trying to have a little fun. We understand. There is no safe or harmless casting. There is always a victim in one form or another. Magics erode the natural order of things and endanger everyone involved. It's an addiction. It really is. Was it exhilarating, casting that spell? Did it make your heart hammer faster than anything you've ever experienced? Did you feel powerful? Important? Like everything you wanted was yours, like there wasn't a stitch of the universe that wouldn't bend to your every whim? Invincibility is a tricky thing. Power like that isn't good for you, miss. It's not a thing we humans are designed to endure. It makes monsters out of good girls. Only God should have the power of God.

"This mimic is mighty red. You're precocious. It takes most witches years to accumulate that sort of supernatural might. Now, it might be raw talent, but something tells me that you didn't act alone, and that's why the magic was so potent. I'd wager you have something of an amateur coven forming. Seeing as the mimic only brought *you* here, you likely were the primary enchantress—you spoke the words, wielded the chalk—but I would imagine that it took more than just you to make that sort of magic. Never worry. We can save your friends as well. It's of the utmost importance that we do. That comes later. First, we work with you.

"You can't talk right now. That's an unfortunate side effect of the mimic, I'm afraid. When we touched its vessel, it activated itself, which tends to reproduce the physical stress of spell casting threefold. No release, just the stress. Freezes you up, as well. I've been told it's a tad awkward. My apologies. We can deactivate the mimic when we've brought you somewhere safe, and then the detox can take place. It's quick and completely painless and you'll never ache again. Levi, Caleb, would you mind?"

"I want to do it," said David, baby eyes wide as his fists. "Let me."

"No," said Caleb.

"If you must," said Abel.

David was practically thrumming. He grinned and clambered up the pool wall, bypassing the ladder entirely. He vaulted up onto the pavement with his elbows and knees, tearing his slacks in the process, and sprang to his feet beside me. His grabbed my wrists, twisted them behind my back like a cop would. My body was limp as a ragdoll and screamed where we made contact. *How dare he, how fucking dare he, the fucking animal,* I howled in my head, but the mimic spell pressed on my chest and smothered any attempt I made toward speech. He was clumsy with me, jerked me like I was a losing show pig at a county fair, eventually arranging me so that I stood in front of him, my back to him, wrists pinned like he was about to slam me across the hood of a car and slap cuffs on me. He shoved me toward the gate.

I couldn't turn my head to see the other three behind us. I barely heard them. Their shoes all but whispered against the concrete and the grass, but their nearness prickled the hair on the back of my neck. I wanted to thrash, to writhe in David's grip, but I couldn't. My feet kept getting caught between his ankles. He limped under my weight.

Someone else reached for me. David yelped and pulled me closer. "I'm doing it," he insisted. "I'm old enough. I can do it." He squeezed harder, hard enough to bruise.

"You're hurting her," said Abel with mild displeasure, as if David was petting a cat the wrong way. He turned his attention to Levi and Caleb, then. "Let's clean this up, will you?"

Clean up *what?*

"I'm not hurting her," David insisted. He hauled me across the yard, past a toolshed, and through the gate of Jing's chain-link fence, to the driveway where a gloomy Lexus waited to receive us. It was navy, recently polished, twice the price of a state school's tuition. I tried to read the license plate, but David didn't shove me at the right angle to see it.

The other brothers trudged up behind us. By a neighbor's watery porchlight, their shadows looked bizarre, distended in ways that didn't make sense to me. One brother—Abel? They all looked the same from this angle—strode up beside the hood. He pulled the mass from his shoulders and slung it between the racks on the roof of the car so that its hooves dipped over the windshield and its nose slumped down toward the trunk. Caleb draped the second doe beside the first one, belly up, and Levi tucked the fawn between the does' bodies. Abel popped the truck, rummaged until he produced a fistful of bungee cords. He tossed them to Caleb, who caught them one-handed. He went to work lashing the corpses in place.

Abel sighed. He unlocked the car, knocked his hands down his shirt, and jogged to climb in the driver's seat. "Three of you will have to squeeze in the back." He shot me a glance between deer legs, flashed an apologetic smile. "Sorry about that. One of us would have stayed behind if we knew we'd be taking a guest back with us. Levi, you've got shotgun."

"Why Levi? Levi always gets it! This is so freaking unfair. He had shotgun on the way here. It's my turn." David whined like he was a fucking baby. How old *was* he? His spittle hit the back of my neck while he complained. He stopped outside of the right-hand back-seat door without releasing me, which felt violating and irritatingly redundant, as I couldn't fucking run regardless, and stomped a monkey brain from a nearby hedge apple tree into a million pulpy pieces.

"Because Levi is hurting, so we're letting him man the music as a consolation. Besides, if it wasn't Levi, it'd be Caleb. Hush," Abel replied, and the engine purred to life.

The cords pulled too tightly over their fur. Skin bulged in

patches. I couldn't stop staring. I felt phantom ropes around my waist.

I was pushed into the back seat, and Caleb and David filed in on either side of me. David's hands stayed firmly on my wrists all the while. He only let go to buckle my seat belt, which he did with too much zeal for something as mundane as buckling a seat belt. He grinned like a damn idiot. The hoof tips jittered as we pulled out of the drive.

I wanted to scream. I wanted to beat the entire lot to death, I wanted to pull the deer off the hood and hold them against me, I wanted to be downstairs, asleep among my shiny new friends, blissfully unaware of the brothers Chantry.

Furthermore, my phone was in the basement.

No one would know where I went.

# SEVEN

# WE WHO ARE FIGHTING LOVE GOD

I had no idea where the fuck we were. It was past the stretch of town that was populated with gas stations and pastel houses, and out into the liminal realm of never-ending cornfields with nary a street sign to be found. They'd turned off from a dubiously paved road onto a dirt one, and now all around the car were scraggly woods. The air outside looked thinner. The trees clawed out of the earth with ragged fingers and twisted elbows, looked like the arms of giants who'd previously occupied this space before the Chantry homestead fell from the sky and crushed them to death with its mass of brick and plaster columns. It was an antebellum monster with long windows and an endless porch. Abel slowed to a halt, and the horrible scratch of tire on gravel ground to silence. Levi killed the Radiohead he'd been playing.

I doubted I'd ever be able to listen Radiohead again.

"Let me disarm the mimic," said David. He made grabby hands across my lap at Caleb. "I never get to do it. I want to do it. Abel, make Caleb let me."

"You could always ask your brother, you know," said Abel.

Caleb audibly scoffed.

"Caleb, please?"

Abel gave Caleb a look in the rearview mirror.

"You'd fuck it up," said Caleb.

"I won't. I'm not an idiot, you know. I know how to do this." Caleb gave him the mimic, and he clutched it close to his chest and leered at his brother, which took bending forward to see him around my body. Then, with a start, to Abel: "How are we going to get her up the stairs?"

"You could carry her bridal style," said Abel with a smile, half joking, or maybe not.

*Not if you want your testicles to remain attached to your body, you fucking fuck.*

"I'll do it," said Caleb as he leaned his temple to the glass. "David would drop her. Stop bitching," he said to David before he began. "You didn't help carry the deer out of the pool, so you're going to help pull them around back."

David huffed and crossed his arms.

The brothers unbuckled, and all but Caleb filed out of the car. The sound of them unlashing the deer overhead flipped my stomach. They pulled them free, jeered at each other, cussed as they dragged them away from the car and around the back of the house. Caleb lingered with me, completely silent, stoic. The sound didn't seem to bother him at all.

When he reached for my buckle, he bent his wrists at odd angles to avoid touching me. His shirt cuffs didn't brush my skin. Maybe it was a twisted form of sympathy, or some sort of shrunken compassion. Not that much compassion, or he wouldn't be an active participant in all of this. Maybe he was just disgusted by the thought of touching me.

Not that disgusted, though. Not enough that he didn't gather me up like a damn doll. One arm snaked behind my back, the other under my knees, and he lifted me up like he was moving a box of china—not tenderly, but with care not to chip the contents.

He paused before he lifted me out of the car. The night air whorled in, and it was cold enough to make my knees shake and the hair on my arms and legs stand up. It set my teeth on edge.

"Blink if you want my jacket," he said. His voice was hushed, even though we were alone.

I must have blinked.

He unhooked his arms from around me and pulled off his jacket, which he draped around my shoulders like he might a little sister's. Then his arms slid back in place and he lifted me out into the night, closed the door with a kick.

He carried me wordlessly up the stairs.

I wanted to shove my heel through his skull.

Someone had propped the door open for us with a wooden stop, which Caleb knocked away as we crossed the threshold. The door slammed behind us with a bodily smacking sound. It rang in my ears like a gong.

The entry room was a hollow, milky cavern, marked only by a staircase and a gaping, hissing hearth. There was a long rectangle on the floor where the floorboards were lighter than the surrounding planks as though there'd been a rug at some point that had since been rolled up and stashed away elsewhere. Above the hearth was a coat of arms, royal blue and gilded with griffins and fasces and a sunny-looking breaking wheel. *Pugnantes Deum Amamus.* Twin lacquered sabers crisscrossed below the symbol, dangling mere inches above the flames in the fireplace. The other brothers were out of sight. I could hear their voices on the walls, but couldn't make out anything distinct. Loud, brassy voices that sitcoms assign to happy, boring bodies in picnics and tennis practices, not to the bodies of boys who dragged girls into cars. Perhaps these weren't separate categories.

Caleb ascended the grand stairs.

These stairs were steeper than the ones outside. My head lolled back, the world spun upside down, and the view between the balusters made my insides quicken. I was hyperaware of how precarious I was in Caleb's arms. I felt his sinews shift with every step, felt the lack of support where his arms weren't holding me. His grip wasn't wavering, but the image of myself dead limp, cartwheeling down these stairs, was enough to make my guts twist. My breath hitched. I felt his eyes swivel across me for a moment, which made me want to punch his throat, because he should pay more attention when he's walking up the fucking stairs.

"*Breathe.* I won't drop you."

We reached the top of the stairs, thank fucking God. Slightly less Spartan than the entryway, but everything was morbid and uncanny from my angle. Trophy antlers thorned the walls, looking bizarrely like human hands on their gold and velvet plaques. White crosses dripped off hooks and painted nails. Beaming family portraits decked the walls between the thorns and windows, and on either side of each portrait was an electric candelabra that resembled a wilting lily. Upside down, the portraits' smiles looked gruesome. They had captions that mentioned full quivers and thankfulness.

Caleb swept me through a doorway, and the drop in temperature crashed over me. It was atrociously cold, cold enough to bleach the air and stab needles into the back of my throat. It made my entire skull hurt, it was so cold. My toes were dangerously exposed. I felt them tinging blue.

"Oh, *Caleb,* lay her in the armchair. Poor little thing. Yes, the blue one, the one your father likes," said someone with the timbre of Grace Kelly. I couldn't see her, but I could guess that she was close enough to touch us, because her perfume smelled like honey and it was wafting by my face. There was the whisper of slippers on the hardwood floor, then a hand placed on my ankle. "Oh, she's freezing! Caleb, fetch her a blanket. I think your father might have started a pot of coffee. If you could fix her a cup, that'd be very sweet of you."

Caleb didn't answer, but he did obediently arrange me on the armchair. He pulled his blazer tighter around my shoulders, placed my hands in my lap, propped my head up with a pillow, and slipped out of sight. His shoes clipped across the floor, and the door creaked shut behind him.

The woman sat down in a chair across from me. She was blond as the brothers were, long-lashed and kitten-faced, and she wore a satin bathrobe that gathered around her waist with a Christmas-perfect bow. Her skin was dewy, flushed despite how late it was getting. I couldn't place her age. She was obviously their mother, but she didn't look quite old enough to have boys my age. I'd have guessed her at an ambiguous thirty-something. Couldn't be right.

"They'll be switching off that mimic soon, I promise. You must feel awful." She smoothed the satin over her knees and sighed. "I hope they weren't too rough with you. Abel and Caleb are good boys, and so is Levi most days, but David can be clumsy with these things. He's fourteen. Just starting out. I'm sure they explained it to you, so I won't bore you by going on about it. We're going to make you better. You can stay in our guest bed overnight, and Caleb or Elias can drive you home after breakfast. Poor dear.

"I'm Grace. I'm the boys' mother, and Elias is my husband. You'll probably be meeting him shortly. It's best that he's the one to perform your purifying rites. Abel could do it, but I think you deserve the smoothest ritual possible after the hassle you've probably had. Elias is the expert. Oh, if the boys were too coarse with you, please do let me know. I'll tell them off. They oughtn't treat a young lady like that." She paused to yawn and stretch out her arms, which looked, to me, like swan necks. "I apologize for how chilly it is in here. David was fiddling with the window the other day, and now it won't shut. Oh, I should go fetch my husband—he might be able to shut it for us. I won't bother trying. Spare us both the embarrassment."

She drifted to her feet and brushed her fingertips over my shoulder. "You've got such thick hair," she said. "It's lovely. I'll braid it later, if you let me. Oh, and I'll get something to clean up those bloody legs of yours. A little iodine and you'll be perfect." She half laughed, winked like I was in on some secret, and ghosted out of sight.

The door locked behind her with a click.

✳

Sensation gushed back. It coursed down my sinews, wove between bones and over odd swathes of skin, and all at once I was aching. It was the kind of ache that usually followed sickness or a mosh pit, a deep, marrow-stinging soreness that pressed the breath out of me. I toppled out of the chair and onto the floor, and I could barely move my hands to catch myself before I hit.

I didn't know how long it'd take for Grace to wander back in here, but something in my gut said that it'd take her splinters of a second to come back now that I was moving. I was the right flavor of unlucky for her and her husband to show up and murder me this instant, or perform their freaky exorcism, or whatever. I scrambled to my feet.

My feet throbbed like yellow-jacket stings and all the blood in my body rushed to my head. My vision splotched. I swayed with my arms outstretched, sucked a hard breath through my teeth. *Fucking breathe, Sideways.* I teetered upright. I had to do something. I had to tell my friends what was going on and get the fuck out of here.

There was a phone on a desk. A real-life, honest-to-God home phone. Curly cord and everything. I hadn't realized that those still existed. I lunged for it, seized the receiver, and shoved it under my chin, then stared down at the dial pad.

What were their fucking phone numbers?

A sweat broke over my back.

I didn't know them. I don't think I'd ever asked. We'd only talked through a messaging app when they'd booked me for the party. Did I know any numbers? Any numbers at all? The phone beeped insistently in my ear and my chin trembled. 911. That was a number! But it was a cop number. No fucking thanks! Boris raised me better than that.

Holy shit! Boris!

I dialed the shop. My fingers were shaking like I had a fucking tremor. I did not, but I couldn't make them move right. What had they done to me? The call went through and I squeezed the phone tighter.

*Got the message. Thank you for calling Rothschild & Pike!*

It was, like, 4:00 a.m. There was no way that they'd be awake. I tried Julian's cell and then Boris' and got nothing. Boris didn't even have his inbox set up.

Come on, brain. We have to know more numbers. Holy fuck. I knew my own number. My phone was on the pillow in Jing's basement. Somebody would pick up, right?

I dialed, it rang, it went to my voice mail. I dialed again. My fingers felt clumsy on the big raised number buttons. I dialed a third time, then a fourth.

"Hello?" It was Yates' voice. In the background, I heard muffled whining, an utterance that sounded like *Who the fuck calls so early? Whoa, like, wait, where'd Sideways go?*

"Yates," I hissed. My knees shook. "Yates, I found the Chett guy. Our hex didn't work, and he and his brothers kidnapped me, but I'm fucking dealing with it. I'm—"

"Wait, what?"

There was a sound outside the door. The groan of floorboards underfoot. Soft voices. "Honey, is that a good idea?"

"Fuck. Later." I slammed the phone down. Grace. Fuck. My blood sizzled inside my guts. Alright. I needed a fucking plan and I needed it now.

I rubbed my palms over the gooseflesh on my arms. Gooseflesh—that phrase felt ridiculously applicable now. I felt freshly plucked and primed for roasting. I tugged Caleb's blazer off my shoulders and slid my arms in the sleeves, buttoned it down my torso. It was ridiculously big on me. The tips of the sleeves hit my second knuckles. I shivered once, jammed my tongue in my cheek.

Oh my God.

The window, the gaping window, the one that was responsible for the tundra inside. It was broad, twice my size or longer. The mothwing curtains gusted around it like shackled ghosts.

I rounded the chairs and made for the window. I felt my heartbeat in my teeth. I slipped my hands through the gap, grasped the sliding pane, and yanked. It opened wider with a squeal.

Below the window was a drop, then rows of slanted pewter shingles. I wagered it was the roof over the porch, because I could eye Abel's car just beyond it. Dying roses twined up the painted lattice directly below me.

I swung one leg over and straddled the skinny sill. My heart thumped too loud. Blood battered in my ears, between my ribs, and I dangled the outside leg a little lower. The lack of anything below my toes stabbed me in the stomach. *This was stupid, this was stupid. Oh my God, I am so fucking stupid.* I bowed my torso under the window and pulled my other leg along with me. The ledge was too small to properly sit on. I was on the verge of freefall, and the moonlight struck me like a searchlight.

I jumped.

I smacked down on my palms and heels. If it hurt, I was thrumming too hard to feel it. Adrenaline hit like a drug. I crawled down the slant with my heart in my teeth and wished, with a bit of spite, that the shingles felt less like sandpaper.

The top of the porch proper was significantly farther below me than I thought it'd be. Potentially femur-snappingly far. I envisioned my body cracking on impact, rolling mangled off the incline, and smashing into jam on the driveway below, hair stained sticky red, bones poking through my skin like white batons. I whipped my head around and tried to remember how to swallow. I felt like I'd swallowed a bee.

There was a tree to my right, a crooked oak with battered

limbs all twisted and gnarled, perfect for climbing. I scrambled for it. The shingles felt electric against my naked feet. I crawled like a feral child, belly close to the ground and clawing, and I prayed to something abstract that I wouldn't accidentally slip off the roof to my death.

*Stop panicking,* I reminded myself. *I can do this. I've dicked around with climbing trees my entire life. Tree-dickery was half my childhood. Just fucking do it.*

I hissed something hideous under my breath, licked my teeth, and launched myself at a branch below me. The moment of falling dragged on, then I struck. The branch was rougher than the shingles, but solid. I clambered for a proper grip and then shimmied lower, balancing myself against the base of the branch.

The gravel on their driveway was corpse colored, jagged like pulled teeth. It was begging to rip the skin off my feet. It'd taken two and a half songs to drive here. How many miles were in two and a half songs? How far back did the gravel stretch? How many steps would it take to bury the Chantry house behind me?

My odds tasted foul in my mouth.

I twisted myself around and braced my back against the trunk. My knees tucked themselves to my chest. What I wouldn't give for some fucking pants! The barely-shorts that Jing had lent me did nothing for the chill. The night had bleached all the color from my legs and left them looking waxy. The blood had dried in thick rivets, and as the moonlight made my skin sallower, it'd made my blood darker.

I looked like I'd been wading in ink. I shoved my hands in the blazer pockets and gnawed at my bottom lip. *Think, fucking think. Come on, Sideways.*

In the caverns of Caleb's pocket, my fingertips brushed something metallic. I traced its edges with a nail, wrapped my fist around it, and pulled it out into the open air.

It was a key. Black around the handle, unremarkable, and as long as the knuckle of my thumb. I'd seen one like it somewhere. It pinged some memory I had, something uncannily vivid and just out of reach. I turned it around in my hand, fiddled with the serrated edge, and realization slapped me across the face. It was the key to a bike lock. I recognized it because I had one just like it.

The bastard had a bike.

I pocketed the key and monkeyed down the trunk, limb after limb, and my feet found the grass with a swish. A worm squiggled under my toes. I shuddered, bounced back, and whirled around.

*Bike, bike, bike.*

Aha. Bikes.

Four glistening bikes leaned against the side of the porch. They looked like horse skeletons under the stars, all chrome bones in strange shapes, and they rested against the roses like they were sleeping. Four bikes for four brothers. It was my own macabre little Christmas. I sprinted over, shoved the key in each lock until I found the one that clicked.

It was a retro model, a well-loved one at that. Must be expensive.

A sloppy grin slid across my mouth.

*Mine now, prick.*

I dragged Caleb's bike to the gravel, climbed on, and flew away.

＊

I was the only thing alive on the road. The drive was as winding as a board game track, curving and convoluted, and the trees stretched on for eternity in either direction. No wildlife. The town's deer population had neglected to infect this stretch of woods. Or maybe not—I remembered the antlers that spiked the Chantry halls and amended my theory: the deer in these parts were strictly past tense. There were no night birds, no opossums, and no scurrying raccoons, either. Nothing. There weren't even half-smashed little carcasses on the sides of the road. The Chantrys had butchered them all.

I pedaled faster. My hair stormed around my cheeks.

Gravel turned solid. The trees broke, and the honeyed glare of a streetlamp flooded the path before me. I could've cried. Sweet civilization gave me a damned streetlamp, and I was in love with it. The streetlamp wasn't going to give me a holy water enema, or whatever else was on the Chantry agenda. I took a left, sped down the empty lane.

The corn loomed high, begging for harvest. It peered over the fences and menaced me as I passed. Cornstalks at night were relentlessly creepy, but they were creepy in a way I was comfortable with. I could handle stalk-roaming monsters. I was higher on the creepy food chain than them, and I'd lived here long enough to make that known.

Post-Chantry family, I'd have to reevaluate my creepy food chain.

A street sign marked the upcoming crossroad. Grover Way and Elm Street, both scribed in milky block letters. My pulse pricked. Grover Way led to Main Street. I needed to be on Main Street. I turned and pedaled faster, faster, and the pedals scraped the underside of my feet. My heart thrashed against my rib cage. I gusted past Lincoln Street, Marsh Street, Tiller Street, flying through red lights, swerving into the wrong lane. I had the street to myself. All the cars were neatly lined up on either side of the road like dead things, sitting stiff and stagnant with the windows rolled shut. Buildings were lightless. Dogs didn't howl.

I wasn't, as far as I could tell, being followed. I didn't look back to check.

# BETWEEN THE FOURTH AND FIFTH RIBS

The sign read ROTHSCHILD & PIKE. Long, spindle-serif letters, each etched as boldly as a proclamation on a headstone. It spilled ivy at the seams. The shop occupied the farthest edge of the last block of brownstones on Main Street, the final business in an endless line of prissy emporiums and bourgeois boutiques. The bricks were matte black, dusty as a chalkboard. Overflowing pansy boxes dangled from the rain gutter. Inside was pitch black. From the darkness inside came my Wild Things to the window, the taxidermy monsters that leered through the glass at passersby, flashing their lacquered eyes and teeth. They reared back with their mouths jutted open, eternally screaming at nothing, or arranged in wicker chairs between mismatched tea sets like the illustrations in children's books. They were a lovely forest-dwelling family, would-be Goldilocks' victims. Around them, lovingly arrayed on oversized bookshelves, lay palmistry kits, limbless mannequins, yellowed newspapers and silver spoons, flapper pearls and unlabeled perfumes.

The door was locked—of course it was locked—but there

was a key in one of the pansy boxes.

I hopped off the bike, tossed it haphazardly against the bricks, and made for the planter box. My lungs were still busted from cycling so fast. Fuck that bike. If someone came and stole that stolen bike in the morning, I'd be jubilant. I'd take the robber out to lunch. I loomed over the planter box, wiggled my fingers, and thrust my hands in the thick of the flora. *Please still be here, little key. You better goddamn be here.* The pansies swallowed my hands to the wrists. They were slick with dewdrops, and they smeared the back of my hands with cold and wet. I combed the soil for something small, something metallic. My nails scraped dirt and the underbelly of leaves, worms, roots, nothing, aching nothing. Then something pricked at my fingers. The relief was as real as a punch to my stomach. It was just the little bite I'd been looking for. I plucked up the key and turned to the door.

I fumbled with the lock. Lots of shoving the key against flat metal, fiddling with the slit, jamming it this way and that to no avail. Jittery. Botched. Must be what being a teenage cis boy is like. The last drops of battery acid I had left in me were fizzling out. It was strange, how quickly hypervigilance gave way to exhaustion.

*Click.*

I pushed the door in, and it swung shut behind me.

The smell was overwhelming. The oxygen inside was laced with copper and frankincense, and it oozed into the ruts in my lungs like a salve, filled me with something holy, something pure and delicious and heartbreaking.

If ball gowns had skeletons, the skeletons would look like our chandeliers. Dozens of them dripped from above, dangling from the ceiling like rip cords from Heaven. They bore thousands of crystal points the size of my pinky fingers. All around, the dark made strange things twist stranger. Bibelots and trinkets stretched on for years in either direction. Book stacks, tarot decks, telescopes, and scratched-up globes mingled with the ancient kitchenware, ornate lamps, effigies of the Virgin Mary. The air was thick with phantoms, with mysteries and revelries. Gilded things. Apparitions. I was not alone. In this space, in the presence of these sacred things, I felt witnessed and genuinely understood. I felt it marrow deep. It made me want to cry, or maybe crash my fists into something over and over again until it was dead.

Home had a way of popping off my scabs. Feeling safe meant feeling, and right now, everything hurt. The numb vanished, and I suddenly remembered that I had feet, and said feet were nearing the point of no return. My toes hollered. Even in the dark, they took on a gruesome shade of blue, a blue so blue that I couldn't just chalk its blueness up to the shadows. There was something wrong with me. My body was a mess. I was a walking horrorshow.

I made my way deeper into the belly of the shop.

Every step stripped the panic off my bones. I didn't have it in me to panic anymore. I was turning into a jellyfish. By the time I reached the staircase, I'd be a ghost-shaped bag of glowing guts and periwinkle slime. No girl in there. No bones. I had neither fight nor flight. It was a sickly feeling, not one I appreciated. I was more comfortable with rage. There was something repugnant about the absence of rage in me. I wanted my fury back. I wanted a bath. And chocolate.

The staircase was discreetly tucked behind a door in the back. There was another staircase, a more customer-friendly, less broken staircase, but that one only led to the second floor of the shop. I needed this here hidden one, which led to our third-floor apartment. I needed to be in my room.

The door was lavender in the light, but night leeched the color from the paint and made it look like a slab of solid glue. Same lock as the front door. I fumbled again, spat, and swore as I tried to shove the key in its slot. Slip, twist, click. I opened it wide and shut it behind me.

It was bleaker than Nietzsche on the staircase proper.

I groped along the wall for the light switch.

Light splashed down from above and I flinched away from it. It was heavenly fire and brimstone, and it stung in places I didn't know could sting. My arms flew to shield my face.

I hadn't found the switch yet. That light wasn't my fault.

"Oh. Oh God. Eloise?"

I peeked between my forearms.

Julian stood on the landing with a Louisville Slugger clutched in his fists. His housecoat, cherry silk two sizes too big, hung crooked off his shoulders, as if he'd just barely bothered putting it on. He made a face like a barn owl. "Lamby, you're *bleeding*," he squawked. He splayed a hand over his heart, and before I could think, he'd fluttered down the stairs and tossed his arms around my shoulders.

Julian smelled like Julian—like soap and books and burnt espresso—and it twisted something in my gut. My throat seized up. Tears threatened to prick. The last cells of power in me gave out, and I went limp against his shoulder. My teeth cut my lip. Breathing was harsher, heavier. I knotted my fists in the silk of his sleeve.

"Let's get you upstairs, okay?" He kissed the top of my head. The baseball bat was awkwardly shoved against my side, and I swallowed, tried to muster up enough snark to make some sort of joke about it. Julian with a baseball bat was about as intimidating as a bluebird with a toothpick. If I was a robber, the store would be thoroughly robbed by now. But I couldn't find the words, so I just nodded instead.

✳

I had scrubbed the top two layers of skin off my back in the shower. Now my skin was sunburn red. The bramble bush that was my hair had been combed flat against my skull, and I sat with my knees to my chest on Julian's chair. It was a privilege to sit on Julian's chair. He was territorial about these things.

This shard of glass was bigger than the last.

Boris fished it out with his tweezers. We hadn't spoken, because he knew me well enough to know when to talk. He dropped the shard in a teacup with the rest, set down his tweezers, and prepped a cotton swab with iodine.

"Your dad wants to call the cops," he said at last. He

smoothed the cotton over the little gash, taking care to sweep away the blood when it started trickling. It stung like salt.

I swore something incoherent.

"He hasn't yet," Boris continued. He took my ankle in his hands and pulled my leg closer to his nose. His gaze switchbacked over my skin, and then he let out a little *aha* and set my leg back down. He reached for his tweezers again. "That's mostly because he doesn't know what he would say. If you want him to, then you should tell him. But I'm giving you that option."

It was weird, seeing Boris without his glamour on. His hair was the first thing he did every morning—he teased it before he brushed his teeth. Seeing him without his pompadour was weird. His fringe dangled all in his face.

I swore again and hugged my arms over my stomach.

"It's five a.m. If you want to skip school tomorrow, be my guest. You need to sleep. You need to sleep for years. I can make you some tea, if you want. Julian might have already started making tea. Either that, or he's nervous baking. Don't worry about staying up until he's done. I can eat whatever he Frankensteins up. Take one for the team."

I licked my gums. Talking was not appealing. If I spoke, I'd probably cry, and I wasn't one for crying. Bless Boris for letting me just be. I sank farther into the armchair, let it swallow me in its corduroy plushness.

"Anything you need, name it. I'm going out to pick up Julian's Truvada in the morning, so if you want anything from the store, I can get it." He leaned back, examined the wreckage.

"You kick a window? I did that once. I was a little older than you. It was not an act of sobriety, let's say that." That sounded rhetorical, thank God. "You're not going to need stitches. If Julian wants you to go to the hospital, it's just him being him. It wouldn't hurt to slap on some Band-Aids, though. Snort if you want the Mickey Mouse ones."

I snorted.

He gingerly selected a few from a plastic box, and I tossed my head back, looked away. The wrappers crackled. The sticky was stuck on me. My gaze traced the cracks on the ceiling.

The fucking curse hadn't worked. Levi was Chett, wasn't he? Shouldn't he have shriveled up and died from even considering abducting me? It'd felt so real when we'd cast it. There was the rage, the rush, the glittering satisfaction. The fucking Ken doll had deformed. The four of us had clicked together like chain links and we'd made something, dragged it out of the universe, and forced it to bloom.

The thought of Levi on Yates, screaming at her, all sneering and snide, made my insides churn. How dare he even *look* at her. He barely deserved to have eyes. My molars ground in the back of my head. I remembered the sound his boot made when it smacked the fawn's spine, how it was quick and gruesome as a lightning strike. That boy, the boy who'd kick a dead animal out of spite, was the same boy who'd dragged the terrified Yates out of the basement and out into the cold. And left her there. And arranged dead animals around her.

And there it was. My anger, vicious and viscous as honey,

bubbled up in my bloodstream like a promise. It was scrawny anger, but anger nonetheless. It'd grow. I could feed it and forge it into something that mattered.

What if they came after me? What if they found me?

What if I clobbered them to death with Julian's bat?

"You're smirking. That's good. I was worried there for a second." Boris clapped his hands. "Voila. Admire my masterpiece. I'm going to fetch some tea." He gave my ankle a squeeze before he stood up. Boris tossed a hand through his hair and winked at me, smoothed his monogrammed pajamas, and wandered off toward the kitchen.

I let my gaze slide down to my legs.

He was right. It was a masterpiece.

He'd layered circular Band-Aids with thumb-shaped ones so that they resembled tiny hearts, and the hearts made a chain from my kneecaps to the tops of my feet. I was crisscrossed with Mickey Mouse hearts. No more cuts.

I knew it was a placebo, but knowing didn't kill the feeling.

I pulled my knees to my chest and traced the ridges of the Band-Aids with my fingertips. It stung a little, but not unbearably so. The hearts sheathed my newborn anger, nestled it somewhere safe. I gave myself a squeeze.

There had to be a hiding spell or something. A don't-stalk-me spell. A spell for being left the fuck alone.

"Dad," I croaked before he made it out the door. "Do we have any new occult books, or anything?"

He paused and glanced over his shoulder. "I theoretically might have found something particularly cool at the last auction. Said theoretical particularly cool book was meant to be a theoretical Hanukkah gift, or maybe Christmas gift, depending on whether we're going to my folks' house this year. You know. Theoretically. However, given the circumstances, my plans could change. Would you like that?"

"Yeah." I ran my nail under the edge of a heart and fought the urge to peel it. "I'd like that a lot."

"Then you shall receive." Boris heaved a melodramatic sigh, and with a wave of his hand and a wink in my direction, he turned again and left. He whistled all the way.

*

There was music. It was barely perceptible, but I felt the chord progressions in some blood-deep way, the same way that I knew how to exhale and swallow. It was instinctual. I let myself be lulled awake with the chorus on my lips.

It was Julian's music. He must be downstairs.

My red curtains stained the light, which stained the walls, which made my waking up warm and hazy pink. Sunlight poured across my Dracula-themed sheets and caught all the spinning dust particles, lit them up, suspended them like a beam from a UFO. My eyelids were sticky. My tongue was fuzzed. I sat up, yawned like a bear, and rubbed my fists against my eyes, which was a bizarrely pleasurable experience. I rubbed and rubbed until I saw spots. My hair still hung wet against my neck, and when I worked up the will to stop mashing at my eyelids, I clawed up my soggy locks and tied them in a knot. Hair ties were optional with curls like mine.

It was eleven, easy. Eleven or noon or maybe later. School started at seven, so I was thoroughly skipping at this point, skipping past the point of Julian changing his mind and making me go. Boris would never go back on something he said to me, particularly something that involved me having a "glorious rebellion against The Man," but Julian was both a lawful good and a chronic worrier. It'd be totally in the realm of things he might do, making me show up for the second half of classes. Did he even know that I was skipping?

I sat up, snatched an oversized t-shirt off my bedpost (where I typically discarded them when I gave up folding), and tossed it on. This was not a bra kind of day. Fuck bras. This shirt, a Siouxsie and the Banshees relic that had been Boris' before I stole it, was big enough to hang off one of my shoulders. I followed it with a pair of mostly clean sweatpants from the floor and willed myself out of bed.

My room was a wreck, but an organized wreck. I knew where everything was, give or take. The walls kaleidoscoped with alchemical diagrams, horror flick posters, pages of blackout poetry. I'd scribbled notes on the blank spaces with lipstick and Sharpie. Candy wrappers were taped to posters, a running record of how much more chocolate I can eat than Boris. There was barely any wall left under all my stuff. I had a thing with Halloween decorations, specifically obnoxious witch paraphernalia, so witchy likenesses cluttered my bedside table and my desk. Coffee mugs sat abandoned, a few growing fuzz. My books sat stacked around the perimeter in crooked, precarious pillars, and on top of the books were sketchpads and mason jars filled with rusting nails, rose petals, and salt. A bestickered television sat in a corner, which was mostly comatose, as Netflix owned my ass these days. Six different incense burners peppered the windowsills, each with its own fragrance. All my stuffed animals (which I refused to throw away) covered the length of my bed. A box of tampons rested on my laptop.

Then, of course, the floor. Two summers ago, I'd painted a ring on the floorboards. It was two fingers thick and one jump rope around, and it vaguely resembled a halo of spilled milk. The ring occupied the space between my bed and my window, and it was the only space on my floor that wasn't covered with clothes, because I'd shoved the catastrophic mess two paces away in every direction. The medicine box I kept my tools in—the chalk, the candles, the knife—sat in the center.

I licked the grime off my teeth.

Time to take the new spell book out for a spin.

# LET ME TAKE YOU DOWN CUZ I'M GOING TO

Babies have gills when they're purple in the womb-dark. They're like little fantastical mercreatures, not quite human, far from finished. They exist suspended in liminal water space, so they need gills to breathe. I picture my own as having been the angriest pink little jaggedy slits, bright as gooey papercuts on either side of my neck. We cannot keep our gills, though. The world outside is colder, thinner. Breathing there requires sputtering. Mouths gasping, flared nostrils, that sort of thing. Babies are stripped of their primordial gills and learn to survive without. The papercuts zip themselves up and vanish, and the babies turn into people who forget they ever had them in the first place. This forgetting is normal. It's nothing to be ashamed about. Everybody who has ever had a body has done it. It's just part of a human life.

Magic is like that. It's intrinsic to who we are, it's innately temporary, and forgetting it is just part of becoming a person. We've all got some ephemeral strangeness that shrivels and fades every day. It's the part of us that doesn't understand how we're separate from the cosmos. If the cosmos is part of us, we can move it like it's part of our body. We could shape it and tear it and flow seamlessly in and out of it, because we *are* it, or at least we were. Keeping our magic isn't possible. This is because the world isn't magically inclined. The fabric of reality as it's been made is defined by this lack of magic. There are laws governing physics. We've got clocks that tell time and standardized ways to measure space. Things don't happen without explanation. There is always evidence and cause and effect. Gravity doesn't make exceptions. The sky is blue because of how molecules scatter light. Sickness is made of itty-bitty beings, and even though you can't see them, they crawl all over every surface and might murder you unless you murder them first with orange-smelling soap. You can't just wish something into being. You've got to work for it. See how magic is a fucked-up framework? You'd be a mess if you kept your magic. You're better off leaving it with your gills. It's not like you'll ever be the wiser.

Scenario: There's a flood.

If there's a flood, and the universe snatches you up and slam dunks you into a whirlpool, you've either got to grow those gills back, or you're going to die. Realistically speaking, you die. How could you not? You barely remember your gills, and even if you do, they're gone. You can claw your throat and thrash and scream, but they won't come back. You lost them in the process of being a normal human person. Your lungs fill until they pop. Belly up.

But sometimes, you live. Ridiculous, no?

She was there when I woke up. My mother, infinitely tall

in a pea coat and Birkenstocks, rapping her knuckles on the kitchen table. She wore at least seven rings per finger. I think a lot about her hands. The ghost of last night's lipstick was still peachy on her mouth, and she gnawed a strip of skin off her bottom lip, smiled at me all crooked. Why don't we get ourselves Italian for lunch? We can split something at that cafe on fourth street. My mother, wondering aloud next about where she left her fake Rolex. Her fingers twisting braids down the back of my head with her shiny coffin nails, tapping the jean pocket where her cigarettes had been before she quit, covering her teeth as she laughed, because I must have said something funny, though I'm not quite sure where the joke was. My mother, the most beautiful being to ever exist corporeally, with features I inherited that actually looked *proportionate* on her face, looked lovely even, neither feminine nor masculine but regal-androgynous like angels must be, telling me that I was going to have to learn to braid my own hair one of these days. She found her car keys in a wineglass and tucked them in her breast pocket. Winked at me, still laughing. Just a few errands. Twenty minutes, tops, then lunch. You're a big girl. Think you can handle it?

Uh-huh, yeah, sure. You betcha.

I could hear it from inside the house. The smack. The strike. It rattled the walls and the windows. It was not a sound that nature could produce, sounded like a spoon-through-a-meat-grinder, a bovine howl, a brittle crunch. The smashing of glass and steel. There went little seven-year-old me, braids a-swinging, darting out of the front door with my disposable camera, hoping in my morbid way that someone had hit the telephone pole with a riding lawnmower again. Little, painfully naive me, taking the time to play hopscotch in my neighbor's driveway before I investigated. Thinking that a noise like that could mean anything other than an irreversible End Of The World.

We only lived five houses down from the tracks.

Someone'd taken a video on their phone and sent it to the local news station. A couple someones, actually. There were enough voyeurs that the station could stitch the shitty flip phone videos into something cinematically presentable. I watched it, of course I did. Knees pulled to my chest, nose to the television screen, chipped nails chittering between my teeth. A passenger train had dragged the smithereens of a cream-colored car two miles before it stopped, and by then, it was barely a car at all. The car was smoldering rubble, crumpled like a ball of paper. They found a body inside, but it was barely a body. They weren't sure who the body rubble had belonged to. I knew, though. It was our car. My mother was in that car. Also, she was not. Parts of my mother's body lined the train tracks just like breadcrumbs leading home.

The rules shattered. How was there a smear where there had been a person? How was twenty minutes also a decade? How was I motherless when I had a mother, who was coming home in twenty minutes to take me to lunch? When I was starving, I wouldn't eat, because I was waiting for her to take me out. I bit the social workers who tried to unbraid my hair. Whenever they tried to explain what had happened to me, I spilled scalding coffee on their knees, or carved notches in the upholstery of their car seats, or broke their office lamps with a mighty swing of my yo-yo and rained sparks all over the desk. Anything to get the explanations to stop. There was no cause and effect. There wasn't an algorithm, or even a vague hypothesis about why she didn't exist anymore that I could fathom. There wasn't anything. What was created had been destroyed. Reality went ragged. I didn't like things that I usually liked. I didn't like things that reminded me of her, but I didn't like new things, either. I liked being nasty, because I hadn't done nasty before, but it'd probably been inside me all along. I liked throwing dishes off the roof. I liked traipsing through doors marked *No Trespassing*. I liked using words that made adults curdle. I liked picking locks, picking pockets, picking scabs. I broke the rules of girlhood. I tossed them in the pyre with the rest.

My mother willed me the lot. It was my very own dragon horde, except that I wasn't allowed to touch it until my magic eighteenth birthday, because that was when I'd grow my responsibility bone, the one that lets you vote and make porn and go to Big Kid Prison. My mother neglected to name who would take me in her stead. Must have forgotten that part. When people asked me, I couldn't name a single blood relative aside from my mother. At the time, I didn't know she had a living brother. I didn't know where she was born or what she did with her time or with whom she kept her company. They couldn't find anything on her. As far as they knew, my mother had started existing when I was born.

Anyway. Sunburned agents pried me screaming from my motherless house to a place where the blacktop was broken and the schoolkids made each other eat worms.

Foster mom had a name, because I wasn't supposed to call her "Mom." I didn't bother to learn this name. I didn't trust her not to dissolve into the next dimension without so much as a note. Not that it'd matter, because she unabashedly didn't care. Maybe somewhere, some luckier kid had landed with a foster mom who loved and respected them, who adopted them and gave them a room and a puppy and a nice little slice of their heart. I wasn't that damn kid. I was half-past rotten, and she couldn't want me, because no one could. Foster mom slapped Nasty Kid on me like a price tag. Well, fuck her. I was too preoccupied with drowning to care. I'd wrap my hands around my neck and search for my gill scars, for places that proved I'd lost something, that I'd been different once, that there'd been a time when I'd been friends with oxygen.

One foster mom was switched out for another. I was periodically asked if I remembered having a clandestine grandpa or something, or if I had the faintest idea who'd fathered me. I still didn't, every time. I didn't even fully grasp that it took two people to make a kid yet. My mother once said that she'd conceived me all on her own, maybe joking, and I'd believed her.

I turned eight. I moved again. Lost teeth, got stitches, had on-again, off-again lice.

Then, the miracle. Deus ex machina. I grew new goddamn gills.

My gills were left on the front porch of my third foster home. No return address. Not even a stamp. It was a parchment-wrapped package, bone white, rectangular, and sturdy. The package was made out to *Ms. Eloise Pike.* If it hadn't been, I doubt foster mom would've let me have it. It was the first piece of mail I received after my mother died, and I didn't know anyone who cared enough to send me packages. Foster mom figured it was an ill-timed birthday present from a social worker, something like that. I'd ripped the package from her hands when she showed it to me. I clutched it to my chest, snarled at her, ran down the street at top speed like a bandit with a bounty. I clambered up a black locust and only unwrapped it when I was sure that no one, not even God, could reach me and take it away.

It'd been tied shut with silk ribbon. It was dark and soft as batwings, and I held it in my teeth as I tore through the paper. There was a note tucked under the first layer of wrapping, and the note was written in the darkest ink I'd ever seen. Dark as the void. Darker than hell. Looping, slanted handwriting, the kind of handwriting that John Hancock would've envied. I could barely read it. I had to squint, sound some of it out loud.

> *Everlasting condolences for your loss. We mourn the tragedy and we remember, we remember, we remember. Heal. Grow. Flourish.*
> —PS

The notecard was illustrated with a tangle of braided

serpents, which ringed the message in glossy scarlet ink. Not quite an ouroboros, because an ouroboros is a single snake, and I counted seven. A wreath of snakes, a crown.

Under the note was a shroud of gossamer wrapping.

Under that wrapping was a book.

The book was heavy. It had gravity. It beckoned like Excalibur or the Holy Grail. It pulled something out of me when I held it in my arms, like it was denser than earthly matter, like it could suck me inside of it and devour me raw. It was bound in oxblood leather. The edges of the pages were dusted with copper. It had a pewter pheasant-claw clasp. The snake pattern appeared again, this time emblazoned on the spine like a scar. It made my fingertips throb, my mouth water, my palms itch.

I opened it, and for the first time in months, I could force myself to breathe.

The title was *VADE MECVM MAGICI, VOL. I.* It was written in thick ink, and it was so shiny that it looked wet, like brushing it might stain my fingertips. There wasn't an author or a date of publication. There wasn't a table of contents. I thumbed through random pages and was consumed.

The first page read like a diary entry, and the page after that detailed a series of botanical illustrations. A lock of hair was embedded in a block of trochaic prose. There were advertisements for children's books with the words blacked out, spiraling geometric sketches, fragments of poetry etched on illustrations of ribs. Two pages didn't have any ink on them, but were entirely written with embroidery, and described the types of objects that can hold curses, and the uses of each phase of the moon. There was a page dedicated to listing feminine names, with a mineral beside the name, as well as a planetary alignment and a time of day. There was a chapter that outlined various theories of the universe, why there is life, why there is death, why these things are all magic, and why magic is everything. The text was broken up with randomly placed illustrations of alchemical symbols, Enochian runes, Roman numerals, and dozens of dead alphabets twisted around ink circles. The captions described the circle and the geometric scribbles within—*this is for healing broken limbs, this is for tearing through the veil, this is for making you love yourself, this is for petitioning the stars.* There was a page that sparkled like fine glitter and listed the benefits of biting the thing you cursed, or kissing the wounds, or suckling poison. There was a page on how to lace a spell into an instrument, and how to entreat cats, crows, and boys with its tune. The chapter on incantation was comprised of red paper and written with white ink, and it repeated the same phrase over and over again: *Cast the word, make it so.* It was written in a dozen different hands and every font imaginable: MAKE IT SO. MAKE IT SO. MAKE IT SO. There was a section on summoning that looked like it belonged in an illuminated manuscript, complete with medieval-style depictions of monstrous beasts. The chunk on sigil making was written upside down, and when the book was held upside down, it was written right-side up.

I read it cover to cover. Then, I read it again.

My *Magici* gave me the bones I was missing. New rules

replaced the withered ones. Time moved forward again. The world made sense. I had guidelines on how to exist without my mother, how to exist in the world at all. Order was restored in my universe. Witchcraft, my life was saved by witchcraft. It was my only mode of survival. It sutured my soul to Earth.

Three days after I received the book, I looked for a spell that might make me feel loved again. I thought, stupidly, that it might make my mother manifest outside my shared bedroom window, that she might reach her long fingers between the curtains and pet my hair, might lure me out onto the roof and whisk me away into the night. The spell looked easy enough. I wrote a stupid little rhyme and drew circles on the sidewalk with green chalk.

Later that morning, the office tracking my case received a flustered call. The call was from one Mr. Julian Pike, who'd only just heard about the death of his older sister, whom he'd lost contact with, and the eight-year-old niece in desperate need of a place to stay. He said that he owned an antique shop with his partner, and he could have everything ready in a week, could fill out whatever forms they needed of him, could make cookies and buy school supplies and, oh God, anything that kid might need.

I moved in with him that Tuesday.

The only thing I brought with me was the book.

✳

I must have been half dead last night, because I'd taken the book from Boris and went directly to bed. No investigation. Nothing. My head hit the pillow and my lights stomped out. I didn't even dream.

Now, in the lucid light of morning, I could behold what Boris had bought me. The looping snakes. The bloody leather. The clasps like hands on a gargoyle. The way it tossed spears in me and flipped on all my switches. I rubbed my thumb over the spine, and it was electric. The snakes pulsed against my skin like they were breathing, crawling under the surface, and my nerves lit up like live wires.

I popped the latch, cracked the book open.

*VADE MECVM MAGICI, VOL. II.*

✳

"Boris. Dad. Where the fuck did you find this, exactly?"

I'd found Boris in the FASHIONS PAST segment of the store, a bordello-red closet lined with half-dressed mannequins. He was in the process of lacing a corset over a Venus de Milo dress form, humming a tune under his breath. The corset boning wound up crooked. The humming abruptly stopped. Boris paused, said something nasty in a language I didn't know, and unlaced the corset. He sighed, started over. He barely cocked his head when I spoke.

"The spell book? At the annual Delacroix House auction," he said, with a cluck of his tongue. He stepped away from the mannequin, tossed his hands behind his head. His hair, as it habitually was, was gelled stiff as a greaser's. "Does this look asymmetrical to you?"

"It's fine," I said. I stepped between Boris and the dress form. "Who was selling it? Was it in a set?" I clamped the *Vade Mecvm* to my rib cage and tried not to sound as thoroughly freaked as I was. It beat against my chest like a second raging heartbeat. My blood rushed quick.

"There was a set on display, but they only let me bid on the one. Pissed me off, you better believe. I wanted to get you the full set. It's like that one you've always had, isn't it? The pretty one? I hope so, otherwise you'll be missing the first volume. They didn't have the first one. Bizarre. There were a lot of volumes in the set, nine or ten, easy, and you'd think they wouldn't display it if it wasn't complete. Anyhow, the binding is so lovely, isn't it? I've never seen anything like it. Maurice—Maurice Delacroix, he owns the House—he said that the books were permanent fixtures in their archives and wouldn't be for sale anytime soon. Which I understand. You know how I feel about those Mapplethorpe prints I found last year—I could never put those in the shop. They're going to live in my bedroom forever, where they'll be safe and I can gaze at them every morning when I wake up."

A giddy, sour something bubbled up inside me.

There were more.

The book in my arms felt suddenly hot, like there was a canary trapped between the pages that desperately needed to crash out the window and fly back to its roost. Like Boris had touched a nerve, and now the book was livid. Livid and lonely and disastrously alive. Like it was me.

"Sideways, did you just wake up? It's nearly three. That's impressive, even for you." He put a hand on my shoulder, gave me a nod. I couldn't tell if he was pleased or concerned, and I was thankful for that. I was in no mood for pity.

"I've been up since noon. Couldn't stop reading this." I ran my fingertips over the cover like it was made of rosary beads. I was in love with the texture. It tickled my palms, made me itch. My heart was overstuffed; it was busting the stitches that held it together. "Thanks. Like. Thank you so fucking much, Dad. I needed this."

"Thought you might," he said.

I kissed his cheek. "Gonna go steal some candles from the display case. Thankyouthankyouthankyou."

He rolled his eyes. "Don't take the big ones."

"Aye-aye."

\*

Volume two lacked foreplay. It skipped to the jugular. I opened it, and I was instantly consumed.

The first page bore a single word, with finely printed instructions just below it. SPECTER: *touch and unveil.* Curious, I traced the lines of the S with my forefinger, then jerked back my hand so fast that my wrist ached. The word SPECTER lit up in violent red. Red like candy. Red like rage. Slowly, like a napkin sucking a spill, it washed back to black. I touched it again. Red as hell. Red as the mimic last night.

I turned the page.

*Hello, reader. You are a witch. That color that swirled over the word matches your soul, and all your magic will be that color. Revere and defend it, for it is the essence of you. Witch souls are rare. We call them specters. They differ from the souls of non-witches in that they possess a higher tolerance for, or even an inclination toward, spell casting and incantation. Magic seeps into reality's cracks and makes it strange, breeds impossibilities in everything. It is antithetical to the great governing apparatus of society as we know it. Specters tend to form in people who don't fit neatly into roles of established power, which opens them to powers less comprehensible. Those who touch this page and see nothing do not have a high enough capacity for magic to constitute witchery. They may be capable of minor magics, enchantments that are stolen or taught to them, but they are not casters.*

*Those who receive the second volume of this text have generally read the first and experimented with the sample incantations provided inside. Reading this means you are capable of magic. If you're going to live as a witch, you've got to know what's coming for you. Witches frighten the masses, and, more pressingly, people who presume themselves to* have unquestionable power over said masses. Witches don't bow to the laws of nature or man. We admit to ourselves what we want, and then create that thing for ourselves, not by some force of industry, but with word and the joint intention of our sisterhood. We don't depend on organized structures. We can simply help each other, and the masses as well, if they so desire. Those that manage the architecture of everything cannot abide witchcraft because of this fact. Our talents are outside of their comprehension, much less their control. Now, while it's possible that some people murdered in European witch-hunts had specter souls, the vast majority of persecuted victims likely did not. Nevertheless, the genealogy of contemporary witchfinders has a specific origin point in the witch-hunts. It is a vital history for new practitioners to understand.

In 1472, a priest by the name of Abner Grier encountered his little sister, Fortune Grier, in the midst of magic revelry. It has been documented that he spied Fortune dancing naked and laughing with flowers in her hair, and knew at once that Fortune was practicing maleficium. She sang over a nursing sow in Greek and Latin, neither of which were languages she should have known. Fortune was illiterate, and had never received any ecclesiastic education, so Abner concluded her knowledge must have been acquired by infernal means. He dragged her by the hair to his chapel, lashed her to his altar, and doused her writhing body with holy water. He then summoned the wealthy men of the village and gathered them around her, instructed them to observe. Over the course of his torture, Fortune surrendered accurate information—the existence of covens, the nature of specters, her methods of casting—and the men, horrified by her confession, vowed to seek out all spectered witches and, for the good of the people, extinguish them. Fortune supposedly taught the witchfinders two spells during her confession: how to make a spectral mimic, and how to extract a witch's specter. They enacted said extraction spell upon her. She died within the hour.

This was the genesis of several witchfinding families, many of which are still active today. While they're predominantly located in England, where Grier's village was, and America, where many of them migrated in hopes of breeding witchless colonies, it is notable that Grier's methods were adopted by French, German, and Spanish witchfinding groups who, via their adjacent colonial projects, spread these *methods across the globe. The success of Grierian witchfinders has largely hinged on their use of stolen magics. In the winter of 1892, a group of witchfinders discovered a sizable coven in New York City. It was a massacre: Not a single witch survived. The deaths were officially listed as the result of smoke inhalation, as the coven's mansion had been burned to the ground. Whatever the witch hunters stole from the Manhattan coven, it made them massively successful. We stopped being able to scry for them. They became effectively invisible. These methods enable them to find witches before we do and destroy them before they even know who they are, what they're capable of.*

I slammed the book shut. The timing of this was uncanny. Why would this book fall into my hands now, after I'd barely escaped the Chantry clan? Why was this aligning so closely to my life? It was eerie and I was nauseous. The word *Chantry* flipped itself around in my skull so many times it stopped sounding like a word. The book was like a looking glass, and all the ugly things in my head spilled across the page and were given definition. The awful and the lovely.

*Witch souls are rare.*

I was something rare.

I took a sharp breath, crossed my legs, and opened the book again.

# TEN

# GATHERING TONGUES WITH WHICH TO SPEAK

Magic's in the invocation, yeah? Well, really cool candles fucking help. It's touched on in both volume one and volume two, and there's a reason why every cheesy Medieval grimoire you see in movies requires fifty-something props. Feeling witchy is a large part of successfully being witchy, and nothing makes you feel powerful like surrounding yourself with gigantic dripping candles. Maybe it was some weird anti-Freudian destruction of phallic symbols thing. Didn't matter. Lucky for me, we at Rothschild & Pike sold them by the dozen. Thank God for Dad and Dad.

Julian had found a strange, Ren-faire-type pair of sixty-somethings who worked as beekeepers and candlemakers, and their candles looked like set pieces from *Hocus Pocus* or *Practical Magic*. Long, fat, oozing candles. Witchy candles. Candles that'd make you feel gother than Wednesday Addams at a Bauhaus concert. I took a few red ones and stuffed them into my pockets.

If I was gonna attempt a stay-off-my-fucking-back spell,

I'd need to feel maximum amounts of goth.

Delacroix House. What the fuck was Delacroix House? Like, was it something that I could Google? Boris and Julian find themselves in some weird circles, and it was possible that this place only existed to the devastatingly weird. I mean, my dads once went to an auction where the only things on the block were "experimental taxidermy art." Most of that auction was apparently too esoteric even for Boris, but they did settle on a Rat King, which now proudly sits atop a refrigerator circa 1952. (The fridge doesn't work, so Boris gutted it and filled it with a stack of retro skin mags that I maybe borrow sometimes.) Point is, it was possible that I wouldn't be able to locate the Delacroix House without interrogating Boris and Julian, which really wasn't what I wanted to do. If I asked about it too much, they might offer to take me. I needed to go, but it wasn't the sort of thing I wanted to do with my parents. Magic was my independence. Going with my dads would feel like some sort of submission, like, *Yeah, mysterious* Vade Mecvm *people, I had to bum a ride off my dad. That's totally cool.* Yeah, no. Unless I couldn't find another way, I'd be doing this myself, thanks.

Maybe I could scry for it. Scrying, that was something new. It hadn't been in the first volume, and while it was mentioned in the other spell books I'd gotten my grimy hands on, the pragmatics of it were never discussed. Mostly, scrying was described as staring at a reflective surface until your question was answered, which is every bit as effective as it sounds. Volume two had actual instructions. Now that I knew it was legitimate enough for a slot in the *VMM*, I had a dire need to try it.

If I had enough spell books, nobody could touch me. Nobody.

Would Boris be pissed if I took a big candle after all? They were so damn badass. I think it was technically stealing, what I did. Taking merchandise and using it without paying *is* stealing, after all. But it's not like my dads didn't know about it, and it's not like they ever did anything to stop me. I only ever took stuff that was easily replaced or not terribly valuable, and if I took too much, I'd work the cash register to make up the difference. But I mean, this was just one candle. He might not even notice. I'd buy him Starbucks later to make up for it.

"Boo."

*Jesus!* My heart slammed against my throat, and I whirled around, fists ready.

Standing behind me was Daisy Brink.

Yates was living morphine. Her arms were around my rib cage and suddenly I wasn't pissed at Daisy for scaring me anymore. I wasn't anything. I was just in awe of her and how soft her cheek was against mine. It sounds stupid, but I hadn't realized how much I could seriously use a hug. I gave her a squeeze and tried to focus.

"We thought you were dead!" Her hair floated free, dark and thick as storm clouds, and it tickled my ear and the side of my neck. "You can't just call us and say that you've been kidnapped and then hang up! Sideways! There was all that blood on the floor. And all the glass? And the deer were gone? And then when you didn't show up to school today, I thought you legit might have been axe murdered. I made Daisy skip cheer so that we could all make sure you were alive. I know that I called the shop a billion times today—well more like twice—and that Mr. Rothschild said you were fine both times, but still! I was so worried!"

Jing, sporting heart-shaped glasses and a black romper, crossed her arms. "Could've called one of us again from your shop phone, you know," she said, eyeing the candles that I was gathering up. There was something metallic about her tone that I couldn't place. "I was having a fucking panic attack intermittently all day. Just freaking the fuck out. All. Day. Nice candles. Going for girth, I see. Good girl."

My hands rolled themselves into fists against Yates' back. "Sorry. I should've called or something. Messaged you. I've just . . . my head's been in a weird place since I got home." I'm not too good at apologizing. That's one of those nice-kid things that was lost on me.

Daisy had been skimming a *Playboy* that she'd pulled off a shelf, but she looked up long enough to snort. Her eyes flashed like a cat's on film. "You can tell us now, can't you?"

I let go of Yates, which felt like ripping off a Band-Aid, but I fought to keep the hurt off my face. There was a voice in my head that didn't want to tell them, that irrationally wanted to pretend that it had happened differently, that it wasn't a huge deal and that I hadn't been completely defenseless, that I hadn't lost control and nearly died. Witches are powerful because they help each other, the book had said. This wasn't the time for my weird internalized faux-macho scaredy-cat bullshit. I put the candle in my pocket and cleared my throat. "My room. Not a shop kind of conversation. Follow me."

*

Jing sat at the foot of my bed. She was mask faced and motionless. There was something direly wrong with her, with how tightly wound she was. She felt volatile, like any sudden movement would pull the pin out of her grenade and she'd bust open and kill us all.

I was done talking. Near tears, but they hadn't spilled out, thank my lucky stars and whatever else. Yates had been appropriately appalled, and she'd spent most of my story curled up with her head on my lap, patting my thigh, wincing when I was too detailed. She took the lulls in conversation to put all their numbers on my phone, like it would retroactively safeguard me against any of this, even though we both knew that it wouldn't. When I talked about Levi, she tensed up against me, and my hands found her shoulders and stayed there. Her empathy was like a low dose of opium—enough to take off the edge and make the world fuzzy, but not enough to kill the pain. Daisy talked the whole time, cussing and spitting, mean as a stray cat. *Dirty pigs. We should burn their house down. I want his head mounted on my wall. I've been needing a new dartboard.* She knotted her fists in my pillow so tightly that the pillow threatened to bust, and when that stopped being enough, she took to beating it, with better form than I would've given her credit for. Probably says more about me than her.

Jing didn't say a word, until she did. "Sideways," she said. She pulled her sunglasses off her forehead, shook a hand through her hair, and slid the shades back on. "Let me see this spell book."

My gut wrenched.

"Why," I spat out, my voice flat as I could muster. I don't show people my *VMM*, and that's a dead rule. It was horrifyingly intimate. My *VMM* was a sizable slice of who I was, and it was a lot to fucking ask, wanting to see inside it. We were practically strangers.

But there was something in the look on Jing's face. There was a sharpness, a nastiness that I admired. Something relatable. She looked feral, just like me. Well, not *just* like me. I'm an ugly, awful, nasty-looking hatchet-faced bruiser, and Jing could be Helen of Troy. But even so, her face felt like a mirror, and I saw myself more clearly than I ever had with glass. Her expression was brittle, jagged, practically begging to snap in half and cut someone.

Despite myself, my stomach in knots, I pushed the book in her direction.

Jing pulled volume two toward her and ran her fingertips over the cover. It felt it sympathetically like she'd brushed my inner arm.

"Open it," Daisy commanded. There was something wildly inappropriate about her tone. My cheeks felt hot. No one noticed, or maybe just Yates, who didn't mention it.

Jing opened to the first page. I watched her eyes trace the S-P-E-C-T-E-R and the phrase just below it. She poised her fingers in the air, hovered them just above the printed word.

Fuck. Abort. What if it doesn't work? What if I'm the only magic one? If it was only my magic at the party, and they were just conductors? The mimic was red, after all. Red like me. Would they stop being friends with me if I was a witch and they were specterless? Hell, if Jing was specterless and the letters stayed black, would she label my magic a fraud? Would the party retroactively seem like a sham? Would it discredit all that we'd done? Or, even worse, would they stop being friends with me if they stopped needing me as their magic toy? If they could do it themselves, would I be obsolete? I needed them to need me. If they didn't, what came next?

She touched the letters, and they stained plum.

Daisy squealed. She clapped her hands in approval.

Yates lifted her head off my lap.

Jing had a specter. Witch to the bone.

"I want to try," Daisy insisted. She made eyes at the book, reached for it with grabby hands. I wasn't so cool with her grabby hands. But I didn't say anything, because what if I fucked up and she stopped liking me? I'm supposed to be missile-proof. Why was I so insecure about everything suddenly? Since when do I care if people like me?

*Since you remembered how nice it is to have friends, Sideways, sweetie.*

Daisy touched the word, and the plum melted into gunmetal gray. It was an inevitable gray, gray like death or the promise of rain. I had to blink a few times to make sure it wasn't the default black.

Yates looked up at me and gracefully extended her hand to the book. Her fingertips tapped the S, and Daisy's gray blurred into opaline blue. It was almost too pale to make out against the page, and it sparkled in the red light. Cinderella blue. It was a stupid-pretty color, if spectacularly un-punk.

They all had specters. All of them.

My heart seized up in my chest.

"What the fuck," said Daisy. Her mouth hung slightly agape. "Yates' specter is prettier than mine."

Yates shrugged and flashed her the sweetest smile I'd ever seen.

"So we'd be targets for them, then. All four of us." Jing ran her tongue over her teeth. "The Chantry boys might come after any of us, or you again, at any time. Right?"

Daisy and Yates looked at each other. Clearly, this wasn't the teasing specter-prettiness-ranking comment they'd been mentally anticipating.

"Yeah." I sucked my teeth. "I guess they might."

"Then we should make a spell against stalking. Something to keep them off our backs." Jing crossed her arms over her chest. "I can't deal with these bastards right now. Until we're showing up to torch their house, I don't want to see, hear, smell, taste, or touch them. And I sure as hell don't want them near us. There's got to be a spell in here for that, right?"

My cheeks flamed and I wasn't sure why. Throat prickly, sticky-feeling down the sides. "There's not." There were lots of little spells, but nothing exactly like that, and it felt a bit involved for us to just make up. The stakes were high. What if a sigil of my design was flimsy and crumbled on us? My Chett hex hadn't done its fucking job, after all.

Maybe if I'd been able to name him. Jab a finger at Levi's stupid face and proclaim him Chett, remind the spell where to go.

But I couldn't speak last night, now could I?

Jing didn't reply. She was on her phone instead, eyes downcast, the glow from the screen bleaching her blond hair blonder. For a second, I was astounded—this wasn't exactly the time—but then something shifted in her expression, and she snapped to attention. She gave us a *Suck it* smile. "Delacroix House. You said your dads found your spell book at the Delacroix House and that they had more. Well, that place is an hour south of here. The pretentious official website says that it's an art gallery that puts on a burlesque-looking dinner theater at night. They're open every night until two a.m."

My insides clenched up and wrenched themselves three degrees to the right. My body thrummed all over. Radiated heat from my core outward. "The third volume might have spells in it we could use." Another spell book. The thought made me shaky, like I'd downed too many energy drinks. The thought thrummed through me.

"Oh, Sideways, we should go!" Yates perked up, black eyes big and sparkling. She pulled her hand back into her lap, and the S-P-E-C-T-E-R resumed its neutral ink color. She leaned back so that her spine nestled against my sternum, and my skin prickled where it touched hers. God, she must be made of silk. Lila Yates, the velveteen witch, who I desperately wanted to belong to, who I was ever so slightly afraid of. She wanted to be my friend. She looked at me like she knew me. She didn't, but, God, I wanted her to. And here she was, asking me to do the thing I wanted to do most, beaming at me like we'd been holding hands since kindergarten.

I felt sick in the head. Why did this feel wrong? It was like I'd swallowed too much candy, and now my body was floating away. I wanted this. I'd always fucking wanted this. Here I was, ringed by friends who understood the witch thing, who were part of it, sitting in my bedroom and listening to me and telling me they want what I want. I was so used to an abundance of nothing. All this was out of my depth. There's gotta be side effects. Fucking—there's always fine print and trick conditions, and saying otherwise was a lie, because that was how life worked. Magic and kidnapping and ancient violence, that much I could fathom. This? People wanting to do things with me? Wanting me around, wanting my opinion, wanting my body beside their bodies? Giving a fuck? I didn't understand. It didn't add up. This wasn't how my story was shaped. I'll never stop being that rotten, mean little vile-tongued brat. I worked hard for my social disclaimer. *Don't bother—this one bites.*

They were bothering.

What had Yates said about all of us and ambiguity?

Jing flipped her hair over her shoulder. "I've got a full tank. I'm going to make a reservation, and *you* are going to put on a bra. Yates, come with me for a second."

Yates crawled off me and bounced to her feet. In the back of my head, I considered scooting to the edge of the bed and pulling her so close to me that my arms snapped in the process. I didn't do that, of course. I hugged my arms across my stomach and tried to scowl, keep myself impassable.

Jing and Yates disappeared through a crack in my bedroom door, and it closed behind them with an audible click. I watched them vanish with my mouth half-open. Why did she need Yates? Why was I so paranoid about where Yates was going? I didn't have a crush on her, I was certain about that. I wasn't jealous. I more just . . . wanted to be where she was. That was a thing, right?

Daisy sidled beside me. Her mouth was curved up at the corners, but it didn't read like a smile. It was malicious and dimpled; promising something unspecified but unquestionably mean. No doubt, she was a crow in a past life. An entire flock of crows. I imagined her as a mob of glossy black birds, clacking and cackling, ripping the meat off a body. She could've been one of those girls in that movie, a *Ghastly* girl. Maybe we all were.

She flickered her tongue between her teeth. "Tell me," she said. "The Chantry brothers. Where did they live?"

"I don't remember," I replied. I hated that it was true, but it was. A few turns off Main, and then off into one of the countless black holes of backwoods mansions. Other than that? Nothing. It could take forever to find the specific private drive, because that sort of thing cropped up a lot around here. This was the right type of suburban hell to breed Chantry-type wealth. There were a plethora of people who bought enough land that they could submerge themselves in pockets of isolation, away from the lowly faces of people less privileged than themselves. "The woods out of town a little."

Daisy cupped her mouth with a hand, lips pursed, hushed like she was spreading rumors in the back of math class. "I wanna find out where they live," she whispered. "I want to go to their house at night and toss firecrackers in their windows. Maybe something better. They need to suffer for what they did to you, you know that? For what they did to you and Yates. I'm not sure if I like you yet, Sideways, but you're with me now. I hate this sort of thing. People don't punish boys who hurt girls, because people don't care about girls. So, when I find 'em—and I will—I'm going to make them drink nail-polish remover. Okay?"

"Okay."

She put her hand back in her lap. "You know what? We didn't know what to think, you calling like that. I thought you were pulling a stunt. A stupid, weird stunt that wasn't funny or cute or even clever. You know, the kid who leaves the sleepover first is usually my least favorite kid? They care too much about the wrong stuff. I was kinda pissed. But I knew pretty quick that that wasn't it, because I cut my feet on that broken glass when we went upstairs looking for you. You really fucked up the kitchen, you know that? Blood everywhere. The floor was all slick and sticky. I didn't want to freak out Yates, but after she went home, Jing and I followed the blood spots down to the swimming pool. Freaky, right? The blood stopped by the poolside, and the deer were missing. Raised a lot of questions. Made us believe you hadn't been lying. Made *me* believe, anyway.

"Jing considered calling 911, but what would we even say? I figured it must not be as bad as we imagined, and we'd shake you down at school. But you never showed. We thought the worst, you know. None of us had your number, not that it'd have mattered, since you left your phone. We're not exactly friends online, either, so I had no idea who to contact to check on you. I asked god-awful Ashleigh fucking Smith about you, and she had no idea where you were. I asked . . ." She paused, squinted. "His new name is Mickey-Dick, right?"

"Mickey Richardson. Mickey-Dick, yeah." I sucked in my cheeks. Poor Mickey-Dick. He got everybody to bleach his deadname and all adjacent nicknames from their memories, only to instantly be presented with a new stupid nickname. He didn't seem to mind much, though. He signs *Mickey-Dick* on pop quizzes, and made a whole thing of it when we read Melville in class.

"Yeah, well, he's a fucking weeb and a half-rate plug and I'd normally never talk to somebody like that, but I did for you. He didn't know, either. So at that point I thought you were probably chopped up in someone's freezer or something. Then

Yates remembered that your folks owned this place, so we came as soon as school let out.

"When I saw you, I kinda wanted to wring your neck. Like, I was genuinely concerned, and I don't get like that. Particularly not for people who aren't mine. But then you told us everything, and I think I know why I cared. We're friends now. Blood is truly thicker than water, is it not? We spilled some blood between us with that glass. If Yates is your sister, I'm your sister, too. And now I have to fucking kill those assholes. Boys don't touch my girls, I swear to *God*. I can be a fucking monster when I wanna be. I'm not good at a whole lot, but I'm *spectacular* at terrorizing people until they've literally lost it. I can ruin people like you wouldn't believe. And I wanna wreck their sorry lives."

I took a beat to let that simmer.

"You know what, Daisy Brink?" I looked at her crooked, spoke with too much gravel in my voice. In an itchy, charred kind of way, this was the most honest I'd felt in a while. It was an honesty that chafed, that irritated my mouth like I was allergic to it, but it was inescapable. Here it was, plain and ugly. "You and me, we're spooky similar, where that is concerned."

She snorted, batted her lashes at me. Objectively speaking, she was Mad Hot, but that wasn't anything new. I should be used to it by now. I wasn't. She and Jing and Yates were all feliform angels. They laughed and sneered and drank pink lemonade. They were vain, self-centered, overconfident. They ran riot and wrecked the world. Who was I, comparing myself to one of them? Daisy could murder someone with a glance. Holy hell, I wanted that. I wanted to be gorgeous and reckless and legendary, or at least somebody people liked. I wanted the privilege of being mistaken for someone like her. I wanted to be her.

No, I didn't.

I wanted to be the leather in her jacket.

We could be despicable together.

Despite the snort, she didn't shoot down my comparison. Did it mean that she maybe agreed? That we were maybe alike?

Daisy slid off the bed, knelt for a moment, and stood back up with a bra and a pair of tattered jeans in her hands. She eyed me, pursed her lips, and shoved the articles of clothing in my general direction. "We're going out to eat. Look less finals week."

"Anything to get us out of here," I said, and I snickered as I fumbled with my bra.

*

I convinced myself to smudge on some eyeliner before we left. It wasn't neat eyeliner, but it was enough to make me look like I might have sauntered in the direction of trying. It was passable by Daisy standards, which were lower than I would've thought. I even went so far as to fish something clean smelling off the floor that wasn't obviously pajamas and put it on before we headed out.

We moved in a pack down the stairs. I walked slightly ahead. Both of my volumes of the *VMM* were stashed in a shoulder bag, and together they were ungodly sorts of heavy. There was something off about taking the lead. Maybe it was just that I wasn't used to being in a group, but I didn't feel justified in walking in front of them instead of beside or behind them. I tried to smush the thoughts before they took too much shape. *Chill out, Sideways. This is what you've wanted since you were, what, twelve? Head in the fucking game.*

When I didn't think about it too hard, this felt spectacularly cool. It was blood stirring and it prickled sweat on the back of my neck. Real friends. Friends who were going to do magic with me, who understood how important it was. Friends I was safe with. Wow.

The shop was intentionally labyrinthine. You could spend hours wandering around and finding things, which of course would make you want more things, or at least present more options. It was a decent marketing plan. I, however, knew the most direct path to the door, and I made a decent effort to steer the flock in that direction.

But Yates saw something pretty, and then we turned left into No Man's Land.

"This is the sweetest little bracelet I've ever seen in my life," she said, her hands fanned over her heart. She'd been caught by one of the jewelry displays; a palmistry hand with beaded bands looped over every finger. Julian had made those bracelets out of my grandparents' broken rosaries. We'd inherited a lot of them when they died. The bracelet that Yates was particularly hypnotized by was made up of freshwater pearls and milky silver that bore an eerie resemblance to a string of baby teeth. "God. Now I need it."

My eyes rolled up in my skull.

They understood that buying stuff involved talking to my dads, which entailed explaining where we were going, yeah? Yeah? No, apparently not. I heaved a sigh, scratched the back of my neck, and trudged in the direction of the checkout counter. "This way, losers."

It was fucking weird, *me* calling *them* losers.

It was left uncontested.

Fuck.

It was Julian behind the counter. He was sitting with his legs crossed, and he was wearing a sweater with elbow patches. His curls were pinned out of his eyes with a copper clip. He sat with Anne Rice in one hand and an Earl Grey in the other, and Schnitzel (a skinny tomcat who lived in the shop) was perched on his shoulder like a vibrating stole. He didn't see us coming, because he was preoccupied with rereading *The Vampire Lestat* for the umpteenth time.

Why'd it have to be Julian? He was habitually concerned for my well-being, which was both very sweet and massively inconvenient. In some ways, I understood. I'd been a glutton for disaster when he first adopted me. If something had the potential to hurt me, I'd throw myself at it as quick as I humanly could. How many fights had he pulled me out of? How many seriously stupid dares had he stopped me from doing? How many times has he forgiven me for disobeying simple rules? I might be dead, or at least in several pieces, if it wasn't for his antics. He cared about me and could potentially have serious issues with me fucking off with girls he hadn't met, particularly if he made the connection that these were the girls I'd been staying with before I came home mangled last night. Or this morning, I guess, technically.

Yates waltzed over to the counter and presented her prospective bracelet. "Hi. Can I buy this?"

Julian startled, jumping at the sound of her voice. He adjusted his glasses with his thumb and forefinger, put down his book, and peered down at the bracelet in her hands. "Oh, you like that one? I'm quite happy with it. I thought they were just the prettiest pearls—I'm glad they're finding a home." He leaned over the counter and blinked a few times, his mouth screwing up at the corner. "Hm. Those bracelets are fifteen dollars. Sound about right?"

Typical Julian, asking his customer if the price sounded reasonable. Also, even more typical for Julian, he hadn't noticed the rest of the group yet, me included. He just looked so *happy*, seeing Yates with his bracelet. Dimples lit up his cheeks like twin suns.

"Sounds right," said Yates, practically bouncing on her toes. "Also. Are you hiring people right now? I could bring in my résumé. I'd really love working here." She glimmered, and I wasn't even sure if she was faking it. She might genuinely be this thrilled about working for my dads. Huh.

"Oh." He paused, tilted his head to the side. And then his

eyes popped wide, and he swiveled his head around to see all four of us. His eyes stopped on me. There was a beat of silence as he loaded this new information, and then he folded his hands together and nodded at me. "Lamby, is this a friend of yours?"

Something inside me shriveled and died.

Lamby.

"Yeah," I ground out, and I locked my arms across my chest. My leather jacket and fingerless gloves suddenly felt drastically less cool. Fucking Christ, I was supposed to be Sideways the spooky lesbian weirdo. I had a fucking reputation to maintain, and it would not withstand a nickname like Lamby. *Lamby.* Goddamn it.

"Well, I was actually looking for someone, as a matter of fact." Julian crinkled around the eyes, which meant I couldn't be mad at him, which sort of pissed me off. "And if you're my employee, then the bracelet will be ten dollars. That'll be ten please."

"Really?" Yates clapped her hands, pulled a bill from her clutch, and smoothed it across the countertop. "Thanks, Julian. When should I come for training?"

"Oh, I don't know. Lamb, could you train her next week?" He blinked, and I felt his eyes trace my obvious going-somewhere non-pajamas attire. "Is there an event or something?"

"We're going to the Delacroix House for dinner." I chewed on the inside of my cheeks and resisted the urge to kick something. I was a decent liar, but not to Julian. If he found out that I'd lied to him he'd be gut-wrenchingly disappointed, and anyone who hurts Julian is the worst human ever to mar the face of the Earth.

I wouldn't have had this problem if *someone* hadn't freaked out and bought something.

Whatever.

Julian parted his lips, but he didn't make a sound. His eyes misted over for a moment. They did that when he was thinking through something. That was his auction face. Schnitzel arched his back, let out a yowl, and hurled himself off Julian's shoulders in a bullet-colored blur. It spooked Julian, and he came back to Earth. Still wordless, he pulled his wallet out of some unseen pocket, and plucked two crumpled twenties from its depths. "They can be quite pricey," he said. He pushed the double twenties in my direction. "Please, for me, don't drink."

Daisy snickered, and I briefly considered skinning her alive.

"Yeah," I said. I pocketed the twenties and gave him a curt nod.

"Have fun, okay?" He gave me a tight smile. I stared at my Doc Martens and tried not to feel how nervous he was. Julian's moods were infectious, and I couldn't afford to be nervous.

"We'll try," Jing chimed. She looped her arm around my shoulder and steered me toward the door.

# ELEVEN

# THE HOUSE OF THE SETTING SUN

As became increasingly apparent on the drive to Delacroix House, sitting in cars makes me really fucking nervous now. I didn't mention it because we didn't need that shit, not when we were on the precipice of something amazing and important.

My hands shook in my lap, and I forced myself to read street signs to calm down. It kept me from scanning the topmost edge of the windshield for deer feet, anyway. That was something.

When we arrived, I felt a palpable wave of relief.

God.

The Delacroix House was a Queen Anne beast. It was infinite stories tall with jutting turrets and frosted gables, and every edge was dripping with filigree lacework. It looked, oddly enough, like a bleached-out Valentine's Day card; all serrated edges and anemic gingerbread embellishments. Candles in every window. It was bloodless light pink and hypnotically pretty, and as we drove up to the lot, I felt something twist inside me. The house was like its own world, complete with impossible gravity and a crisp, mysterious air. I ached to belong to it. I never wanted to leave. It gave me the strangest déjà vu. Something coiled in my stomach and I suddenly forgot all the things I'd wanted to say.

This was the anxiety right before the roller coaster drops.

The lot was half full, and nearly every parked car was glossy black. Jing's cherry convertible was an inappropriate pop of color; a spot of blood on clean black scales. Vermilion leaves plastered themselves across windshields, and powdered sugar gravel shivered under the wheels. We pulled to a stop between two luxury cars, each darker than the next, and Jing turned off the engine.

We filed out of the car in sync. I tried not to make a big deal about how happy I was to be on solid ground.

The breeze picked up, tossed fistfuls of leaves in our direction. It caught our hair and tossed it around our shoulders. Yates' skirt fluttered around her thighs. My jacket whipped around my torso, and I clamped my arms to my ribs to keep it in place. The chill cut through fabric and skin alike. It smelled ever so slightly of copper and rain.

Unreasonably large jack-o'-lanterns stood sentinel around the borders of the house. Each pumpkin was the size of a sow. Candles inside their mouths made their whittled teeth flicker orange, and their eyes followed us as we made our way up the entry staircase, a trick of the light. Daisy moved to kick one and was stopped by Jing, who grabbed a fistful of her shirt and yanked her onward.

The doorknob was ice in my hand. For a second, I was

afraid that I wouldn't be able to open it, but I pressed my shoulder to the frame, and it clicked.

Inside, the house was swollen with music, live music, the sort that I assumed had died decades ago. A piano jaunted over minor keys and devil's fifths. There were brass horns and rolling drums, and above the instrumental chaos was a languid soprano spinning jazz. I couldn't quite make out what she was saying, but I heard the word *witchcraft* more than once.

We stood on a Persian rug underneath an imposing crystal chandelier, the likeness of which I'd only ever seen in *The Phantom of the Opera*. A neon sign on the wall read DELACROIX HOUSE in florid violet, tinging the air with ultraviolet light. The jazz was coming from our left, behind a set of double doors. Dead ahead was another staircase, and to the right was a triplicate of skinny doors and a hallway that wound out of sight.

A person in red lipstick approached us. A choker just above their collarbone read THEY/THEM in silvery pearls. They gleamed like a movie star, not looking even vaguely like a server—slim hipped, long limbed, with a velvet dress that swayed around their strappy ankles as they approached. They wore glitter on their eyelids. They clasped their hands and smiled. "Welcome to Delacroix House! Have you made a reservation?"

"It's under Jing Gao," said Yates.

"Of course. We've been expecting you," they replied. They took a stride in the direction of the jazz room, probably expecting us to follow. "Are you here just for dinner, or have you arranged for a gallery tour as well?"

"I need to see the archives," I said too sharply, cutting them off. I didn't mean to be snappish, but I couldn't help myself. I needed to see the rest of the volumes and I needed to see them immediately. I needed it like a blood transfusion. I crossed my arms and stared at the floor.

The server shifted their gaze so that their eyes, dark and unimpressed, rested squarely on my face. The corner of their mouth quirked upward. "The archives aren't on display for general admission, I'm afraid. We can show you the art galleries, however. There's quite a lot to see."

Something ugly unfurled in my gut. "It's important," I said between my teeth. "Vitally important." It took considerable mental effort not to cuss them out and kick a hole in the nearest wall.

The server said "ah" and their penciled brows shot up into their hairline. "Well, I can put in a word with my manager. See if something can be arranged. In the meantime, let's sit you lot down, shall we?"

"Sounds marvelous," said Jing. She strode after them, and Yates and Daisy fell in line. The three of them walked in automatic synchronization, heels stabbing the Persian carpet, then tapping against the checkerboard tiles beyond, but my boots felt glued to the floor. I wasn't ready to concede and go eat without confirmation that we'd get to see the books. *Word with my manager* sounded fake. Yates glanced over her shoulder at me, gave me a look, and then snapped her head back.

I set my jaw. *Fucking fine.* I trudged across the floor
behind them.

✳

We sat on wingback chairs around a little marble table, as
lofty and whimsical as the court of the Queen of Hearts, and
beside me, Daisy Brink was going ballistic.

"I feel like Marie Antoinette," she hissed. Her eyes were
enormous. Her teeth looked like shards of a porcelain plate.
She bounced in her leather chair, swung one of her legs on its
studded side, tossed her arms behind her head. Friendship
bracelets clattered from her wrists to her elbows. She had just
ordered herself cheesecake for dinner, which was served with
three scoops of homemade ice cream and hand-picked
raspberries from the Delacroix garden sprinkled over the top.
It sounded ridiculously delicious. It was also sixteen dollars
for a slice of cheesecake. "Coming here was a good idea. We
should come more often, no matter if the witchery shit works
out. Do you think they card?"

"Wait until after Sideways has her answer to find out,"
said Yates, tearing off a piece of bread. Delacroix House, like
any respectable overpriced restaurant, gave us baguettes on a
silver platter before we'd even ordered. The baguettes were
toasted golden and brushed with olive oil and minced herbs,
and the slices felt unduly elegant in my red-knuckled hands. I
should've used some forethought, put on something fancier.
Did I have anything fancier? I'd worn a blazer and slacks to

the wedding of one of Boris' friends, and surely those were somewhere. Under the clothes mound, probably. Jing and Yates and Daisy, while a tad more scantily dressed than most of the patrons, at least looked like they were used to this sort of treatment. Or, scratch that, Jing and Yates looked fine. An older woman in pearls was giving Daisy the evil eye from the next table over.

The server who'd greeted us hadn't come back with their manager. Their absence was crawling under my skin. It'd been five minutes, nearly six. I kept checking. I'd checked so many times that Jing had threatened to take my phone away. Now, with my phone on time-out in my pocket, feeling anxious and vaguely bitter, I sunk deeper into my armchair and crossed my arms across my chest.

These people were milking the Supernatural Darkness thing for all it was worth. There were game heads on the walls, but instead of furs and foggy eyes, just the skeletal head and shoulders of each animal were displayed. Flowers, black ribbons, and Spanish moss dangled from hollow jaws and looping horns. Above our table was a bluish portrait labeled ROMAINE BROOKS, and a Dutch-looking still life was mounted above the table beside us. Wasn't quite a standard still life, though. There was a pack of cigarettes tucked in the side of the vase, and a milky unrolled condom. Farther down the room, there were works I recognized and works I didn't, with labels that read Francis Bacon, Michelangelo Merisi da Caravaggio, Mickalene Thomas, Laura Knight, Andy Warhol, Beauford Delaney, Frida Kahlo, Aubrey Beardsley. Looked like originals, too. Julian could spot that sort of thing from fifty yards. I wasn't anywhere near as good, but still. A part of my heart that wasn't fixated on getting into the archives was acutely aware of what kind of place I was in. No wonder Julian and Boris had been here. There was a Sir Lady Java poster that I would bet Benjamins they'd bought off my dads. None of the art matched, per se, but it shared a kind of off-kilter decadence. Bloody purples, erotic reds, cream and slate and pitch. It felt deliberately burlesque-ish, insistently witchy and cluttered. It kind of reminded me of my bedroom, if bigger and plusher and significantly higher quality.

I could see this sort of place housing the *VMMs*. It felt right that they exist in an *Addams Family*–esque personal library, displayed among the art and pricey cheesecake. Anything less than this would be criminal. But the proximity to the books was more than I could bear. Being in the same building as the rest of them made me itch, and if that damn server didn't come back with news soon, I might go berserk and kill something. Probably Daisy. She was sitting the closest.

"So, Sideways. What happens if they bring out your food and it's like, Austin Grass, sliced thin over rice pilaf?" Jing took one of her long nails and tapped it on my knee.

"Ugh. If it is, don't eat it. He'd probably be all rancid and bland." Yates scoffed, took a fourth piece of bread. "Also, if it is Austin, it's your own fault for ordering the special without asking what it is."

"Fault? You make it sound like a bad thing. God, I'd be

damn excited if it was Austin," said Daisy. She flicked the tip of her tongue between her teeth. "Butchering that boy would be the best thing that ever happened to him. It's what pigs deserve. I'd steal a bite or two, just for the satisfaction."

"You sound like Hannibal Lecter," I said. I meant it approvingly. I decided not to mention that they'd seemed to be on jokey/antagonistic but still non-combative speaking terms until literally two days ago. Felt like not mentioning it was becoming a habit of mine.

Despite having eaten nothing but bread all day, my appetite was shot. If the portions here were big, I would be screwed, and then I'd feel guilty for wasting Julian's money. I wasn't even sure if I could finish my slice of baguette.

Still a little nauseous from the car ride, too.

The pianist who'd been playing with the band stood up, and the room rolled into applause. Daisy was clapping unnecessarily enthusiastically, which might have been mocking, or her just being Too Much. She stopped abruptly, mewled in pain, and flicked a piece of crust at Jing, who was sitting pretty, like she totally hadn't meant to stomp on Daisy's foot.

Yates clapped like a normal human being.

Then, all at once, the world unhinged and spiraled into chaos. My heart crashed into my rib cage and I rocked forward, knocked by its momentum.

Up on stage was Madeline Kline. It had to be her. Her hair was slicked over her skull, twisted tight against the back of her neck just above the tip of her brocade collar. Her pocket square was the same violet as the unbuttoned button-up shirt she wore under the blazer, paired with pressed slacks with inappropriately scuffed-up shoes below. Her heavy eyes were rimmed with pink, and she sang with a crooked smile, weary poise, a slow, dripping sigh. She ran her fingertips up the microphone stand and gave the crowd a nod.

My lungs knotted up.

The band resumed playing.

Madeline opened her mouth and sang. Her voice was harsh at the edges, but buttery and sweet as burnt sugar, and the melody was infectious. I knew this song; I knew all the words. It was one of those jazz pieces that was covered a billion times, made soft and ritualistic by the words of countless starlets and horn players. It must have been in a movie somewhere or played overhead in a boudoir boutique. I found myself mouthing the words.

This was too perfect. Madeline, who'd cast with me, was here, here in this magic place, looking like a dream creature under the blue stage lights. My arms turned to gooseflesh.

"Sideways." Daisy shoved a finger in my ribs.

"What?" I reflexively scowled, hugged my arms closer to my chest. I peeled my eyes away from the stage long enough to glare at Daisy, who'd resumed a normal sitting position and was watching me with a grin.

"You've gotta talk to her," Daisy whispered, eyes glinting. "Seriously. You've gotta."

"It's true. You must. You don't have a goddamned choice." Jing was watching the stage, eyes fixed on the crooning

Madeline. Maybe she was thinking what I was thinking. We were on the same side of the proverbial spectrum, after all, but if Jing decided she wanted to court Madeline as well, I'd be finished before anything started. Jing lifted a skinny slice of bread to her lips and tore off a chunk of crust with her canines. "I'd put money down that she knows something about what happened at the party. That spell you two did, at least. I want details. Besides. I want you to get lucky on my behalf."

"Jesus," I said. "Doubtful." Yeah, no, straight-up sleeping with Madeline wasn't the goal here. Hookups weren't in my wheelhouse. I barely qualified out of virgin category, and even then, my exemption was only on technicality. Was virginity a thing for girls who like girls? There was that tryst I'd had at improv camp with Mickey-Dick's ex-girlfriend, Tina, but did that mean I wasn't a virgin, even if the same actions wouldn't register as sex at all on a straight girl? Sleeping with Madeline seemed like an unrealistic, if ridiculously pleasant, scenario. I was significantly more interested in, I don't know, making her a playlist and a personalized cache of dreadful memes. Maybe taking her to the movies. We could watch *Ghastly* and complain about the end together. Or whatever she wanted to do. Hell, if Madeline offered to beat me up, I'd probably weep with joy and give her a hearty tip when she was done.

But saying that wouldn't exactly lend me any much-needed coolness.

I leaned back, swiped my tongue over my gums. *Play it cool.* Cool meant being quiet and not smiling like an idiot whenever I thought Madeline might be singing to me specifically, which she wasn't, but I can dream. No smiling. No blushing. No hugging my arms around my stomach. Minimal swaying.

Our server emerged with a tray of glorious, steam-billowing food, all of which made my stomach go animal inside me. Even Yates' salad managed to look appetizing, and I have moral issues with eating salad as a meal. The special I'd ordered turned out to be a gleaming slab of meat, which was draped over wild rice and morels and pomegranate seeds that looked like little rubies scattered on the plate. We were to dine on bone china, apparently. I was suddenly very grateful for the forty dollars in my pocket. I hadn't asked the price, and steak and morels and pomegranate seeds probably wouldn't fit my usual eight-dollar maximum budget. The dishes were set before us, and my lost appetite came crawling back.

As our server was leaving, Daisy caught their arm, whispered something in their ear. The server nodded, whispering something in reply and shooting their eyes at me as they spoke. Daisy rubbed her hands together conspiratorially.

Jing leaned toward me, eyes still on the stage, and cleared her throat. "Feeling hungry?"

"Yeah, right." Color was pooling in my cheeks. I fondled the serrated knife as it was placed before me, started the process of slashing my steak into bits.

The server, apparently done gossiping with Daisy, straightened back up. "Oh, miss, my manager is very busy tonight, and I doubt he can come and talk to you. It's possible that you could come earlier tomorrow, and he might be able to work something out then. Sorry about that."

It was like they'd pushed ten thousand thumbtacks into my chest. I wasn't hungry anymore. My pulse flared up, my fingers buzzed, my vision flickered red. My heart, coupled with my soul and my ability to be chill, plummeted somewhere by my toes. "You don't understand. It's really important," I said, speaking slow, trying to keep myself from crying or screaming or both. I chewed the words like they were made of leather.

Yates cleared her throat.

"Right. Which is why I'm sorry. I really am." The server gave me a look that illustrated exactly how little they cared about my urgent situation, and slipped back out of sight with their tray.

I stopped sawing at my steak and dropped my knife. I placed my hands on my lap, dug my nails into my thighs, inhaled too deeply for comfort. The meat, black and tan and rosy pink, was perfectly cooked. It smelled delicious. I never wanted to see it again.

Jing watched the server go. The overhead lights made her glow, illuminated her profile in a vibrant maraschino red. Her expression changed quick, faster than a blink. I saw it happen, but couldn't catch any specifics. She rolled her eyes back at us after a moment, shoved her tongue in her cheek. "Fuck them," she said. She sounded dismissive, but not too upset.

"We should curse them," said Daisy, who was probably joking, but possibly not.

"I'm sorry, Sideways." Yates looked down at her salad and thoughtfully speared an artichoke heart. "God, they didn't have to be such a jerk about it."

Daisy paused. She froze mid-bite of cheesecake, eyes wide, and then something feral blossomed in her expression. She shot Jing a look, wagged her brows, bent her mouth up into a hook-shaped smile. Under the table, I heard her foot rhythmically tap away, pounding out a beat like cardiac arrest.

Her enthusiasm must mean something in some strange, unspoken language that the two of them shared. Jing perked up, leaned toward her like she'd heard her name called. They made eye contact, and both of their expressions changed. Sharper, wider, more saccharine than before. The air itched with telepathy. Daisy's eyes flashed, and Jing inclined her head, something to the effect of a nod. She swept a lock of hair out of her eyes and tucked it behind her ear. Jing and Daisy glanced at Yates in tandem, who shrugged, but not disapprovingly. All three of them looked at me.

For a moment, I forgot that we were friends. They didn't feel like my friends. They felt like the three heads of Cerberus. I felt like a bite-sized deer.

"I was asking the server about Madeline. That's what we were talking about. They say that Madeline takes a break after five songs. This is her fourth song. That gives you about five minutes to eat, give or take, so eat fast." Daisy spread her hands on the table like she was claiming it. "We're going to get you your spell books, Sideways. And Madeline Kline is going to help us do it."

✳

I was vaguely seasick.

Without the band playing, the restaurant felt hollow. Random discordant notes broke through low voices and clattering glasses as the musicians retuned their instruments. The pianist played a scale in E-flat minor, pausing halfway through to lean backward and talk to the bass player beside her.

I had put my jacket back on. It was an extra layer between myself and the heavens, so that if the sky decided to open and hail its wrath on my back for what I was about to do, the jacket might deflect the worst of the onslaught.

Madeline had slinked off the stage and was drinking water out of a wineglass on a set of rickety steps. She was chatting up the sax player, and they were talking animatedly with snickers and overzealous hand-waving. He said something musical, and she put her hand over her mouth and cackled, all snide and coy and throaty sounding. There was a distinct possibility that he might be her boyfriend, and that was unnerving. He was handsome enough—good cheekbones, long lashes, thin cornrows—and if I were inclined to have boyfriends, he might register as a viable candidate. He had a nice smile on him. Looked like he'd tell good stories at parties. Looked like he wouldn't approve of me talking to his friend with the intention of stealing spell books from their boss.

Atrociously, and undeniably, he was prettier than me.

Something in my gut slammed on the brakes. How could I just edge myself into a conversation with her if she was talking to her boyfriend? How was that possible? If I was with my significant other and some random from a party interrupted valuable flirting time, I wouldn't exactly want to chitchat. Particularly not about the subject matter I was about to be bringing up. I might deck me in the face.

The boy looked up and saw me, and something lit up in his expression. He waved me over with dimples in his cheeks, moving casually, invitingly. His cuff links shimmered in the scarlet lights, blinked like little eyes on his wrists.

It was like being challenged to a duel. I couldn't back out now, or I'd mark myself a loser. Daisy might skin me alive. I'd certainly skin me alive. I huffed a breath, squared my shoulders, and trudged toward them like I knew what the fuck I was doing. My boots scuffed the tiles underfoot. I might have been the only person in the room with boots on, and I wasn't sure if that was a good thing. They were cacophonously loud against the marble floor.

Madeline swiveled her head to look at me. The rings under her eyes were plum colored, vaguely and inexplicably iridescent. Crow colored, almost. Her mouth screwed up at the corner.

A shiver snuck down my spine.

"Yo," said Madeline.

"Hey." I gnawed on the inside of my cheeks and tried for a smile, but it fell somewhere in grimace territory. Too many teeth, too sharp, too hungry. Probably made me look like a jackass, which wasn't entirely off the mark. I fiddled with the lining of my pockets and shuffled my weight from foot to foot.

"Oh, do you two know each other?" The boy's expression warmed up, and he looked back and forth between us, wagging his brows. There was something private exchanged between them, something that made me sour and jealous. Inside jokes that I'm not inside of make me spiteful. The boy winked at Madeline, then extended a hand for me to shake. "I'm Jacques. Haven't seen you around before. It's nice to get new faces in here, though."

"Sideways." I took his hand and shook it, gripped a little harder than I needed to. *Firm shake. Assert dominance.* My power play didn't register on his face, so I squeezed even harder, then let go like it hadn't happened in the first place and put my hands back in my pockets before they could act out.

"I was hoping I'd see you again." Madeline ran a hand over her mouth, nodded at me. "I was sorry I didn't snag your number."

It was like she'd reached up, took me by the shoulders, and hurled me against a wall. My vision swam, my lungs constricted, my heart fluttered and promptly stopped. All the punk in me evacuated. She wanted my number in a potentially gay way. Oh God, I wanted to die.

I opened my mouth to respond, but it just curled up higher. It was a stupid, slapstick smile, the kind of smile that rendered me useless and dizzy. It felt like walking down Jing's stairs and seeing the chalk scribbles drip down the walls. My soul felt so light that it might float out of my body and get lost in the rafters like a stray balloon.

"Same," I said.

*Same.* Fucking hell.

Jacques cracked a laugh. "You know what? I'm going to go get something to drink before we start playing again. You two have fun. Pleasure meeting you." He inclined his head in my direction, clapped Madeline on the shoulder, and bounced to his feet.

Madeline watched him go without moving her head, pupils rolling under her lashes, and then she settled her gaze back on me. She patted the chair beside her with one hand, cocked her finger with the other.

Nerves on the fritz, I obeyed. I sat beside her and bit my tongue.

"It was pretty spooky, what you did." Something sparkled low in her voice. God, was she doing this on purpose? She continued, speaking lower still, inclining her head. "You know, that was the most fun I've had in a long time."

"Yeah?" I felt my eyebrows disappear in my hairline. My cheeks hurt. God, I must look like an idiot. I bounced on the balls of my feet.

"Really truly." She placed her hands on her knees and leaned toward me, all serious-like. The light caught the gel in her hair and scattered it. It was so glossy it was distracting. "I keep having these weird dreams about it. About the party, and your spell. Is that weird for me to say?"

"No. God, no. Tell me about it." I blanched, held my breath.

"So, it always goes like this. We're sitting by the circle downstairs, and the music is playing and all those lights are spinning around—those lights were so gorgeous, I haven't shaken them off—and then everyone stops dancing. No, not stops. It's like they turn to stone. Everyone freezes. It's like God hit pause on everybody, except for us. And so I take your hand and we wander away from the circle, out through the crowd, but the room stretches on and on and on. Much bigger than Jing's basement. It's endless. The dancers' eyes follow us, but they can't turn to watch us go. They watch us wander around and around, until finally some stairs show up in the middle of the floor, and we climb those stairs for what feels like forever. We open the door, and right outside is the porch. No living room. It's dark as death outside. And as soon as we walk out, the door slams behind us and disappears. Then you change. Your leather jacket still looks pink and blue, glowing like we'd never left the basement. You double over and grab at your stomach like you're in agony, but there's this smile on your face. You're smiling like you just ripped the world in half. Like it was fun. You look up at me, and you hold my hands, and you start casting your spell, but I never remember the words. And then you let go of me and reach up into the sky and pluck the moon out of the stars. It's the size of a tennis ball in your hand. Shines like a lightbulb. You peel it like a clementine and pop it in your mouth. And then I wake up." Madeline Kline looked lost. Her eyelids drooped, half-moon and slate, and she had an uncanny wistfulness about her. Her eyes never left my face, and she looked at me like I was something to look at. She didn't blink.

My ribs ached.

"You know, I don't have my phone on me," she said, "but if you give me yours, I can put my number in it."

I fumbled at my pocket and yanked out my phone, which I clumsily unlocked and thrust at her in all its shatter-screened glory.

Her fingertips danced across the screen, and I made myself look away.

Over at my table, the clique was sitting prim. All of them had their right leg crossed over their left, because I guess it made them powerful when they all did the same thing. Daisy was eating my steak. Yates was scribbling on a receipt with a fluffy purple pen. Jing was watching me intently, hands folded professionally on her knee. I felt her pupils dissect every awkward stray movement of mine.

I cleared my throat.

"About that night," I said, nervously running a forefinger over the metal fringe of my zipper, resisting the urge to stare pleadingly at Jing or dissolve on the spot. The spell books, the spell books were somewhere in this endless house, and that's why I was talking to her. She might have an inkling about where they'd be. I chewed on my tongue, tried to construct a sentence that wasn't horrific. *Ask her about the books!* "That spell. I learned it from a book, and I've heard they have the rest of the set here, somewhere. Think you could be an angel and help me find them?" My voice didn't sound like my voice when I spoke. It was too high, too halting to be mine. None of my usual faux-cocky harshness. Breathless, I pulled my bag off my back and set it crookedly on my lap. My cheeks burned. I saw spots. I opened my bag and stretched it wide, wide enough for her to peer inside it. My books didn't move, remained worldly and serene, but even so, I felt them whispering, squirming, shifting to soak up the chromatic light. They felt heavier than they did five minutes ago.

Madeline's eyes popped open, and with my phone still in her hands, she leaned forward to glance inside and see the books. She abandoned my phone in her lap, dove her hands into my backpack, wrapped her fingers around one of the volumes and hefted it from its resting place with a firm tug, like she was pulling a loose tooth from my bag's leather gums. "God, it's heavy," she exclaimed, and she set it on the table with an audible *thunk*. She stroked the little notched scales on the snake emblem and tilted her head, glazed her eyes across the details like she was admiring a Monet. It warmed something in her expression, and as she ran her fingers back and forth along the spine, over the edges of pages, across the binding's seams, a little smile melted across her face. She scrunched her nose, crinkled her eyes, looked up at me like I'd handed her a drop of the sun.

My palms felt cold and thawing. Sweat prickled down my neck.

"You know what?" Madeline looked up at me from under her lashes, a wry little something flickering in her smile. She tapped her index finger on the snake seal. Her nails were painted two shades paler than the leather binding. I watched the tapping like it was in slow motion, the repetitive knocking as rhythmic and decisive as a judge's gavel, and I felt my heart rush to sync up with it. She rolled her stray hand into a fist and leaned her cheek on it. "I've seen this before."

I unclenched my jaw. "Seen it where?"

"Upstairs," she mused, pulling her hands into her lap and out of sight. "I think I saw this when I was fooling around in the stacks. Maurice keeps the coolest things in the archives, and I try and sneak up there whenever I have the chance. Lots of *Hocus Pocus*–looking stuff."

"Do you think you could show me around? I'd kill to see them."

"You know . . ." She paused, and her hair drifted out from behind her ear to fall in her face. She glanced up at the stage, and then back at me. She sloped her back, brought herself closer to me, and dropped her voice to a gossipy whisper. "I need to go back onstage in a minute, but I can tell you where they are. People are never up there, and the security cameras are only in customer areas. If you walked up the back set of stairs instead of the main set, you wouldn't get caught. No one would ever know. Don't take them, of course, but I don't see the harm in you looking at them. The archives are on the third floor, and they aren't usually locked during workdays. Maurice doesn't go up there very often, and he's the only one who spends much time there. Besides, he's off at an auction today. I think we might be getting a real da Vinci, can you imagine?"

"Right," I breathed, nodding too vigorously. There was

something intoxicating about the idea of sneaking upstairs, something glorious enough that I could ignore the sour fear that was reminding me of just how bad an idea this was. "I majorly owe you. Like, anything you want. Thank you."

"You don't have to owe me if you take me out sometime soon. Do you like that little coffee shop downtown? The Rosewood Grind? Just get me coffee and you can consider us even." She winked and stood up.

My jaw hung slack.

I nodded once, dumbstruck, and stood in tandem with her. Unlike Madeline, I shoved the chair at an odd angle when I stood, and it screeched beneath me. I couldn't muster the ability to care about the awful sound. My brain wasn't computing anything anymore. I'd lost my ability to process. My whole chest was vibrating like I'd swallowed a beehive, and now my insides were honeyed and stinging and struck with thousands of wings.

"The back stairs are at the end of that hallway over there. That's where the restrooms are, so it wouldn't look strange if you all walked over. If you stay quiet, you should be fine," she said with a tone of reassurance. She smoothed her trousers. "Good luck, okay? Promise me that if you find anything curious, you'll tell me all about it when we go out."

"Stick a needle in my eye," I said. I meant it. I dropped my phone in my pocket and tossed my hand through my tangles.

"Cool," she said. She dimpled, turned from me, and went up the stage steps.

My pulse felt electric. It zapped through my arms and buzzed in my skull. This jacket was too hot. I was drowning. This was real, and this was happening. It was so lovely that I might die.

# TWELVE

# CURIOUSER AND CURIOUSER

The hallway was slim, decked with portraits and scarlet Victorian wallpaper. It was longer than I thought it should be. The restroom doors were on either side, and at the far end was a flat, black door. It sported a silvery plaque, and the closer we got, the more obvious it became that the plaque said EMPLOYEES ONLY. It was starkly simple amid all the grandeur, sharply minimalist, and something about it was genuinely foreboding. I felt like I might be cursed if I touched the knob.

Luckily, I didn't have to. Daisy surged forward and gave it a twist. We followed her single file through the doorway. Jing closed it behind us. It sealed with a neat little click. The new room we were in was surprisingly small, completely bare except for a spindly spiral staircase. The steps were mostly exposed, and only a bony rail separated the walking path from certain death by falling. Yates tossed her head back, her mouth gaping. The staircase stretched upward and upward and upward, like a spring pulled taut, and my gut said that putting too much weight on it might send the whole thing snapping down on us. It didn't look like something built for human use.

Jing pulled her sunglasses off her brow and put them on properly. The little hearts made her face look sweeter, but her expression turned nasty and prim. Business face. She clicked her tongue. "Third floor, right?"

"Right." I shoved my hands in my pockets and forced myself not to ogle the staircase of doom. Ogling might lead to wussing out. No sir.

Jing swore. "That's not that high. I'll walk in front, and you losers can keep pace behind. If any of you hyperventilate, I'm pushing you off. Capisce?"

The three of us mumbled "capisce" in response.

Jing rolled her shoulders and swaggered toward the staircase. She stepped slowly, evenly, onto the first stair, and when it didn't give, she stepped onto the next. After five, she looked back at us and stuck out her tongue. "Last one up is a rotten egg."

Daisy grabbed Yates by both wrists and tugged her toward the stairs. Daisy looked like a happy gremlin. Yates looked like she'd seen the Reaper.

I followed behind, hands in my pockets, eyes straight ahead.

My entire body tensed up when I started my ascent. The stairs were stable, but the exposure made me think they weren't. Still, it wasn't nearly as terrifying as the Chantry staircase. At least now, I'd be responsible for my own falling, not some overgrown fuckboy in a suit. I picked up my pace, which made Daisy and Yates speed up in turn. Daisy was giggling, and Yates shushed her, and my stomach tied itself into butterfly knots. The helix motion was making me dizzy in the worst way. The bits of steak in me were threatening to rebel.

God, did I not pay for it? I hadn't stopped to slap down money.

*Fuck, fuck, fuck.*

If the server came over and I hadn't paid, would they come looking for us? And find us here, on the stairs behind the clearly marked NOT YOU sign? We'd be thrown out. Not only thrown out, but likely forbidden to return.

The stair opened onto what I assumed was the second floor. Jing wasn't waiting there. I climbed faster, and in the process, I let my gaze fall downward.

Between the steps, I could make out the checkerboard tiles below. Miles away, surely. I was in the sky without a net.

I stopped mid-step.

A cold chill shot down my body. I couldn't make myself move, couldn't make myself look away. If someone was coming up after us, they'd snag me without a hitch.

There were a set of feet in my line of sight. They were feet in fuchsia heels. Slowly, agonizingly, I made myself look up at who they were attached to. Daisy stood there with one hip popped. One of her eyebrows was arched above the other, and she looked rather smug, smiling at me with all her dimples. She placed a hand on my shoulder. For a fraction of a second, I thought she was going to push me back. She didn't. Her grip was cast-iron, and the pressure of her fingers on me reminded me that I needed to breathe.

"You aren't gonna puke, are you?" She poked my cheek with her free hand. It hurt, but not enough to piss me off. The sensation was grounding, and strangely comforting. It felt like something a friend would do, not that Daisy and I were friends—or were we? Admiration had to be mutual for friendship. I was coming to really like Daisy Brink, but she was impossible to read.

"No," I said. I wiggled my jaw and tried to summon up words to speak with. "I think I forgot to pay. If they see the unpaid tab, they might come poking around for us. I don't know."

"Nah. You didn't forget. You've already paid. They're not going to come after us," she said. She blew a bubble of sky-colored gum and snapped it in my face. "Stop freaking out. We have trespassing to do."

"I didn't pay," I insisted. Her gum smelled vaguely of raspberries, but it was hard to tell with the mysterious blue flavors. It didn't smell like imminent demise, though, so I appreciated it.

"Yes, you did. Your tab is paid. You left a damn good tip, too, if I say so myself." She rolled her eyes. Daisy's hand slid off my shoulder and knotted in the fabric of my shirt, and she gave it a tug, propelling me forward. "Come on, Sideways. Move your gay ass. I wanna see this witchy shit."

I moved forward, lured by her knuckles against my sternum. She walked up the staircase backward, which was terrifying, and made me somehow doubt Daisy's initial hesitation at the bottom of the stairs. She was a powerful type of fearless. A dangerous type. Anyone who walks in reverse up a spiral staircase while chewing gum and dragging another person isn't the type of person that one should take for granted.

Wait.

"Did you ... ?"

She scoffed, pulled me harder. "I swear to God, don't mention it. I'll push you if you thank me. Now. Do you want gum? I lifted it from the gas station. Tastes like victory."

"Yeah, I'll take a piece," I replied, and I fought the urge to hug her or punch her or both. "Don't do it again, alright? Next time is my turn."

"I don't take turns. I just do whatever I want and either people play along, or I sacrifice them to the bleacher gods." She twisted her gum into wispy strands with her tongue.

"What the fuck are bleacher gods?" The door was in sight, thank the bleacher gods, and the two of us strolled off the stairs and onto a hardwood landing. Jing and Yates were waiting there, blowing bubbles, and looking bored.

Daisy pulled a box of gum from her blouse and tossed it toward me. I caught it one-handed, fumbled for a piece. She cracked her knuckles. "The bleacher gods are the mighty monsters that live under the football field. You know how we've never lost a home game, not in, like, two decades? It's because we feed the gods. I like to feed them fuckboys. I push them off the bleachers, and we score."

I was fairly certain we'd lost the last homecoming game,

but I grinned like a jackal, nonetheless.

"It's locked," said Jing. She said this like she was announcing the weather: No big deal. Nothing of importance. "So. Who's going to do the honors, eh? Daze, it's you or me."

Daisy bounced on her toes. "Me. God. Totally me. Dibs."

"Be my guest." Jing stepped aside, and Daisy dropped to her knees before the door. She reached into her hair and pulled out two pins, which she straightened and artfully plunged into the slit below the knob. She fiddled them around with her ear pressed against the lock.

Yates winked at me.

Within moments, Daisy jerked herself upright and wiggled the knob, and the door sprung open with a satisfactory click. She turned toward us, ecstatic, and took a bow.

I clapped despite myself.

Jing stood close to me and brushed the curls off my cheek. "She's the family delinquent," she breathed. "We love her dearly for it."

Yates peeked around the door on tiptoe and looked back at us with a nod. "I think we're alone," she said. She danced through the crack, and Daisy, Jing, and I all rushed in behind her. The door shut without our prompting.

The archives were dripping with ghosts. White sheets covered chairs, tables, tall cylindrical somethings, boxes the size of cars. The darkness stretched back forever, and the ghosts around us were the only points of reference. There must be a handful of windows somewhere in the blackness, because I could make out the raw edges of cases and racks, but nothing was distinct.

Yates moved for the light switches, but Jing stopped her with a flick of her wrist. "Phone lights," she said, and she pulled out her cell as an example. Yates nodded, pulled out her own phone, and added a twin point of light. Daisy followed suit.

I took out my phone, and the first thing on the screen was the effervescent Madeline Kline. She must've taken a selfie for her contact. Her likeness had a lopsided smile. I turned on the flashlight and pointed it into the black.

"If we split up, we can cover more ground," said Jing.

"Screw that. This place gives me the creeps. Besides, that's how people die in horror flicks," said Yates.

"We're less horror flick and more *Scooby-Doo*. Besides. Remember *Ghastly*? The witches in the sisterhood split up, and they were fine," said Daisy.

"No, they were killed by that stupid jock," said Yates.

"We're alone up here. There's no one to kill us. And if an axe murderer does show up, Sideways can take him. We split up, and whoever finds the books first texts the rest of us where they are. Yates will stay by the door and tell us if someone's coming. If anyone shows, we hide. There are ten thousand white sheets in here. Hide under one of the covered tables or something, you'll be fine," said Jing. She said it like a punctuation mark. There was to be no discussion. "I'll take the left flank, Daisy'll take the right. Sideways moves down the middle. Are we clear?"

"Clear as crystal," said Daisy.

"Good." Jing nodded at us and pivoted on her heel. She strode off toward the left. Daisy snorted, ducked to the right. Yates retreated and tucked herself beside the door.

I was alone. I started forward.

✳

They must make their floral skull trophies themselves. On either side of me, shelves upon shelves of dry bones lined my path. There were some whole skeletons, wired together and posed in lifelike positions, as well as some in pieces. I spotted several half-finished rib cages wired to a few stray vertebrae, lacking arms and hips. Above each display piece in progress was a strip of masking tape with words like *Raven* and *Grey fox* and *Jackalope* written in fine-point Sharpie. One slot, which was mostly bare aside from a skinny white stick, was labeled *Possibly human*. Beside the corpse bits was a fish tank. I shone my light over it with morbid curiosity and recoiled as soon as the light hit the contents. Long black beetles scurried over a meatless shoulder blade. I turned my phone back to the path and picked up my pace. My heart was in my teeth.

The books on my back were like magnets. They rushed me forward, lurched at the slightest hesitation. The rest of the set were close, they were so damn close. I walked past the bones and into a sea of rectangles wrapped in corrugated carboard. They were large, flat, stacked with obvious care. The paper was marked with masking tape like the bones had been, mostly with names and dates. I didn't pay much mind. Then, passing by a particularly large rectangle, the name on the label caught my eye. *Simeon Solomon,* it said, without a date. I caught myself, made myself look a little closer. Simeon Solomon? Boris had a thing about him. Made us all drive three hours to see a traveling art exhibit with literally only three of his paintings in it once. What the fuck was up with this place? Why wasn't this on display downstairs?

My bag felt increasingly heavy.

I quickened my pace.

These ghosts were shaped like people.

It was undeniable. The white sheets rippled over heads and spilled past shoulders. They were motionless and taller than me, all lined up like servants meeting their master. The stillness unnerved me. I took a step back, convinced myself to breathe slowly. Statues. They had to be statues. Tall, broad statues.

I gnawed on my tongue and reached for a fistful of sheet. The fabric was cool to the touch, softer than I expected it to be. I gave it a yank.

The fabric came tumbling down.

It wasn't a statue beneath the sheet. It was a suit of fucking armor. Gleaming, quicksilver armor. It looked like it'd just waltzed out of Avalon. Its eyes were like coin slots, and it was muzzled with a strip of metal that jutted up like a beak. A ridge ran down the chest plate. The shoulder plates were rounded, iced with tiny floral insignias. Between its clasped hands, the suit held an elaborate broadsword, the blade of which was the same color as bubblegum foil.

Alright. Kinda rad.

"You scared the life out of me," I mumbled in the armor's direction. Curious, I tested the sword's edge with my finger. It slipped through my skin like I was made of butter. I pulled away, curled my lip. "You don't have to be a dick about it." I recovered the suit with the sheet and stuck my bleeding finger in my mouth.

I took a few strides farther down the path.

It hit me like a train. I pitched forward, braced myself against a shrouded metal chest to stay upright. My mind spiraled. My phone flew out of my hand and onto the floor, where it skidded toward another suit of armor. I fell to my knees, which made all my little cuts scream, but this was good pain. It was pain I recognized like an old friend. My phone buzzed, which meant I'd received a text, but I already knew what it was about. I felt it in my gut. Someone'd found the books. This thing I was feeling, it was magic, no doubt. I saw spots and pawed for my phone, snatched it up.

The message was from Jing.

**Found it first, bitch. Second row from the left, toward the back.**

My mouth twisted up. I heaved myself to my feet, made myself stand despite the magic malaise. God, spell craft felt good in my bones. I didn't usually feel it until I was working on some ritual. What were the other volumes like? Maybe they hadn't sold them because the pure concentration of magic between each page was too much to sell. The sort of power that shouldn't be put on the market. It made my mouth water. My vision wobbled, but I blinked through the blurriness and ran. I broke forward past endless shelves and stacks. The pathway narrowed and the unfinished exhibits loomed higher and higher, but I didn't let up. My insides felt tight. My phone light strobed as I ran, bouncing over nameless shapes, making them look alive.

I hit the end of the aisle. It opened into a wider path, one that branched off into other aisles filled with other bubble-wrapped unknowns. This place could be the behemoth mother of Rothschild & Pike, what with all the rarities and weirdness. Even in the back of the room, there were still enough bundled treasures to fill a modest museum. I held my breath, wrapped my arms around my stomach, and counted off rows until I reached the one Jing had texted about.

Something girl shaped shifted in the dark.

I paused, panting, and the shape stood up. Jing. Her phone's light swiveled in my direction. I winced, shielded my eyes with the back of my hand.

"What the fuck are you waiting for?" Jing waved me over, returning her light to a shelf. "I haven't opened them yet. You're welcome."

My hands shook. I took a step, then another, and then I couldn't stop myself and sprinted to Jing's side. I stood so close that our arms brushed. Her light was aimed at a spot just above our heads, and I raised my phone to join it. Together, we lit up the entire shelf, bleached it of all its color. I threw back my head and wanted to cry.

There were seventeen volumes. Seventeen sublime volumes in dark leather, each more heartbreaking than the last. Something like love or hunger struck my chest. I thrust my phone at Jing, who caught it with a feline swipe of her hand, and I reached up with both hands to touch the books. It was like praising holy relics. I laid my hands across the spines, which shot a chill down my spine. My palms were hot, throbbing against the leather, and I plucked one of them from its place and brought it close. I held it against my stomach, wrapped my arms around it so tightly that they might've fallen off, and let my throat grow tight and itchy. Jing be damned—I didn't care if she saw. She didn't know what they were to me, and she didn't have to. I fit my fingers on the snake emblem like I was pressing frets on a guitar and marveled at how neatly its corners fit against my body. It was like it used to be a part of me, some dark extra organ, and I was holding it close to its origin. My chest was where it was made. I felt my pulse in the binding. God, how was I going to let it go?

I sat down, and Jing sat beside me. I placed the volume on my lap. Its weight on my thighs was delicious. I stroked the edges of each page, took a deep breath, and opened it wide.

### VOLUME V

Wasn't the next one, but who gave a fuck? I bit my tongue, turned the page.

My still-bleeding thumb swiped across the paper, and the red smear soaked into the blank page and disappeared. The cut on my thumb zipped itself up.

Ink bloomed across the page where I'd touched it. The letters floated up from the whiteness and arranged themselves in neat rows, drifting ever so slightly, like they were suspended in liquid.

*Hello, Sideways. This is not your book. It is someone else's book. We only reveal our pages to those we've been given to, I'm afraid. Also, do not touch blades. They are designed for splitting skin, as you've observed, and the results are both messy and painful. We've fixed that for you.*

*Hello, Jing. Reading over people's shoulders is generally considered rude, but we are not judgmental. We would highly advise reading the first two volumes in their entirety. The contents might be to your liking. We feel like you might have an aptitude for it, based on your ability to read this alone.*

*We thank you both for your time and apologize for any inconvenience.*

*Best,*

*Volume V*

The words sank back into the pulp, and the page was blank again.

I stared at the blankness and waited. I didn't breathe. My tongue was a dry, shriveled thing between my gluey teeth. I didn't move. I didn't blink. I waited for words to come back and spell something different. *Congratulations, Sideways— you passed! That was a test of your tricky patience.* But the page stayed blank. It was spilled milk. I stared until my eyes watered, or maybe they watered on their own.

I closed the book, rose to my feet, and gently nudged it back in its place between two adjacent volumes. It was like I'd never taken it in the first place. All the books in a neat little row looked unassuming and undisturbed, much happier without my meddling fingers poking between their pages.

Undeterred, I pulled the one on the end. Volume three, that was. Didn't bother sitting down, just undid the latch, pushed up the cover with my thumb, looked down at the first page.

*Hello, Sideways.*
   *Reading in chronological order won't change our answer.*
   *Our apologies. Take care.*

I put the book back unceremoniously. It made a hollow little clacking sound as the cover struck the shelf. The sound zapped through my capillaries like a lightning strike, and every single nerve in my body lit up at once. The books didn't want me. Why would they? They were not mine. They would never be mine. They belonged to someone else, and why the fuck would they want to be mine when they could belong to literally anyone else on the planet?

I took a breath, gnashed my teeth, and turned on my heel. Behind us were rows of antique vases, all blue glass and porcelain. I seized one by its skinny neck and dashed it against the floor. It exploded outward like a giant white raindrop. White powder and jigsaw shards skidded in every direction, and the sound echoed off the walls and ricocheted around in my skull. It sounded like everything crashing at once, the whole world and myself and everything I'd ever wanted. My heart bashed itself against my sternum, and now my whole body ached, and my lip trembled, and my hands rolled up into fists.

Hands on my shoulders. Hands on my back. Cold hands, moving deftly as they pulled tassels of hair off my face. Straightening my jacket across my shoulders. Tracing down between my scapula. Resting there, at my core, while I remembered how my body worked well enough to sob. Jing didn't say a word when the crying started. If she watched, she didn't gawk enough for me to notice. I felt her nails press through the leather of my jacket, felt them etch little figure eights into the fabric. They danced back and forth, and I choked a little, twisted my mouth into ugly shapes.

The rumble of adolescent magic was still raw inside me. Maybe that was the crying? Crying always turned my insides sour. Probably that. I wrapped my arms around my stomach and heaved another sob, but my eyes couldn't give any more, and my throat ached too much to make a sound. Everything in me was curdled. I wanted to curl up tight and die.

Jing pressed her face into the back of my neck. "I can make something up when the girls ask. Say they weren't here. Say we couldn't find them. They'll either believe it or play along.

They'll never have to know."

I didn't say anything, mostly because I couldn't. If I spoke, I might scream. Get us caught. Get us tossed out, not that it'd matter now. I knifed my teeth into my bottom lip and let her fingers crisscross over my back, let Jing breathe on my mass of curls.

There was a stab of light out of the corner of my eye, something broader and brighter than a phone flashlight. A notification from Yates. Jing pulled away from me, swiped her thumb across her screen, and swore. Her hand clamped around my arm, and she yanked me down the aisle and around the corner. We passed three aisles before I slammed my heel into the floor and she jerked to a halt. She whirled her head around to scowl at me. Something dangerous flickered in her. I bit my tongue.

A table-shaped sheet ghost sat unassumingly to our left. Jing dropped to a crouch and lifted a fistful of sheet, cast a seething glance at me, and dragged us both into the dark below the table.

It was darker under the table than it was in the archives proper. Black-hole dark. I rubbed my fists in my eyes until I saw bruise colors, and when I pulled my hands away, I could just barely make out the edges of Jing's blond head as it swiveled against the shadows.

"Fuck," she hissed. She whipped out her phone and grabbed mine, turned off the flashlights, and brought down the brightness until the screens were barely visible. She thrust my phone back at me, and I caught it with my rib cage. Her thumbs flew across the screen.

**Daisy fucking Brink, where are you?**

There was a pause, and Yates responded.

**She's not with you??**

I wrapped my arms around my stomach. My mouth filled up with blood. I must've bit my tongue. There wasn't pain. Just a salty taste. Maybe it was my nerves sizzling.

The fluorescent lights hummed to life above us. Someone must've flipped them on.

**Oh my God. Someone just walked past me.**

Jing's face, blurry now, but visible, turned vicious. She shot me a glance, and my phone blinked with a notification, which I checked with my heart in my teeth.

**Do you think that book snitched?**

I looked up at her and my insides flipped.

Fuck. Everything.

These books were my Judas Iscariot. My stupid daydreams had damned us all.

Heels to our right. Slow, deliberate footsteps, gingerly clacking back and forth beside our hiding place.

Jing froze, but her eyes followed the movement back and forth.

"I know you're here." The voice was cloyingly familiar and smooth as melted butter. "There isn't any need to hide. Come on out, own up. I won't bite."

Jing scoffed, punched something into her phone.

**No fucking thanks, mister.**

"*Vade Mecvm Magici.* Some of the best spell books around, in my humble opinion. You've got good taste . . ." The footsteps trailed away, and the voice became muffled as he left.

Still no reply from Daisy.

Whoever was out there cried out.

Jing snapped her head up.

The voice spiked an octave higher. "What the hell have you done? Jesus *Christ.*" The footsteps weren't deliberate anymore. The stranger ran, shoes echoing across the tiles like thunder. I heard the door slam behind them like a slap across the face.

Jing's eyes shot wide. She scurried out from under the table, I followed suit, and we stood shaking under the fluorescents with our hands rolled into fists.

"Why the fuck did he run, Sideways?" Jing panted. She spun around once, eyes on all the aisles, which were startlingly clear with the lights on. "What the fuck is he running from?"

"I don't know," I said. My knees buckled beneath me.

"Whatever. Let's find Daisy and fucking leave." Jing swore, ripped her fingers through her hair, gnashed her teeth into a tight line. She marched toward the far wall, the direction Daisy was supposed to be searching in. "She probably dropped her fucking phone somewhere."

If she had dropped her phone, she'd be staggering around

in the dark. How do you lose a working flashlight in a black room? You don't. Daisy just wasn't checking her phone. That must be it. I hurried after Jing and shoved my own phone in my pocket, wrapped my arms around my stomach, dug my nails into my sides.

We glanced down each aisle as we passed it, and all of them were Daisy-less. They stretched back forever and ever, but they were devoid of movement, and Daisy was Daisy. Even if she hadn't heard the stranger leave, she would've moved around or fidgeted or something, wouldn't she? I barely knew the girl and I knew she couldn't hold still. Maybe she was moving away from us—maybe that was it.

We hit the last row in the right half of the room. It was stocked with books and boxes and embellished mirrors, each more intricate than the last. They glinted like long eyes under the lights.

Daisy's phone, flashlight still shining, lay abandoned on the floor.

# THIRTEEN

# THIS CHAPTER IS UNLUCKY

"She's not here." Jing splayed her fingers across her face. Her mouth twisted up into a hysterical arch, and she sank her teeth into her palm. Her breathing became ragged. "She wouldn't leave without her phone. It'd be like leaving her liver behind. She wouldn't. But she's not here. There's only one door, Sideways, and Yates is guarding the fucking door. Where the hell is she?"

"I don't know," I spat. My hands trembled, so I dug my nails harder into my skin. "I don't fucking know."

"This isn't like her. She doesn't vanish. Daisy's like a damned lighthouse. You see her miles away. She doesn't pull Houdini stunts. It's like trying to hide a firecracker. It doesn't work." Jing jerked her hands away from her face and plucked the phone off the floor. "She left the light on. Damn it, Daisy."

A wave of nausea rocked me. I leaned back, squared my shoulders against the wall behind me, and forced breath into my lungs. All the synapses down my spine vibrated. My limbs tingled. Pins and needles in my chest. I'd felt the sickness earlier, the magic malaise, but it was building now. I was teeming with it. My mind was TV static. I lolled back my head.

"Holy hell," I said. "It's Daisy."

Her body was suspended in air.

She was twenty feet above us, held up by nothing, all loose limbs and swaying hair. Her skirt opened like a lily, and her arms were stretched out on either side of her in bloodless stigmata. Her fuchsia heels dangled from her toe-tips. Her head was tossed back. I took a step back, craned my neck, and I saw her face.

She wore a grin.

"Jing," I breathed. "Jing. Fucking, just. Look up."

Jing scowled, flipped me off, and obeyed. The scowl dropped off her face. "Oh my God. Daisy!"

"Shut up," I hissed. A shiver raked my spine. "What happens if she fucking falls? She'd break her back, or worse."

"How the fuck did she get up there?" Jing spun around, eyes turned up, mouth agape.

"No idea." Instinct struck. "Call Yates. We'll need Yates, too."

"She's guarding the door!"

"If someone comes back up, we'll get thrown out. Whatever. Just do it, okay?" I dropped to my knees, yanked the bag off my back, and fished out the second book of the *VMM*. "We need her. It works better with more people."

I felt Jing's eyes on me.

I set my book on the floor and cracked my knuckles.

Jing dialed Yates and spoke in harsh tones. I tuned her out, opened the book wide. Blank pages. It took a moment, and then ink scrawled across the page. Diagrams poured themselves into strange shapes. Inscriptions ringed each spell, and I flipped through the pages, scanning for something, fucking anything that looked appropriate. There was a thought in my head about how this book wasn't fessing up about the ones that rejected me, but I swallowed it. Focus. "Levitation," I spat, thumbing through chapters upon chapters of health spells and herbal drivel. "I need something on levitation."

The pages flipped themselves.

Blue and black ink folded together, stretched into a sigil I didn't recognize. For flying and falling. I bit my tongue, rubbed my hands together. "Jing."

She plunked down beside me, crossed her legs, and seized my hands. "Tell me what to do."

I shook my head. I was swimming in my jacket. Everything was sultry and thick. "We're gonna use the page as our spell. No time to redraw it. It'll have to work."

Yates sprinted up the aisle and screeched, her hands flying up to clasp her mouth and her heart. "God, Daisy! How did—"

"Sit down." I swiped my tongue over my gums. "We need you."

She nodded, sank between Jing and I, and we gathered up her hands. The page rippled, added another phrase to the chaos.

*Invocate.*

I coughed, opened my mouth. "Come down, Daisy. We enchant you to fall slow."

She stayed in place.

"You're flying," said Jing. She threw back her head and gazed up at Daisy, lashes fluttering, mouth screwed at either side. "You're flying, just like you always said you would."

"God, it's not working. It's like the Chett curse. It isn't working. She's going to be stuck up there," Yates cried. She started to pull her hand away, and I grabbed it tighter.

"You're fucking flying, Daisy," Jing continued. "We're watching you fly. What a fucking story to tell. Behold Daisy Brink, who broke the law of gravity."

Yates' chin trembled, but she shook herself off. Blinked a few times and said, "You've always been our flyer, Daisy. This is the highest you've gone yet. We've seen you fly at football games, at the top of a girl pyramid, where you belong. We've seen you fly before. But this? This is impressive, even for you. I've never seen you so close to the sun before."

The magic quickened in me. I cleared my throat, spoke up. "I barely know you and I see it. You're flying. You're up there with the stars, shining like you should be, like you oughta be. All Hail Daisy Brink, human victory flag."

"When you come down, come slow, okay?" Yates squeezed my hand so tightly that my knuckles cracked. "I want you to come down as slowly and gently as a feather off an angel's wing. I want you to come down so you can tell us all about how you did it. I want to hear the story of how Daisy Brink flew. Come down, Daisy. Please come down, okay? Slow and soft."

"Slow and soft," I echoed.

"Daisy," said Jing. She looked ashen. "Come on down. For us. *Right now.*"

A shiver circuited through us. I saw it start in Yates, and it fluttered through me and into Jing, and we all shook together like the gears of some strange machine. Our pulses moved in sync. "Come down," we said in unison. "Come down."

We looked at each other. Then we looked up.

All the fluorescents flickered in tandem. Daisy floated downward. She moved like a ghost, seamless and fluid, her hair and skirt swishing around her as though she were submerged in water. Her eyes were shut. Her mouth was still curved up in a jackal smile. Her wrists brushed the tiles first, and then the rest of her body floated down between them. Her neck braced on the bridge of Jing's hand and mine, and her head landed on the open page like it was hitting a pillow.

As soon as Daisy's body brushed the floor, Yates and Jing unclasped their hands. Her eyes shot open.

The lights went out.

I felt Daisy bolt upright in the darkness. She panted, tossed her arms around herself. I couldn't make out her face, but I felt her grinning. It was a radioactive smile. It was infectious, slightly noxious. It'd probably kill me.

I dropped Jing's and Yates' hands and felt around for my book in the dark. The page was warm like skin. I gathered it up, shut it, fumbled around for my bag. Yates turned the flashlight on her phone back on, and she shone it in my direction. I tugged my bag toward me and shoved the *VMM* back inside, zipped it shut.

"Let's get the fuck out of here." Jing stood up and groped in Daisy's direction. "You've got some fucking explaining to do when we're home, you understand?"

Daisy didn't say anything. She clawed at Jing, clambered to her feet, and slung an arm around Jing's neck. One of her hands shot through the darkness and grabbed at my shoulder, and she pulled me close, used me as leverage as she straightened herself up.

Yates pointed her flashlight ahead of us, and the four of us lumbered toward the door. "I can hear my heart beating," she said under her breath. She led us deeper and deeper into the room, closer to the door, away from the spot we'd cast in. "It's beating so loud. God, I feel like they can hear it downstairs."

"Don't worry," said Daisy. Her voice was raw. "I can hear your heart beating, too."

We sped up our pace.

"You better be able to walk on your own by the time we get to the stairs," said Jing. "I am not carrying you down. If you can't walk, you're scooting on your ass the whole way down. Like a two-year-old. You hear me?"

"Crystal clear, baby." Daisy slumped her head on my shoulder. "Don't you worry one bit. I can walk. Just remembering how to make my legs move, that's all. So, did you find your book?"

"Fuck off," I said.

"Gotcha," Daisy replied. She wobbled on her feet, then abruptly stopped, dropped to the floor, and resurfaced with her heels dangling from her hand. "Insert something cliché about sensible shoes, right?"

"Put them back on before we get downstairs. Looks less conspicuous. We're gonna have to play it super cool, especially if whoever that guy was snitches on us. No small talk, nothing. We walk out and drive away. And we do it looking as gorgeous as when we came in. If our server sees us or anything like that, we say that I felt sick and all of you were keeping an eye on me. That's our story. Understood?"

"Yeah," said Yates. "Sideways, you've got eyeliner all over your face. I'll wipe it off, and we can pretend like it wasn't there in the first place. Let's hope the band is playing so people's eyes are on stage. Plus, the food here is delicious, and people came in groups, so their attention is divided. It's all good. We'll be fine," she said, but her reassurances trailed off and she halted mid-step.

Jing bumped into her. "What? Fucking go."

"I saw something move." Yates took a step backward, smooshing herself closer to the three of us. "I'm not joking. Something totally just moved."

"You've got to be kidding me," said Jing, exasperated. "We don't have time for this shit. The longer we're up here, the more likely that someone else is gonna come poking around, and then we'll be fucked. We don't need that, you hear? Move your ass."

"There's something there," Yates insisted. She pointed into

the abyss beyond the flashlight's glow. "I saw it. I'm sure of it."

"You're scaring yourself. Come. On." Jing unhooked herself from Daisy's arm, turned on her own flashlight, and walked out in front of us. "Let's go." She took a few steps, paused, then spat a curse.

"*See?*" Yates' voice spiked higher.

"What the hell is going on," I growled. My tongue ran dry.

"There's someone over there." Jing squinted, leaned toward the dark. "Someone. Something. It's by the door."

"How the fuck are we going to leave if there's something by the door? Guys," said Yates, whose voice was turning shrill. "If even the group skeptic sees it, we're screwed. God, I refuse to die here. Jesus. Sideways?"

I swore, pulled out my phone, and turned on its flashlight. I added its light to where Jing's was pointing.

Something danced just out of sight.

"Whatever the fuck you are, you can fuck right off," I said. My pulse thundered in my skull. "Not in the mood right now. Move along."

The darkness spoke. "Oh, hush. 'Good evening' would be more polite."

My eyes popped wide.

"I wanted to thank you. I've been in that vase an awfully long while. Much too long. Oh, stretching feels *divine*. What coven do you all belong to?"

"Excuse me?" said Jing, sounding equal parts bewildered and terrified.

"What coven is this? I count four of you. There are never

four witches in a group without them being in a Group. A coven of witches, like how crows have murders and sheep have herds. Surely you know which coven you belong to, my friends. Pythons or Goldies or Star Thieves or Corbies? Something more modern, perhaps?"

"We're our own coven," said Jing. She paused, took a step toward the shadows.

"Please stop that. I'm not so fond of light," said the voice. "Now. Your own coven, you say? I like that. Fresh scapegracers, making their own little band. Doesn't happen much anymore."

I swallowed, gawked at the darkness. "What are you?"

"Me? Oh, I'm Mr. Scratch. Nothing for you to frighten yourself over. Why, if anything, I'm your friend. I'm in your debt. Mosey along, now. The folks downstairs might have some feelings if they catch you up here, but I think you'll be fine if you leave here now. That boy might not even tattle on you, now that he's got me to worry about. I'm more important, I'm afraid. Hurry along now, baby coven. Go seek your happiness somewhere safe."

✳

We sat in the car in silence.

The lot was drenched with nighttime, but the clock in the car said that it was only nine. Rusty leaves plastered themselves across the windshield. The wind howled like a pack of dogs. The heater hummed, but it wasn't quite working yet, so the cold air swirled around without warming us.

After an eternity, Jing spoke. She raked her nails down the back of her neck. "What the fuck is Mr. Scratch?"

"Sounds like something out of a kid's cartoon. A seriously fucked-up kid's cartoon." I put my knees up on the seat in front of me. "I'll try to find something on it in volume two. I don't know. There's gotta be something on it somewhere. I'll google it, if all else fails."

"Daisy," said Yates, who had lain herself across the seats and rested her head in my lap. Her hair was soft against my thigh—I felt it through a rip in my jeans—and I put a hand on her shoulder, gave it a squeeze. She stuck her tongue in her cheek. "Why were you floating? Like, how did you do that?"

"I don't remember," said Daisy. She pulled the hair off her cheeks and gathered it into a knot at the top of her head. "I don't remember what happened. I just remember the feeling. God, it's like paradise, floating like that. I wish I remembered how I did it. I'd do it again."

"If I walk into school tomorrow and find you floating around the ceiling, I swear to God, I'm getting a broom," said Jing. "I'm literally going to bash you out of the rafters, you hear? And then I'm going to stab you sixty times with a pencil and leave your buoyant ass in a dumpster somewhere. No more fucking floating. Particularly when you're alone. I'm putting a ban on floating."

"Don't be mean, Jing," said Yates. "Only ban, like, public floating. If we're all there, maybe we could make it safe. We got her down, didn't we? I don't know. A Daisy balloon could make for a stellar party trick."

Jing sighed, and her bristling gave way to thought. "You know, you might be right. But still, it's banned unless we vote on it. All in favor?"

Yates and I mumbled agreement.

Daisy snorted, stretched her arms above her head. "Let's just go home."

"Agreed," said Yates. She toyed with the rips in my jeans, plucked the threads like strings on an instrument.

Jing revved the engine and rolled out of the lot, away from Delacroix House. I leaned my forehead on the window. Yates pulled herself off my lap, and I pretended it didn't make me feel a little lonely. There weren't any stars above us. The car vibrations drilled my temple, and I shifted, tried to find a place where I was comfortable.

I don't think cars are ever going to be comfortable again.

Especially not now that it's dark.

Daisy twisted in her seat so that she could leer at Yates and me. She wagged her eyebrows. "I don't regret anything. Tonight was awesome. I'm fucking pleased. We need to do more shit like this. The four of us are special. We make things happen. Even if you didn't find your books, we proved we can make magic on our own. The party wasn't some fluke. You know what? I say we find some place, hold another party Friday night. We can pull out all the big guns. Scare the fuck out of the whole student body. We're gonna be legends. They'll talk about us forever."

"You think so?" Jing slapped her dashboard, and her radio

flickered on. "We'll start planning as soon as we think of a protection spell for the four of us. We brought Daze down. We should be fine without the book. We're naturals. Speaking of . . . hey, Daisy, find something to fucking listen to. I hate driving without music."

"Yeah, yeah." Daisy turned away from us to fiddle with the radio. After three stations of staticky ads, she reached for the AUX cord and sent us all back into sleazy pop hell, which I'd protest, if I had the energy.

"Hey, Daze," said Yates, scooting forward in her seat. "That choker is pretty."

"Oh?" Daisy's hand flew to her throat, and a grin broke over her face. The choker in question was a thin strip of velvet, from which a little silver pendant dangled like a grape. I hadn't noticed it before. Daisy gave it a pat. "It's new. I think it suits me."

"Daisy fucking Brink, tell me you didn't steal a damn necklace from the Delacroix House." Jing rolled her shoulders and curled her lip into a smile. "You are such a prick."

"I didn't steal anything," Daisy said indignantly. She scrunched up her nose. "It's mine. Can't steal what belongs to you."

"I mean, sure, it belongs to you now. But it didn't ten minutes ago. I'm right, aren't I?" Jing snorted. "I don't know if I should clap you on the back or knock you upside your head."

"It's not stealing if your name is on it." Daisy ran her fingertips over her pendant and lolled back her head, fluttered her lashes. Her face was serene. Her serenity was anxiety inducing. "My name was on it. It's mine."

"Shut up," said Jing. "No way."

Daisy popped fresh bubblegum between her teeth and leaned back, stretching her neck so that Yates could examine the pendant. Yates reached for it and scooted closer, brought her nose to the smooth metal. She furrowed her brows. "Sideways. Flashlight, please."

God. I groped at my phone and shone the light at Daisy's throat. It cast shadows when she swallowed. Vampire vision.

Yates tilted her head, narrowed her eyes, brushed the velvety fabric with her thumb. "She's half right," she said. "It says Daisy. Daisy Stringer. You're Daisy Brink. Doesn't really work, sweetie."

"My mother's name was Daisy Stringer. So, it's mine." Her eyes glistered, and I understood. All my arteries filled with the understanding, the link we had now. It was like iron.

If I focused on Daisy, it almost wasn't like I was in the back of a car in the dark in the woods. If I looked at Daisy, I'd be fine. Daisy who was like me.

I cleared my throat. It was filled with nothing, but still felt gunky. Nerves made my whole body feel grimy thick. "How'd she die?"

"Vicodin overdose." The car fell silent, but Daisy looked at me long and hard, and something magnetized between us. Yates tensed up. Jing's eyes flashed in the rearview mirror. Daisy blew a bubble. "Yours?"

"Train crash," I said.

Daisy nodded. "Helluva way to go. Flashier, but less bored

housewife. Was she a bored housewife? Mine was."

"No." I paused, made myself think for a second. What had she actually done for a living? My mom often went off to work, but I couldn't for the life of me remember what exactly that work *was*. She saw customers, and she complained about them sometimes, told me coy little stories about who did what that day. But not what her job was. I shrugged. "She was a salesperson. She would've been a really bad housewife. She wasn't even a wife to begin with."

"You two can borrow my mom," said Yates as she fiddled with the hem of her skirt. "She's a professor of Molecular Physics. She's boring, but I love her. And she's, you know, alive."

"Mrs. Yates is a hell of a woman. I fucked her good last Tuesday. We're getting married after I graduate and moving to Paris. Delicious," said Jing. Her eyes flashed up, and the crooked smile fell off her face.

Out of the corner of my eye, I saw the red-blue flashing. My guts wound up in knots.

"Shit," Jing said, and she spun the wheel, pulling the car to the side of the road. The car rolled to a stop, and she killed the radio, letting us all sit in hovering silence.

Jing fixed her hair in the mirror, fluffing bangs and smoothing flyaway. "Daisy Brink, if you say a single word, I will personally hand feed tiny pieces of you to Yates' Yorkie-poo." When she deemed herself to look appropriate, she rolled down the window and beamed at the approaching officer. Her lashes batted like a butterfly caught in a web.

The officer, a pale white man, swaggered over to Jing's car. He smiled at us as he approached. He was tall, broad, but very trim, and the way he walked suggested something predatory, something purposeful. They were hunter's steps. I'd seen the likes of those steps before.

"Oh, God. He's not a traffic cop," said Yates, who pressed her nose to the back window. "That's a sheriff's car. Jing, why would a sheriff want to talk to us?" She shrank in her seat, wrapped her fingers around her knobby knees. "God, he has the hat and everything. I hate the hat."

"Hush," I said. I swept my fingertips over Yates' forearm. Jing was hot. Jing would be able to flirt her way out of this. I told myself how hot Jing was like a chant, and I made myself hold still against the seat behind me.

"Good evening, ladies. It's a bit late for a cruise, don't you think?" The sheriff bent over, peering inside Jing's convertible as though he thought he might find something. His blue eyes scanned back and forth—blue, ridiculously blue, blue like rat poison—and I felt them trace my shape for a moment. He showed us his teeth, which was meant to be charming, but wasn't.

"Oh, we're driving home from dinner." Jing dimpled, and she pushed a lock of hair behind her ear. "Is there a problem, sir? Anything we can help you with?" I hadn't ever heard Jing use that tone of voice. It was thicker than any customer service voice I'd ever heard. It was coquettish, sweeter and more viscous than cough syrup. I had a toothache by proxy. My jaws ached. I made myself unclench them.

"There's been strange activity around these parts lately. We've been doing random stops to see if we can gather any information. Have you ladies seen anything unusual?" He swept his eyes around the car again, and I made myself stare at my shoes. I didn't like him. I didn't really care for cops, or anyone with too much authority, but there was something particularly off with this fuck. Had he blinked yet?

"Nothing unusual, sir. We haven't even seen any deer this evening. Sorry if that doesn't help much." Jing stuck out her bottom lip, a distinctly Daisy-ish expression, and I wanted to smother everyone with a pillow. Seeing Jing like this was as impressive as it was nauseating. I genuinely felt queasy. There was bile in the back of my throat.

"Not a problem at all, miss. I'd rather you not see anything and be safe than the other way around. You ladies drive home safely, alright?" He patted Jing's wrist and turned away, straightening himself back up to full height. He walked back toward his car, and the four of us collectively exhaled.

"I just died a little." Jing threw back her head and whistled, eyes popped wide as coins. "I thought he was pulling me over because he recognized my license plate. Oh. My God. That could've been so many kinds of bad."

"Why would he have recognized your plates?" I coughed until I smiled, and the smile turned into my infamous nervous laugh. The bile taste was overwhelming. I swallowed it, muffled myself with the back of my hand. Was I going to have a panic attack in this convertible? Likely.

"Uh, because I'm into drag racing and I haven't paid a fine

in my life," Jing said matter-of-factly.

My laughter pounded out harder. I clutched at my sides and howled. I mashed my forehead against Daisy's headrest and laughed until I couldn't breathe, then I bit my tongue, forced myself to stop. My lungs weren't deflating. My head swam with little lights.

"That could've been bad," said Daisy. There was an odd look on her face. I couldn't place it. Her mouth shaped an inverted rainbow, and her eyes were bright as July. "Did you catch the name on his tag?"

"No." Jing creased her brows. "Why would that even matter?"

"Because his tag said *E. Chantry,*" Daisy said. She turned the radio back on. She switched songs, skipping a tame breakup ballad in favor of a raunchy clubbing track. She opened her mouth and sang. She danced in her seat, twisting and snaking and rolling her wrists, and she shouted each profane lyric like she was chanting for cheer. The pendant drifted in the hollow of her throat, never quite resting where gravity commanded.

# FOURTEEN

# THINGS THAT SPREAD LIKE WILDFIRE

We had a hell of a time thinking of protective sigils that didn't feel stupid. The four of us sat in a circle scribbling on pieces of paper until it was so late that Yates nearly fell asleep sitting up. Jing was determined to make a spell tonight, though, and so we shook Yates awake and focused harder on the computer paper, like that would make it any easier to think of something succinct and potent and powerful and honest.

I shoved my paper under my bed for a moment, because looking at my scratched-out ideas was making my stomach hurt. It already hurt. It and my lungs were worn ragged from the ride home, and the nerves didn't just ice themselves when I got out of the car. They were still here. Still with me.

Under the bed, the piece of paper swam with ink. Lines bubbled up in the pulp, made neat little arcs, clean lines, soft loops. A few phrases unfurled below the blooming shapes, emerged letter by letter on the center of the page. The three of them didn't notice, busy drawing and cussing and yawning and shoving each other, but I couldn't tear my eyes away.

The sigil that had drawn itself had given itself a little signature.

*Keep the incantation. This should hold for a little while, I think. All my best. Keep safe.*
*—Your friend, S*

I didn't tell them about the signature. I didn't tell them that I felt like I was going insane. But I did tell them about the sigil, that I'd thought of something that would maybe work.

We drew what Mr. Scratch had given us, spoke an invocation, and rode out the rise and crash that magic brings. It felt appropriately staticky and it ached the right amount. We were satisfied. Jing took everybody home.

All the while, I felt my eyes flicker to the corner of my bed, to the dark space just beneath. I thought I might see movement. I caught an inky smell.

✳

I dreamed about Mr. Scratch that night. My brain couldn't pick a singular face for it. Him? Her? Them? Fucking zir? It was a Mr., so I guess he/him would do. Anyway, I tried to put a shape to what he looked like. I stole masks off Hollywood slashers and internet creeps, hollow eyes and long pale faces, double-wide grins with yellow teeth. Horns and scales and slimy bits. Hooves and a barbed tail. I made it look like a relatable monster. A boogeyman I understood was less intimidating than some shapeless indescribable monster.

What had it really looked like? What on earth had I done?

I dreamed it had crawled inside my backpack and devoured both of my spell books. I pictured it wriggling around in my drawers like a slick black eel, awaiting reaching fingertips to gnash on. I imagined it hiding in the darkness under my covers, curling up beside me with its fluid, massless body. I made myself bolt my closet with a chair before I went to bed. I shut my blinds, locked my door.

But it'd helped me, hadn't it?

It'd helped keep me safe.

I woke up without prompting. It was dark outside, nighttime dark, and my arms and legs were tangled in three different blankets. My hair clung to my face like an itchy scarf. Across the room at eye level, glowing red, was my alarm clock. I really, truly hated my alarm clock. It was going to scream like a nuclear microwave in T-minus two minutes. Six thirty in the damn morning. Who thought it should be legal to make a bunch of teenagers do algebra after waking up at six thirty in the morning? A significant part of me wanted to throw things at my alarm until it broke. That way I could sleep forever, and Julian and Boris wouldn't make me go to school.

But they totally would make me go to school. Also, I recalled my imagination's warped rendition of what Mr. Scratch might look like, and the thought made school sound almost appealing.

I dripped off my bed and onto the floor and laid there for a second, relishing the cold hardwood against my back. That is, where I could feel the cold hardwood. There was something else under my back, and I wasn't quite sure what it was. In a room like mine, there's never a decent way to tell. I heaved myself upright, peeled something that didn't smell like death off the floor, and threw it on.

What I'd peeled up turned out to be an enormous sweater that had belonged to Boris, once upon a time. It was a black cable-knit riddled with gashes, and the sweater paws it provided me were divine. I was swimming in a wooly Shangri-la. No matter that it was kinda sticky and smelled a little sour. Everything was beautiful and nothing hurt, or something like that. I found a pair of jeans and wrangled them on.

I grabbed my school bag, slung it over one shoulder, and wandered into the bathroom. I splashed my face, scrubbed my teeth, ran cheap liner around my eyes. I tried not to look too closely. I wasn't a fan of mirrors. I avoided them whenever possible. Mirrors meant looking at myself, and I hated my face, because it wasn't mine. When I was little, I would pretend my reflection was my mother, alive again in a smaller body. We've always looked startlingly similar. Julian used to say so all the time, before he knew what it did to me. He almost never talked about her, but he would say that much. *You and Lenora could've been twins,* he'd say. *If you miss her, look in a mirror.* Biology is a strange, uncanny thing. Mirrors scratched the scar tissue off old wounds. I'd see her eyes again, her cheeks and jaw, her nose, and the curve of her mouth. Now the wounds are past picking, but it still reminds me that they're there in the first place.

I am not worthy of her bone structure.

It was too early for fucking angst.

I scribbled my eyeliner on a little thicker and headed toward the kitchen. That's where Julian usually was, and it always smelled utopic when he was there. He liked nursing sauces and simmering fragrant stews and doting on soups for hours on end. He woke up at six every morning to make coffee and breakfast and drive me to school, because he's a stupidly good person, I guess. This morning wasn't any different. He was already dressed, looking like a Gorey sketch come to life, flipping crepes and sipping tar-black coffee out of a moon-shaped mug. He didn't look up, but he glanced at me out of the corner of his eye, and I found myself wandering to his side.

"G'morning." I pressed my forehead into his side, which was my non-sappy way of giving him a hug. "Food smells delicious, Dad. Thanks for that."

"Good morning, Lamb." He took another sip of his coffee and furrowed his brows. "Did you have a good outing last night? Did you talk them into lending you another volume or two?"

"It was . . ." I hesitated, yanked on a lock of my hair. "It was a night, that's for sure."

"Oh. That doesn't sound good. I'm sorry about that, then. Well, I made crepes. And blueberry sauce, but I'm afraid it isn't sweet enough. There's ricotta for them, too. I figured you could wrap it up like a burrito and carry it with you. Portable breakfast. Oh. There's coffee. It's Boris coffee, though, so it's flavored. He's a weirdo. Sorry about that."

"I like flavored coffee." I frowned. "You like coffee to taste like coal. I like it to taste like hazelnuts. Which one of us is the weirdo?"

"Still you. You look like an angry panda." He smiled at me, flipped a third crepe. "Did you do all of your homework?"

"Yes," I lied. But that's what first period study hall was for. That, and dicking around while teachers weren't watching. "Do you have anything cool planned for today?"

"Do I ever?" He turned off the stove and moved his pan off the heat. "So. New friends. That's good. I don't know if I've ever seen them around before. Are they in Drama with you?"

"Nah. I don't think they're into it." Admittedly, given Jing's sheriff-schmoozing skills, she'd probably kick ass where that club was concerned. We don't exactly have a lot of killer talent in our little band, passionate though we may be. "I think I'll be hanging out with them a lot, actually. We're going to make a coven."

*Coven.* Why was that word so sexy?

"Interesting." He nodded, and his eyes creased, which was the Julian equivalent of a raucous grin. "How do you make a coven?"

"I don't know." I shrugged and spooned liquid blueberries over a crepe that smelled like God. The syrup on the spoon stained my fingertips, just a shade bluer than the bruises on my knuckles. That douchebag's face sure did leave an odd impression on my hands. Robin's-egg knuckles. I whistled through my tooth gap. "Thanks, Dad."

"I hope it all works out. This town could use a proper girl gang. Too many meathead jocks prowling around and terrorizing establishments for my liking." He frowned and downed the rest of his coffee. "You could have matching jackets. It'd be very cool."

A crooked little smile found my mouth. Julian said "cool" like most people said "laundry." He had the inflection range of an air conditioner. I elbowed him as I crossed behind him and moved to make myself a cup of coffee, which I relished. I should be prescribed coffee. I needed it in an IV drip.

"I'm not surprised you didn't have much luck at Delacroix. They're loyal customers of ours, and they have the most beautiful art galleries, but they seldom share their toys. They wouldn't even let us bid until we mentioned that our daughter would love it, and then suddenly they were willing to sell. How odd is that? Cheap, too. A book that lovingly bound should have gone for at least seventy-five dollars. We bought it for ten. Bizarre, no?" He drizzled blueberries on a crepe and rolled it up, sprinkled it with powdered sugar. "We'll try and find you one at the next auction. Normally they have another one closer to New Year's, and we can go then. You could come, if you don't think you'll be bored to death. I think I might be the only person in the universe who genuinely enjoys auctions. Even Boris doesn't like them. Boris just likes seeing artifacts and oddities, but once the paperwork comes out, he gets cold feet. Oh, *Boris*." He thoughtfully took a bite.

Oh, *Boris*. Ick. They were as mortifying as they were endearing.

"I'd like that." Assuming they didn't recognize me and not sell to me on principle. I sighed and chugged my coffee, successfully scalding off all my taste buds in the process. "They said the books were in the archives, but they wouldn't show us the archives because the manager wasn't there."

"Maurice is a good man. If we lived closer, I think we might be friends. I see him whenever Boris and I go to Dorothy's." He nodded toward the door, plucked his keys off the countertop. "You ready to go?"

Saw him at Dorothy's, eh? Dorothy's was a gay bar about five miles out of town. I'd go myself with my fake ID if I wasn't terrified I'd run into my parents inside. Even though I was pissed at Maurice for not being where I needed him to be, that somehow made me almost like Maurice, or at least the abstract idea of him. Maybe I could go back, explain how important these books are to me. Maybe they belonged to him, and him giving the book to me would mean I could read them. Fat chance.

Whatever. "Yeah, I'm ready."

"Good." Julian waited for a moment, eyeing the coffeepot. "Should I unplug it? I don't want a fire to start while we're gone. But then it'll be cold, and Boris won't drink it. Oh God."

"There won't be a fire," I said. I wolfed down my crepe and rubbed my mouth with the back of my wrist. "That was delicious, by the way."

"Oh, was it? I was afraid it was bland. The recipe never turns out the way I had it in my head. I like crepes to be thinner than air . . ." He trailed off and meandered in the direction of the door. "Come along. I'd hate for you to be late."

The wall clock, which was five minutes fast, said we had a half an hour until school started. We lived ten minutes away. I wasn't awake enough yet to harp on him for it, though. I trudged behind him, stopping only to grab my boots along the way.

✳

So, my school is repulsive. It's a crumbling mass of rats and rusty lockers. There was supposed to be a new high school three years ago, what with the asbestos problem and all, but the funding always ran dry before it could get anywhere. No doubt we'll all die in West High. It was like a Venus flytrap for happiness. I walked toward the main doors alongside my emotionally anemic peers and, like them, considered turning around and running as quickly as I could in the opposite direction. But I didn't. I skulked my way inside and shouldered through clumps of denim-clad teenagers, pushing and shoving a path to my locker. I wished that I was as cool as Madeline had been at the party. She'd spliced crowds like it was her profession.

The hallways smelled like weed. This was normal. All the vents in the building looped back to the girl's bathroom, which proved a blessing for the West High stoner population and a curse for the administration. If someone smokes early in the morning and blows little cannabis rings into the air vent, the smell permeates the entire school, and then everyone else can smoke as they please with no fear of being caught. Basic part of West High hazing, actually. Someone has to be the first to light up.

My locker was between Mikayla's locker and Hotaru's locker. Hotaru was nice enough, and she had the courtesy to be habitually tardy. We never had to brawl over elbow space. Both of us got on better that way. Besides, it wasn't fair to fight with Hotaru, because it's hard to fight with anyone that blissed out. Mikayla, on the other hand, could be problematic. She always managed to arrive within three minutes of me, and she didn't grab her shit and leave like a normal human being. No, she had to linger in her locker and play with an ancient Tamagotchi until first bell. Our lockers are too skinny for this shit. I never have enough room.

Sure enough. Mikayla. I could always tell it was Mikayla from across the hall, because her egg-shaped head makes her look like an alien. A weird, pasty Tamagotchi-worshiping alien. I soldiered over to my locker and took care not to bump her as I opened it. For as stringy as Mikayla looked, it was no secret that she (along with the rest of the field hockey team) had curb stomped our rival team's star player before a game last year. That was a little too much even for me. Not today. I hauled a few textbooks out of my locker and dropped them in my bag. It was like stuffing my bag with bricks. I slung it back over my shoulders and reeled forward, sucked in a breath. Would it kill the school district to order lighter books?

I turned around and wandered in the direction of my study hall. Study hall was in the cafeteria, the other side of school from where I was now. It would be a damn long walk from here to there. I popped in my earbuds, cranked up my music, and headed toward class with anesthetizing shoegaze crashing around my head.

The cafeteria was still mostly empty, save for two JV cheerleaders and Austin fucking Grass. They stood huddled together, snickering and squealing, heads angled toward the floor. Sequined hairbows bobbed. Austin laughed loud enough that I heard it over my music. There was a heather-yellow shadow on Austin's nose that stretched from one cheek across the other. He'd slapped a flesh-toned Band-Aid across the center of the bruise bloom for some reason, and, much to my amusement, his un-fucked-up skin was the same damn color as the Barbie-plastic bandage. My hand thrummed sympathetically.

Curiosity possessed me, and I turned off my music, kept my earbuds in.

"Oh my God. Like, ew! Why are there roaches? This is a cafeteria. Isn't there, like, a health inspector or something?" One of the JV girls, wearing her hair in a distinctly Daisy-inspired style, bounced in her sneakers as if the roach was about to rear back like a cobra and bite her. "God, Austin. I'm literally gonna hurl."

"Isn't that the cheer squad's favorite diet plan?" Austin laughed in the back of his throat. "It's just a little roach. Look at it, wriggling around on its back like that. Looks like one of your squad girls, am I right?"

"God, Austin, you're awful," giggled the other JV girl. She touched his arm, leaned her head against his chest. "Are you sure you're okay? It's pretty screwed up that Ethan threw a football at your face. Like, you should kick his ass. He totally did it on purpose."

"Oh, he probably did. It's chill, though. I screwed his girlfriend, so we're even." He stretched his arms over his head and yawned. "If you ladies want proper revenge, though, I could always make him eat this here cockroach. Oughta teach him."

I painted an image in my mind of my boots on Austin's neck.

Wait. Opportunity. I stood up a little straighter, squared my shoulders, thrust out my chin. I took a few wide strides and shouldered my way through the group, taking care to shove Austin in the process. Slowly, deliberately, I leaned down and plucked up the roach by one of its legs, cupped it in my hands.

"Oh my God!" squeaked the girl to my right.

"Oh, come on, fresh meat. You two best get used to roaches around here." I gave them a wolf grin and turned around, beaming up at Austin, who looked petrified. "Good morning, Grass."

"Austin," said the girl to my left.

Austin said nothing. He froze like a tiny gazelle in a lion's path. Hadn't he heard that the whole freezing thing doesn't work? I licked my teeth, waggled my brows, rose onto my tiptoes, and tenderly dropped the roach down the front of his shirt.

He balked, squealed, and flailed his hands around his torso.

Fucking loser.

I nodded to the girls and walked away, over to the hand-sanitizer dispenser fixed on the far wall. Austin cussed and writhed behind me. One of the JV girls was laughing, and I felt radiant. I squirted a dollop of hand sanitizer on my hands and rubbed away until my skin felt tacky and gross, which meant it was working, I think. I doubled back and took a seat close to the fray.

Other people were drifting in, chatting and moaning, creeping toward the greasy benches with sleep still on their faces. I paid them no mind. I didn't have any friends in study hall since Mickey-Dick was almost always a solid forty minutes late to school, and we were really more like acquaintances, so I wasn't sure if I minded that much. It did mean I was more likely to use study hall to actually get work done. Or sleep. Whatever. I swung my bag onto the table and ferreted around for my algebra homework.

Fucking sentence problems.

> Joaquin is interested in buying a gym membership. Fitness Fun has an initiation fee of $100, with additional payments of $25 per month. The Happy Health Hut has an initiation fee of $150, with additional payments of $15 per month. If Joaquin wants to keep a membership for a year, which membership is a better deal? Show your work with an equation and a graph!

I stared at the problem for a moment and felt my eyes

glaze over. I didn't know what was more painful, names like Fitness Fun and The Happy Health Hut, or the inevitable butchering of a name like Joaquin in class. My math teacher wasn't exactly good at pronouncing names that weren't Megan or Tom. We've been in school over two months and he still couldn't grasp that Alexis Nguyen's last name wasn't pronounced *na-goo-yen*.

Thank God he only graded for completion.

I drew two lines at random on the graph paper. Joaquin should go to Fitness Fun, not because it's cheaper, but because going to a gym called The Happy Health Hut would literally be worse than death. I BSed my way through an equation and crept through the rest of the worksheet, barely skimming each question, writing down random numbers where it felt appropriate. My math teacher seldom did more than flip through the pages and scan for handwriting. This should be more than enough.

Something hit the back of my head.

What the hell?

I pawed at my curls and found something crinkly. I tugged it out of my hair and set it on the table, eyeing it before I opened it. Violently pink paper, pink as Hello Kitty hell. Definitely not from Austin Grass. I uncrinkled it, spread it flat across the tabletop.

> *Hey sexy. Guess who. Also, your hair looks fucking weird today. It's like you're wearing a Persian cat for a wig.*

The scribe dotted her *i*'s with hearts.

I turned my head, and Daisy Brink glowered back from two tables behind me. She waggled her fingers at me, half waving, half spooky spirit-fingering. I caught myself smirking and turned back around, scribbled a line beneath hers.

> *Did you see Austin's face? Classic.*

I crushed the note back up and tossed it back.
Seconds later, the little ball hurtled back.

> *He looks so much better like that. He's telling everyone that you worship Satan and have a voodoo doll of him in your locker. People are believing it, too, after that party. Should I confirm or deny? XOXOX*

I snickered, muffled my mouth with the palm of my hand.

> *Surprise me. Are we pretending that you're not doing witch shit too?*

I made eye contact with one of the custodians as I tossed the note back to Daisy. He winked, went back to absently sweeping. Ricky the custodian was a good guy. He and I got on. He wasn't going to rat on us.

> *Texted Jing. She's down with us all coming out of the witch closet. I'm about to scare the living fuck out of Austin. Prepare to die laughing.*

I glanced out of the corner of my eye toward Austin's table, where he sat with the JV girls and some jock asshole whose name I couldn't remember. I couldn't see Daisy from this angle, but I did see a piece of pink paper sail toward his table.

He smirked, elbowed his guy friend, and unfolded the paper. His smirk fell away. "What the *fuck?*"

"Language, Mr. Grass," said the overseeing teacher, looking up from her laptop long enough to stare razors toward Austin's table. "Study hall is silent. No talking."

"Sure thing," said the boy beside Austin. He looked pleased. Austin, however, did not look pleased. He gawked down at the page and stared at Daisy behind me, and then turned his gaze at me, his eyes the size of his fists.

*What the hell did you write?*

I tossed the paper back at Daisy, literally snagging my tongue between my teeth to keep from laughing.

*I told him that he only lasted three minutes with his girlfriend because we hexed his cock. Good guess, right?*

As predicted, I died. I put my head on my algebra book and broke into laughter. My sides shook. My diaphragm burned. My sweater's stickiness felt like it might be squirming around. I chose not to think about that too deeply.

"Is there a problem, Ms. Pike?" I felt the overseer's eyes on my back like they were made of pokers.

"Oh, man. It's just this algebra homework. Good stuff." I raised one of my thumbs and held my breath, tried to beat my laughter into submission.

Overhead, the bell rung thrice.

I pulled myself upright, stuffed my homework into my bag and chucked the bag back onto my shoulders. The lunch tables groaned as everyone moved. A rat scurried across the floor, eliciting scattered curses and squawking from the students in a five-foot radius. I rolled my neck, strolled toward my next class.

Daisy caught up to me. She wrapped her arm around my shoulder and leaned up on tiptoe to kiss my cheek, and I felt myself turn red. I grinned like mad. She skittered her nails over my shoulder, which was affectionate, I think.

"That party is literally part of the school mythos now." She locked step with me and swept her eyes across the crowd, meeting everyone's gaze, beaming at them. "Everyone who's everyone knows. For real. Three girls asked me this morning how we did it. They're all so fucking thrilled, but not half as thrilled as I am. This weekend should be killer. We need something fucking big for it, you hear? And it's closer to Halloween, so we can up the creepy factor without being tacky. It's gonna be sublime."

"Are we going to have it at Jing's again?" Tentatively, I moved my arm around her waist, moving slowly enough to catch it if she protested. She didn't. I let myself relax. Walking through the halls with Daisy Brink on my arm, even platonically, was like wearing an invincibility star. I felt like a rock star, or maybe a cult leader. Her hair smelled like strawberries and cream.

A couple of people shot us nasty looks. I was used it, but the looks weren't directed at me, per se. They were a little to my left.

Had anybody ever looked at Daisy with disdain like that?

Was I contagious, or something?

"Nah. Her folks are back in town. We're scoping out a new location, something private." She fooled with a hole in my sweater, seemingly oblivious to the gazes of lesser mortals. "I have a few places in mind. When we have it narrowed down, we'll let you know. It'd be sick if we could set up all the sigils and stuff before the party so that we could get down to business quicker. Waiting around isn't hot. What class are you going to?"

"Math." I grimaced. "You?"

"History." She rolled her eyes. "It's so fucking bogus, you know?"

Math and History were in the same hallway, for some godforsaken reason, which gave us a few extra seconds of walking together. I leered at someone who gawked too long, defensive even if Daisy wasn't. "Not a fan?"

"You kidding? I fucking love history. When I go to university next year, I'm taking Classics as a double major with prelaw. Veni, vidi, vici, bitch." She yanked a piece of yarn out of my sweater and twisted it around her finger, cringed when it stained her finger Sharpie black. "The teacher just isn't on my level, that's all."

Huh. Wouldn't have guessed. We neared my class, and she unhooked herself from me and blew me a kiss. I dodged my feelings by flipping her off, and we nodded at each other before we split. I pushed my way through the door.

The bell rang before I was in my seat.

"Late," said the teacher.

"Bite me. I'm here, aren't I?" I took a seat toward the back of class and pulled my homework out, smoothed it flat, smiled as if to say, *Screw you, sir.*

The teacher blinked. He coughed once and stared at his computer screen. "Roll call."

I felt my mind leave my body as he went down the list.

"Eloise Pike?"

I rubbed my temples. "It's Sideways."

"Sideways isn't a name," he said. His brow winkled up like a shar-pei's.

Alexis, sitting beside me, piped up. "Literally everyone calls her Sideways. Everyone. Her name is Sideways."

"Why would you go by *Sideways?*" He grimaced, looking between Alexis and me like we were twin bugs.

"It's because I'm not straight." I shot gun hands at him.

He blanched and returned to roll call.

Alexis held out her fist for me to bump. I obliged.

Holy shit. Is this what being recognized as a human being by your peers is like? This was not bad at all.

Directly behind me, I felt the jab of a pencil eraser. It butted against my spine insistently, tap-tap-tap, like a stupid rubber woodpecker. I chanced a glance over my shoulder, and there was Mickey-Dick, teal green undercut and all. His eyes looked sleep chapped behind his glasses. Crusty.

I mouthed, *What gives?*

He leaned forward far enough that his nose was stuck in the curls above my ear. Hot breath, dank with last night's weed and something sweet. "Saw you with Daisy Brink this morning."

"Yeah? What of it?"

His voice dropped a few steps, ground out between his molars. "She's a total bitch, Sideways. Since when do you hang out with breeders, anyway? She's bad news, she and her friends. You're so much cooler than them. What the fuck are you doing?"

The spit in my mouth tasted mildewed all of a sudden. I scraped at my tongue with my teeth. "You know that's sexist bullshit, right, man?"

"Don't be like that." Mickey-Dick shifted around, arranged his elbows on the desk, propping himself on the nearest edge so that his whole torso stretched over his notebook and homework and secret little gaming console. "She's straight, Sideways. I'm looking out for you."

"I can't recall asking you to look out for me, funnily enough. Fuck off for a while, yeah?"

The teacher clasped his hands together, and I used it as an excuse not to look at Mickey-Dick, or Alexis (who was definitely watching), or at anything at all. I glared into the middle distance and felt a wobble of nebulous doubt cloud my gut. "Everyone hand your homework to the front. Today, we're learning about the quadratic equation. I've prepared a PowerPoint. Take notes, please."

# FIFTEEN

# REMEMBER THAT EDUCATION IS GOOD FOR YOU

By fifth period, I was officially numb to any attempts to teach me. This was mostly because fifth period was English, which I usually enjoyed, but we were spending the period reading *Frankenstein*. I've read *Frankenstein*—Julian loves him some Shelley—so the reading period was essentially Study Hall 2.0. Before this weekend, I would've spent class passing notes back and forth with Mickey-Dick, but I was still pissed at him. And besides, more pressing matters demanded my attention.

I hauled out volume two of the *VMM* and thunked it on my desk. It was a conspicuous book, but now that my village witch status had ascended into canon law, being flashy sort of worked. I relished the stares and delved in.

It was more straightforward than volume one. The chapters were mostly chronological, and while the ink flowed in and out of focus, the pages stayed the same no matter how many times I opened it. This book was blissfully honest. For each basic enchantment, there were four or five different sigils or runes, each describing different ways the enchantment is commonly performed. Some of the methods were opposites of each other, and there weren't connective threads to link them together. The only concrete advice offered at the bottom of each page was that combining favored elements and adding a few personal touches was the best way to ensure results. In other words, if I directly used a sigil from the book, I'd damn well better make up my own incantation, or it'd be as good as wet matches.

I found the levitation page again.

Yates was right. Flight magic really would be a good party trick. Making sure it was safe was one thing, but it looked doable. Floating people a few feet above the ground should be manageable, particularly if they held still. The real difficulty was apparently in actual flight. According to the book, flying like a bird over town would take considerable power and incantation levels beyond what the book could provide. But lifting a small group of people should be possible if everyone participated in the incantation, and one person stayed on the ground to manage the ordeal.

I shoved back thoughts about how this might be the last fucking spell book I ever got, about how the other volumes in the collection were completely uninterested in me, about how I wasn't half as special as I thought I was. I couldn't afford to think about that.

This party was going to be wicked.

I pulled out a piece of scrap paper and jotted down a few shapes that spoke to me. One sigil was made of interlocking crescent moons, joined with arrows and quills, and it was supremely cool. I copied it as best I could and closed my book, slipped it back into my bag.

The bell rang and everyone stood up. I folded the paper and stashed it in my bra, rising with the rest of the class. We jumbled out through the door in a mob.

✳

The cafeteria was packed to bursting. The lunch line snaked halfway down the hall and then wound back around, and word was that the kitchen had already run out of all the food that wasn't gluey pizza. Bless Julian, for real. He was petrified of the whole rat/roaches situation we were in, so he made it a point of packing me a lunch every day. I didn't know exactly what he'd packed today, but it was undoubtedly better than gluey pizza.

Spotting the girls in the mass of people was trickier than I thought it would be. The room was sweltering, garbled with distorted conversation and the clatter of trays, and picking faces out of the sea wasn't something I was used to. I mean, there were days when I ate in the library so I wouldn't have to find people to sit with.

The first thing I spotted was Yates' cat-shaped backpack. It was holographic and covered with little floral stickers. I couldn't think of many people besides Yates who would be able to make it look cool. I weaved between tables and sat beside her.

Daisy and Jing were playing "Miss Susie Had a

Steamboat." Their hands flew so fast I could barely track them, and Yates chanted the song as she filmed them playing. Some of the lyrics were different than I remembered them. "Flies are in the meadow. Bees are in the park. Miss Susie and your boyfriend are fucking in the d-a-r-k, dark dark dark dark." Yates paused the filming and clicked her tongue. "Twenty-four seconds. Again."

"Fuck," Jing hissed. She slapped the table with her hand. "Daisy, you're too slow."

"Am not," she said. She tugged on one of her ringlets. "I'm perfect. You're slow."

"Faster than I could go." I pulled out my thermos and opened it. Bless Julian's soul. It was mac and cheese. I stabbed a forkful and stuffed it in my mouth. My eyes rolled up in my head.

"That smells orgasmic," said Jing. She peered over the table at my lunch, reached her own fork toward my thermos.

I batted at her hand. "Get away, vulture." I crinkled my nose and ate another bite, feeling smug.

Jing had packed her lunch as well. It was, as far as I could tell, scrambled eggs with chucks of tomato mixed in. She saw me looking and shrugged. "It's better warm," she said.

"So. The next party." I pulled the paper out of my bra and thrust it toward Jing. "I have a hell of an idea."

She picked up the page and scanned it, lifted a quizzical brow.

"Turns out that it's not all that hard to make three people levitate. Not a lot, but a few feet off the floor. I mean, we'd all have to chant, and it'll take a while to draw the sigil, but if the next party is somewhere where we could draw on the floor ahead of time, then it wouldn't be too much work, and I think we could float you three for a minute or two. It'd be sick."

Jing cocked her head to the side. "If we pull it off, it'd be amazing. It'll look good on camera, too. More convincing for people who weren't there." She eyed the page, lined the sigil with her thumb. "You've got my vote. Ladies?"

"Hell yes," said Daisy.

"Um," said Yates.

"Um? Why um? You were game last night." Jing leaned across the table and poked Yates' arm. "If you've got doubts, speak 'em."

"Um, I don't want to float away like a balloon, that's what," she said with a frown. "Like, is there a foolproof way we could reverse it? I agree, it'd be really cool. And everyone would remember. And fame and glory, I get it. But I'm not sold until I know that we're not floating to the moon."

"Floating to the moon sounds cool," said Daisy.

"The details are in the incantation. We can set it up so that you levitate a good four feet off the ground, stay there for a second, then drift back down." I scrunched my brows together, took another bite. "It's pretty safe, all things considered. I don't know what Daisy did. Like, there wasn't a sigil, and if she cast an incantation, she doesn't remember it now. Right, Daisy?"

"Right," she agreed.

"So that means the circumstances were different. Daisy hit

a weird spike of magic. I guess it's like what happened at the last party. I don't know how that happened. But we should have more control over this." I finished up my food and took a swig of water. I was only half lying. I mean, *technically*, I was right. The spell *should* work. But then again, it was magic, and magic didn't always abide by rules.

"So. Yates. Verdict time." Daisy clucked her tongue.

Yates shrugged, waved her hand. "I guess."

"Badass." Daisy rubbed her hands maniacally. "This is gonna be killer."

"Sideways." Jing folded the paper diagonally and tucked it into her pocket. "Real talk. Have you texted Madeline yet?"

"Ah." I sucked in my cheeks. "Haven't thought about it."

"Jesus. Hand me your phone." She tapped the table expectantly.

". . . Why?"

"Because you light up like the Fourth of July when you talk to her, and I want you to get laid on my behalf, idiot. Why else? Pass the phone. Or, you know, do it yourself. But do it. For me." Jing pursed her lips, looked pleased.

"Seconded," said Yates. She gave one of my curls a tug. "You'd be so cute together! It'll be adorable."

"You have to." Daisy made a face like a Cheshire Cat. "Like, right now."

I grinned despite myself. "I don't know how to do the flirting thing. Like. Do I just say hi? Is that what I do? Come on. You guys are probably experts at this."

"We are." Daisy flipped her hair. "'Hi' works. Do you use

emojis? If you do, use emojis. If you don't, it'll be awkward if you try."

Emojis were strictly reserved for texting Boris, and even then, it was usually just a series of different cat emojis to communicate when I was hungry, or whatever. I shook my head and pulled out my phone, laid it on the table before me. My palms clammed up. My throat turned to leather. Yates danced her fingertips over my shoulder blade while I typed.

**Hey it's Sideways**

"Put a heart after *Sideways*! That'd be cute. And it doesn't feel desperate, either. It could totally be an innocent heart. I put hearts in my texts all the time. It makes people imagine you smiling when they read it."

"Hearts are totally not my style." I eyed her, made a face.

"Put, like, a purple one or a blue one there. Or a black one! Like. Alternative kindness. That's your style, isn't it?" Yates pressed her cheek to my upper arm and gazed down at my screen. "Just remember to put it in the same text as the message. Putting it afterward is weird."

"I didn't know there were so many rules to this." I hit send and set my phone facedown on my thigh. "I mean, she might not even text back. It might wind up being nothing. That's how hitting on girls usually goes. Besides, I'm not totally sure if she was flirting with me or just trying to be cute. I don't know. Hard to tell sometimes. Some girls, like Yates over here"—I paused to jerk my chin at her and smirk—"like to send little hearts with simple messages. It's like: are you gay or friendly?"

"She could be gay *and* friendly," Yates protested, and I snorted.

My screen lit up against my thigh.

**Sneaking texts in class. Naughty. Santa's gonna bring you coal.**

I rested my face in my fists and marveled down at the screen. My heart wailed against my ribs like a canary in a too-small cage. It sang and suffered and lost air. I was dizzy, pleasantly dizzy. I cracked a smile.

**Coal is a non-renewable resource. Thanks Santa. Bring me lots. I'll sell it and make bank. Fuck the planet, I guess**

The response was nearly instantaneous.

**Are you free on Thursday night?**

"Yes, you are. You are so free on Thursday. If you have Thursday plans, I veto them." Yates clapped her hands together and bounced in her seat. "That was adorable! I mean. You two are weirdos. But still, really cute."

"Christ, already? How'd that happen?" Jing stretched her neck for a better view of the screen, but Yates shooed her away with a wave of her hand.

"Madeline is happy *and* gay, that's how. They're going out on Thursday after school," Yates said in a diplomatic tone, which she bolstered by sitting up straighter and batting her lashes. "It's going to be grand."

**I'm free Thursday, yeah. Wanna grab coffee?**

Daisy ran her thumb over her choker's velvet edges. She watched me incredulously, a little toothy smirk on her mouth, and she leaned across the table toward me like she had a big secret to tell. "Invite her to the party. She was into you at the last one. Ask her to join in. You and Jing and Yatesy, you three can practice the levitation spell under the bleachers while I'm at cheer. Practice until it's seamless. Then offer to have her help again, like she did at the last party. We dangle her in midair for a few minutes and lay her back down. Come on. If that's not a way to nail someone's heart to the wall, I'll be damned."

Jing considered, then nodded. "Agreed, but do it tomorrow. We can finalize plans for the party by then. If you ask her in person, then you can tell her all the juicy details. Scratch that. Just say it'll be better than last time."

"I feel like a Halloween party would be a good place for you to start something. It's kind of your season, Sideways." Yates clasped her hands together. "Are we doing costumes? Is it time?"

"If we do, we need to be cohesive, or it'll be stupid." Jing paused for a moment, glared at her nails. Her head jerked up. She snapped her gaze at Daisy, and then both of them turned to look at us. Matching murder smiles. Jing waggled her eyebrows. "I know what we're doing."

"Care to share this information?" I coughed once, scratched at the nape of my neck.

"We're gonna be girls from the sisterhood. Remember *Ghastly*? We're gonna be *Ghastly* girls. Boy-killing, school-conquering *Ghastly* girls." Daisy nodded exuberantly. She rubbed her palms together like she was trying to start a fire. "It'll be stellar. All the costumes will match, but we can pick different colors so we don't look like clones. Everyone's seen that movie, or at least a poster or two. They'll get it. It'll be perfect."

"Okay," I said. I closed my eyes for a moment and conjured an image from the movie: a circle of pastel dementors ringed around a zip-tied jock, reading aloud their grievances, brandishing pink knives. *So, like, die.* I clicked my tongue. "Here's the thing, though. How the fuck are we going to find *Ghastly* girl costumes? I don't think any of the costume shops will carry them, because the movie's so new. They might be online, but there's no way we could get them shipped here by Friday."

"Oh, don't worry about that." Daisy gathered up her hair and started braiding it, smirking all the while. "Haven't you ever wondered why you've never seen my clothes anywhere before? Or why Jing and Yates and I always have cohesive looks? Or, God, why my family's so fucking rich? The Brink side of the family is made up of bankers; my aunt Chelsea on the Stringer side is a big deal in the fashion industry. She's had stuff in Vogue. You can find knockoffs in mall chains and everything. Best of all, she's drying up again in a rehab center just outside of town and bored out of her mind, and she fucking loves making me stuff. For real. If I give her our measurements and a few screenshots of the movie, she can make us something fucking amazing. She's grateful for anything to do that isn't talking about her feelings to other bottle hiders." She finished her braid with a band around her wrist and tossed it behind her. "So, yeah. Totally doable. It's gonna be sick."

"Hard to argue with that," I said. Anticipation made me jittery. My face felt stupid and loopy, twisted up like this. "Can mine be red?"

"They were pastel in the movie," Yates said, but Jing cut her off with a wave of her hand.

"We should try to get close to our specter colors." Jing stabbed a chunk of tomato and popped it between her teeth. "No one will get it, but that doesn't matter. Feels like a good idea. We'll just wash out those colors. Sideways, you can wear, like a bruisy pale red. I'll wear lavender, Yates will wear baby blue, and Daisy will wear silver. Who knows? Maybe it'll amp up the spell work. Make us feel witchier. Set the mood."

"Fine by me," said Daisy. She whipped out her own phone and fluttered her fingertips over the keyboard. "Hey, Sideways. Text me your measurements, will you? Across your shoulders, shoulders to ankles, shoulders to wrists, and around the tits."

"Uh." That sounded like a really good way to feel awful.

"I can measure you," said Yates. She opened a bag of M&M's and slid one toward me. "It won't be a big deal at all. I'll swipe a measuring tape from my science lab next period and measure you after we practice the spell."

"Fine," I said. I set my jaw for a moment, let myself brood.

The bell screeched above.

We all stood up.

My screen lit up.

**Yeah. Coffee works. I'll pay.**

# SIXTEEN

# IF TEENS DON'T HAVE SPIRIT, THEN WHAT'S THAT SMELL?

The football field was hypnotically green. It was also probably toxic enough to kill several people. God knows how many different chemicals had been churned into the soil to keep things green and weed-free. Heaven forbid the football players play on slightly yellow grass, right? The field was so luxurious, so money-green, that you nearly forgot that the cafeteria had a roach infestation. And that the choir program had cut all but two sections because they couldn't afford new music. You know.

Jing and Yates and I sat in a circle. Yates' notebook was open to a blank page, and Jing and I took turns etching lines, erasing stray marks, renegotiating boundaries. The shape of the star warped and was replaced. Jing wanted longer lines, I wanted tighter turns. We didn't argue, but the more we drew, the more the shape felt stilted, overworked, and generally unusable. Yates said it hurt to look at. Earlier, she'd picked a few phlox flowers out of the school garden and tucked them into the loops of her corkscrews. She looked like Persephone.

Also, she was right. We turned a page, tried again on a blank slate.

"The incantation should have a refrain. Is that a thing? Like, we all chant, but there's one phrase that we all say together to keep things even. I feel like if we give it a rhythm, it'll flow better, so we don't choke up and stop talking. That could be a disaster." Jing streamlined three straight lines into one 3-shaped curve.

"That makes sense. So long as it isn't distractingly kitschy, I feel like a refrain would help. That, and if our audience sees us chanting together, it might look really cool. Rehearse until it doesn't look rehearsed, you know?" Yates looked at Jing's 3 with her brows drawn together. "A little softer, I think."

Jing shrugged, adjusted.

"The problem is going to be keeping things spontaneous. If too much is planned, then there won't be that visceral improvisation," I said. "Like, nothing I ever did on my own worked if I had it completely memorized."

"I don't know. I feel like we could riff off a refrain without too much trouble. Remember when we took Daisy down? We seemed to settle on a few words, and we repeated them over and over, with other phrases tucked in here or there. 'Come down slow and soft,' you know?" Yates cocked her head to the side. She spun the page upside down. "You know, I think I'm starting to like this. Like, a lot. Could you draw that arrow again, the one you had on the first design?"

I pierced an arrow through the 3-curve and brought the ends of it down on either side, puncturing the circle and lacing back around. I leaned back, narrowed my eyes. It really was gorgeous. Cleaner than anything I'd made on my own. Crisper. I nodded, licked my chops. "This looks fucking awesome. And we can make it again, that's for sure." Something clicked. "I think I catch your point, Yates. Jing, have you ever done an improv scene?"

"No," she said. She erased the smudges around the circle and scrutinized the angles of each line. "But go on."

"In an improv scene, the ensemble normally has marks. Cue lines, something like that. They know point A and point Z, but there's wiggle room in the middle. We could do it that way. One mark can start the levitation, one can hold you still in the air, and the third can bring you back down. The middle casting, the important stuff, that can ride on instinct. But Yates is right. If we start and end with chanting, that'll make sure that we aren't drifting apart halfway through. Remember how we broke the circle at the last party and it killed the magic for a while? We don't want that to happen again. It was cool as all fuck, but it was unpredictable. This time, we need to have control."

Jing stood up, took a step away from the notebook. She cocked her head to the side and scanned it up and down. "Is it going to work if Madeline doesn't chant? It'll still be cool as fuck without her, but it's going to be all kinds of heart-snatching if we levitate her, too. How can she resist that? You damn deserve it."

"Daisy wasn't chanting when we brought her down." Daisy also wasn't chanting when she floated herself twenty feet in the air. Without a circle or a sigil. Or anyone casting. But whatever. "I think we can make it work. We'll just clue her in on the steps and see how that goes."

"I'm thinking we should do this as a coven. Like, introduce ourselves that way. With the robes and the circle and all these sigils, we're going to look the part, that's for sure. I'm sick of people being horrible to you, Sideways." Yates tangled her fingers in the grass. "You're with us, now. You're part of the clique. If we all come out and say we're a coven, people are going to have to deal with that."

"Yeah, agreed," Jing said. "You're not going to be Sideways the Satanist loner lesbian anymore. You're gonna be with us. You *are* with us, and we're with you. The world can suck our collective dick."

My vision blurred. Throat felt bee-stung. I looked at the sigil, buried my hands in my pockets and took a few slow, deep breaths. *Jesus, Sideways.* I shook it off, nodded. My voice barely crackled when I spoke. "Are we gonna have a sick coven name? I feel like covens should."

"I'd say we should call ourselves the *Ghastly* girls, seeing as we're going to do the costumes and everything, but that feels too trendy." Yates made a face. "Plus, they were terrifying villains. I don't want that to be me. Can I read your texts with Madeline, Sideways? I'm curious."

"Yeah." I pulled my phone from my pocket, unlocked it, and tossed it over.

Jing crossed her arms. "On the name thing. You remember what Mr. Scratch said to us? It called us scapegracers. I like that."

"Scapegracers," I repeated.

"It's a bit archaic, I know. Means you've escaped the grace of God. It was up there with *rascal* for a while. Implied a particularly nasty kid. I like it." After a long pause, she held up her hands in defense. "I'm a fucking English nerd. Sue me."

I bunched my sleeves up around my elbows and rubbed my hands together, cracked my knuckles. There was something on my wrist. My eyes fixed on it. Tiny lettering, like I'd written a phrase there with pen, but I hadn't. I recognized the handwriting, though.

*I'm so flattered. Scapegracers is a lovely name.*

Oh boy. Oh fuck.

"Oh my God," said Yates. I snapped my head up, yanked my sleeve down, ignored the ringing in my ears. She clasped my phone to her chest like it was a bouquet of roses. "Sideways. You two are so perfect. I wish boys texted like that. The last three boys I've texted have asked me if I was a virgin. This is love. It has to be."

"You are so melodramatic," said Jing. She crinkled up her nose like a rabbit, but she wasn't fooling anyone. Her grimace was barely a grimace. "Give me a rundown. I don't want a play-by-play, but I want the outline."

"We talked about astrology and a true crime podcast we both like." I shrugged, felt my cheeks heat up, and tried to shove the whole *things writing themselves autonomously and without my permission on my wrist* thing to the brig of my brain. "Wasn't anything huge, you know? The conversation just sorta rolled. Like, we talked about going to roller derby sometime, and how we both really like Halloween. It's, whatever."

"It's not whatever." Jing stretched her arms above her head so far that her shirt rose over her midriff. "It's fucking fantastic. Now. Yates. Ready to float?"

✳

There was a strange reverence in watching Daisy cheer. Not the pom-pom jittering, or the sporadic twitchy chants, but in the pure gladiator thrill of it. Watching girls hoist themselves onto shoulders, piling girl on top of girl into a breathing monument. It was kind of terrifying. Hairless legs, pleated skirts, iron cores, and sugary nail polish. Weren't they supposed to be flaky? I'd always coupled cheer with bitchery, and bitchery with weakness. Maybe I'd gotten it wrong. This wasn't even the real thing, and I still got the shivers. *Daisy was the flyer,* said Jing. She was the one at the top of the pyramid who they tossed in the air and usually caught at the bottom. She'd explained this dryly, like I'd asked her how to use a remote.

It wasn't all that unlike magic, was it? I mean, they weren't spontaneously shouting power stanzas at the universe, but they were all shouting, and that was part of it. They shouted, threw their bodies, and the crowd went wild. Maybe that was the spell. This chant plus these lines plus these contortions equaled spectacle. I couldn't tolerate sports, and I was allergic to school spirit, but something told me that neither of those things served as motivation for Daisy Brink. This was about being a starlet. Everyone would look on and cheer. Death-defying feats of ridiculous acrobatics on chemical grass wasn't all that far removed from her floating stunt at Delacroix.

There she was. She'd pulled her hair into a high pony and sauntered toward the triangle of girls like she was about to eat them, and when she hit her mark, someone counted off. On one, they grabbed her wrists. On two, they bounced her between the two girls on shoulders, who balanced her shoes on their thighs. On three, they tossed her in the air, where she soared high, flipped twice, and then dove into an arm cradle far below.

To my right, Yates clapped her hands and hollered Daisy's name at the top of her lungs. Jing and I did not. The two of us exchanged glances and chanted a little faster, gave a little punch to our words. Our lips weren't synchronized, but we were saying the same thing in rounds, switching words here and there, fluttering around syllables for extra emphasis. I felt like we were thicker than thieves.

Yates was hovering about five inches off the bench. She had been for the past ten minutes. She hadn't touched the ground in a solid half hour. The flowers in her hair looked even bluer in the afternoon sunlight.

Cheer was coming to a close. The girls all dismounted and huddled close for discussion. The coach, looking leathery, said something that sounded both encouraging and terrifying. The girls mostly didn't listen. A few of them were on their phones. Daisy, being Daisy, just cartwheeled back and forth behind the coach, blatantly ignoring every word out of her mouth. One of the other varsity girls, a pyramid base, filmed her flipping. The coach clapped her hands and the group disbanded, each wandering in slightly different directions. Daisy made a break for the bleachers, and she jumped up the benches like they were overgrown stairs. She was outside the stadium in a matter of seconds, looking glowy and slightly pinkish.

"Did you see that last one? I felt like a damn bird. That stunt is, like, three inches from being illegal, and I love it so much." She wiped the sweat off her brow with the back of her wrist. "Why are you two whispering? Do we speak in tongues now? Why are you . . ." Daisy trailed off, looking between the three of us. Her eyes flicked from face to face, and then up at Yates, whose eyes were well above where they usually were. She broke into a smile. "No. Fucking. Way."

"You can put me down now, ladies," said Yates, who patted the side of her afro affectionately. "Like the flowers, Daze? Oh, and by the by, you looked like a shooting star up there. Just so you know."

Jing and I elbowed each other, nodded our heads, and changed up the words, barely speaking aloud. "Come down slow. Come down soft." Yates descended, landing gracefully on the titanium bleacher, her hands folded neatly in her lap.

Jing rubbed her cheeks, flicked her fingers. "God, that's itchy. It's like static electricity, you know? Man." She stood up and kicked the bleacher in front of her. "Daisy. We're coming out as a coven next party, right? Right. I say we call ourselves the Scapegracers."

"What, are we in a band, now? Do we need a name?" Daisy sneered, but she leaned forward, nonetheless. "If we're in a band, I call dibs on being the drummer."

"You just want to be the drummer so that you can hit stuff," said Yates.

Daisy shrugged.

"That wouldn't be our band name." I shook my hands through my hair and finger-combed it until it stood up. The wind was making it deflate. Can't have that. "If we were in a band, we'd totally call ourselves The Dental Damned. And I'd be the drummer. You give me more of a lead guitar vibe, Daze." Daze. Was I allowed to call her that yet?

If she noticed, she didn't care. "What the hell does that mean?"

I blinked. "Really?"

Jing screwed up her face. "Why the fuck would we call ourselves The Dental Damned?"

I looked at her with bewilderment. "Wait. Seriously, Jing? Like. Google *dental dam*."

Sure enough, she pulled out her phone and typed away. Her face turned slightly red. Slowly, she closed her browser and slipped her phone back into her pocket. "Sideways. I need training on how to be gay. I'm missing key details."

"Yes, you are," I said with a snort. "That's fixable, though. I should take you to Dorothy's sometime. It's the gay bar outside of town. You can be with your own kind and learn how this whole not-straight thing works in practice. And, you know. Dorothy's is sick as hell."

"Isn't Dorothy's the place out past Pine Street?" Daisy pulled the band out of her hair and shook it loose. She smacked her lips. "That's on the way to Aunt Chelsea's rehab center. I was planning on taking her fabric shopping, for the costumes and all. I could give you two a ride. You couldn't stay long, only an hour or two, but still. Enough time to pump some pride into Jing, am I right?"

"I could kiss you," I said. "That sounds fantastic."

"I'd let you." She winked.

*Sigh.*

"Oh, can I come with you and Aunt Chelsea? I love Aunt Chelsea. And I want to help pick out costume supplies." Yates uncrossed her ankles and sprang to her feet. "Besides. If the three of you all go somewhere without me, I'd be so lonely. It'd be terrible. I might have to, you know, hibernate for the next thousand years."

"Ain't we only going for, like, three hours, tops?" I stopped finger-combing long enough to stick my tongue out at her. She brushed it off.

"If you're only going to be gone for three hours, that's a shame. Three hours of fun for an eternity without Lila Yates. It'd be tragic."

✳

Dorothy's, looking like a bit like a drive-in diner or a ritzy fifties laundromat, wasn't typically busy at this time of day. Uneven coats of lavender paint rippled down the brick walls, and the sign, looking shabby, was rimmed with golden lights. Not that the lights were on when we pulled up. The OPEN sign flashed in the window, alongside a neon HAUNTED sign, and a sign that said NOT A STRAIGHT ESTABLISHMENT. The lot was seldom full (aside from the notorious drag nights), and Daisy had no problem pulling directly up to the door. Even with the door closed, I could hear the tinny sound of British Invasion pop music, which made the place seem even gayer than it already was. Boris and Julian drank themselves silly every few weeks at Dorothy's bar, but tonight was a work night, so the chances of meeting them there were relatively slim. I wasn't worried.

"We're gonna be back in two-ish hours. Hook up with as many people as humanly possible. Like it's a race." Daisy looked back at us with a devilish expression. She tapped the side of her nose. "Hope you brought your fakes."

"Thanks," I said with a nod. I climbed out of Daisy's car with Jing. Daisy barely took the time to flip us off before she wheeled away. As her baby-blue car zoomed off, people in either lane beside her audibly cussed and shook their fists, because she drove nearly twice the speed limit and her music made the air shake. I snorted a laugh and shoved my hands in my pockets. "She and Yates are so getting pulled over."

"Doubtful," said Jing. She took a step in the direction of the bar, and I followed suit. "Daisy and I have been drag-racing and hill hopping since we had licenses. Daisy's badder than I am. She'll do donuts at three a.m. with her music blasting loud enough for satellites to hear her. She's done it before. That's her third car. She totaled her first two. But never has any cop ever had the guts to give her a ticket. Seriously. Last night was the first time I was ever pulled over, and that wasn't even for speeding. Cops around here don't care about that kind of nonsense. I mean, freshman year, Alexis had a bag of weed in her purse, and a dog found it during one of those drug sweeps. The cop just took it. Didn't get her in trouble or anything." She shrugged.

I blinked. Wasn't quite the response I expected. It didn't seem out of place, though. Doing donuts in the dark sounded exceedingly Daisy-ish, and so did getting away with it. She and Jing and Yates were immortals. No one was stupid enough to screw with them, not in this town. Some people were just innately powerful.

"For the record, don't buy anything alcoholic. My dads hang out here, so, like, the bartenders know how old I am, and they'll guess you're in school with me," I said as I held open the door for her. "It's chill, though. Their virgin margaritas taste like the real thing, sans the hangover."

Inside, the air was saturated with violet lights. Only a smattering of people sat around the bar, and there was an open space toward the far end. I took a seat on one of the precariously tall bar stools, and Jing sat down elegantly beside me, crossing her feet at the ankles. She twisted her hair around her fingertips, and her bleach-blond locks looked bluish under the lights as she eyed the place. When the bartender sidled over to us, Jing waved a hand and said, "I'll have what she's having."

"Hey, Sideways." The bartender, a stocky ginger with hipster glasses, gave me his customary smile. His name was Drew, and he didn't need to ask me what I wanted to drink. My order hadn't changed in the two years since I started coming. He cleared his throat and set to work. "It'll be right up."

Jing's gaze had settled somewhere on the far wall, about twenty feet away, on the other side of the makeshift dance floor. It was covered with images of patrons past. Pictures of couples kissing, dancing, clattering their glasses together in frozen cheer were displayed in mismatched frames. Somewhere toward the upper right corner, a much younger Boris and Julian glittered down at the dance floor. Younger them were clasped together tight, caught in the middle of a halting laugh. Julian's glasses were stuck eternally falling off his nose. I couldn't tell exactly where Jing was looking, but I had the feeling that it wasn't at one fixed point, but rather, a synthesis of the wall as a whole.

"I've known for a while," she said slowly. Her voice was distant, and she didn't blink. She sat perfectly still in her seat, so still that I couldn't see her breathing, but her eyelids drooped half-shut, and her mouth tugged up on one side. It wasn't a particularly regal expression, which made it strange on her face. She looked contemplative and starkly honest. "Since I was ten or eleven. Maybe longer."

"About being bisexual?" I squashed my cheek against my fist.

"Yeah," she said. "And about magic. I've known about one as long as I've known about the other. I just didn't have words for it. Now I do." In that moment, illuminated by the neon lights, Jing looked like what a witch should look like. Menacing and lovely. She was pure and raw and radioactive. She was more vivid than anything else in the room. I looked at her and marveled. She went on. "I've been friends with Daze since before the big bang. We've always been best friends, and we will always be best friends. We were such sweet little monsters. Writing on the walls with lipstick, playing dress up with her aunt's haute couture, running down boys in my pink Barbie Jeep. We once made fifty bucks selling lemonade on her front lawn.

"And I was with her when she found her mom's body in the garden. That's when things changed, Sideways. It wasn't just about us anymore. The world was bigger and meaner than two nasty little girls. We'd always had complete reign over our little patch of reality, but Daisy's mom dying spoiled that sense of control. She needed it back. We both did. We stopped tormenting small-scale. We made a market for ourselves. We were ridiculously cutthroat about the whole thing. People who were with us could be new royalty, and those who opposed us found themselves on the meat hook soon enough. Like, there was this girl who was mean to Alexis in the fifth grade. The girl had a stupid name, I forget what. She called Alexis an ugly bitch, something like that. Stuck gum in her hair. Shoved her off the monkey bars. In fifth grade, that sort of thing was a big deal. So Daisy and I threw a huge party on the same day as her birthday, and not a single person turned up at the little gnat's house. Wasn't enough, though. She still wouldn't leave Alexis alone. So, you know what we did? We put her bike in a tree. Told her we'd haul it down when Alexis told us to, but she never did. It was always public, what we did. People knew where they should put their loyalty.

"Then there was Lila Yates. She moves to town during eighth grade, looking like a goddamned archangel, and my heart just breaks. She was so pretty, and no one is pretty when they're fourteen. She's pretty and quick and nicer than me. I remember telling Daisy that I needed her to be friends with me. I needed her to be our *best friend*. So, Daisy chats her up for me, and soon they're talking resorts in the Bahamas and Tiffany diamonds. Summers in Montenegro. Golf courses and ballet lessons. My family's doing alright, but both of them are dripping money. They had luxury in common. I did not. For a while I was so *jealous*. I felt like Daisy would leave me, that she'd be Yates' best friend instead of mine, and I was crushed. And God, that crush was something nasty. I was so lovestruck. I'd never loved anyone before, not like that. I'd never loved anything. But Daisy's no Brutus, and she stuck by me. The two of us became the three of us. Yates understood without asking.

"I don't love her anymore. I mean, I do, but not like that. I don't think so, anyway. Sometimes it crawls back up and I'm sick with it for a little while. It's not fair. She's *Lila Yates.* Loving her is compulsory.

"The three of us are one monster now. We're like

Cerberus. Or, we were. I've had my eye on you for a while, Sideways. I mean, we'd always noticed you. You were the skulky gap-toothed weirdo who was into occultism and knocked people's lights out if they looked at you funny. For a while, I wrote you off as being a store-brand metalhead type. You looked enough like a freak Satanist type who murders squirrels that I was sure it had to be an act. But you know, Yates was genuinely put off by you, and she normally only gets squeamish around the Real Thing. That's why we invited you to that party. You gave Yates the creeps." Jing smirked, and it was the first time her expression had changed since she'd started talking. "Look. All this stuff is coming together. Now our three is four. That magic thrill we always wanted is real, and it's because of you. With you, we're powerful. We have magic. We're fucking marvelous. No one better dare screw with us.

"And I'm even sort of out now. Out-ish. Out in a small way, and I don't do things in small ways very often. I'm usually a big deal. This feels different. It's special."

Our virgin margaritas had been sitting in front of us for a few minutes now. I took one and raised it, and Jing mirrored me. Salty rims knocked together in a silent toast. I brought it to my lips and pretended that it could make me drunk, because there was a peculiar sensation in my chest, and I didn't know how to deal with that other than drowning it. It felt like a bundle of candles was burning down to the quick inside me. My tummy was all fire and liquid wax. Goddamn.

I wondered if Yates ever planned on telling her about

being queer, but I held my tongue about that.

"So that's my damn life story," Jing said with a cough. An easy smile slipped over her lips. She pushed her bangs off her forehead and made a face like a Halloween monster with her lips scrunched up and her nostrils flared. I cracked a laugh, and she let go of her hair, straightening herself up. "Fucking. Your turn. Be vulnerable, or some shit."

"Pass," I said. I licked along the rim of my glass. Jing stopped fixing her bangs long enough to shoot me a withering look. "Right," I said. I looked somewhere in the direction of my lap. "Ain't much to say. I grew up with just Mom and then she died. Someone sent the *Vade Mecvm Magici* to my foster home and I used it to find my uncles. I didn't have a friend to be my partner in crime, though. I didn't have any friends at all. Just me and my spell book. I mean, there were people I talked to in class, but that's where the relationship ended. God, I hate that. I'd rather be a stranger than someone's casual friend. At least with a stranger, there's things to unwrap about each other. There's a mystery there. People don't care about their acquaintances' mysteries. Why the hell would they? I don't. I only went to parties because people didn't know how to politely avoid inviting me. You lot were weird. You went out of your way to invite me, a fucking Wild Thing, to your huge party, with the explicit instruction to be as me as possible. You wanted me to be a horrorshow. I don't care if I was a gimmick. People never asked me to hang out with them as myself. Meant a fucking lot, even if I didn't know it at the time. Then you all drag me into your clique, and suddenly I've got friends who want me around. Before you, magic only worked in bursts: levitating bottles of nail polish, flickering lightbulbs, bubbling flat water without touching it. Small magics, nothing like what we've done. I thought I was damn cool for it, too. Seems like hopscotch now, you know?"

"You're thoroughly ours now. In case there was any doubt about that. You're what we were looking for." Jing took a slow sip of her drink. "Besides. I've never talked to anyone who wasn't straight before. I don't think I have, anyway."

Drew the bartender made a sound of strangled shock under his breath. "God, you haven't? You poor thing."

I sniggered, waggled my eyebrows at her. Typical Drew antics, half listening to everything but only ever chiming in where being gay was concerned. We clinked our glasses together and took a drink in tandem.

Drew's eyes slipped over our heads. A smile broke on his face, and he nodded vigorously, so vigorously that his glasses nearly clattered off his nose. "Maurice! It's been a while. How are you this fine afternoon, eh?"

A man in a crisp red suit sat down beside us. He sighed, inclined his head, smiled ever so slightly. He looked thoroughly exhausted. Something had stained his long brown fingers the color of ink, and he rubbed at them slowly, which only served to spread the dark stain across his knuckles and the backs of his hands. Finally, he looked up at Drew, and his expression warmed a few degrees. "It's been a day, I'm afraid. I'd sell my soul for an Irish coffee."

"Sure thing," said Drew, who set off to work.

I stared at the man. So did Jing. We gawked together in a moment of shock and understanding, because without a doubt in my mind, this was the elusive Maurice from Delacroix House. If he sorceried his way into reading my mind, he might have a serious bone to pick with me. I watched him with my mouth slightly agape as he reached for his coffee, slid a twenty-dollar tip to Drew, and downed the scalding drink in one gulp. Then, when he was done, he gently placed the cup down and leaned back on his stool. He smiled at Drew and asked for another drink, then shifted in his seat to turn his attention toward us. He gave us a nod and a smile. "Good evening."

I blanched.

Maurice wheezed a laugh, which sounded slightly deflated. There was something of a smoker's edge to it that made him sound older than he looked. "Wasn't meant to be threatening. Sorry about that." He folded his splotchy hands into his pockets, out of sight. The man inclined his head in an odd gesture of respect, and when he straightened back up, his eyes swept between the two of us with a glint of recognition. "Jing and Sideways, I assume?"

Jing's eyes narrowed a notch.

The man shook his head. "You're not in trouble. I'm not mad. Truly. It's simple enough for anyone with a specter to walk right through our wards, because really, anyone with a specter is *allowed* up there. I'd have gone with a different series of spell books, though, if I were you. *Vade Mecvm*s were written for a closed coven. They don't share too often. Not the most straightforward texts, either; that series has a particular knack for being mysterious for mystery's sake. And a bit elitist, if you ask me. If you'd have gone for a Book of Chaos, that might've worked out better for you. They're not as particular with who they read for."

"Right," I said. My palms were itchy. I didn't dare look away from Maurice, not while he was watching us. In all his pleasantries, I hadn't seen him blink. His eyes stayed focused intensely enough to X-ray us both if he'd liked.

"I'm Maurice, by the by. Maurice Delacroix. The house is always open to those like us. It's neutral ground between the covens, as a matter of fact. We provide lodging for traveling covens, storage for their supplies, and a neutral forum for inter-coven relations, on those rare occasions everyone feels like talking. Covens don't typically do that. It's like herding cats.

"By age alone, I'd guess that the two of you aren't properly aligned yet, even if you've started making prospects. Pythoness Society girls to be, I'd expect? It's the Pythonesses who write the *Vade Mecvm Magicis*. Old-world coven, very dignified, well esteemed. A prestigious pick, though you'll have your work cut out for you working your way into their inner circles. They don't seek out recruits often. Invitation only." The exhaustion on his face echoed in his movements; it looked like it took something out of him to reach his hands out of his pockets and thumb through his wallet. There was a tremor in his fingertips. He placed a ten-dollar bill on the bar and returned his hands to his pockets again. He cleared his throat.

"You should've told someone why you were there. They'd have told you anything you needed to know. Well, when you come back around, I'm sure that we can chat about things. I'd imagine you'll come back. Find a spell book that'd take you. I could put a word in with Guadalupe and see if you could have one of our *Vade Mecvm*s. She's a Pythoness contact of ours. Helps out with auctions from time to time."

The sheer audacity of the moment was enough to knock all the words out of my mouth like loose teeth. This was wholly contrary to what I'd expected. I stared at Maurice, mouth agape, and tried to riddle through the frankness that he'd laid out. He knew. This man knew about the only thing that'd tethered me to the Here and Now for years. He knew and he was willing to talk. But this was too convenient. The universe didn't just *align* for people.

Instinct moved my body for me. I felt my hands grip my bag, tug the zipper open, and reach deep inside. I felt myself pull my *VMM* volumes out of the bag and rest them on the bar before me. I looked at them, and then at Maurice, and my voice found its way out of my mouth. "I was invited."

Maurice raised a brow. Jing looked at me beseechingly, but I didn't look back. My pulse pounded like a snare drum in my temples. I placed my fists on the bar and swallowed, ground out the truth. "My name is Eloise Pike. Someone sent me the first volume after my mom died. The note was from 'PS.' That's gotta be the Pythoness Society, right? They wrote these books, didn't they? So I was invited. But I couldn't read the other volumes. The book gave me lip when I tried."

Maurice sat for a moment, then downed his second drink in one swallow, as if the liquor was medicine. The stains on his fingertips might have spread higher, or perhaps that was an illusion, and I was just confused. He set down the shot glass. It clinked on the countertop. "Eloise Pike, you say?"

"Yeah. But Sideways is better. Whatever." I ground my molars, which made my jaw ache, but not enough to make me stop. "What's it matter?"

"Pike, as in Rothschild & Pike?"

My brows meshed together. "Yeah."

Maurice made a sound in the back of his throat. "That is curious, then. The books didn't recognize you? Guadalupe seemed content to sell one to your father when he said it was for his daughter. She doesn't typically allow for that. We usually put a line of grimoires up in auctions to mark who we are to other covens, but it's just for show. We don't sell them. They're all unique. Irreplaceable. I didn't question Lupe's judgment at the time, but if she'd given one of them to you, it'd make more sense for the other books to follow suit. I could have a word with her. I'm not in the Pythoness Society; the *Vade Mecvm Magici* only address me for security purposes. Perhaps there's some ritual you need to partake in before they all reveal themselves? I don't know. Lupe is traveling right now, but she'll be back in a month or two. If you come by the House soon, I'm sure that I could arrange for you two to talk. Negotiate. Whatever you need."

Jing, who'd been silent, cleared her throat.

Maurice looked at her and smiled wearily, wavering on his

stool. He shrugged. "Perhaps Lupe will speak to you, too. We can find a place for you girls. We'll sort this out. It's unwise for you to practice without a coven. Dangerous, even. There are unsavory sorts about, all of whom would love to get their hands on unattached witches without the power of a coven to back them. You girls best lay low where magic is concerned, at least until we've got the Pythoness business sorted. Don't make any scenes."

Jing fished a cherry out of her mocktail and popped it between her teeth. Her stare hadn't broken, glittered maliciously. It was like Jing was sizing him up for a fight that she very much intended on winning. "Did you follow us here?" Her tone was casual enough. "Kind of weird, running into us. Recognizing us, and all."

Maurice snorted, a reaction that made Jing blink. His mouth flickered into a smile, and perfect dimples buttoned either side of his face. "Dear, no. This is a gay bar. I am a gay man. I am a gay man who's had a very long, very trying day, and who just so happens to have a Sigil of Intuition carved on the back of my wristwatch. I came here for a drink, but my sigil is buzzing and I made a guess. It's quite handy, having one of these around. I'd recommend it."

Jing did not look convinced.

I cut in. I refused to let Jing pick a fight with the first helpful person I'd run across. I pulled one of my fists off the table and slid it down the nape of my neck. "What happened today?"

Maurice sighed, shrugged his shoulders slightly. "Something nasty got loose in our storeroom, and we've been searching for it all morning. I don't blame you two. I imagine it freed itself. Strange things are prone to that."

Jing and I exchanged a look.

"Hard to tell you what it is, really. Bugaboos, boogeymen . . . you'd think there'd be more appropriate words for such creatures. Words that make them sound a bit more urgent." He slumped his shoulders, swaying forward. "Devils. Tragic little bastards. Even our kind has trouble catching them. It's like trying to catch a shadow with your hands. We've been interrogating the creatures in our storage for information, and undoubtedly one of them will know something of its intended whereabouts. We'll find it soon enough. Neither of you should worry. They're easy to follow. They stain everything they touch. Just be aware: if either of you find yourself in the dark and something smells like a broken pen, make sure to turn on a light. They hate light. It fades their ink."

"Ink." Jing repeated the word with an incredulous look on her face. "The boogeyman has ink?"

I felt a funny thickness in my throat.

"It's made of ink. Ink and ash and charred scraps of leather. Keep away from it. It's nothing but trouble, and I don't want you girls sticking your fingers in things that could hurt you," he said slowly, eyes fixed on Jing and me with a burrowing intensity. I felt his gaze like it was a physical thing.

"Sure," said Jing. She sounded dismissive. Maurice did not look amused. Before he could open his mouth to say anything else, Jing's phone chirped in her pocket and she fished it out, held it at arm's length. "Sideways," she said sharply, not bothering to look at me as she spoke. "Our ride is here."

I gritted my teeth.

The spike of her heel ground into my foot.

"We're off," said Jing succinctly, and she slapped a twenty on the bar. "Come along."

I flared my nostrils, hissed in a breath. I wasn't done, but my foot screamed under Jing's heel. I swallowed and stood up, shaking off Jing's foot in the process. "Whatever," I said under my breath. I felt my shoulders hunch forward defensively and stuffed my books back into my bag.

Jing's hand found my wrist and she yanked me away from the stools. I turned my head to say something, anything, to Maurice, but he just gave a lazy half salute and motioned for a third drink. I looked ahead, my throat tight. Jing's hand slid down from my wrist to my hand, and she looped her fingers through mine and led me out the door.

"I wasn't done," I said.

"You should've been." Jing didn't look at me. Her fingers were cold against my skin. "I don't trust him, and we shouldn't keep Daisy waiting. She hates that."

The sticky feeling inside my sweater wriggled around my stomach, like I had an eel curled up against my skin. Several eels, a whole wreath of them. The feeling crawled up me, squirmed up to my collar, ducked beneath my hair.

"Thank you," it said with the smallest, highest voice. It was so slight that I could've missed it, could've written it off as a trick of a stupid, weary mind. "If he put me in a vase again, I think I'd eat myself alive."

# SEVENTEEN

# THE HOUSE HORROR WARNED YOU ABOUT

That night I balled up my sweater and hurled it across the room. I stood on my bed and stared at it, waited with Julian's baseball bat in hand for it to move.

"What are you?" I bounced on the mattress, shifted from foot to foot. "Why have you been following me around, huh?"

My sweater stayed a sweater. It didn't grow giant crab legs and scuttle away. It didn't even shiver.

"I know you're in there." Swung the bat around to prove a point, or at least suggest one. I wasn't sure that hitting this thing would work, or if it was even something that could be struck.

The sweater didn't move, but it looked a shade lighter now. All its darkness seeped into the carpet, rushed under the bed in an amalgam of milky black droplets.

My guts flew up to hit the roof of my mouth.

"You freed me. You didn't turn me over to the Delacroix House. I want to be your friend, Sideways. I want to help you, if you let me." The silky, slipping voice came from all around me. The sound of it coated the back of my throat.

"I don't need help." I swallowed, but the feeling wouldn't leave me. "I don't need you to follow me."

"I have nowhere else to go."

I opened my mouth, but I lost sight of the inkiness. The devil melted itself into the creases of my room, blended with the shadows.

"Just for a little while," it said. "Just until I find people to be with, if I cannot be with you. But consider it, Sideways. It'd be my honor."

My mouth clamped shut like a bear trap. My pulse hammered in my ears. I sat down, still clutching my bat, thought about wailing at the open air. But that thought was beat out by a stupid, cloying sympathy.

I remembered being a sticky devil-something without anywhere to go. "Just for a while," I said. "Don't make a scene, okay?"

"Okay," it said. "Now get some sleep."

✳

I dreamt that there were dead deer all over my floor and that the Chantry boys stood around my bed with their hands on my arms and my shins. They pressed down, mashed me into the mattress. Their palms were cold like metal. The deer around the bed piled up like leaves.

*Oh my God,* dream-me said. *Oh my God, oh my fucking God, get the fuck off me, get away from me.*

One of the dream-Chantrys clucked his bright pink

tongue and *tsk*ed. "Come on, Eloise. There's no need for profanity."

✳

Classes blurred into one another. The mundanity of it all was stifling. Could I care about math more than I cared about magic? I hadn't cared about math in the first place. My life was full of friendship and ink devils and witchfinders and, holy hell, Madeline Kline, and I couldn't stomach our state-mandated curriculum. Anticipation for this weekend sizzled like Pop Rocks in my bloodstream, and it was all I could do to take notes and pretend to listen to the katydid drone of teacher after teacher, none of whom cared any more than I did.

My phone burned in my pocket. Madeline had only texted me once, but that singular sentence rattled around in my head.

**Psyched for tomorrow.**

I'd texted back something stupid and short, seen at 10:00 a.m., and she hadn't said anything after that. I know she didn't because I'd checked all of twenty times. Nothing. But it was a positive nothing.

By the time I took my lunch to the Scapegracer table, Daisy was already entrenched in conversation with Jing. There were the usual flyby fans of theirs, people who said hello and woefully showered them with panicky compliments as they passed by, but I thought there were fewer than normal. A few people seemed more interested in just staring. On the stage, Mickey-Dick, Ashleigh, and Tina made a show of pretending to gag themselves with sporks. Anyway, Jing and Daisy were discussing something about a fight that'd occurred between first and second period. According to Daisy, there was still blood on the lockers. Jing's face said that this was total bull, but Daisy seemed convinced, or at least pleased to keep the story going. Meanwhile, Yates was bent over what looked suspiciously like Physics homework. I sat beside her and saw, to not much shock, that the homework Yates was looking over was already finished. She was highlighting key phrases.

"Hey, Sideways," she said without looking up. "Does this look right to you?"

"Lila Yates, your homework is fucking immaculate," said Jing, pausing mid-sentence to stick her tongue out at the open notebook. "It's always right. You're our baby genius."

"Baby geniuses like second opinions, too," said Yates.

I stifled a laugh. "You want *my* opinion on Physics?"

She nodded vigorously.

I eyeballed the page, understood none of its contents, and gave her a vague thumbs-up.

This was apparently enough.

"So, do you have anywhere to be after school? No? Awesome. We're showing you the place we're throwing the party." Daisy tucked a strand of hair behind her ear. "My aunt has already started the costumes. They'll totally be done in time. She's super excited about it. We have to take a lot of pictures for her, but that's a given."

"They can put the pictures in the museum they're going to make about us," said Jing with a smirk.

"I think you're going to approve of the venue, Sideways." Yates looked away from her homework long enough to pop a grape into her mouth. "It's awful."

"It's perfect," Daisy insisted. "Absolutely perfect. I'm beyond psyched for this, alright?"

"We'll meet you at my car," said Jing. "Try not to dawdle, okay? I want to beat the traffic out of here. We need to set up a little, though the real setup will be right before the party."

"Will do," I said. My stomach, which had been screaming all day, reminded me to open my lunch box. Inside was a sandwich, strawberries, and not one, but *four* lollipops. *Julian.* I sighed, rolled my eyes, and passed them out.

Yates perked up. "Aw, thank you, Sideways!"

"It was Julian," I said with a wave of my hand. "He's a sweetie." He was probably just excited that I have friends to give candy to, honestly. This was his indirect Julian-style attempt to ensure that I still have friends by the end of the week.

Jing stuck the sucker between her teeth. "Thanks. Right. Sideways, you have our sigil sketches, yeah?"

"Yeah."

She gave me a sharp nod. "Good."

✳

I kept checking the time. It was getting compulsive. Classes couldn't go fast enough, and when the final bell finally rang, I was out the door before most kids were done packing.

Still no texts from Madeline Kline.

Was Mr. Scratch with me? I couldn't tell. My clothes all smelled kinda tart, and lots of them were sticky. I wasn't sure if it was me or him.

Jing's cherry convertible played a song with heavy bass. The song was cranked high enough that I felt the beat pulsing through my shoes, and a haphazard crowd of friends and admirers flocked around the bumper, seemingly oblivious to the pounding music.

Daisy was sprawled across the hood. She playfully kicked some boy who was trying to lean in closer. She didn't seem to like him terribly much. "You're boring," she sneered, jamming the toe of her cheer sneakers squarely in his rib cage. The boy coughed, then chuckled, and the cycle repeated.

Jing honked, and a group of girls who'd been leaning against the trunk jumped. Jing leaned her arm out the window, pulled her sunglasses down a notch, and snapped a gum bubble. "There you are. Get your ass in the car."

I rolled my eyes, felt a smirk come on, and pulled myself into the back seat. Yates had been waiting there. She was drinking a bottle of orange soda as though it was a vodka martini. She waved and jerked her thumb toward Daisy, who was still sunning herself on the hood.

"That's Dylan," she said. "Daisy's current nothing. It won't last. I don't think he knows that, though."

"Idiot." Jing looked at her nails. "Boys are replicable."

"I don't think I've ever seen him before," I said. He didn't look particularly remarkable. He had clear skin and a ginger buzz cut. Letter-jacket type. Not my thing.

"He's JV. I give him a week, tops," said Yates.

Jing scoffed. "I give him an hour."

Daisy, seemingly sensing that it was time to leave, slid off the hood and flounced around to the passenger's seat. The boy gave a half wave that she didn't return. She turned to the radio and fiddled with it, and a different song, something raunchy and electric, poured out of the speakers.

We sped away, and I chanted a bit of our protection sigil's incantation for defense under my breath. Repeating bits of the spell without a ritual attached didn't reinforce it or anything, but it reminded me that the spell was there and keeping me safe, and at least it was something to do that wasn't fixating on the car's engine sounds. Town was to the left, but Daisy pulled to the right. As far as I knew, nowhere worth going was in this direction. Sycamore Gorge proper was only about six miles around, and beyond that was a wasteland of cornstalks, construction sites, and Wi-Fi-less wilderness. Also, one would assume, a gorge. The colonizing town founders were real clever, clearly. Regardless, driving this way made zero sense. I couldn't see us having a party in a crop circle, at any rate.

*Stalk not, witchfinders. Don't see me and stay very fucking far from me. Stalk not, stalk not, stalk not.*

"Where the fuck?" I started, but Daisy and Jing didn't look back. I doubted they could hear me over the sleazy lyrics. Instead, Yates looked up and curled her lip.

"Slasherville," she said.

Jing took a turn off the main road, and the pavement turned to gravel. The tires crunched. Trees whorled by like outstretched arms caught aflame. There was a lurch in my gut. Fuck cars, fuck cars in the woods, fuck cars in the woods crunching over broken asphalt. My whole body swept with shivers. I kept my eyes open and I fixed them on the back of Daisy's head.

The road snaked back and forth without explanation. No mailboxes, nothing suggesting a hidden rich-folk retreat. Trees and trees and more scorching trees. Crimson leaves clustered in heaps across the road. Something deer-shaped flashed beside us.

"How much farther?"

Yates shrugged. "Not much."

Jing slowed to a halt.

The road (or path, more like) opened into a clearing. There was enough space for thirty cars max, a sort of makeshift cul-de-sac, likely for turnaround purposes. Zero signs of civilization. The trees stretched back forever.

"Get out," Jing commanded. "Sideways, take your notebook." She opened her door and stepped outside, and we all followed suit. Daisy looked ecstatic. Yates had her arms crossed securely over her chest. She left her pop in the car. The three of them veered left, and I trudged close behind with my notebook tucked under my arm.

They stopped. Daisy wolf whistled. It took me a moment to process what I was seeing.

A rickety wooden staircase descended from the lot. Half the steps were crooked, and all of them were rotting. The guardrail was growing mushrooms. Beyond the stairs, looking like a carcass, was a house with a rickety porch. Where the windows weren't boarded up, the glass was cracked and dingy. The white paint peeled off in ribbons. The shingles were gray green with lichen and looked like unbrushed teeth.

"We found it while exploring a while back," said Jing. She gave the house a nod. "Totally abandoned. We looked it up. It's condemned. Nothing we can't do to it."

Daisy patted the backpack on her shoulders. "We're not using chalk this time round. We don't want someone scuffing it up. We're spray-painting this bitch all over the floorboards."

"How the hell will people find this?" I shifted my weight. The house was a death trap, sure, but they had a point. No one would give a singular fuck what happened to it. And it certainly had the right vibe. Made my skin tingle. I wanted to go inside.

"They'll find it," said Jing. "It's easy to get to, it's just out of the way. Simple instructions: right past the high school, take a left, and keep going. They can't fuck it up."

Yates grimaced and we made our descent.

Inside, the house was cavernous. The decaying spots smelled like rain. Most of it was one open room, with high ceilings and crumbling molding. The walls were grimy and finger smudged. A few slouchy armchairs sat across from a long couch, but someone had slashed them all open and yellow stuffing sloughed out the sides. A back window was patched with newspaper and duct tape, and it made the light that filtered inside look sallow.

Jing pulled her bag off her back. "We're drawing the sigils now. I want as much set up before Friday as possible." Lo and behold, Jing produced three cans of spray paint from her bag. She tossed one at me and I caught it. My jaw hung slack. "You sure about this?"

"Positive," said Jing. She blew a bubble and popped it.

Yates sighed, pulled the notebook out from under my arm, and leafed through it. "If we're doing this, we need to make sure we get the lines right. There's no redoing it if we dick it up."

"Aye-aye," said Daisy. She took the third can of spray paint and shook it hard.

Yates rolled her eyes up into her skull. "Great," she said. She knelt, placed the notebook on the floor, and motioned for us to gather round. "We're starting with the circle, then working inward, alright?"

Jing clicked her tongue, which meant yes.

Yates pulled a ziplocked bag out of her pocket. "*I* brought chalk," she said matter-of-factly. Sure enough, she withdrew a pale blue stick of chalk from the bag. She held it like a pen. "I'm tracing everything out, and then you three can go over it with the paint. If you screw up what I draw, that'd seriously suck. I'll be grumpy. Avoid that."

I shook my can of paint and grinned.

Yates pressed the chalk to the floorboards and the line work bloomed.

*

I had paint beneath my nails.

We stood back and admired our work. There was something ridiculously sexy about the way sorcery looked spray-painted across the floor. We'd outdone ourselves. The red lines splattered in swirls and zigzags over the warped floorboards. Confident lines. Power strikes. The sigil spiraled from the middle of the room outward, ending about three feet from the walls in every direction. The far wall read REIGN OF SCAPEGRACE, courtesy of Daisy, who might have been a little overzealous.

It looked ever so slightly like a crime scene. There were wannabe violent-kitsch Satanic rituals in the eighties where they slaughtered randoms for Baphomet's glory, weren't there? If so, this could pass for one of them. It made the hair on my arms stand up. This was more official, more damning than that chalk had been. It would not be washed away. Whatever happened on Friday night was going to last forever.

We hadn't stopped at the spray paint, though. Jing and Daisy and I had nailed a few hooks into the walls at Yates' behest. It wasn't a bad move. Hooks meant that we could suspend our lanterns over the party, ensuring that people didn't kick them aside or accidently stomp on them. Made for a better display of our handiwork, too.

Daisy checked the bathroom downstairs. The water lines must've been cut at some point, so the bathroom situation was dubious, but bathroom situations were always dubious at parties. Not like the aftermath would be our problem. We avoided the top floor. Gave us bad vibes. We decided we'd caution tape it up and avoid its weirdness altogether.

The couches and chairs were shoved against the walls. The papered windows were left papered. We cleaned up some broken glass, but that didn't take long. Our venue was, for all intents and purposes, finished. It'd be cold in here at night, but all those bodies packed close would help correct the situation. We'd friction our way to warmth. Besides, our robes would trap all our body heat. It'd be like wearing a blanket around. Thank God we hadn't picked something skimpy.

"This place gives me the creeps," said Yates, eventually. We'd been admiring it for a while now. Jing had been taking pictures. Yates stood apart from us, more toward the center of the room. She stood in the sigil's center, the place where I would sit. She hugged her arms to her chest, gnawed a strip of skin off her bottom lip.

Jing and Daisy abruptly looked up from their phones. Daisy's distracted stare split into a grin. Jing looked over her shoulder at me, and something flashed in her eyes. She glanced back at Daisy, then at Yates, and then she quirked her brow. "Go on," she said. "What kind of creeps are we talking, here?"

"Gives me the shivers. Prickles the hair on my arms, you know?" Yates shook her head. "I don't like it. It's weird. This whole room is weird. It was already slasher city. Now it's, like, *begging* for Jason Voorhees to pop out and stab us all to death."

"Fantastic," said Jing.

Daisy bounced.

I slid my hands in my pockets. "Did I give you the shivers when you met me?"

Yates paused. Tilted her head to the side. "Yeah, I think."

"Lila Yates, I adore you." Jing rubbed her hands together. "I think we're done here, fellas."

"Agreed." Daisy flipped her hair over her shoulder and shifted her weight from foot to foot, like she was getting ready to fight someone. "God, I'm so hype I could kill something."

"And maybe you will," said Jing. "Save that for Friday, though. We need to be here at eight. They'll be here at nine. It's going to be apocalyptic."

"Dope." Daisy took a selfie, tucked her phone in her bra, and gave me a crooked glance. "Let's take Sideways home before her daddy and her daddy get nervous."

"Let's," Jing agreed. She turned away from our masterpiece, took me by the wrist, and led me toward the door.

✷

"I'm going to be out on Friday night."

I sat across from my fathers, who looked gaunt under the electric chandelier. We were nearly done with dinner. Yellow bones, now stripped of meat, sat in stacks on mismatched china. I played with a saltshaker. Julian was doing a crossword and Boris was supplying the ambiance with some story about his travels abroad.

Julian screwed up his mouth, stuck his pen behind his ear, and looked up from the newspaper. Ink blotted his fingertips. "Out? Didn't you go out last weekend?"

Boris scoffed, clapping Julian's shoulder. He waggled his brows at me, flashed me a smile. His hair, more lacquered than usual, caught the light like it was plastic. "Julian, Julian," he said. He moved his hand from Julian's shoulder to the nape of his neck, smoothed down a few rebel curls. "Sideways is going to be in college next year. Learning how to balance a social life with schoolwork is important. Wouldn't you rather her explore things now than in university? Remember what happened when *you* waited until university, sweetheart. We don't need that for Little Miss Black Sheep, now do we?"

Julian's eyes popped out of his head. He opened his mouth, made a strangled sound in the back of his throat, and looked between the two of us beseechingly. "That's not fair," he started, then stopped. The pen behind his ear slipped and landed on his dinner plate. The clatter echoed off the walls. Julian sighed, plucked it up, and wiped it on his sleeve. "I'm not saying that you're not responsible, dear. I'm just concerned. I'm not going to make you talk about last Sunday, not if you don't want to. I just want you to be safe. Whatever you're doing, I'm not positive that you're doing it responsibly."

"Trust me." I leaned back in my chair and forced my eyes to stick to the tablecloth. It looked like a slab of Victorian wallpaper, yellowed at the edges and everything. I licked my gums. "This weekend isn't going to be like the last one. I'll call you if anything goes wrong."

"Ah." Julian did not look convinced. He looked at me for a long moment, unblinking, like there was something specific he was expecting to discover. I don't think he found it. He looked back down at his crossword, absently outlined the edge of the puzzle with his nail. "Five letter word. Means 'To influence with allure or magnetism.'"

"*Charm*," said Boris.

"*Witch*." I leaned back in my chair, rocked it on its hind legs. "Thanks for dinner. I'm going to bed." I rocked the chair back into place and stood up, pushed it in. Pulled fistfuls of my hair off my face and turned and headed toward my room.

"Good night," Boris called after me.

"You know," said Julian as I walked away. "*Witch* fits."

"Then use it," said Boris. "How often do you get to throw around a word like *witch*?"

✳

There were papercuts in the darkness. Together, they read *3:04.*

Shapeless shadows floated around my room, and my furniture lost its edges. Everything flowed into a single, hazy mass. My eyelids were sticky. I rolled over, pressed my face into my pillow, and tried to smother sleep back into me. Fuck waking up at 3:04. I had better things to be doing.

Before reality had yanked me back, I'd been somewhere else. I think it was vaguely the football field. Not our football field, but the one from the movie. The grass wasn't green like it should've been. It was pale, soft, the color of mint chip ice cream. I was lying on the grass. My wrists were zip-tied behind me.

My mind left out the ritual part. There wasn't a circle of *Ghastly* girls, either, or at least, not anyone from the movie. There was only one girl. She knelt beside me and pushed my hair out of my eyes. Her nails crisscrossed over my scalp, down the back of my neck. Eyes half-shut. Lips parted.

Damn 3:04 to hell. I wanted to go back to the part where Madeline Kline was murdering me, thanks.

The sheets snaked between my ankles. It was too hot, but not hot enough to kick all my blankets off. If I went without, I might catch hypothermia and wake up without fingers, or something like that. I rolled again, faced away from the alarm clock. I stared at a spot on the wall.

There just so happened to be a mirror on the wall. The mirror reflected 3:05 with excruciating brightness. Once I noticed it, I couldn't un-notice it. It was like a mosquito bite, ugly and red and unignorable.

"Screw off," I said to nothing. My voice was thick and gluey.

"Oh, don't mind me. Just stretching. You have school tomorrow morning. Ought to rest up, don't you think?"

I snapped my jaws shut. My eyes froze on the mirror. My lungs hurtled to a halt.

"Hush. Go back to sleep, baby Scapegracer. Close those heavy eyes. Dream about spell craft and pretty, wicked women. Dream that you are dreaming right now. You'll wake up in the morning and be ready. All is well."

My eyelids fell obediently shut. Muscles uncoiled. The bed seemed to swell, swallow me up. The crooked springs turned soft. Everything was easy, everything was smooth. My breathing slowed down.

"Who are you?" I barely moved my lips, barely had the energy required. Something might've moved across my foot. My toes felt cold and wet. There was the slightest pressure against my shins, like something had been placed there. That something smelled like ink. "What are you?"

"I'm the devil, dear. I'm what happens when you burn a living spell book. We'll talk about it later. Sleep well."

# EIGHTEEN

# THE PERILS OF NOT BEING LOVELESS

The coffee shop was a hipster catastrophe. The bricks were all painted different shades of pink and blue, and Christmas lights dripped from every available surface. Broken mugs hung from the doorway where another place might've hung shrunken heads. Jing and I sat outside. We'd rolled to a stop, and her music was low enough for us to hear each other. It was just the two of us. Yates had gone home separately, and Daisy was busy slicing necks at cheer practice. We sat in front of the shop, half-parked, and Jing reapplied her lipstick in the rearview mirror.

"You look nervous," she said. "Stop that."

"I'm not fucking nervous," I lied. My knees were propped up on the dash. I'd been screwing with the frays in my jeans for a solid five minutes. The fashionable holes were now full-fledged gashes. I looked a mess.

"Bullshit. You're nervous. Don't be nervous. You're hot as hell."

I snorted.

Jing lowered her lipstick and glowered at me. "I'm serious.

Look, riddle me this: do you want to date her, or do you want to screw her?"

I blanched. "Fucking hell, Jing."

"So, both. Good. Dating her shouldn't be a problem. Just screwing her could go worse. As far as weirdos go, you're as good as they come. And she agreed to come here, so, clearly, she's into weirdos. That means you don't have anything to worry about."

"If you tell me to be myself, I'm punching you in the nose."

"I'm fake as hell, Sideways. Why would I tell you that? No, I'm telling you to play it cool. You know how to talk to girls. You're doing it right now. If she doesn't like what she sees, so be it. I'll buy you a *Playboy* and we can move on with our lives. You're going to kill it. Understood?"

I flipped her off and huffed a sigh, tucked my hands against my ribs.

And there she fucking was. Madeline Kline, dressed in a snapback and slashed-up shorts, sauntered into the coffee shop with a swish of impossibly black hair. She didn't look nervous. She looked cool, casual with her braided leather bracelets, her Sharpie-scribbled kicks.

Jing gave me a shove. "Showtime, sweetie. Remember not to bite unless she asks."

✳

Madeline had already found a table. It was tucked in the back, crammed between two wide windows that made the tabletop shimmer holographic. Madeline had pulled her ponytail loose and her hair spilled over her shoulders. She sat with her chair turned backward, straddling it, her arms propped on the back. Tipped it forward so that it rested on two legs. Her hair swept the tabletop. She gave me a cocky little nod, flashed her teeth at me, waved me over. Jerked a thumb at the seat across from her.

My palms tingled. My fingertips twitched. My coffee was hot against my hand, and it matched the way my insides felt. I sat across from her in my preordained spot. Forced myself to look up, and tried at a smile.

If I started nervous laughing, God could just butcher me right then and there. Random lightning strike. Kaboom, death.

"You look killer," said Madeline. Her gaze was even, unblinking.

Impulse struck. I flipped her off, rolled my eyes.

She laughed. Thank God, she laughed. Her laugh was harsh and low in her throat. It reverberated down my spine.

"So. Sideways. Tell me about magic. Tell me how it works." She leaned across the table and her hair swished in to frame her face. "Tell me everything."

I took a sip of coffee that scalded my tongue, sizzled on the way down. Her eye contact didn't break, which was weird and spooky of her, and it made me want to lean over and plant one on her.

I touched my burn to the roof of my mouth and told Madeline everything. She must've done something to me, because she'd busted the floodgate. I opened my mouth and couldn't shut it again. One thing fell out after another, and soon everything that'd happened to me was spilling all over the table. Madeline didn't mind. If I slowed down, she urged me on with a nod. She didn't look away. Didn't drop her attention. Didn't even check her phone or drink her macchiato. She let me drift on and on, only reacting when I asked for a reaction. I told her about the *Vade Mecvm*s. I told her about scribbling with chalk. I told her about specters and the color of my soul. I told her how to hex someone. I told her how I'd tried to hex my science teacher when I was twelve. I told her how I'd tried to bless the acne off my back once, and how that had failed because it was too mundane for the universe to bother with. I told her about language and how it snares things, how it makes reality and twists the world around us. I told her about my mother, only briefly. I didn't tell her much about Jing and Yates and Daisy, but they were present, even if I didn't mention them by name. They'd wormed their way into my narrative. Yates' theory of ambiguity came up once or twice. I told her how magic kept me going. About how for a while, it was the *only* thing keeping me going. About how I used to underline passages in my English books because certain lines crawled off the page, because those lines were magic and they meant something on a cosmic scale. I told her everything, absolutely everything.

I felt like a damn idiot when I was done. How long had I been talking? I wasn't a big talker, not like this. A cackle ripped out of me, and I hated it as soon as it came. It was a giddy, nasty laugh. Awkward laughter always sounded mean when I did it. I drank my coffee, which was lukewarm now.

Madeline broke her gaze. "I need you to do something for me, Sideways."

I swallowed my coffee wrong. My lungs seized up and I hacked a cough, lurched over, wheezed into my elbow. My cheeks torched. I set my teeth, wiped my mouth with the back of my wrist, and looked up at her with a blink. "Sure," I managed. Furrowed my brows. "Anything."

"I need you to make a sigil for me." She didn't blink, didn't waver. Leaned forward across the table toward me. Reached to brush her fingertips against my sleeve. "Could you do that?"

I nodded too quickly. "Yeah. Yeah I could." I ducked under the table, clawed at my bookbag, and produced my shabby notebook and a busted pen. I put the pen in my teeth, dropped the notebook on the table, and rifled through it until I found a clean page. Looked up at her with a brow raised.

She didn't look at the paper. Her eyes stayed on me, deep and dark and endless. She licked her lips. "I need it to mean *This is mine.*"

"This is mine?" I mumbled the words around my pen. "Could you be more specific?"

"I've been in a bad way lately. Need to reclaim some stuff." She lowered her eyes for a moment, unfocused them. I couldn't parse what she was thinking. She cocked her head to the side. "I need it to surrender and to take back. Does that make sense? I need to give myself power. Something to get me through the day."

"Like for self-esteem?" I pulled my pen out of my mouth, twirled it around my fingers. She didn't react. I bit my tongue, swallowed my extra questions. Vagueness be damned. "Surrender and take back." I drew a few lines, swooping, swirling lines—an S for surrender, an arrowhead for taking things back. Vague as it was, the lines came easy. I glanced up at her for confirmation, and she nodded, clenched her jaw.

I set my coffee cup on top of the sigil and traced a circle around it.

"I feel like it needs something," Madeline said.

I frowned. "Yeah?"

She tapped her index finger on the middle of the glyph. "Can you put an X here? A big one."

"Like crosshairs?" I looked at the sigil crooked, tried to imagine an X over top of my lines. That might change the vibe a bit, adding an X. Make it more strident than it might've otherwise been.

Madeline was quiet for a moment, before nodding, crossing her arms. "Yeah."

I drew the X and she was satisfied. Extended her right hand, placed it beside my notebook. "Could you draw it on me?"

There was a rustling under my sleeve. A cold, wet writhing that shaped letters in its wake. I hadn't even realized that I'd brought Mr. Scratch with me, and the feel of him squirming against me made my stomach flip. I yanked my arms under the table and pulled my sleeve up, tried not to be obvious as I did so.

*Do not do not do not draw it on her absolutely do not do that please don't do that Sideways do not!*

"And who the fuck asked you?"

Madeline blinked.

"Sorry." I felt my face turn red. My insides burned and I shoved my sleeve down over my arm, tried to scrub away the message with a twist of my wrist. "Sure. Yeah. I'll draw it on you, whatever you want."

The inkbody under my sleeve went ballistic.

I shook my pen, scribbled a bit on the edge of the page, and pressed the ballpoint to Madeline's skin. I had no idea why Mr. Scratch was being so weird, but I frankly didn't care and would do basically anything that Madeline wanted, because holy fuck! A girl wanted me to do magic for her. A really hot and funny girl. Anything thing she wanted, literally anything. Fuck it. The lines looked bluish across her knuckles. I tried pressing lightly, tried not to bite the ballpoint into her skin, but when I'd nearly finished she gave me a look and I went over the lines again, pressed them harder, carved them out.

It looked almost pretty.

Madeline wiggled her fingers. Made a fist. Something fell over her expression and she looked up at me unsmiling, her brows drawn together in a V. "That's good. Thank you."

"Anytime," I said. I stuck my tongue in my cheek. "The incantation's a little vague, but if you focus on it, I think it'll work. Some of the best incantations are improvised. It should be fine."

Sleeve was going absolutely wild.

"Stellar." She withdrew her hand, hid it under the table. Didn't look at me for a moment. I felt her gaze float vaguely near my collarbone. Her mascara clumped like spider's legs. "I appreciate that. I really do."

Then there was silence. How do you follow making a sigil together? The hair on my arms prickled and I wasn't sure if it was the hints of magic or the proximity to Madeline that did it to me. Knocked the breath out of me, whatever it was. My head buzzed. First dates were supposed to be shallow, were they not? Small-talk babble about stuff we vaguely cared about, not a life story paired with impromptu glyph making. Assuming this was a date. Assuming she was interested.

I nibbled the inside of my bottom lip. Formulated something coherent. "So, are you doing anything tomorrow night?"

Madeline's gaze flickered up. Shot holes through my head. "Nah, why?"

"My friends and I are having another Halloween party." Felt confident when I said it out loud. The Scapegracers, they were my friends. Not a single damn doubt in my head. If our clique had a name, it was official, wasn't it? Right, right. I jammed my tongue against my hard palate. "It's gonna be pretty dope. We're doing more magic. Better magic. I'd like you to be there."

"You're doing magic at another party. Well, damn." She whistled through her teeth and rocked back in her chair. Her expression phased into something else, something identical but darker. Her eyes glossed up. When she spoke again, there was strain in her voice. "You know what? I think I have to be there. Got no choice."

"Costumes encouraged." I shrugged, tried for a smile. "I can text you the address. It's kind of a weird place, but I think you'll dig it. The whole thing goes down at nine."

"I'll be there." Madeline sucked her cheeks in, furrowed her brows. Gave me a nod. "Yeah, I'll be there. Thanks for this, by the way. Been too damn long since I went out with a hot girl, you feel? Anyway, I gotta jet. I've got basketball practice in twenty minutes and Coach will split me if I'm late again. But thanks. Seriously."

"Yeah." My cheeks flashed, and I nodded, sat up a little straighter in my chair. My pulse hammered in my temples. "Yeah. We should do it again sometime."

Madeline paused for a moment. I watched her throat move as she swallowed. "Sure," she said. She stood up, threw her bag over her shoulder. Then something flashed across her face—she flushed, eyes hazy, teeth against her lower lip—and she leaned across the table. Her hair swooshed down on either side of her face and she brought herself nearer. Brushed her lips against my cheek.

Madeline smelled like matches. Matches and patchouli and a sharp edge of sweetness, something I couldn't place. She stood upright and gave me a crooked little smile. I sat there like she'd taken a pipe wrench to my rib cage. My heart splattered against my spine. My whole body tingled, and she pulled her hair back into a ponytail, tied it up, gave me a nod.

"Tomorrow at nine," she said.

"Yeah." My eyes fell half-shut. "Tomorrow at nine."

Her lipstick had left a deep purple stain on my cheekbone. It glistened like a cut. I stared at my reflection in my blackened phone screen, marveling at its redness, its sparkle. She'd barely kissed me. The whole thing had lasted five seconds, max, but I pulled the moment apart, made it last a millennium in my mind. Her hair and her skin and her nearness, her electric nearness. The cool, slick sensation her mouth made when it touched me. I worked myself into a fit over it. Thought about it on repeat. Madeline Kline, who played basketball and liked witchcraft and *girls*. Liked me. Liked me enough to agree to a second date. The impracticality of it made my mind shake. Madeline, Madeline—damn, did I even know a single thing about basketball? I didn't, but now I had a burning desire to see her play. Wanted to see her run around in ill-fitting polyester, being a warrior, slaughtering another team. Wanted to know if she smiled when she won. Was she good? She must be. I couldn't imagine anything else. What were Madeline's friends like? If I went to one of her games, would they mind me screaming encouragement alongside them? If East High played West High, would I be crucified for cheering on the wrong team? If I was, the public execution would be worth it. Madeline could bring popcorn. Enjoy the show.

I made a point of not looking under my sleeves at whatever weirdness Mr. Scratch was on about. I didn't know him, so he didn't get a say. What did he know, anyway? He's been stuck in a vase for God knows how long.

The hood was down, so the wind threw my curls around

my face. Stung my neck and my shoulders. Jing had said very little thus far. She'd picked me up, and now we were sailing back home toward Rothschild & Pike. We listened to her music so loud the car shook. We received nasty looks from moms in minivans. People I didn't recognize shouted and waved.

"You look shaken." It wasn't a question. Jing's blond braids ruffled, glittered in the dying light. "Did you screw her?"

"Where would I have screwed her? The bathroom?"

"Sure." Jing shrugged.

The world outside her convertible looked candied. Scarlet leaves rushed over top of pastel homesteads. Chain-link fences lined the hopscotched sidewalks. Boxed pansies hung under windows. Fake ghosts dangled from the limbs of trees. Skeletons peered out of windows and over porches. A kid roller-skated in circles. The air was gummy worms and fire. Sycamore Gorge glowed, and I was glowing, too, and time moved slower than it ought to.

"Nah," I said. "She asked me to make her a sigil." I leaned my head back, looked up at the sky as it churned past. Sheep clouds, dreamy clouds. Suburban paradise, some shit like that. Pollution made the sky damn pretty. I heaved in a breath through my teeth. "She said she'd be there tomorrow."

"She better be." Jing snickered, took a turn. Main Street bloomed on either side of us. Jing turned the music down a touch, but not enough that pedestrians wouldn't hear the filth that poured out of her speakers. "If she plays you, I'll have her blood."

"Nah," I said. I breathed in slow. The air was crisp in my throat. "No need. I have a good feeling about this, Jing. About her. She's kinda spooky, you know?"

"Jesus Christ, only you would say some shit like that about a girl you have a crush on." Jing crinkled her nose. "You win the spooky contest, if we're having a spooky contest. Just saying."

"She listened like none other, alright." My heartbeat hummed in my fingertips. I pressed them against my cheekbone, against the lipstick gash. My nails scraped. My eyes fluttered back. "Is it normal to feel this stupid after someone kisses you?"

"Fucking no. I've kissed a lot of boys in my life, Sideways. It's like watching nail polish dry."

"Ever kissed a girl?"

"Not yet." She pulled up next to Rothschild & Pike, stopped the car. "But even if I did, I don't think I'd act all dopey after the fact. You're lame, Sideways. You get any more Disney about this and I'll shove your ass in a locker, you hear?"

"As if my ass would fit in a locker."

"Bite me."

I arched my back, knotted my fingers in my snarly curls, pressed the toes of my boots into the cheetah-print carpeting. "How exactly am I supposed to wait until tomorrow? School's gonna kill me, Jing."

"You'll live. You're a big kid." Jing adjusted her bangs in the rearview mirror. "I'm confident in your abilities to buck up and take it. Just over twenty-four hours, babe."

\*

Just inside the shop, Mr. Scratch found it in him to speak. He nestled his wet body against the back of my hair at the place where my curls met my collar. "I don't think you should talk to that Madeline anymore. I don't think that she is a safe person to talk to."

"She's the only girl who's been interested in me, ever. I don't see why you'd get a fucking say, Scratch."

"Sideways," he said faintly. "Sigils like that aren't any good. They're—"

"If you're going to be a nag, you can hop off me right now. I'm not carrying you around anymore." I curled my lip and whirled around, but he wasn't behind me, of course. He was too close for me to see. "Leave me alone. Live in my room for all I care, but don't follow me, and don't butt in."

"Are you sure?"

"People don't just *like* me. People never just like me. Don't go ruining it for me when they do." I shoved my forehead against a wall. "I don't even know you. I mean, what are you? How can you be a burned book *and* a devil? How does that square, huh?"

"I'm called a devil, and I was a book," he said. His voice was high, not just in pitch, but in tone. Windy and brittle. "It's not safe for baby witches to run about without a book to aid them, Sideways. I just want—"

"I'm not a baby, and you're not a book. You're a lump of

ink in my hair. Just. Just go, okay?"

Mr. Scratch didn't say anything else. I felt him drip off my body and pool around my boots, and watched his dark form as it oozed between the cracks in the floorboards.

# NINETEEN

# A LITTLE NIGHT MUSIC

I drew Madeline's mark on every piece of paper I touched. It overlapped ill-conceived equations, bounced in *Frankenstein*'s margins, bloomed on the edges of the French Revolution. I drew her symbol on my thigh, where my skin peeked between the rips. I drew it on the inner crook of my elbow, on my ankle, on the bones of my wrist. All of school was devoted to sigil drawing, and I ignored the rest of the world. Classes rolled by seamlessly, dull and throbbing, without distinguishing detail. I didn't talk all that much, unless it was about the party. The party was starting to find press, though. I wasn't sure how, but people spoke about it just out of sight. I heard whispers in the hallways. Saw people nod at the Scapegracer girls, make notes about what was to come. Mickey-Dick and Ashleigh made a huge show of cringing whenever we walked by. Most people seemed chill, though, or at least the people who weren't awful to me as a rule. Alexis made a point of telling me she was pumped, even if she refused to DJ after our last party broke her speakers. I told her that Jing was handling it, because as far as I knew, she was.

Madeline's sigil was damn pretty. Even when I briefly got distracted, I came back to it, tracing and retracing it over and over again. Madeline had been right. The X did make it better. Even without an incantation, it made my skin prickle, and I hyped myself up, revved for magic to come.

The final bell rang, and I was unshackled at last.

Daisy, as one might guess, had a football game that night. The game would run from six until about eight, which meant that Yates and Jing and I were responsible for all the preparations. Jing and Yates picked me up at seven and we drove to a seedier stretch of town, where the less-favored restaurant chains and drug dealers loitered around hoping for business. We ordered quick, ate salty drive-through french fries in the back of a sleazy lot, watched the sun phase out of the sky overhead. We took turns cursing classes and braiding each other's hair. Discussed what would've happened if the *Ghastly* movie had gone differently, how much cooler it'd be if the sisterhood had won.

"Is it true that you locked Natalie Crouching in a closet last year, Sideways? Like, with magic?" Yates dipped one of her french fries in her chocolate shake. "Because I've been hearing people say that she called you ugly, and you were so pissed that you shoved her in a closet and hexed the door shut behind her. No lights in there or anything. She didn't have her phone on her, so she had to wait three hours for a janitor to finally open the door."

"Bullshit," said Jing before I could. She had her seat fully reclined and lay back with her arms behind her head, her feet propped up, her mouth twisted in a lazy purple scowl. "Natalie Crouching's in the closet of her own goddamned accord."

"You think so?" I raised a brow, shredded a chicken nugget with my nails. Wasn't appetizing, but that was fine. Least it gave me something to do.

"Sure as death," said Jing. She closed her eyes, raked her fringe out of her face. "No girl who kisses other girls at parties that much is straight. Unless she's an asshole who gets all of her happiness from performing porny fake lesbian shit for the worst kind of guys. There's always that possibility."

Hadn't Natalie and Daisy done that once?

We passed around a bottle of Coke and the conversation wandered. The sky above our heads tinged black.

In the back of Jing's car were backpacks full of battery-powered lanterns and strobes, bottles of water, speakers for our music. Jing had considered Halloween deco, but had ultimately decided against it. It was tacky, she explained. Overkill. Our raggedy house was already a murder palace, and suiting it up with ghosts and ghouls would be a mark of disrespect. Like slapping a BEWARE OF DOG sign on an obviously lycanthropic household, constant howling, bellowing at the slightest intruder. BEWARE OF DOG. Like, fucking obviously.

We headed over at eight. It was dark enough for our headlights to bleach the red leaves pink. Our music echoed off the black bark, bounced back around our heads. I focused on the music, on Jing's hair flashing around her face, on the glow of lights in Yates' curls. This was not the Chantry car, I reminded myself, but I still closed my eyes through most of the ride. The gravel made the car grind, and it flipped my stomach. I sucked in a breath through my teeth. "Can you turn up the music?"

Yates cranked it even louder.

I rubbed Madeline's sigil where it still showed faintly on my elbow, and I rubbed her sigil on my thigh. Taking stuff back, was that it? Reclaiming power, or something like that? How about my cool? I'd like that back, thanks. Madeline's scribbles, give me strength. Let me stress less about country roads at night.

We arrived at our destination before my prayers could take hold, but that was fine by me. The gravel crunch stopped, and my stomach stayed inside my body. I made myself open my eyes.

The three of us hopped out of the car. Yates and I went around back, started heaving bags of supplies over our shoulders, and Jing went on ahead. She reached into one of her pockets and withdrew skinny, unsnapped glow sticks, which she proceeded to rip in half. She held them at arm's length and they gushed. Jing walked down the path toward the house with oozing glow sticks outstretched, and droplets of neon light drizzled along the handrail. Blue and pick splotches glared through the dark.

Yates and I followed her down. Between the two of us, we managed to carry everything we needed. My arms screamed under the weight. The rickety steps groaned under our feet, but they didn't break, didn't pitch us down into the darkness.

Our dead house looked sicker by moonlight. Jing broke a fresh set of glow sticks and smeared them all over the front door, mixing pink and blue and violent violet together into a psychedelic blur. It shone holographic, like ectoplasm or Wonderland. Made a beacon for us to aim for.

Jing held the door for us and we carried the bags inside. It was crushingly dark in the house, smotheringly silent. It was like stepping into outer space. I wasn't confident that my boots would find floor with every step—my foot might fall through and I'd tumble forward, bags flying, into the shapeless black.

Something grabbed me by the shirt collar.

"*Fuck!*" I jerked away from the grip, but it tightened, held me in place.

"Jesus, relax. Hold still. The lanterns are in that bag." Jing's voice. I could almost hear her smirk. Her hand slid lower, toward one of the bags on my shoulder, where she fumbled with a zipper. I felt her rummage around, then she let go of me and something clicked.

My shadow fell across the floor. Everything was amber, and the gutted furniture looked jagged and weary, like the light had just woken it up. Jing walked around me, lanterns swinging from her fingertips, and hung them on our makeshift hooks.

REIGN OF SCAPEGRACE.

We put down our bags.

Jing and Yates attacked the speakers. They tucked them in the corners, where they stood like robot sentinels, and stuck them full of wires which they attached to Jing's laptop. They hooked the laptop up to an external battery, one of three or four they'd brought. The air hummed with static.

The front door opened behind me.

Jing and Yates snapped to attention. I spun on my heels, my heart hammering in my teeth.

Quicksilver haunted the doorway. Liquid, rippling fabric tumbled off skinny shoulders, sparkled like crushed glass and starlight, swished with every click of high-heeled shoes. Manicured fingers stretched out from the sleeves and flew up to yank back the hood with lacquered, knife-shaped nails, revealing a flash of glittered eyes, a button nose, a savage grin. "Good evening, gashes."

I broke into a grin.

Yates clapped, Jing wolf whistled, and Daisy—lovely, hooded Daisy—flipped her hair over her shoulder, gave us a wink. She swept up beside me and pulled a satchel off her shoulder, clawed inside of it, and withdrew a bundle of faded red fabric. She tossed the bundle at my head, and I caught it one-handed. The fabric was buttery soft.

Jing and Yates pulled on their robes, and I locked my attention on the fabric in my fist. I loosened my grip and it unfurled. The color was ghostly, a hazy, bruisy red. Pink wasn't right—no, it was eerier, shimmering in shades of crimson and maroon. Looked like something that a figure in a tarot card might wear. Like a violent daydream. I shouldered off my jacket and slipped it over my head, and the robe spilled around me, fluttered to my ankles.

Yates was baby blue across the room, and Jing fiddled with

her glistening lavender hood. The two of them looked like they'd waltzed out of a fairy tale. Jing cracked her knuckles, looked us over.

Something crashed over my head, something that wasn't real but felt very cold. Chills. My body ached like it'd been whip-cracked, and all the meat on me hung limp off the bone. Head swam, stomach corkscrewed, guts tangled and kicked high.

It felt like magic breaking.

I looked at the three of them, and all of us, a little shivery and pale now, peered at one another.

"Must be the fucking mold," said Jing. "Don't think about it. No worries."

"Mold," said Yates. "I hate this place."

"Just mold," I repeated. The word didn't seem real anymore, but I told myself it was plausible. The four of us all felt nauseous at the same time because it was kind of poisonous in here. No other reason. Nothing to worry about.

"Adds to the mood," Daisy said.

"Right," said Jing. "Now, someone fucking help me set the music up, yeah?"

✳

The bass made the floorboards throb. I'd guess around sixty people tangled in the living room, but it could have been more. They all blurred together into one hydra-shaped monster. The bodies knotted up and pulsated, and our frozen, hollow, murder house found a new circulatory system in their twisting, ecstatic jamming. A girl with a four-jawed rubber mask hooked her body around someone with a plastic knife in their temple, and they grinded against zombie princesses, classic slashers, generic spooky people-eaters. Michael Myers made out with Vampira. Someone in a wolf mask and a flannel leered from a corner. The room wasn't cold anymore. Heat shimmered off the bodies in waves, thick and salty and metallic. Naked limbs drifted in the air, clawed at nothing, flashed in the seizing lights.

I was nervous enough to wreck something. I stood in the center of our sigil, and the trinity took up three of the four points on the circle. Jing was drinking, Daisy looked ravenous, and Yates kept wiggling her fingertips, straightening her cloak, looking around for our missing point. Madeline hadn't shown. In all the writhing bodies at our party, Madeline's face was nowhere to be seen, not even in the farthest corners of the dance floor. We were an hour in, and she wasn't here. She wasn't fucking here.

# TWENTY

# PERMISSION TO CROSS THE THRESHOLD

Jing crushed her can in her fist, tossed it to the floor, and crossed the room to stand in the center with me. She did a 360, gaze cutting through the crowd like hot razors. "Son of a bitch," she said. "You seen her?"

"No."

"Son of a bitch." Jing cracked her knuckles, ripped her hands back through her hair. "We need to start soon. Call her."

I curled my lip, shot up my brows. Ha, no. "*Call* her? Jesus, Jing, call her? Am I her fucking babysitter? If she ditched, she ditched."

"Fuck that." Jing took a step closer, cracked a raucous smile, spoke crisply enough to be heard through the sickening bassline. "Ladies and gents, we need ourselves a fearless volunteer. Step up, if you're not too gutless for us." She held up one of her hands, and it felt like a rallying cry—people turned away, or else looked on with smirks and awkward glances. No doubt, the crowd was having a mass flashback to last weekend.

The whole thing made me nervous. Ye olde random participant might ruin our whole circuit, shatter my concentration, dampen the magic. Make this whole thing a bust. Thinking about it made me feel like I'd dry-swallowed a AAA battery. No fucking thanks. This mass of flowy fabric felt smothering all of a sudden. It clogged my pores. My body couldn't breathe. The hair on my arms stood up. I had a distinctive urge to find one of the speakers and stomp it.

The wolf-mask kid sauntered up. Long strides, shoulders forward, hands stuffed deep in the pockets of their Levi's. I couldn't really place their gender—shame on me for trying, but fucking whatever—because red flannel shirts do a decent job of swallowing a person's body. Their jeans were shredded, maybe naturally—they were the kind of holes that came from skidding concrete and snagging chain-linked fences, not factory-reinforced aesthetic tattering. Sharpied high-tops.

Oh.

Wolf-head, who now stood at the edge of our circle, shoulders sloped, one leg crossed over the other, was Madeline. The edge of her sigil peeked out from under her sleeve. What the fuck had she been doing, lurking in the corner instead of saying hi?

I let out a little huff. Smiled crookedly, hoped it wasn't as anxiety drenched as I felt. Yates' brows shot up to her hairline, and she pulled her mouth into a dubious horizontal line, but I ignored her when she opened her mouth to comment. Blood was pooling in my temples. I stepped forward, reached out a hand. "Thought you wouldn't show."

Madeline gave me an exaggerated shrug. If she said something, it was smothered by the wolf mask, which she wasn't taking any steps to remove. The big cartoony rubber fangs were motionless. Rubber yellow eyes stared unseeing. After a pause, she took my hand, and I dragged her toward her point on the sigil. Her hands were dry as chalk.

Daisy bounced on her toes like a prize fighter and moved her hands in fluid waves, an arc that curved from her wrists to her knuckles. She jammed the tip of her tongue between her incisors and dove downward, took a seat at her point, and held out her hands to either side of her. Jing and Yates exchanged a look before they sat. Took her hands in theirs. The two of them then reached for Madeline.

For a moment, I thought she wouldn't play. She sat motionless, hands in her lap. Rubbed a thumb into her opposite palm. Her shoulders bobbed when she breathed. Daisy grinned at her, teeth bared in a show of dominance, and gave Madeline a delirious little nod. The whites of her eyes were enormous.

Madeline took Jing's and Yates' hands and the magic began.

It poured like ice down my back. My sides seized up with shivers as strong as convulsions, and my hands shrunk into fists. Copper on my tongue. Copper in my nose, in my jaw, down the seams of my throat. My arms quivered. My arms, then my shoulders, then my rib cage, and every button in my spine. I shook, quaked, thrummed like a plucked string. The robe was too hot. I wanted to take it in my fists and rip it off my spine, to stand mad and naked and panting. My skeleton was swelling beneath my skin, and it needed space to expand. I was like Alice. I was going to unfurl and grow twenty feet tall, bust through the walls and the ceiling with my immensity. My pulse was an industrial drill. It hammered quick enough that my teeth chattered, clacked together in hyperdrive.

I smiled so hard that my face ached.

Magic would be the death of me. I was wholly, unflinchingly fine with this. I cleared my throat, tossed back my head, and threw both my hands toward the vault of heaven.

"Who wants to see some *fucking magic?*"

A collective cry from the crowd. Nervous laughter, roars of approval, snickers and sneering and faux-cynicism—I relished it. My hair fell out of my hood, snarled around my cheeks, absorbed all the evil energies that flooded the corpselike room. Dancing had stopped, but the rush of it hadn't—all the kinetics of thrashing and grinding alchemized into something else, something unearthly. The shadows glowed. The Scapegracer girls around me, gripping each other and Madeline tight, looked up in tandem. It wasn't choreographed. Three faces split with enormous, monstrous smiles—even Yates, ever pretty, looked ooky and ravenous—and the rubber mask over Madeline's head took on a shade of realism it hadn't had before.

Drugs could not accomplish this. Nothing chemical could make my heart twist and deform and metamorphose into something this strange, this volatile. I was silly with it, enthralled. My voice didn't sound like it should. It sounded like the voice in my head, like how my thoughts sound, like the whisper roll that plays when I read something.

"We are the Scapegracers, and the cosmos belongs to us." I rolled my shoulders, wiggled my fingertips. "When we want something to happen, it happens. When we want to grab physics by the throat and shake it to death, we do. Fuck your perceptions. Forget about reality. Gravity isn't relevant anymore, not to us." Damn, did hubris taste nice against my tongue. I flared my nostrils. Cleared my throat. Spoke a little louder, diaphragm all in knots, and the girls joined in. *"Higher."*

The chant was high and harsh. Jing and Yates and Daisy's voices were distorted, only audible where the fricatives struck. Their consonants were clipped, discordant, bouncing between savage sopranos and low, wicked sighs. My vision splattered red. I was swaying, but I wasn't sure how—the chant had a current and it rocked me. My organs threatened to burst out of my bones. I was too big for a human body to hold anymore. I was too swollen—magic marrow deep and throbbing, oozing glitter into my bloodstream, into my consciousness. "Gravity isn't real. Gravity is optional. Gravity is a lie they told us when we were kids."

Cameras flashed like a thousand dancing eyes in the darkness. They stung like pinpricks on my skin. I liked it. Every gasp, every curse and overexaggerated gesture from the crowd melted together into a single, dripping force. It was a mirror to bounce off of. My voice rattled my skull, echoed off the ceiling and the walls. "Scapegracer girls are impervious to gravity. Higher, higher—this whole house can't manage us anymore. The world can't manage us anymore."

Something flittered in the corner of my eye, a liquidy movement blooming in silver, lavender, and baby blue. The robes. They dangled in a circle around me, loose and rippling, unhindered by legs, which were still crossed, floating somewhere around rib cage height.

Under my feet, the spray paint glowed like crimson floodlights. It illuminated the ceiling in a gory, glorious red, and it sparkled and waved like the glare off a swimming pool. People clapped and hollered, but that was far away, way on the other side of the world. All I could see were my Scapegracer girls, suspended in space. Chanting, grinning, glistening.

I could only see Jing's face properly. Her eyes were rolled back, her mouth agape with chanting, her face flushed and flawless and raw. Was that what I looked like? Jing, whispering magic, breathing it, was a different kind of beautiful. A kind of beautiful too sharp to describe as beautiful. There was a magnitude of power in her, in how simultaneously relaxed and tense she was. Her hair twisted around her shoulders with no regard for logic, moving fluidly, floating like a bleach-kissed halo. Her lips were crooked, hiked higher on one side.

Beside her was the wolf-head. Fake teeth didn't snap, rubber eyes didn't blink. If Madeline was rapturous under there, she didn't show it. Tendrils of inky black hair crept from underneath the mask, drifted upward like vines that twined up the rubbery neck and around the pointed ears. The body underneath was still, sneakers hanging limp from its ankles.

Then the wolf-head turned sideways. Madeline stayed like

that, head whipped back, rubber snout jabbed out into the darkness, for just a second before she wrenched her hands out of Jing's and Yates' and curled them to her chest.

The spell snapped.

It sucker-punched me like a freight train through plaster. The world inverted, flipped red and crooked, and my insides wrenched around, rearranged. My hands found my knees. Fire quaked through my esophagus, flooded my shoulders with a sour feeling, and my tongue, suddenly too big for my teeth, tasted bitter and sick. The music was too loud. It closed in on my skull like a vise and squeezed, threatened to crack through bone and flatten my brains and send gore flying everywhere. I was about to splatter. People were screaming. I think they were happy, but I could barely make out the crowd.

Through the chaos, someone grabbed me. I still couldn't see anything, but I could feel their nails in my wrists.

Something kept trying to lurch me forward, but I didn't want to go. I dug my heels into the hardwood, but the pulling was desperate. Fingers gripped hard enough to leave marks. There was a yank, and my weight gave way. I crashed forward in the direction of the person pulling me. My vision spun. Monster-painted teenagers, half-cackling, half-horrified, kaleidoscoped everywhere I looked. Faces warped, distorted. I couldn't recognize anyone, couldn't match the beastly faces to names. My feet moved without my permission, one falling after the other.

We rounded a corner, and everything was dark.

Whatever force was dragging me did so faster. There were

fewer bodies to navigate around, fewer wires to toe and jump. This part of our corpse house was cold. It smelled sweet, like rot and drywall. Whoever was pulling me stopped, and I stopped, too. There was a scraping, a clatter—the chairs we'd blocked the staircase with, they'd moved them aside. I was shoved up a set of stairs, boots smacking the planks unceremoniously, and they dragged the chairs back behind us. Put their hands between my shoulder blades and pushed.

Stillborn magic had stolen my center of gravity. I pitched forward, nearly smacking the floor, but they grabbed a fistful of my robe and caught me, hauled me upright. Put a hand on my shoulder to steady me, and kept it there as they climbed, bringing me with them.

It felt like I'd swallowed honeyed sawdust. My throat was raw, sticky thick, and my voice had to knife through the gloom to be heard. It was too hoarse, too raspy to sound like mine. I tasted copper on my teeth. "What are you doing?"

They didn't say anything back. We'd reached the top floor, and they put an arm around my waist, hoisted me down the hall. My eyes were adjusting, but there wasn't much to adjust to. We were going somewhere darker than where we'd been. A black hole in the shadows. A doorway.

They let go of me and my knees shot out. The floor came up around me and I smacked hardwood, mashed my floating ribs. My tongue swelled up, tasted red. I jerked myself up onto my hands and knees. The floor was clammy, slick with wet decay and tufts of something itchy.

They shut the door. They must've pulled a phone out, or a

flashlight—the brightness stabbed my eyes and I shrunk back, tossed an arm over my face.

My eyes adjusted.

The wolf knelt in front of me. I could hear denim rustling against the floor, the squeak of folding boot leather. Then, they—she—spoke. "I'm sorry." Low alto, melodic, rough around the edges like she was on the verge of tears.

I recognized the voice.

My heart lurched. I coughed and managed, "Madeline?"

She put down the phone. Pulled off her wolf mask and shook her head, let all that black hair fly loose. The blackest black I'd ever seen settled around her shoulders, split her face in odd places, looking like cracks. Eyeliner ran in rivulets down her cheeks. Her eyes were huge and splotchy, harsh pink framed with spider-legged lashes, and her brows knotted up in the center of her face. "I am so fucking sorry."

"Madeline," I wheezed, wiping my mouth with the back of my sleeve, "what the *fuck* are you doing? What's wrong?"

"I was gonna wait. I was going to wait and do this when we were alone. And, God, when I saw *his* car, I nearly bailed. It's too dangerous, me being here. It would be easier to do it later. And, I mean, I wanted to spend more time with you. I like you, Sideways. God, I fucking *like* you." Madeline spoke out of the corner of her mouth. She didn't blink, didn't look away, didn't move those huge eyes off my face, but she started to shiver. Her whole body trembled, shuddering like a weathervane in a storm, and she reached out, put her hands on the back of my neck. "But he's here, and that means he'll be after you, too, and I couldn't let that happen. I need you too much to let that happen. I need this for both of us, for every girl like us. Just, just know that I'm sorry. I mean that."

Who was this *he* she was fixated on? "Madeline, I don't know what the fuck you're talking about—I'm not going anywhere. What is going *on?* Whatever it is, you can tell me." There was a strange, tart twinge in my stomach. I shook my head, narrowed my eyes a touch, tried not to notice how chilly Madeline's fingers were against my neck. How her fingertips were calloused as they scraped the base of my jaw. My heartbeat was too fast. I couldn't pinpoint why. Everything was too much.

Madeline leaned forward. Kissed me between the eyes.

My lungs stopped working.

She hovered by my forehead, pressed her nose into my hairline. Her exhalation was harsh, clipped. Wandering. Whispering—she was whispering something. I couldn't make it out, but she was saying the same phrase over and over again. The consonants tripped over each other.

The side of my neck burned where she held me with the hand I'd drawn her sigil on. The pain was immediate, electric. I jerked away from her, but her grip was too tight and dead magic made me groggy. She held me in place. I lifted my hands up, shoved at her shoulders, her chest, but my arms were numb and leaden. Flannel slipped through my fingers. The pain sharpened. It seared me now. My whole body recoiled. I spasmed, then thrashed—kicked out both of my legs, got my feet under me, tried to stand.

Pain ripped through me. My skin, at the point where she was burning me, bonded itself to her hand, and when I tried to stand up the skin pulled, threatened to tear. I froze, jaw stiff, eyes wide, fixed on the shape of Madeline in the dark. She whispered faster. I could see her face more clearly now—there was a red glow on her nose and across her shoulders. It floodlit her features in a violent, glittering crimson. It struck her eyes. Maybe that's why she was crying. Her makeup, black as her hair, dripped down her cheeks, dripped off her chin in toxic, muddy droplets. Drops landed on my neck. She looked at me and curled her lip.

"It isn't personal," she said. Stabbed her tongue in her cheek. "I'll give it back. I'll take back what's mine, and then you can have what's yours. You have my word on that." Her voice was ragged. Her breath was hot, tainted with an edge of alcohol and something sugary, something that made me nauseous. "Hold still."

"Stop," I hissed, and I thrashed again, lurched backward. Her hand was still adhered to my neck, and she came crashing after me. My head smacked the floor, and one of her knees struck my abdomen, slammed the air out of my lungs. I sputtered. I saw spots. I tried to writhe and kick her away, but my arms and legs weren't moving like they were supposed to. They were numb. Everything was numb, save for the pain at my throat, which lit up my nerves like the Fourth of July.

Madeline scrambled up, adjusted herself, pinned me in place with her legs. She straddled my ribs, kept my breathing shallow. Curved her spine like a candy cane, leaving her face dangling lash-length from mine. Her hair spilled everywhere, curtaining the two of us in a glossy, brilliant red. She kept one hand, the one with the sigil that was stuck to my skin, on my neck, and grabbed my jaw with the other. Shoved until my cheek pressed the hardwood. All I could see was her hair, her glowing hair, but I could feel where she was looking, regardless. She was watching the place where her fingers met my skin. She was transfixed.

Something flickered off and died. It was like she'd taken a wrench to my sternum, pried my rib cage apart, and tore my sneering, hissing heart out of its resting place. My body stopped feeling like a body. It wasn't mine anymore. It was nothing.

I rolled my eyes up to see her. Her hand wasn't on my neck anymore. It was aloft, inches above my face. The sigil I'd drawn on her was bloody red, and between her curled fingertips glimmered a light, brilliant and blinding as a sliver of sun. She looked at it instead of me. Then she tossed back her head, opened her mouth, and lowered the light between her jaws.

I couldn't breathe. I couldn't make a sound.

The glow slid down Madeline's throat, illuminating its path from her neck to her chest, where it vanished. I couldn't feel my fingers. I couldn't feel my tongue. Madeline let go of me, and I didn't lash out and strike her, because I couldn't make my arms move. My body felt crushed, like I'd been hit by a train, or hurled down a well in a bag. If there was sensation, that sensation was the ache, and nothing more.

"You're prickly," she said. Her voice was odd. Breathy, silky. Her eyes rolled back in her head. "It feels like barbed fire all the way down. Fire with fangs and hooks and chunks of glass." Madeline ran her hands down her throat, then slid them down to wrap around her torso. She gave herself a squeeze. "You're like eating electricity, Sideways."

She stood up. Wiped the tears off her cheeks with the edge of her sleeves. "Thank you. Seriously. I fucking owe you, Sideways Pike. And remember this: If a bunch of blond guys ever come asking about your magic, you don't tell them a thing. Not a single thing." She swayed a little, pulled a face. "Not that they could do much to you now."

"You're Addie." My tongue was heavy. I made my head roll to look at her. Iron-flavored anger bubbled in my stomach, radiated through my body, through every stinging vein. If I could move, I'd be on her. I'd throw her down the stairs.

She looked down at me. Narrowed those enormous eyes of hers. "If you're my ex, yeah. No one else calls me fucking *Addie*." Madeline's voice was venomous, and she spat out *Addie* like it was the foulest word she'd ever heard. She wiggled her fingertips, rolled her shoulders, and slipped her hands into her pockets. My sigil filtered pink through the denim. The glow was insulting. I wanted to kick out her teeth.

"Speaking of. His car is outside, which means he's probably downstairs. Can't do much to you now, though. Witchfinders go for the specter and, I mean, your specter is thoroughly fucking taken at this point. So, yeah." Madeline sniffed, took a few steps back. "Don't look for me," she said. Turned away from me. "I'll come find you when you can have it back."

She closed the door behind her as she left.

## ✳ TWENTY-ONE ✳

# SYMPATHY FOR, WELL, YOU KNOW

"You're not dead. Did you know that?"

I'd clawed myself halfway to the door. My legs didn't want to work, and I couldn't stand yet, but I had enough rage feeding my furnace that I could manage a slithering, desperate crawl. My hands scraped the floor in front of me, driving splinters under my nails.

I stopped mid-motion, wheezing, woozy. No. This was not the fucking time to lose my head. I needed to slither down those stairs, shove my hand down Madeline's throat, and fish my bloody soul out of her stomach. I needed to get to the door, but my forearms were bruised and sticky, the ground was slick with mold, and I was too damn tired to keep this up if I didn't focus. What would happen if I fell asleep? How long had it taken Fortune Grier to die?

"I imagine her ex-boyfriend taught her that trick. A witch willfully fraternizing with a Chantry boy—it horrifies me, it makes me roil just to think it. I knew that sigil was bad, Sideways. I knew it. It smacked of witchfinder torture."

The smell struck and it was overwhelming. Ink. Sour,

acrid ink reeked from every direction. I choked on it. My lip curled up, and I sucked in a breath, hard. Tried not to retch.

"I felt your protective spell break earlier. I knew it wouldn't hold long. The Chantry boy downstairs must've assumed that Madeline would be at this party and sensed your spell when he was scrying for you before the party. Witchfinders are very good at breaking protection charms. I am sorry that I was not here to reinforce it. I couldn't get to you any quicker than this, not with the Delacroix witches after me, not when I wasn't sure where you'd gone. I am so sorry. I'm sorry that I'm not faster.

"I did one thing for you, though: I arrived when that girl was eating your soul, and I slowed things down inside this room. What took ten minutes for you was ten seconds for the human bodies downstairs. That's why your friends didn't come to save you. They couldn't. It hasn't even really happened in their sphere of reality yet. I know that might seem cruel, but I need you to believe me: it probably saved their lives, or at least spared them from sharing your fate. None of you know offensive magic. None of you can cast on command. You're fledgling witches, without a spell book of your own. With the Chantry boy downstairs, if I had let things move at a normal pace, your friends would all be snatched up by now. An entire coven, snuffed out in a night. I couldn't bear that. I lost my coven. I would never forgive myself if I saw them destroy another. I think I would cease to be me.

"Book devils need witches as much as the other way around. We amplify spell work for you and record all your brilliance, and you give us materials and the kinship we need to survive. The world is not habitable for us, Sideways. Everything wants us dead outside of the likes of you. I want to be your friend. You could use a friend like me right now."

One of my nails split. Pain wasn't bad. It was a concrete thing I could feel and I relished it, even though I wanted to sob. I spat, scraped my tongue with my teeth. "Go on."

"I want to help you. A devil is what makes a spell book a spell book. Every coven has at least one devil among them, to fill the pages of their books, to give them magic and have it returned. We are living archives. We—I—take pride in seeing our covens grow. In providing spells and sigils. In remembering for them. In instructing them. Witchfinders *burned* my old coven, Sideways. They made my daughters cough their souls out and locked their bodies up, set our house on fire. They burned my book body. That urn you broke was a shell for my ashes. An urn to let me mourn, they said, to let me rest in remembrance. It was an urn to trap me—hateful, *vengeful* me—in a cage, out of sight. Witches were afraid of me. They were afraid I would hate them for failing to protect my daughters, or that seeing my pain might mean having to admit that they aren't safe; aren't invincible and strong like they pretend to be. Nobody was punished. For decades, I was trapped.

"And then came you. You and your girls, you freed me. Offered me a glimmer of hope—what could be more hopeful than a new, bookless coven, bright-eyed and cunning, knocking me free of my urn? I want to be your strange thing,

Sideways. I want to get you your soul back, and I want to burn the witchfinders, and I want you and your girls to make a new book for me to live in. Will you let me be yours, Sideways? Would you like me to be your friend?"

Raspy, at the tip of my tongue: "*Yes.*"

"Splendid." The ink smell swept over me, and something touched against the burn mark on my neck—something cold, slick, and sultry. "Now, you've got to go save your friends, dear. You'll need magic for that."

I wanted to scream.

"Hush, hush—no need to fret. I need to live inside you for a while. I won't stay forever. I would hate that as much as you. I much prefer paper to platelets. But I can keep you alive without your specter, and I can let you use the magic in me to protect yourself and your friends. May I climb through this little wound that Madeline made in your neck?"

"You asking to possess me?" I cracked a mirthless laugh, went limp against the floor for a moment. Breathing hurt. I rolled my head to the side, and tried to fight the tightness in my throat. My eyes felt wasp-stung. They swelled, blurred. I bit my lip. "Fine. Let's fry him."

"Lovely."

The coolness pressed against me, prodded the broken skin. It tickled for a moment. Then, it poured itself inside. It was like a drink of cold water that skipped my mouth, jumped straight for my throat instead. My body was drenched inside out and everything hurt at once. It felt like a billion dancing pinpricks, like my body had been asleep and only now could the blood rush back. I found my feet. Pulled myself upright. My head swam. My body brimmed with static and I felt like I'd zap everything I touched, like billions of volts lived in my fingertips and were itching to slip out.

"Very good. Now. Let's go downstairs, shall we?"

✳

A song I liked was playing. People still had phones out, but the crowd, drunk with voyeuristic magic rebound, were slipping back into dance mode. Arms flew in the air and the crowd throbbed like a single, beating organ. There was a clearing in the middle of the room where my Scapegracers were pulling themselves upright. Daisy looked ecstatic—I could make out her face across the crowd. She didn't seem mad that she'd been so unceremoniously dropped on the floor, she just seemed confused. Then I watched her expression change. She was staring at something, or the lack of something. The lack of me, which left the middle of the sigil empty.

Madeline. Where the fuck was Madeline? She'd left her wolf-head upstairs, and I couldn't spot her in the crowd. Every head of dark hair seemed like it could've been her—but those people were dancing, dressed in gory little nothings, mindless to the hell that'd happened upstairs.

I elbowed my way through the crowd. My shoulders collided with dancers, who by and large ignored me—until one of them grabbed my arm, wheeled me around. It was

Alexis. She was a Frankenstein monster, I think. She gave me a huge, gaping smile that made all her painted-on stitches crinkle up.

"That was amazing! How did you do that? Seriously, I can't believe it! Jesus H. Christ, Sideways—people are gonna be talking about that for years!" Before I could say anything, her arms were around my waist. I tensed up and peered over the top of her head, toward the rest of the crowd. Madeline, Madeline, where was Madeline? Where the hell had she gone?

My mouth was full of Scratch's ink. The taste was distracting. If I opened my mouth, would Alexis see the blackness between my teeth?

Whatever. I kept scanning for Madeline in the crowd. There was dark hair everywhere, and then a discordance. I spotted a flash of blond out of the corner of my eye. It was too light, too sugar white to be mistaken for anyone else. I whipped my head around, tried to track the towhead in the crowd. It wove between clustered dancers at a fast pace, strides long and self-assured. Levi. My blood sped up, felt quick, poisonous.

Inside my head, Mr. Scratch said, *I wanted to eat him alive.*

"Shut up," I hissed under my breath.

Alexis shifted, pulled away from me. Blinked at me, incredulous. "What the hell?"

"Not you," I said. I shook my head, tried to focus. My curls stung like nettles where they slapped my cheek. Bit at me. "Don't worry about it. Talk to you later, alright?"

"Okay, I . . ."

I pulled away from her, trudged deeper into the fray, after the blond hair that was slipping farther away from me. Where was he going?

Toward the sigil, of course. He was covering ground fast. I picked up my pace and forced my way between a couple in the throes of heavy petting, crunched a discarded beer can underfoot. Threw myself in his direction.

In my direct line of sight, two yards away from me, was Yates. She saw me, opened her eyes wide, and waved me over. Then her expression seized up. Her eyes fixed on something just in front of me. Fixed on the face-side of the blond head. Her brows steepled. She took another step back, but the wall of dancers was too thick. She turned and he was already there, inches from her. His pale hand flashed in the darkness, clasped her shoulder, whirled her around.

My heart slammed against my teeth.

I felt the ink course through me, felt it rev up every facility in my body. All the floodgates busted. I jabbed a finger at Levi and snarled, lip curled up in a sneer, and the voice in my spine and I said: "*Chett.*"

He buckled. Fell forward onto Yates, who kicked him away like he was a rat. He hit the floor with a smack and writhed, clawing at his neck. Gurgling. His sneakers skidded on the floor. The crowd largely ignored him.

The acrid taste was overwhelming. I choked, then brought my wrist to my mouth and spat, smearing the insides of my lips between my carpal bones. My saliva was tinged with black.

It looked like I'd gnawed on a pen nib until it burst between my teeth. It left smudges on the back of my hand.

I lunged forward and dove beside Levi. Seized him above the elbows, dragged him upright. Sank my nails into the fabric of his jacket. The veins down the backs of my hands looked darker, looked like they were raised over my bones like interwoven leeches. I shook him, snarling like a fucking dog, and his mouth popped open wide. His eyes bulged out of his head, swiveled in their sockets like lottery balls. A thin, sketchy line had snaked itself around his throat. It glimmered there, dark and thirsty. The sigil circle we'd drawn around our Ken doll's neck looked uglier on him, like a poisonous, angry choker.

Levi pulled against my grip, had to strain his neck to glare at me. He curled his lip and spat something that sounded like *Bitch*. With a jerk of his arms, he wrenched himself free of my grasp, shoulders heaving, ribs spasming under his jacket—

And the whites of his eyes turned scarlet. Levi doubled over, threw his hands over his face. I grabbed him by the hood and yanked him toward the door. He buckled, and suddenly there was a second set of hands on his shoulders. A third seized his wrists, a fourth his hair. Flashes of silky, liquid fabric swept around his body, dragged him off the dance floor. The fists in his hair released him to prop open the door, and the four of hauled him through it, into the cold beyond. The door slammed shut behind us.

Standing on the porch was like the first jump into a lake. Sound dulled, cold sliced bone deep, and we were alone in the dark, surrounded only by neon splatter marks and shapeless, swaying trees.

"So," said Jing. She shoved Levi to the ground, placed her foot between his shoulder blades and shifted her weight against his spine. Levi gasped, clawed at the lichen-stained concrete, but Jing didn't let up. She peered down at the back of his head with disgust, and then looked up at me. Cocked a penciled brow. "Who the fuck is this?"

"That's Chett," said Yates. She wrapped her arms around her stomach and her chin quivered. Upon her pronouncement of "Chett," Levi convulsed again, and I imagined the ugly black line growing a little thicker on his throat.

Daisy sneered. Spat beside his head, then tossed an arm around Yates' shoulders. Yates leaned into the half embrace and Daisy rested her cheek against Yates' forehead, gave her a little squeeze.

"Thought our spell didn't work," Jing mused, twisting her wedge heel between his vertebrae like she was snuffing out a cigarette. "This is the sicko who child-snatched you, isn't it, Sideways? Shouldn't it have worked then?"

"I couldn't talk." My voice was brittle, jagged. I felt like my insides were melting. My organs were all tangled and fucked up. The ink smell made me sick. "Couldn't call him Chett. Guess that was part of it."

He swore, shuddered, whimpered.

Yates flinched and looked away.

"Damn." Jing stepped off, knelt by his side. Rubbed her hands together and took a fistful of his hair, jerked his head up to make him look at her. If he *could* look at her. I had an inkling that looking at her might go poorly for him. "Hey there, witchfinder. If I ever see your simpering face again, I'll smash it in. Are we clear?"

Levi, between wheezes, managed a broken, toothy smile. "Clear as day."

"Fuck you." Jing released him, stood up. Delivered a neat little kick to his ribs. "Run now. Go."

Levi peeled himself off the concrete and half staggered, half fell down the porch steps. His steps were even, well placed, but he shook at his core and his movements looked zombie-like, agonized. In the light of the half-moon, I could just make out a shadow on his back, a dark smear where Jing's foot had been.

My vision blurred.

*Your friends are nicer than I am. I would've eaten him raw, teeth, bones, and all. I would've split him like a salmon and flipped him inside out, and I would've swallowed his insides down my throat and relished it.*

The world spotted, flickered like the swan song of a dingy florescent light. My head swam. Colors inverted and I buckled, swayed forward.

Something caught me, hauled me back, held me in place. I knew without looking that it was Jing. I could tell, somehow.

She pressed her nose into my hair, spoke just loud enough for me to hear. "Hey. Hey. What the fuck happened? You were there and then you vanished."

I rocked back on my heels. Swayed against her, bracing my

weight against her arms and her hands. She held me firm, like a second spine.

"Madeline Kline was Addie."

Levi was a pinprick in the dark. The night ate him up, black as ink, and I couldn't spot his shoulders against the trees anymore. He was gone. I thought I heard an engine rev somewhere out of sight.

Madeline was gone, too.

Madeline was gone with a slice of me inside her.

Part of my body wasn't inside of me. It felt like she'd taken my lungs and my stomach, too. All my guts were gone.

Jing traced her nails down my arms, toward my elbows, and up again. "What do you need right now, Sideways?" Her voice was warm above my ear. "Talk to me. What's wrong?"

Daisy and Yates glanced at us, leaned in closer.

I looked up at the patch of sky above us that shone through a hole in the slanted porch roof. My voice felt disconnected from my throat and it took concentration to fish it out of my chest cavity, hook it through my teeth. "Madeline took my specter." My gaze fell, fixed on the vague spot where Levi had vanished. "Because of him, I think."

Jing went rigid. The air between the four of us went cold, and she breathed something at Yates and Daisy that I maybe could've caught if I tried, but my ability to focus on anything was dissolving fast. I thought I heard her say, *Well, tell them*, and *We should*, and *What time is it?*

"Got it," Daisy said, sounding prickly, but genuinely affirmative. She went back in the house and barked something, and without warning, the music fell dead. I could hear people inside complaining, and the rotting house groaning underneath them.

"Sideways," Jing said. She adjusted her grip on me, moved until she was in my line of sight. "Delacroix House should still be open if we leave right now. Do you want to go see if they know what to do? Or you can go home if you want. Whatever you wanna do."

My head nodded, jostling my eyes around in their sockets. "Delacroix House sounds like a good idea. Let's go there."

"Of course," said Yates, all eyes and twisting mouth.

"We'll leave in ten minutes, tops," Jing explained to me. "Daisy's breaking up the crowd, but we don't have to wait for them to go. She'll yank the equipment, or pay somebody else to do it, and then we're gone. Okay?"

There was a well of something in me that burst. I tried to say *thank you,* but I couldn't move my mouth. I just hugged her instead. She had the mercy not to comment on the fact that I was crying so hard that I thought it might tear my lungs up.

He felt chilly under my skin. *Delacroix House?* Mr. Scratch nestled himself between the rungs of my rib cage. *Just my luck.*

# TWENTY-TWO

# ABOUT THAT HOLE IN YOUR HEART

My body wasn't crying anymore, and I certainly wasn't running, but my abdomen screamed like I'd just sobbed through a marathon. I was in the passenger seat of Jing's car, and the world rushed by my windows in a slurry of night-muted color, but I felt far away. Felt myself finally slowing down, panicking about safety, about whether or not he'd find me here, whether or not he could see me, about how long I could stay.

Those weren't my thoughts. They were Madeline's. Guess she was having a bad evening, too, huh?

Yates had called Delacroix House as soon as we got in the car. She told the receptionist exactly what we needed—that we were a bunch of witches who'd had a run-in with one of their employees and also a witchfinder and now one of us was without a specter; that we didn't know where else to go, that we needed to talk to Maurice, it was urgent.

The receptionist had apparently gone very quiet, said that she would tell Maurice right away and we didn't have to worry, that they'd hold the door for us and make sure we got whatever help we needed.

At least, that's what Yates said they said.

We were nearing the house now. My brain zigzagged between not wanting to focus on being in a car and not wanting to focus on being inside of Madeline Kline. I tried to pick the third option, which was listening to Mr. Scratch awkwardly work his way around my circulatory system, which he clearly thought inferior to flowing between paper signatures.

*It's similar, I think,* he was saying, from the inside of the top of my head. *You've got a spine. And skin—plenty of devils have books made of skin. It's usually stretched and shaved, and very flat, and without any blood. But it's similar enough. It's very nice in here, really.*

He hated it. Clearly, he hated it.

Better than him loving it a lot, I guess.

We got out of the car and I took a step onto the gravel like I could support my own weight. Totally could, absolutely could. I didn't want any more help than I was already receiving. Then my boot made contact with all the baby-tooth stones and I pitched forward. Daisy caught me by the elbow and hooked her arm through mine. She hoisted me upright, used some of that magic cheerleading core strength to brace me while I found my footing.

We walked between all the pumpkins. Their mouths glowed a forgiving orange warmth and made long shadows fall behind us like a train.

Someone opened the door for us before we climbed the stairs.

Maurice and a fistful of other people hovered in the foyer, witches of all genders and ages. Their hands fell over our shoulders and they closed the door behind us, and the motion was one big blur of hushing velvets and satin ties. Somebody with big glittered platform boots led us to a studded leather couch. Somebody else in a baby-blue suit fetched glasses of water and hot black coffee, which they served in a teacup with a pitcher of cream. Daisy answered questions vaguely about our names and how old we were.

The person who'd served us dinner last time whispered something in Maurice's ear, then cleared most of the people out of the room until it was just the four of us, Maurice, and the saxophonist we saw perform with Madeline. Jacques, I think it was. I remembered being so jealous of him.

I felt sick to my stomach. Inky inside.

Mr. Scratch squiggled all over inside me, seemed nervous about being inside this place again, so I wrapped a hand around my wrist and squeezed, hoping it'd feel reassuring, maybe. At least it might get him to hold still.

"So, what exactly happened?" Maurice looked at me, mostly. Guess it was obvious that I was the fucked-up one here. Or perhaps Yates had mentioned that on the phone?

I chewed on my tongue and then told him everything.

Maurice rubbed a hand over his mouth. He took a moment, rocked back in his seat, and shot a look at Jacques. Jacques didn't return it, though. He was staring at his hands. After a moment, Maurice took a sip of water, then rested the glass on his knee. "I'm glad you're alive."

Daisy blinked. "Why wouldn't she be?"

"It's possible to live without your specter, but the extraction process is physically and spiritually traumatic," Maurice said. His eyelids hung low and glossy. "From what I understand, lots of witches don't survive it. Most don't. Ironically, it probably helped that Madeline had you make the extraction sigil yourself. I bet she thought she was being merciful. It at least means the spell fit you, perverse as that is. Kept you from dying during the ritual. Even then. I've heard of good witches, strong, healthy witches, dying just weeks after an extraction takes place." He looked me in the eye, moved his head so that we were level, dead-on. "I would normally be very wary about letting one of the vase devils upstairs out for *anything*. I would advise you girls to stay away from them. They're dangerous, single-minded creatures. Pain has made them that way. We respect them for their service to our community, and mourn for them and the violence done to them and theirs, but we don't get too close. It's too risky, I'm afraid."

Mr. Scratch seethed in my skull. It must have left a trace in my face. Darkened the vein in my forehead, or something like that. Jacques was looking at it with a mix of horror and something darker, something crushingly sad.

"However," Maurice said as he rested his chin on his fist, "your circumstances are unique. A book devil has more than enough magic to keep a witch alive, provided that it wants to help. If you're serious about forming your own coven, you'd need one, too. It's just that this one"—he closed his eyes, took a deep breath through his nose and out his teeth—"is complicated. There are fresh book devils you could summon. Ones that have never had a coven before, have never been a book at all. Or, even better, you could find an older, established coven and let them take care of you. That would be the responsible thing to do."

"We can take care of each other, thanks," Jing said.

*We can take care of each other,* Mr. Scratch repeated. He curled ribbons of himself around the inside of my head. *I will take care of you and your sisters, and you will take care of me.*

"Mhm." Maurice nodded like he thought she'd say that. "In that case, I'm not going to risk any exorcism attempts, because Sideways' life is more important than my discomfort. Just be safe, is all I ask."

"Madeline," said Jacques. "I knew there was something wrong, but I didn't know that she'd— I didn't think she could do something like this. I knew she had a bad ex-boyfriend, but I didn't know who, and I definitely didn't think it'd be a Chantry boy." He ran a hand over his head.

"Can Sideways grow a new one?" Yates shrank a little, as though her question might not be allowed for some reason. "Her specter, I mean. Or find a new one?"

Maurice and Jacques looked at each other, then looked at Yates. Maurice said, "I think a better use of your time would be finding Madeline."

"Her specter must've been taken out for her to need mine." I sucked my cheeks. "Are you going to do something about that?"

"We'll tell the Sisters Corbie," Maurice said. "She's a formal initiate of that coven. It's in their jurisdiction what happens to one of their own. They'll find her."

"Please. If you ever need anything, come to the Delacroix. We'll help you out," Jacques stressed. "Anything at all, and we'll do our best."

"We'll remember that," Jing said. She stood up. "Come on, guys, it's late. We should head home."

"Thank you," Yates said. "Thank you so much."

Daisy didn't say anything. She and Yates stood up on either side of me. Yates held a hand out to me, and I took it. Put my boots on the red carpet and made my knees extend.

Once the door had shut behind us and we were a fair ways into the lines of jack-o'-lanterns, Jing let out a breath through her teeth. "Jesus, that place gives me the creeps. Let's crash at my place, guys. I'll make spaghetti."

✳

Jing's lilac rug felt like a thunderhead. I crackled, sizzled with the devil's ink, and the faux fur was too fine to be real. My *Ghastly* robe was balled in my fists. The fabric was a tactile hell. It rubbed between my fingers and lingered there with phantom softness, red as the specter in Madeline's teeth, and it made me sick. It was like holding a bloody rag. It was like I'd poured my insides out and it had soaked up all my red and stained that way. My soul was somewhere else. It wasn't in my body and neither was I, not properly. The lilac rug and I were far away, on the flip side of the universe. Jing and Yates and Daisy, sitting around me in a ring, they weren't beside me at all.

But when Yates touched my wrist, I felt it.

Mr. Scratch thought a joke in the stupid cartoon we'd turned on for white noise was funny; he laughed so hard that my whole body fizzed like pop.

I was here. I was right here.

"I'm gonna rip Madeline's throat out with my fucking teeth." Jing said this unblinkingly. She ghosted her fingertips across my temples, rubbed circles against my skin. Our empty bowls of spaghetti hung out by our ankles. Still smelled good. "We're getting your specter back, Sideways. We'll get it back if it means torching the entire town. The entire state. The fucking nation. You'll get what's yours, I swear it."

"I can't believe she set you up like that. It was premeditated. It's just. You shared your magic and she snatched it up and ran." Yates sounded distant. She rubbed her thumb between my knuckles. In my mind's eye, her lip quivered, and she bit it, held it in place. Or maybe she didn't. I wasn't sure of much of anything right now. "What she did, it's like a kind of murder. I never thought girls did this kind of thing. In my head, it's always boys. To think that stealing specters like that is how the Chantry boys attack witch girls— if Chett had known about me, do you think he would've taken mine before I even knew I had it?"

"Probably," said Daisy. Her voice floated over from behind me. "That's probably what they were planning when they dragged Sideways to their mansion. They were gonna rip her fucking soul out, just like Madeline did. What kind of a traitor does that make her?"

"The lowest," said Jing.

"Her ex-boyfriend pulled *her* soul out," Yates said.

"Was that fucking sympathy?" I imagined the way Daisy's face must look right now, how taut it must be stretched. "I don't give a singular fuck about her and what might've happened to her. Fuck, if she'd fallen in Sideways' arms and asked for help, I'd be torching the Chantry house right fucking now. Whatever she needed. But she didn't. She ripped Sideways' insides out, and now she's dead to me, completely dead to me. If I see her, I'm hooking my fist through her jaws and clawing around her throat until I find Sideways' specter, and I'm knocking all her teeth out when I drag it back up."

"Daisy, stop," Yates said. She gripped my wrist a little tighter, tight enough to hurt. "Just stop."

I heard Daisy scoff, mumble something fanged and poisonous under her breath, but I couldn't make out any words. Then silence.

Jing broke it. "Let me see this sigil, Sideways." She spoke slowly, like I'd hit my head and was only just now floating out of a coma. Gathered the hair out of my face.

I rolled my head to the side, stretched my neck to show off the brand, the lines that'd seeped from Madeline's hand into my skin. It stung when touched by open air. Stung like an uncovered burn. There was a vague worry in the back of my head that it'd fester when exposed to light, but I didn't know how microbes and magic mixed. I avoided eye contact.

"Jesus H. Christ."

"Why does it look so charred? Is that the Sharpie, like with our Chett curse?"

*That'd be me.*

"No." I swallowed, swept my tongue over my hard palate and my teeth. It felt like my mouth had been gathering dust, and the grit clogged between my canines and my incisors. I felt chalky. "That's the ink. Mr. Scratch's ink."

"Right," said Jing eventually. She ghosted a fingertip over the sigil. It wasn't as abrasive as it should've been. "Right. Send our thanks to Mr. Scratch."

*You're very welcome.*

I snorted, passed along a nod.

*Say—I have something to say, Sideways.*

I opened my mouth and let him speak.

"Helping Sideways is only natural. After all, you three and Sideways helped me." It didn't sound quite like my voice. It was stilted, the kind of brassy mid-Atlantic accent that only ever showed up in black-and-white movies. I closed my eyes, but my mouth kept moving. "I was a spell book once," Mr. Scratch said from inside my mouth. "I was the most glorious spell book. My leather glistened like oil on water and my tips were edged with plated gold, and I weaved the loveliest spells for my brood. I kept their histories and their philosophies. They read from me, wrote in me every day. My old coven was filled with performers, dancers and sword-swallowers, divas and poets and heretics, wonderful girls, the whole lot of them.

They were called the Honeyeaters. I taught them how to slow time and sculpt light. I recorded what they taught themselves. They gave me a school and I poured magic into them. I loved them very much. Then witchfinders burned my body and robbed the souls from my children and all of them were dead. I fought for them in the way that I can, but books are bound to the pulp we reside in. Pulp is not designed for violence. There was nothing I could do.

"You girls freed me. You freed me and showed me your talent and cunning and curiosity, your marvelous disregard for authority, your relentless care for one another, and then I watched as your Sideways was stripped of her self like my daughters had been. There was little I could do, being what I am, but I offered myself to her. She accepted, so here I sit and speak."

*Sit up, dear. I need you all to join hands.*

I willed my body upward, and I dragged my wrist over my mouth, tried to rub life back into my face. My gums tasted like ink and rust. Yates still held me, so I reached for Jing and Daisy. They all understood, bless them. They locked hands with each other and watched me, weary, wary.

"I'll get Sideways her soul back. I'll teach you how—that's what I'm for. I'll show you everything you'll need, my dovelings, but you need to be my coven for that. When we're through, you four will make a book for me. You will read from me, and you will tell others what you read. You will be witches like there haven't been for centuries, and I will be a spell book again. Say that I'm yours, O Scapegracers. Say it as one, and it shall be so."

The voice fell, settled back where it belonged, and I opened my mouth again. There was fear on Yates' face, and a flash of concern, but her mouth popped open as well, as did Jing's, and Daisy's. We all snaked in a slow breath, and on the exhale, we said together: "It shall be so."

The ink spiraled through my arteries and shot out through my fingertips, coursed into Yates on one side and through Jing on the other. It rushed through Daisy, met itself in her sternum, and then surged around the circle back to me. I could see it in their eyes, in the way they stiffened for a moment, shuddered as it passed. When it slipped back into my limbs it felt lighter, thinner, doused in syrup and lightning. The world flickered for a moment.

Mr. Scratch purred and spoke. "Then Scapegracers you shall be," he said.

I felt him descend in my chest. I released Yates and Jing, pulled my hands to my belly. My *Ghastly* sisterhood robe was in a heap on the floor where I must've dropped it, and I reached down and took it by the fistful. My body trembled. I bit my lip. Yates reached out and grabbed me around the middle, pulled me toward her. I went slack, pressed my temple to her sternum and heaved a sob that was not a sob. No tears, just the reeling. Just the ache.

After a moment of grieving, I went for more noodles. I numbly scooped some out of the pot. They really smelled amazing. I gave Jing the smallest thumbs-up.

"So. Sideways," said Daisy. I saw her out of the corner of my eye, sitting strange, with her knees to her chest like a beast might rest. She had one of her hands to her lips, a nail snagged between her teeth. With the other, she tapped on her phone screen. She peered down through her spidery lashes and knotted her brows together, then she looked at me with a twitch at the corner of her mouth. Her gaze was too strident to reciprocate. "It's trending."

"What are you on about?" Jing, looking exhausted as the grave, had lost the edge in her voice. She just sounded croaky, now. She brushed her fingertips over my ankle.

"The party. It's trending. It's fucking everywhere. Someone uploaded a video and now it's *everywhere*. Sideways, your magic is kinda fucking famous. It's real. Everyone knows it's real."

Yates shifted above me, pawed around for her phone. Her thumb danced across the glass and she held it by my cheek, scrolled by post after post until it was obvious that she didn't need to scroll anymore. #REIGNOFSCAPEGRACE flickered back and forth, and there we were, suspended in midair over a spray-painted sigil. There we were, and there we were again, from a different angle and a different partygoer's mechanical eye. Yates switched apps, and there was the corpse house, the strung-up lanterns, the girls floating over the crowd. Half the posts were speculating how we'd pulled it off, but I didn't mind that. There were believers. They believed and they shot that faith into the ether, and now it nestled against my bones and made me think, for a moment, that I was nearly whole again.

"It was a hell of a party," Daisy said distantly.

"Sure was," Jing replied.

Yates pressed a kiss to the crown of my head. Her fingers found the nape of my neck and stayed there, and I sucked in a slow breath. There was ink in the grooves of my lungs, and it was acrid and harsh, but it kept them breathing in time. Slow and easy, in and out. Breathe like a prizefighter. Broken ribs, but standing.

I sank against Yates and stared down at her phone, at the people who'd been staring at me. The Scapegracers were real now, the world as our witness. My magic wasn't something to snicker about.

Not that I had it anymore.

"Hey." Yates wrapped an arm around my stomach, but she was looking between Jing and Daisy, and I had a feeling she wasn't quite addressing me. She sucked her lower lip between her teeth. "What if we had a private party for Halloween proper? Just the four of us and some goofy, spooky kids' movies, you know? Some cute pumpkin-shaped cupcakes? I could make my dog a little costume. He could be a baby witch. The babyest Scapegracer."

I blinked. My tongue felt dry and funny.

"Yeah," Jing said after a moment's silence. "That sounds fun, actually. Like, an old-school sleepover. We could do special-effects makeup on each other. Give candy to trick-or-treaters."

Daisy shrugged affirmatively.

Yates looked at me. She gave me the softest squeeze. "Does that sound like fun, Sideways?"

"Yeah," I breathed. I shook my head. "I just didn't think you guys would want me to come to a party like that. One without magic, I mean."

They looked at each other. Then they all looked at me.

"Duh, of course we'd want you to come," said Daisy.

"Yeah," said Jing. "Now eat your spaghetti before it's nasty and cold."

Far away, I sprinted. Madeline was running, and my soul rubbed raw against the lining of her esophagus. My lungs burned with the effort, my calves heaved, and the tendons in my limbs twitched, but I hadn't moved a muscle. My red soul was churning in Judas' throat, and I was here, unmoving, out of reach of myself.

But here I was with friends, real friends. We leaned against Jing's bed together, watched a bit of the old cartoon. I leaned my head on Yates' shoulder, and I shut my eyes and just listened to them breathing, and the kitschy spooky score.

The devil squirmed around inside my head and asked, rather politely, *Hello, Sideways? A pumpkin-shaped cupcake. What is that?*

# ACKNOWLEDGMENTS

Thank you to Abby Schulman, my amazing agent. Thank you to Liz Gorinsky for being such an insightful editor, and thank you to the innumerable mentors who've influenced this book and me in some way or another, including but not limited to Jeremy, Sara, Anita, Patrick, Jody, cris, Steve, Margaret, Rhonda, Benjamin, and all my fellow Lambda Fellows. Thank you to the weird coffee shops that I used as makeshift office spaces, and thank you to all the people I've lived with who've tolerated my late-night writing antics, most notably the Circle and Dan. Thank you to my best friends, and to the communities I've found across schools. Thank you to Daniel Handler, Leslie Feinberg, Libba Bray, Samuel Delaney, Carmen Maria Machado, Tamora Pierce, Octavia Butler, Ursula K. Le Guin, Holly Black, Anne Rice, Toni Morrison, Cassandra Clare, Maxine Hong Kingston, Shirley Jackson, Han Kang, Angela Carter, Alice Sheldon, Renée Vivien, V. E. Schwab, and Philip Pullman for writing stories that have made me who I am. Thank you to younger me for surviving high school in rural Ohio while being as gay as I am. Thank you to the universe for making me a Leo sun and a Capricorn ascendant, rendering me unstoppable. Thank you to Sarah, Rosie, and everyone else who reads the unreadable drafts. Thank you to my mother, who gave me fiction, and my family writ large, found and otherwise.